A

LYDIA

A Home for
LYDIA

VANNETTA
CHAPMAN

HARVEST HOUSE PUBLISHERS
EUGENE, OREGON

Cover by Koechel Peterson & Associates, Inc., Minneapolis, Minnesota

Cover photos © Koechel Peterson & Associates, Inc.; Arsty / Dreamstime.com

A HOME FOR LYDIA

Copyright © 2013 by Vannetta Chapman
Published by Harvest House Publishers
Eugene, Oregon 97402
www.harvesthousepublishers.com

Library of Congress Cataloging-in-Publication Data
Chapman, Vannetta.
    A home for lydia / Vannetta Chapman.
        p. cm. ~ (The Pebble Creek Amish series ; bk. 2)
    ISBN 978-0-7369-4614-8 (pbk.)
    ISBN 978-0-7369-4615-5 (eBook)
    1. Amish~Fiction. 2. Wisconsin~Fiction. I. Title.
    PS3603.H3744H66 2013
    813'.6-dc23
                                                                            2012027223

Printed in the United States of America

13 14 15 16 17 18 19 20 21 / LB-JH / 10 9 8 7 6 5 4 3 2 1

For my mother-in-law,
Barbara Elizabeth Chapman

Acknowledgments

This book is dedicated to my mother-in-law, Barbara Elizabeth Chapman. We have enjoyed many evenings together, and I count it as joy that she accepted me into her family. She has been such an inspiration to me—a real-life example of a woman who lives with grace, compassion, and a sense of humor.

Although Pebble Creek doesn't actually exist, the village of Cashton does, and I would like to thank several folks in the Driftless region, including Anita Reeck (Amil's Inn Bed and Breakfast), Kathy Kuderer (Down a Country Road), and Pete and Nora Knapik (Inn at Lonesome Hollow). Richard Lee Dawley (author of *Amish in Wisconsin*) was also kind enough to answer questions while I was conducting research.

Many of the items described in Aaron's Plain Shop can be purchased at www.downacountryroad.com, which is in the Cashton area and supplies items made by local Amish artisans.

Thanks to Suzanne Woods Fisher and the *Budget* for their endless supply of Amish proverbs.

My editor, Kim Moore, is a dream to work with, and the excellent staff at Harvest House have been superb. I'm also indebted to my agent, Mary Sue Seymour. Donna, Kristy, and Dorsey, I need you every book. Bobby, Mom, and Pam—thank you. Kids, every single day I thank God for you.

I've always been drawn to rivers and cabins. There have been many places, such as the cabins along Pebble Creek, where I have found a respite from the world. I am extremely grateful they exist.

And finally...*always giving thanks to God the Father for everything, in the name of our Lord Jesus Christ* (Ephesians 5:20).

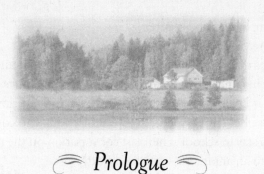

≈ *Prologue* ≈

Wisconsin
May

Lydia Fisher pulled her sweater around her shoulders and sank down on the top step of the last cabin as the sun set along Pebble Creek. The waters had begun to recede from last week's rains, but the creek still pushed at its banks—running swiftly past the Plain Cabins and not pausing to consider her worries.

Debris from the flooding reached to the bottom step of cabin twelve. She could have reached out and nudged it with the toe of her shoe. Fortunately, the water hadn't made it into the small cottages.

Almost, though.

Only two days ago she'd stood at the office window and watched as the waters had crept closer to the picturesque buildings nestled along the creek—watched and prayed.

Now the sun was dropping, and she knew she should harness Tin Star to the buggy and head home. Her mother would be putting dinner on the table. Her brother and sisters would be needing help with schoolwork. Her father would be waiting.

Standing up with a weariness that was unnatural for her twenty-two years, Lydia trudged back toward the front of the property, checking each cabin as she went.

All were locked and secure.

All were vacant.

Perhaps this weekend the *Englisch* tourists would return and provide some income for the owner, Elizabeth Troyer. Guests would also ensure that Lydia kept her job. If the cabins were to close and she were to lose her employment, she wouldn't be able to convince her brother to stay in school. Their last conversation on the matter had turned into an argument—one she'd nearly lost.

Pulling their old black gelding from the barn, she tied Tin Star's lead rope to the hitching post, and then she began to work the collar up and over his ears.

"You're a *gut* boy. Are you ready to go home? Ready for some oats? I imagine you are."

He'd been their buggy horse since she was a child, and Lydia knew his days were numbered. What would her family do when he gave out on them? As she straightened his mane and made sure the collar pad protected his shoulders and neck, she paused to rest her cheek against his side. The horse's sure steady breathing brought her a measure of comfort.

Reaching into the pocket of her jacket, she brought out a handful of raisins. Tin Star's lips on her hand were soft and wet. Lydia rubbed his neck as she glanced back once more at the cluster of buildings which had become like a small community to her—a community she was responsible for maintaining.

Squaring her shoulders, she climbed into the buggy and turned toward home.

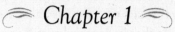 Chapter 1

Aaron Troyer stepped off the bus, careful to avoid a large puddle of rainwater. Because no one else was exiting at Cashton, he didn't have to wait long for the driver to remove his single piece of luggage from the storage compartment. He'd thanked the man and shouldered the duffel bag when the buggy coming in the opposite direction hit an even bigger puddle, soaking him.

The bus driver had managed to jump out of the way at the last second. "Good luck to you, son."

With a nod the man was back on the bus, heading farther west. A part of Aaron wished he were riding with him. Another part longed to take the next bus back east, back where he'd come from, back to Indiana.

Neither was going to happen, so he repositioned his damp duffel bag and surveyed his surroundings.

Not much to Cashton.

According to his uncle and his dad, the town was about the same size as Monroe, but Aaron couldn't tell it. He supposed new places never did measure up to expectations, especially when a fellow would rather not be there.

The ride had been interesting enough. They had crossed the northern part of Indiana, skirted the southern tip of Lake Michigan, traveled through Chicago and Rockford, and finally entered Wisconsin in the south central portion of the state. Aaron had seen more cities in the last twenty-four hours than he'd visited in his entire life. Those had been oddities to him. Something he would tell his family about once he was home, but nothing he would ever care to see again. But passing through the Hidden Valley region of southwestern Wisconsin—now that had caused him to sit up straighter and gaze out of the bus's window.

There had been an older *Englisch* couple sitting behind him. They'd had tourist brochures that they read aloud to each other. He'd caught the highlights as he tried to sleep.

He heard them use the word "driftless." The term apparently indicated a lack of glacial drift. His *dat* would laugh at that one. Not that he discounted all aspects of science, but he had his doubts regarding what was and wasn't proven as far as the Ice Age.

According to the couple's brochure, Wildcat Mountain to the east of Cashton was teeming with wildlife and good hiking. Any other time he might be interested in that piece of information, but he wasn't staying, so it didn't matter much to him.

He also learned that small towns in the Driftless Area were at risk of major flooding every fifty to one hundred years.

Staring down at his damp pants, he wondered how much rain they'd had. How much rain were they expecting? He hoped he wouldn't be here long enough to find out.

Aaron glanced up and down the street. He saw a town hall, a tavern, a café, a general store, and a feed store. A larger building, probably three stories high, rose in the distance, but he had no desire to walk that far because it could be in the wrong direction. Already the sun was heading west, and he'd rather be at the cabins before dark.

Several streets branched off the main one, but they didn't look any more promising. Pushing his hat down more firmly on his head, he cinched up the duffel bag and walked resolutely toward the feed store.

Instead of heading toward the front door, he moved down the side of the building to the loading docks, where two pickup trucks and a buggy were parked.

Fortunately, it wasn't the buggy that had sprayed him with rainwater and mud. He would rather not ask information of that person, though in all likelihood the driver had no idea what he'd done. Folks seldom slowed down enough to look outside their own buggy window—even Amish folk. It appeared some things were the same whether you were in Wisconsin or Indiana.

He approached the loading docks, intending to find the owner of the parked buggy.

"That duffel looks heavy...and wet."

Turning in surprise, he saw a man leaning against the driver's side of the buggy. Aaron could tell he was tall, even though he was half sitting, tall and thin. Somber brown eyes studied him, and a full dark beard indicated the man was married. Which was no surprise, because a basket with a baby in it sat on the buggy's floor. The baby couldn't have been more than a few months old, based on the size of the basket. He couldn't see much except for a blanket and two small fists waving in the air.

"Duffel wouldn't be wet if someone hadn't been determined to break the speed limit with a sorrel mare."

The man smiled, reached down, and slipped a pacifier into the baby's mouth. "That would probably have been one of the Eicher boys. I'm sure he meant no harm, but both of them tend to drive on the far side of fast."

He placed the walnut bowl he'd been sanding with a piece of fine wool on the seat, dusted his hands on his trousers, and then he stepped forward. "Name's Gabe Miller."

"Aaron Troyer."

"Guess you're new in town."

"*Ya.* Just off the bus."

"Explains the duffel."

Aaron glanced again at the sun, headed west. Why did it seem to speed up once it was setting? "I was looking for the Plain Cabins on Pebble Creek. Have you heard of them?"

"If you're needing a room for the night, we can either find you a place or take you to our bishop. No need for you to rent a cabin."

Easing the duffel bag off his shoulder and onto the ground, Aaron rested his hands on top of it. "Actually I need to go to the cabins for personal reasons. Could you tell me where they are?"

"Ya. I'd be happy to give you directions, but it's a fair piece from here if you're planning on walking."

Aaron pulled off his hat and ran his hand over his hair. Slowly he replaced it as he considered his options. He'd boarded the bus ten hours earlier. He was used to long days and hard work. Though he was only twenty-three, he'd been working in the fields for nine years—since he'd left the schoolhouse after eighth grade. It was work he enjoyed. What he didn't like was ten hours on a bus, moving farther away from his home, on a trip that seemed to him like a fool's mission.

"Sooner I start, sooner I'll arrive."

"Plain Cabins are on what we call the west side of Pebble Creek."

"You mean the west side of Cashton?"

"Well, Cashton is the name of the town, but Plain folks mostly refer to Pebble Creek, the river."

"The same river going through town?"

"Yes. There are two Plain communities here—one to the east side of town, and one to the west. I live on the east side. The cabins you're looking for are on the west. The town's sort of in the middle. You can walk to them from here, but as I said, it's a good ways. Maybe five miles, and there are quite a few hills in between, not to mention that bag you're carrying…"

Instead of answering, Aaron hoisted the duffel to his shoulder.

Throughout the conversation, Gabe's expression had been pleasant but serious. At the sound of voices, he glanced up and across the street, toward the general store. When he did, Aaron noticed a subtle change in the man, like light shifting across a room. Some of the seriousness left his eyes and contentment spread across his face.

Following his gaze, Aaron saw the reason why—a woman. She was beautiful and had the darkest hair he'd ever seen on an Amish woman. A small amount peeked out from the edges of her prayer *kapp*. She was holding the hand of a young girl, who was the spitting image of the man before him. Both the woman and the child were carrying shopping bags.

"I was waiting on my family. Looks like they're done. We'd be happy to take you by the cabins."

"I don't want to be a bother," Aaron mumbled.

Gabe smiled, and now the seriousness was completely gone, as if having his family draw close had vanquished it. As if having his family close had eased all of the places in his heart.

Aaron wondered what that felt like. He wanted to be back with his own parents, brothers, and sisters in Indiana, but even there he felt an itching, a restlessness no amount of work could satisfy.

From what he'd seen of Wisconsin so far, he could tell he wasn't going to be any happier here. He'd arrived less than thirty minutes ago, and he couldn't wait to get back home.

Gabe was already moving toward his wife, waving away his protest.

"If it were a bother, I wouldn't have offered."

≈ Chapter 2 ≈

Miriam held Grace's hand as they crossed the street.

She wasn't actually worried about Rachel. Gabe's smile assured her the baby was fine. Her anxiousness was more of a natural thing, as if a string stretched between her and the infant. When she was separated from her for more than a few minutes, the string began to grow tauter until she had trouble resisting the pull.

"Who is that man with *dat*?" Grace asked, clutching her package of drawing supplies close to her chest.

"I'm not sure, but I imagine we're about to find out."

"He looks a little dirty."

"Could be the mud."

"*Ya*. Suppose so. Hunter is awfully dirty sometimes, but he's still a *gut* dog."

Miriam smiled down at Grace as they rounded the corner of the buggy.

"Miriam, meet Aaron Troyer. He's new to Pebble Creek. Aaron, this is my *fraa*, Miriam, and my *dochder*, Grace. Our youngest, Rachel, is in the basket."

"Hello." Aaron nodded and shuffled his feet.

Miriam noticed he seemed impatient to move on. "Nice to meet you."

"I'm nine," Grace proclaimed.

"Nine. That's a good age to be." Aaron looked uncertain how to continue.

"We came straight to town after school to pick up more feed and buy drawing supplies." Grace closed her mouth suddenly and stepped closer to her father.

Miriam had noticed she was doing that more lately since the baby was born. She'd have a rainfall of language before clamming up as if she was afraid that perhaps she'd said too much.

Gabe smiled at her, and Grace relaxed.

The small interchange brought back memories of Grace's silent time, memories of all that had brought them together.

Miriam handed Gabe her package from the general store and reached for Rachel as the baby began to fuss. "What brings you to the Cashton area, Aaron?"

"Actually, I was asking your husband directions to the Plain Cabins. He offered to give me a lift, but I don't mind walking."

"Oh, we'd be happy to drive you. We know exactly where they are. The cabins are near my *bruder*'s home."

Aaron shrugged, apparently too tired to argue further.

"There's room in the back for your duffel." Gabe moved the baby basket onto the backseat, accepted Rachel from Miriam, and tucked the baby in.

"I don't mind sitting in the back—"

"It's no trouble. This way Gabe can tell you about the area," Miriam said as she settled on the backseat beside Grace, who was peeking into her shopping sack.

Grace glanced at Aaron Troyer, at the mud that had dried on his clothes, and then she stared back down into her bag.

"You can take out the tablet," Miriam whispered.

Carefully folding down the top of the paper bag, Grace set it on the seat beside her. "No. I'll wait until we're home. I wouldn't want anything to happen to it."

"All right. Maybe safer is better."

"*Ya*. Safe is *gut*." Grace reached into the basket to rest her hand on top of her baby sister.

"First time to Cashton?" Gabe asked the younger man.

"*Ya*. My bus left Indiana before daylight this morning."

Gabe murmured to their gelding, Chance. A large dark bay with white tips, he was the same age as Grace and quite spirited. To Miriam, he seemed as eager to be on the move as their new acquaintance. Gabe directed the buggy onto the two-lane road. As soon as they left the parking area and the horse's hooves crossed onto blacktop, Chance picked up speed.

"Long ride from Indiana," Gabe said. "I'm from the Nappanee area myself. Been here almost a year and a half."

"Seventeen months," Miriam murmured.

"I've been to Nappanee," Aaron said. "I'm from Monroe."

"Southeast of Fort Wayne?"

"*Ya*."

"Well, I went to Fort Wayne once, but never Monroe."

Aaron shook his head, staring out at the countryside. "My *dat* says he wouldn't give the *Englischers* either of our donkeys for all of Fort Wayne."

Gabe laughed and glanced back at Miriam. "Your *dat* sounds like a smart man."

"We have a donkey," Grace piped up. "His name is Gus, but he tends to find trouble at least twice a week."

"Sometimes more than that," Miriam admitted.

They rode in silence a few minutes, the sun casting long shadows across the hills and valleys of southwestern Wisconsin as the afternoon brought its chill.

Aaron cleared his throat. "My *onkel* owned the Plain Cabins, owned it for the last ten years. I'm here because he recently passed."

"I'm sorry to hear that," Gabe said.

Aaron struck Miriam as young, though he was old enough to shave. She guessed he was probably in his early twenties, but he still impressed her as being more boy than man. There was enough

difference in their ages that he could have been one of the pupils in
her classroom when she first began teaching. She waited for him to
say more, which took another minute.

Finally he offered, "*Dat* says it was *Gotte's wille.*"

Gabe, his voice as soft as the late afternoon light, asked, "And
what do you say?"

"I say his passing is a shame, and I shouldn't be the one who has
to clean up his mess."

Lydia peeked out the window as a buggy pulled into the cabins'
parking lot. She was already late leaving, and obviously these were
not tourists. The last thing she needed was to become caught up in
a long conversation with an Amish family.

Amish families were rarely paying customers.

She shuffled the paperwork she'd been fussing over into a desk
drawer and locked the office door behind her. As she made her way
down the steps, two men, a woman, and a young girl exited the buggy.

"Lydia?"

Stepping closer, it took her a few seconds to recognize her former teacher. It had been so many years. Since before the move. Since
before they had lost the farm.

"Miriam." Lydia hurried to cross the distance between them and
accept a hug. "How are you?"

"I'm fine. I didn't know you were working here."

"*Ya.* More than a year now."

"We were in town and happened to meet—" Miriam turned to
introduce the younger man, but she never had a chance.

"I'm Aaron Troyer." Stepping forward, Aaron glanced around at
the cabins. His expression changed quickly from curiosity to disappointment to contempt.

Lydia could read him the way she could read the *Englischers'* looks
when they came for three nights but stayed only one.

She pushed down her resentment and aimed for pleasant. "Aaron Troyer. So you're Ervin's—"

"He was my *onkel*. Yes."

"I'm sorry for your loss. Your *daed* sent a letter saying someone would be coming, but we didn't know who or when or even what to expect."

"You could have expected we would want you to keep the place in better repair than this." Aaron dropped his duffel bag onto the ground and placed his hands on his hips.

He wasn't overly large, as men went. In fact, he was quite a few inches shorter than the man with Miriam, who must be her husband. Lydia had heard the teacher at the school at Pebble Creek had married the year before. Aaron only topped Lydia by an inch or so, and she was barely five foot six. That didn't make her short for a girl, but she often felt short—short and round. She pushed the thought away and studied Aaron Troyer.

She guessed he was near her age and unmarried—and with his attitude that didn't surprise her. Even with his jacket on she could see he was muscular, and from the look of his tan he was more than likely a farmer. Light brown hair and chocolate eyes scowling at everything completed the picture of a very unhappy man.

Great. That's what she needed around the place—one more disgruntled person at the cabins.

Why was he staring at her with that frown? She had an urge to reach up and pat down her hair, which had no doubt frizzed out from its braids and was peeping from the corners of her *kapp*, but she resisted. She looked presentable enough. Nonetheless, the sour look on Aaron Troyer's face raised hackles along the back of her neck. The way he frowned at the cabins and then her snapped the last string of her patience.

Lydia forgot her hair and the dirt she'd smeared across her apron while dusting under the beds. Suddenly, the last thing she was worried about was how she looked to this out-of-towner who had only just arrived but was already judging her and the cabins.

"Has it been flooded in the last few days or does it always look this way? Have you made no attempt to clean it up recently? The place looks deserted."

Lydia's cheeks flushed, and she took a step back from both Miriam and Aaron.

"I'll have you know I've been working very hard since your *onkel* passed. It's not as if there are a lot of hands to help with the place. I'm the only employee. And, in case you haven't noticed, there are twelve cabins."

"It doesn't look as if there's a lot of business, though. You should have had plenty of time. It looks…it looks…" He seemed as if he were at a loss for words.

They all turned to study the cabins.

"It looks as if everything is falling apart."

Lydia sucked in her breath and promptly bit her lower lip. It was the one thing proven to keep her from speaking her mind.

The man standing next to Miriam bent down and whispered something to the little girl, who ducked back into the buggy.

When she was out of earshot, he stepped in between them.

"Aaron, I'm sure you're tired from your trip. Perhaps it would be better if you rested before saying anything else to…" he paused and glanced at Miriam.

"Lydia," Miriam said. "Gabe, this is Lydia Fisher. She was one of my better students in the years I taught at the Pebble Creek school."

The words were said so simply that instead of embarrassing Lydia, they managed to calm her emotions. She pulled in a deep breath, stared down at the ground, and fought to settle the feelings struggling within her.

She would not cry.

She was exhausted, late heading home, and angry, but she would not give in to tears.

This arrogant stranger was rude, but he was going to be her boss. She would not break down and bawl like a calf in front of him.

In fact, she'd rather scream and show the temper her mother

often warned her about, but she couldn't do that in front of her former teacher. So instead she stared at the ground.

"I don't..." Aaron snatched his hat off his head and ran his hand over his hair, which could stand a good cutting. Ramming the hat back on with much more force than was necessary, he added, "I don't see how resting will make this place look any better."

"Maybe a few days of working instead of complaining—" The words were out of Lydia's mouth before she had a chance to weigh them.

"Lydia, why don't we fetch a key for Aaron so he can stay in one of the cottages?" Miriam tucked her hand into the crook of Lydia's arm and tugged her toward the steps of the office. "Gabe and Aaron will see to your buggy. We've kept you late, and I'm sure your parents are waiting for you."

"*Gut* idea. We'll see to the buggy." Gabe nudged Aaron toward the barn, calling out to the girl as he went. "Grace, watch out after your sister. Your *mamm* will be inside the office if you need her."

The last sight Lydia had of Aaron Troyer was of him storming across the parking area toward the barn. It occurred to her that Tin Star would be looking for his raisins and that neither of the men had any.

Gut. Maybe Aaron would be the one who was nipped. It wouldn't bother her at all if he was. That might take the edge off of his temper.

☙ Chapter 3 ❧

As soon as the two men walked into the barn, Aaron started harnessing the black gelding. Gabe stood back and watched him work. Apparently, he needed to spend some of his pent up energy, not to mention some of his frustration.

"Debris up to the porch steps." Aaron pulled the gelding out of his stall.

"Shutters falling off the windows." He worked the collar over the horse's ears, not bothering to speak to him or show him any affection.

"Cabins look as if they haven't seen any paint in years." He straightened the horse's mane, but wasn't too gentle about it. He did, however, check the collar pad and unhook the lead rope properly before rehooking it to the halter.

"And did you see how the trees need trimming?" Aaron turned to Gabe, waving his hands toward the direction of the cabins and the offending trees. "They look as if they're taking over the cabins in places."

The black gelding had been trying to catch Aaron's attention, obviously searching for a treat. When Aaron didn't respond, and when he moved toward the front to check the harness, the gelding gave him a slight nip.

"What was that for?" Aaron jumped back, shaking his hand up and down and checking for blood.

"I believe the horse would have appreciated a little more attention, rather like you're saying the cabins need." Gabe stepped forward as he searched in his jacket pocket. He came up with a few sugar cubes, which he kept for Chance. The gelding sniffed them twice before gently taking them in his teeth and crunching them contentedly.

Aaron sank back against the door of the horse stall.

"How bad did he get you?"

"Not that bad." He stuck his hands in his pockets. "The way this day is going, I should have expected it."

"So let me see if I have this right. You're upset about the river flooding, the shutters falling off, the buildings needing paint, and the trees wanting trimming."

"Ya." Aaron's voice sank even lower. "Among other things."

"And which of those things did you expect a young woman like Lydia to have the resources to take care of?"

He waited for Aaron to answer, but the young man continued to stare at the horse's hooves. Lydia's horse finally reached forward and nudged his arm.

Gabe dug a few more sugar cubes out of his pocket and dropped them into Aaron's hand. When Aaron held the cubes out to the horse, the treat immediately disappeared.

"Horses are spoiled here, same as at home."

"Ya, that's true."

Gabe followed Aaron as he pulled the horse out into the last of the afternoon light. They both turned and faced the cabins. The setting sun cast light on the group of buildings, hiding most of the scars and leaving them in a charming glow.

The river continued to rush past, still pushing at its banks. As they watched, a crane flew down and plucked a fish from the steel-blue water. Gabe thought that this was a picture Grace would like to draw. Grace would see the beauty in it, but the young man beside him could only see the work waiting beside the river and all that was lacking in the group of cabins.

What could he say to change his mind?

Perhaps that wasn't his job.

It had taken Gabe some time to recognize the beauty in his own place, and yes, it had needed quite a lot of repair when he'd first bought it. Grace had described their place as the sad barn and the droopy house. He still had the pictures she'd drawn, which depicted the buildings quite accurately. Though she'd labeled them "sad" and "droopy," her drawings had also highlighted the good aspects of their new home. She had that gift—of seeing the best in things and sharing it with others through her drawing.

It had taken him longer to be able to see past the despair.

After seventeen months most things had been repaired, but he was learning that Wisconsin winters were hard and springs unpredictable. The summers and falls, though? They were things of beauty.

Whether Aaron would stay long enough to learn those secrets was up to the young man and God.

The women joined them as Aaron hooked the horse up to the buggy and accepted the keys Lydia offered him without another word.

"This one is for the office. A pantry there has some food. It's minimal as I had no reservations for the night and didn't know you would be here." Aaron nodded without commenting, so she continued. "The other key is for cabin four. Before your *onkel* bought the place, it was the manager's cabin." Without another word, she climbed into the buggy and called out to her gelding.

They stood and watched as she turned onto the two-lane blacktop.

Gabe offered to stay until Aaron was sure he had what he needed.

"No need. *Danki* for your help."

"It was nice meeting you," Miriam said.

"Same."

"If you need anything, Lydia will know how to contact the bishop. His name is Atlee." Gabe leaned in to the buggy where Miriam was tending to the baby. After talking with her for a few moments, he ducked back out and spoke again to Aaron. "Miriam's *bruder* lives on this section of Pebble Creek. His name is David King. Have Lydia contact him if you run into any unexpected problems."

He thought the man wouldn't speak, but then his hands came out of his pockets, and he pointed at the cabins as if Gabe should be able to see what he saw. "This...is all unexpected."

"*Ya.* I suppose it is. Good night, then."

They had barely begun moving when Grace opened up her bag of supplies and began sketching in the backseat of the buggy. Gabe glanced back at the cabins and saw Aaron once again shoulder his duffel bag.

Once they were home, Grace had no time to spend with her new drawing supplies. They had a quick dinner, and then she took care of her chores—which included caring for her mouse, Stanley, who now had a small family of his own. That being the case, he'd been moved to the barn.

She couldn't blame Miriam. Most people wouldn't want a family of mice living in the mudroom.

While she was in the barn she spent a little time with their new puppy, Hunter, brushing him and being sure he had fresh water and food in his bowl. He was a German shorthaired pointer. Hunter was the prettiest thing Grace had ever seen, next to her sister, Rachel. His floppy ears and snout were a warm chocolate brown. His tummy was chocolate too, but his body was sprinkled with black, brown, and white.

He was born from a litter that Pepper had fathered. Pepper was Miriam's dog, and he had saved Grace's life once, back when her voice was broken. She'd gone outside and managed to get lost in the worst snowstorm of the year, maybe of the century. Stanley had escaped from his box, and somehow she'd caught the little mouse, which was a real miracle, but she couldn't find her way back home. All she could do was hide under a tree in what became a snow cave. Petting Hunter, Grace thought about that snow cave and goose bumps popped out on her arms. She might have died in there, frozen with Stanley in her pocket, but she hadn't. God had watched over her and sent Pepper. The hunting dog had found her, buried under the trees in the snow cave and barked and barked until the men he was guiding had dug her out and carried her home. It seemed to her that Pepper was pure angel, so probably Hunter was part angel.

Part angel and part puppy.

The part of Hunter that was angel was precious.

The part of him that was puppy was a mess. He would pounce on something and fall over. He'd try to eat from his bowl and step in it. He'd chase his tail until he was dizzy before falling into a heap on the ground. Puppies didn't make much sense, but they were adorable.

She also had a kitten named Stormy. He wasn't much of a kitten anymore. He had grown into a big tomcat who liked to chase things, especially Stanley if he had the chance.

Grace thought she was all done with her chores in the barn when she heard Gus knocking around in his stall. Gus loved Belle, Miriam's horse, and Chance, her dad's horse, but what Gus didn't love was being alone in his stall. He was dark brown with a white muzzle and stood about as tall as Grace. She couldn't help loving the little guy. He would be perfect for pulling a cart, and she was almost old enough to drive one. She ran her hand down his mane and scratched behind the tips of his ears, hoping that would settle him down.

Her dad had been right about Gus. Gabe hadn't wanted the donkey at all. He'd warned her that donkeys were a lot of trouble, but their little donkey was still as cute as the day she'd first seen him at the benefit auction—the day she had begged her dad to enter the woodchopping contest. He'd won too, which still surprised her. After all, he was somewhat old, but he'd chopped wood faster than the younger men. He had been determined that day.

All for a donkey he didn't want. She would probably never understand grown-ups.

By the time she was finished in the barn, she was more than ready to crawl into bed, but then she heard her little sister making baby noises in the sitting room. How could she ignore that?

"It seems as if she's growing every day," Grace whispered as she leaned over the cradle and kissed Rachel good night.

The baby stretched, tiny arms reaching over her head. She gazed at Grace and popped the corner of her small right fist in her mouth.

"You used to suck on your fist," Gabe said.

"I did?"

"Don't you remember?"

"*Dat*. I can't remember that long ago."

"Oh. I thought you remembered everything."

Grace rolled her eyes, walked around the cradle, and gave her dad a big hug anyway. He might be the silliest person she knew, but he also smelled just right and his arms around her felt *wunderbaar*.

"Want me to come and tuck you in?"

"I'm nine, *dat*. I don't need tucking in."

"Oh." Gabe tugged at his beard, looking confused.

"Miriam can come, though."

Miriam smiled as she set aside the quilt top she was working on. "Gabe Miller, it sounds to me like you have *boppli* duty."

"Oh."

Grace had noticed he said "oh" a lot lately, as if it was the one word that came to mind.

"Can you handle it?" Miriam asked.

"*Ya*. Is her diaper clean?"

"It was last time I checked. You'll smell it if conditions change."

Gabe groaned, which made Grace giggle. When Rachel soiled a diaper, the smell was worse than a dirty stall.

"Grace and I are going to have a little girl time." Miriam picked up one of the gas lanterns sitting on the side table.

"Good night, *dat*."

"Good night, Gracie."

Grace sighed as she slid her hand into Miriam's and they headed toward her bedroom. She'd been worried when Rachel was born that Miriam might not have time for her anymore. When Miriam was her teacher, she used to dream about one day having a new mother. Dreaming was all she did, because praying for it seemed like asking God for too much.

Then Miriam and her dad married, and for a while Grace felt as though she were walking an inch off the ground. She had a whole family again, complete with another set of grandparents here in Wisconsin.

The hitch was she didn't know if she should call Miriam her *mamm* or not. After all, she had a *mamm* in heaven. When she'd confessed her worries to her dad and Miriam, they had both told her a name didn't matter as much as a person's heart. And they both knew she loved Miriam as much as her dad loved her.

As much as Miriam loved them.

What mattered was that they were a family.

So Grace still called her Miriam, though sometimes lately in her head she said *mamm*, and in her heart she was starting to feel okay about using that word.

"Did you have a *gut* day?" Miriam asked as she pulled back the bedcovers.

"*Ya.*"

"You found the supplies you wanted at the store."

"They're perfect." Grace climbed into her bed and pulled the covers up to her chin. It wasn't cold, but the covers made her feel nice and sleepy.

Miriam set the lantern on the floor beside the bed. It cast funny shadows across the room. She pulled the flashlight out of Grace's nightstand and tested the batteries, same as she did every night. Then she set it on top of the nightstand where Grace could reach it if she needed to get up and it was dark.

"Do you know what I was thinking about?" Grace yawned so big her eyes squeezed shut, even though she was trying to keep them open.

"Gus?"

"No."

"Hunter?"

"I love that puppy. No, not Hunter."

"What, then?" Miriam settled on the bed beside her.

Grace liked how Miriam was never in a hurry, even when she must be tired. When her stomach had been *huge*, Grace had worried that she might roll off her bed, but she hadn't. And now they had Rachel.

"Are we going to have another *boppli*?"

"That's what you were thinking about?"

"No, but when you sat down I was remembering how big you were before, and how you looked like you had a volleyball under your apron."

Miriam started laughing, and then Grace started laughing. Soon her dad's voice came booming down the hall. "You wouldn't be giggling if you were changing this diaper."

"I thought she might do that. She usually does an hour after she eats."

"Should you go help him?" Grace asked.

"Nope. Your *dat*'s a smart guy. He can handle it."

"So what about it? What about another *boppli*?"

"Usually takes longer than that. Can't say for sure, but I wouldn't expect another right away."

Grace thought about that a minute. Finally she nodded as if it made perfect sense. "I adore Rachel."

"I know you do. You're a *gut schweschder*."

Grace folded her hands to say her prayers. As she was thanking God for her new drawing supplies, she remembered what else she was going to tell Miriam.

"Lydia's cabins..." She yawned again, trying to keep her eyes open.

"I'd like to go back and draw them. I tried to do it while we were riding home, but it was hard to catch the details, hard to remember."

"I'm sure it's difficult to draw while riding in a buggy."

"Did you see the way the river wound behind the cabins?"

"I did." Miriam leaned forward and planted a kiss on her forehead.

"The light was just so..."

"It was."

Grace fought to keep her eyes open. She wanted to talk more with Miriam, but things felt so warm and snuggly and *right*.

"Rest now, dear. If *Gotte* wants you to draw the cabins, He'll make a way."

Chapter 4

Aaron thought he would toss and turn in the double bed he found in cabin four. He'd expected dust on the small table, sheets that hadn't been washed, and a lumpy mattress. He'd thought the inside of the cabins would disappoint him as badly as the outside had.

He was pleasantly surprised.

All of the furnishings were certainly dated. The small table, four chairs, bed, a single nightstand, and one rocker all looked as if they were at least twenty years old.

Which didn't matter at all because the workmanship was simple and excellent.

The bed was constructed from oak and Amish made. As he peered down and studied the way the headboard was fastened together, he was sure of it. Running his hand down the post, he appreciated the solid feel—no plastics, no fabricated wood.

Had his *onkel* Ervin made it? Had he made all the furniture in this room? Long ago, Ervin had worked with wood—before he'd left the family in Indiana and struck out on his own. His dad had told him some of the history.

Much of it Aaron hadn't listened to very closely.

At the time he'd been in a hurry to be back in the fields. He hadn't had much time for remembering about the old days. Family stories were fine, but what use were they when a field needed planting or a horse was sick? The farm was what concerned him, not old stories about family members he could barely remember. He had been so sure his future lay outside the kitchen window, in the Indiana fields, and now he was here...

He was here and he was clueless.

Pulling out the chair, he dropped his provisions onto the table. Maybe it was his exhaustion, or maybe it was his low expectations. Whatever the reason, the clean room and Plain furnishings helped ease the tension from the day.

Lydia had been right about the food supplies in the office. Basics were there and nothing more. He'd found crackers on the shelves and a package of cheese and sausage in the gas-powered refrigerator. Interesting that the office had a phone but no electricity.

Did their bishop not allow it? Even for businesses?

Questions sifted through his mind as he sliced the cheese and sausage, placed them on the crackers, and ate until he was full. Chasing his dinner with cold water, he realized the food was exactly what he'd needed—simple but sufficient. Tomorrow he'd figure out a way to cook.

Would he need to cook? How long would he be staying? Was his job to sell the place or to clean it up?

Every time he sought to find an answer, he uncovered three more questions. So instead he pulled off his work boots, washed at the sink, and sank onto the bed, grateful for the firm mattress and soft pile of blankets.

The questions persisted, though.

Things he needed to know about the cabins, about his *onkel*, even about why his father had sent him. As his eyes grew heavier with each persistent hoot of the owl outside his door, his final questions were about the girl.

Except she wasn't a girl. She was a woman. That much was plain. She no longer had a girl's body or a girl's mannerisms.

The first thought embarrassed him and the second made him laugh out loud in the empty room. Lydia Fisher did not appear to be the kind of woman who would easily back down.

Was that why his *onkel* had chosen to hire such a young person to help oversee things? Because of her stubbornness?

How young was she? Why did she have such an explosive attitude?

The questions circled and echoed through his mind as sleep claimed him.

Sleep that seemed to last hours. He dreamed of Indiana, of working the fields and watching the crops grow tall. He could smell the corn, run his hands across the stalks, walk down the rows, and see his shadow in the afternoon sun.

Too soon, sunlight woke him. He felt disoriented, unsure at first of where he was and feeling as if he'd put his head on the pillow less than five minutes earlier. It wasn't the light that had caused him to sit up in the cabin's bed, though. It was a noise.

He had been awakened by the sound of a horse and buggy pulling into the parking area. No doubt this had been the manager's cabin because it was positioned to hear any comings and goings. He groaned and rolled out of bed, pulling back the shade that covered the window.

Looking out, he saw the beast that had nipped him the day before. The sun was barely over the horizon.

Did she always arrive at work so early? What was her name? Linda? Laura? Lydia.

That was it.

What was she doing here? She must have left when the sun was scratching the first field. Why? Perhaps she was checking on him, to see how late he slept.

Aaron wasn't about to be outworked by a woman. Running water over his face, he attempted to comb his hair, but he could see by the small mirror hung over the sink that he wasn't making it any better. How he looked didn't matter. Hats were made for covering unruly hair. Quickly brushing his teeth, he searched in his bag for clean clothes, threw them on, and bolted out the front door.

The scene from his porch stopped him cold.

A crane similar to the one he'd seen the night before stood on the far side of the river, catching its morning meal.

Smaller birds called from the trees, some he recognized from Indiana and others he didn't. He didn't glance up for long. His eyes were drawn to the beauty upstream, standing in the river near the next cabin.

White as a new moon and easily twenty pounds, the trumpeter swan upended, searching for food. As he watched, the bird's head darted out of the stream. Stretching its long neck straight, water dripped off its black beak and splashed back into the river. It swallowed once, before upending again.

Aaron could have stood watching for hours, but the cry of a hawk startled him. He turned his head and peered up into the sky, following the sound. When he looked back, the swan was gone. Perhaps he'd found better waters around the bend.

Was every morning like this?

Was all of Wisconsin like this?

He placed his hand on the railing as he leaned forward, and the wood cracked, splintered, and nearly gave way beneath his weight.

It figured.

As he walked down the steps, he dodged two hummingbirds that dove past him, headed for the flowering bushes bordering the far side of the porch, practically taking over that side of the building even up to the roof.

His heart wanted to remain focused on the wildlife. His brain was moving toward work, and he was surprised when his stomach began to gurgle.

Last night's cracker sandwiches had left him. Their nutrition was as fleeting as the sense of wonder he'd just experienced. Walking past cabins three, two, and one, which were in desperate need of repair, his shoulders began to tense as he worried over what he should do first.

One thing he knew for certain. It was time to demand some answers. And the one way to do that was to confront his only employee.

Lydia started the *kaffi* and placed her mother's oatmeal cake on the table as soon as she walked inside the office. She had passed by the window and was looking toward the river when she saw Aaron Troyer step out of cabin four's front door. He stepped into the morning light, hat pushed down over hair that needed a good trimming, and something in Lydia's heart tripped a beat. She tried to deny the fluttery feeling, knowing no good would come of it, but hopes and dreams stirred regardless of her good common sense.

Best to ignore them and focus on other things.

She had always liked cabin four. It allowed a good view of the bend in the river, but Aaron probably didn't pause to notice that. He probably saw only the rotten part on the railing that needed replacing. No doubt he noted the fact that the shrubs needed trimming.

Didn't he think she realized those things? She wasn't daft. But there was a limit to how much one person could do.

He still hadn't started toward the office. What was he doing on the porch?

Maybe he had fallen through the rotten rail.

As she began to wonder if she should check on him, he came walking down the steps, frowning at the other cabins as he trudged toward the front of the property.

Humph.

It seemed Aaron woke with the same mood he had carried to bed—a bad one. Well, she'd had customers like him before, she certainly had a younger brother like him, and she'd once had a boy-friend like him.

The customers never stayed long enough to be more than a pass-ing problem.

The younger brother was bound to grow out of his surly disposition.

And the boyfriend had broken things off when he'd realized Lydia had obligations to fulfill and not much time for buggy rides and Sunday evening singings. She'd come to realize she was better off without him.

But what about handsome Aaron Troyer? How long was he going to stick around?

Her instincts told her not very long.

Then the door to the office rattled open, and she didn't have to rely on her instincts. The expression on his face told her all she needed to know. He'd be out of Pebble Creek before Monday's bus left town.

"*Kaffi?*" He stood just inside the doorway, as if he hadn't decided whether to walk inside any farther.

"*Ya*, and some oatmeal cake from my *mamm*."

"Smells *gut*."

Lydia didn't offer to pour his drink or cut a piece of the sweet *kaffi* cake for him. She wasn't sure what her role here was, but she didn't think fetching *kaffi* for the boss was in her job description. At least, it hadn't been with his *onkel*. She missed Ervin, and once again she found herself wondering about God's wisdom in taking the kindly old man when He did.

Of course, it wasn't her place to wonder about God's decisions, as her mother was fond of pointing out.

Aaron fixed his *kaffi* with two sugars and no cream. Walking back to the table, he cut a large piece of the oatmeal cake—Lydia's *aenti* called it a Lazy Daisy oatmeal cake. She had never learned why, but as a child she remembered finding a handful of daisies in the pasture and running into the kitchen so that her mother could add them to the batter.

Aaron didn't sit but instead stood with his back to the window, next to the table, eating and studying her.

Lydia didn't speak, figuring she'd let him begin.

"I'm going to need a pen and some paper to make a list of all the repairs that need to be done."

Lydia walked to the desk and pulled the supplies he needed out of the drawer. She set them on the table in front of him.

"Are the cabins always completely empty?"

"Weekdays, most of them are."

Aaron closed his eyes, but he continued chewing. Maybe her mother had known what she was doing, sending the cake. Perhaps butter, brown sugar, eggs, and cinnamon soothed the soul when little else could. Maybe they would help with all Aaron would learn today.

"Weekends?" he asked.

"Some better."

"How much?"

Lydia shifted from one foot to the other. She realized she was responding the way her youngest sister, Sally Ann, did when she was caught in mischief—which was often. Lydia forced herself to stop fidgeting and stand still.

"How much better?" Aaron repeated, refilling his *kaffi* mug and adding another sugar.

She found herself wondering if his family had a history of diabetes.

"Some weekends half the cabins are full."

"And others?"

"We start with half full, but they leave."

Aaron leaned against the counter, studying her as he drank his *kaffi*. Was he noticing the ten pounds she'd been meaning to lose? Maybe it had crept up to fifteen. Not that it mattered. He wouldn't be around long enough for courting, and if he was staying he wouldn't be courting her. There were plenty of eligible girls in their district to choose from—girls who weren't responsible for a family of eight, girls who had better attitudes and thinner waistlines. Worrying about weight was a prideful thing. She shouldn't care unless it affected her health, which it didn't. Though at the rate Aaron was devouring her *mamm*'s cake, he might need to be letting out his suspenders in the next year. Did he always eat so much? And so quickly?

He took another drink of *kaffi*. At least he didn't slurp it. She could not abide a man who slurped, though it wasn't as if she'd be around him long enough for it to matter. From the look he was giving her, slurping was the least of her problems.

"Why do they leave?"

"Most the time they don't say."

"And when they do say?"

Now she turned and began fiddling at the desk, which was already in perfect order.

"Lydia, when they do say anything, how do they explain their leaving?" When she didn't answer, he walked across the room and stood directly in front of her, close enough that when she looked up she saw that his eyes were exactly the color of her mother's *kaffi* after she'd stirred a measure of cream into it—a nice warm brown, completely opposite the chill in his voice.

"They must have a reservation," he said. "If their reservation is for two or three nights, they must have a reason for leaving. Certainly they tell you something when they—"

"Always they give an explanation. All right? They come up with some excuse, and it's plain that it isn't their real reason." Lydia stepped back from the desk. She wanted more distance between them. She had worked here alone for two months now, and she'd found a comfortable rhythm.

Ervin, he knew the way things were. He understood about the *Englischers*. He caught on before she did.

Somehow they had shared the knowledge together, stumbled through it together. They had even scrounged up enough money to keep the place running. Perhaps they had allowed a few repairs to remain undone, but it had stayed between them. There had been no need for Elizabeth to worry, and Lydia had been able to keep her job.

Now, looking at Aaron, she knew those days were over.

She half turned away from him so she could gaze out over the cabins. "They always tell me something, but I can see the looks of pity," she said quietly. "They stare at this place as you do, as if they can't drive away fast enough. As if they can't possibly rest here or appreciate the flow of the river or hear the cry of the birds. Instead, they run away because of all that is wrong. All that Ervin couldn't do then, and I still can't do now. I see it in their eyes, I see their pity, and I don't know what to say."

Aaron walked over to the sink and rinsed out his *kaffi* cup.

"Does Elizabeth know? Has anyone discussed this with my *onkel*'s wife?"

She had expected sympathy in his voice. His cold hard tone was almost a relief. He turned and pierced her with his stare.

"No. Your *onkel* tried to protect her from how poorly the business was doing."

"Tell me where I can find her."

⌒ Chapter 5 ⌒

On Friday mornings Miriam was in the habit of visiting her mother. After she'd seen Grace off to school, she would bundle Rachel up and head in the opposite direction.

Part of her heart tugged when Grace walked down the lane with Gabe. Eli Stutzman still gave her a ride to school. They were at the edge of the school's boundary, and it was too far for a young girl to walk. Gabe could have taken her, but Grace was in the habit of riding with the Stutzman children, including her best friend, Sadie. Miriam knew all too well the scene that would greet Grace once Eli delivered her to the doors of the little schoolhouse along the banks of Pebble Creek. Having been the teacher there for eight years, she could picture the students tramping inside after pausing to stomp the mud off their shoes. She could practically feel the chalk dust on her fingers. She could hear the children's voices as she prepared to ring the first morning bell.

She glanced over at little Rachel, riding contentedly in her basket, staring up at her with those beautiful brown eyes. Belle moved down the road at a steady trot, and Miriam's restlessness began to ease.

There wasn't even one inch in her heart that regretted giving up teaching to marry Gabe and live in the droopy house with the sad barn...though neither was sad or droopy anymore. But when Gabe

39

smiled and touched her face in the glow of the lantern light, when he asked her gently what was wrong, she was honest enough to admit she missed the schoolchildren at times.

Grace didn't require much tending when compared to a classroom full of students. Even the birth of her baby didn't add a lot of work; Rachel was easy to care for as far as babies were concerned. She slept well. She ate well. Her delivery had been easy.

Miriam wasn't complaining. She directed Belle into her parents' lane, though the mare knew the way. They had traveled home every weekend while she taught at the one-room schoolhouse.

Gabe had understood when she'd admitted to being more than occasionally bored. He'd suggested visiting with her mother one day a week. Perhaps there would be additional work once they could put in the summer vegetable garden, but even Gabe's fields were still too wet for planting. She wouldn't have that distraction anytime soon.

Her father walked out of the barn before she'd pulled the buggy up to the house. Pepper followed him but then hurried ahead to greet her. The German shorthaired pointer was at her buggy by the time she'd pulled to a stop.

"I think he misses you." Joshua King had coal-black hair like Miriam, something of an oddity among Plain people. Both his hair and his beard were streaked with gray. Other than that, he didn't seem a day older than when she had started teaching.

Tying Belle to the hitching rail, he reached for the basket, and his expression softened into wonder. "She's smiling, eh?"

"At you, apparently." Her daughter smiled for Gabe and her father, but she had yet to smile for her. As Joshua carried the baby toward the house, Miriam stooped to pet Pepper. "Don't worry, boy. All the men seem taken with her. You and I still have each other."

Joshua turned and studied them. "No need to be jealous over a *boppli*. A man naturally feels this way about his *grossdochdern*."

"Even when he has so many?" Miriam reached into the buggy and pulled out her quilting bag, and then she hurried to catch up with him, Pepper trotting at her heels.

"Oh, *ya*. More definitely makes it sweeter. Now I know what to expect."

"Such as?"

"Well…" Joshua carried the basket with one hand as if it weighed no more than a loaf of bread, and he tugged on his long beard with the other. "I know she'll be starting school soon, so I need to appreciate these little visits."

"*Dat*, that's years and years away."

"I suppose by the calendar you're right. But in moments of the heart…" He looked to the sky, where a bird lighted in the sugar maple tree near the house. "She'll fly as quickly as that bird."

He winked at her before opening the back door, which led into the mudroom.

Miriam stopped him, reaching out and resting her hand on his arm. "How's *mamm* feeling today?"

"*Gut*. Today is a *gut* day."

Stepping inside, he hollered into the kitchen, "Abigail, Miriam and Rachel are here."

"*Wunderbaar*. I just pulled raisin bread from the oven."

Miriam followed her father into the house. "*Gudemariye, mamm*."

"And to you, dear. How's Rachel this morning?"

Her daughter chose that moment to let out a healthy cry.

"There now. See? She doesn't like bread without the icing. She took one look and let out a holler."

"Joshua King. She did no such thing."

Miriam took the baby into the sitting room, sank into the rocker, and proceeded with her midmorning feeding while her mother reminded her father of the reasons they were cutting back on his sugar intake.

It was an old lecture—one that had been going on for at least two years.

Although Joshua was good about following Doc Hanson's recommendations, he seemed to enjoy giving Abigail a hard time about her new recipes. Their conversation in the background was much like the gurgling of Pebble Creek—familiar, pleasant, and comforting.

As Miriam settled Rachel at her breast, Abigail walked into the room and placed a cup of warm tea next to her chair. It was hard for Miriam to believe her mother was fifty-five years old. Though many Amish women tended to gain weight as they aged, probably because their diet was high in carbohydrates and sweets, Abigail had managed to stay small. Glancing at her, Miriam realized again that her mother was too thin. She could stand to gain a few pounds.

She'd talked to her brothers about it at the last Sunday meeting, but they had only shrugged and reminded her that Abigail insisted she was fine. When she spoke with her two sisters-in-law, she'd found they were both concerned too.

Anna, David's wife, had stopped by and caught Abigail napping in the middle of the day, which was unheard of. Miriam had never known her to nap. And Abigail had confessed to Ida, Noah's wife, that she'd suddenly begun losing her hair.

Her beautiful thick hair. Unlike Miriam's coal-black hair, Abigail's was a light brown. Miriam could remember as a child waiting for bedtime, asking if she could brush it out for her. She'd been awed by the length and weight of it. She'd asked repeatedly when hers would grow past her shoulder blades.

Was her mother ill?

Perhaps they had been worried over nothing. Today Abigail wore a dark gray dress with a black apron, her hair pulled back and tucked into a fresh white prayer *kapp*. She seemed like her old self. She seemed almost healthy and certainly not old. Maybe it wasn't a focus on appearance that made Abigail seem young. In fact, she practiced humility as much as anyone Miriam had ever known. No, it was something else.

Perhaps it was the way she accepted life.

It could be the calmness in her manners. Miriam had seen her handle many emergencies, such as when Gabe had shown up on their doorstep torn apart with grief that Grace was lost in a winter blizzard.

Abigail could be counted on to be a port in any storm.

When Miriam was a teacher, her mother's ways had made sense. Since she'd become a mother, she had a lot of questions.

"Your *dat* likes to grumble, but I believe he's enjoying the new recipes." Abigail sat down and reached for her knitting. The yarn was a soft pink-and-white, and it looked as if she were making a small blanket. Hard to tell though. Her mother's knitting skills were far superior to her own and what looked like a blanket could quickly turn into a child's sweater.

"He eats whatever you fix now? Even the low-sugar recipes?"

"Oh my, yes. Yesterday he asked for me to bake this particular bread. I believe he's lost the craving for the sweets, but he enjoys giving me a hard time."

"And his diabetes?"

"His blood sugar level is improving. No longer borderline. He went for another check last week, and he still doesn't need medicine or daily monitoring according to Doc Hanson."

"That's *wunderbaar* news."

"*Ya.* We were very thankful. Now tell me about Rachel. What new thing has she done this week?"

The morning passed quickly. Soon they were eating lunch, and she remembered to tell them about picking up Aaron Troyer the night before and to ask them about Lydia.

Miriam saw the look that passed between her parents.

Over the years, she'd learned that look usually meant one of two things—either they knew something about someone they didn't think it was proper to share, or they weren't sure it was something Miriam needed to know. She couldn't imagine why it would be improper for her to know about Lydia, who was once her student, or Aaron, who was a complete stranger.

So they must be worried about spreading gossip. But she didn't want rumors. She wanted to know how she could help.

"The reason I ask is that Gabe and I were wondering if we could somehow lend a hand to Lydia or Aaron. They seemed somewhat...lost."

Abigail reached for Rachel and rested the babe against her shoulder, rubbing her back in slow gentle circles. "You taught Lydia."

"I did. It was years ago, though, and so many girls passed through my schoolroom. Sometimes I have trouble keeping them straight. Lydia I remember because she was a very *gut* student. She especially loved math, which was unusual for girls her age. I don't recall what happened after she graduated. Didn't her family move out of our district not long after she finished her schooling?"

When neither of her parents spoke, Miriam fought harder to remember. "It seems I recall the entire family moved to the other side of Pebble Creek, but I can't recollect why. It seems as if I should know why they sold their farm."

Joshua glanced at Abigail. The unspoken thing passed between them again, and she nodded her head ever so slightly.

"Lydia's family lost their farm." Joshua spoke matter-of-factly as he studied the sunny day outside the kitchen window. "That's the reason they moved to the west side of Pebble Creek. They bought a smaller place, one with no acreage to work."

No one spoke for a moment. Miriam became aware of the sounds in the house—the crackling of the fire in the stove and the contented small murmurs coming from Rachel sucking at her fist.

"But, if there was a financial problem, our district would have helped them. There would have been a benefit, or a..." Miriam's voice fell away as questions filled the space between them.

"Ella and Menno, Lydia's parents, had their reasons for allowing things to happen as they did." Abigail gently laid the baby down on her lap. Rachel looked up and smiled—waving her hands. Her head reached Abigail's knees and her feet were pushing against her *mammi's* stomach.

Miriam thought she was a perfect little bundle of joy.

She tried to piece together the small scraps of information her parents were and were not saying, but too much was missing. She knew it was no use asking questions. If her parents considered explaining more about Lydia's family as gossiping, there would be no extracting more information from them. She'd have to try a different tack.

"So Lydia has worked at the cabins for some time?" Miriam asked.

"*Ya*, I believe so." Abigail reached for her tea. "Her *mamm* tells me she enjoys the work."

Another piece of information. Abigail still spoke with Lydia's mother. Why would that be? The more Miriam aged, the less she understood about her parents.

"So this Aaron is here to work in his *onkel*'s place?" Joshua asked.

"*Ya*, but—"

"That's *gut*. It's *gut* to see family take care of family. That is the Amish way." Joshua stood and carried his dishes to the sink.

"But I'm not sure how long he's staying or exactly what his plans are. How are we supposed to help if we don't understand the situation? Gabe tried to talk to him last night. He seemed upset when he saw the cabins. I think he expected them to be in better shape."

"I haven't been by there in several years myself, but I'm sure Ervin did the best he could." Joshua bent and kissed his granddaughter on the cheek and then glanced toward the plate of cookies Abigail had wrapped up for Gabe and Grace.

Abigail shook her head once and Joshua shrugged. "Can't blame a man for wishing."

Patting Miriam on the shoulder, he added, "I'll have Belle ready for your trip home in thirty minutes."

"*Danki*."

When he was gone, she tried one more time to find out more from her mother, but it was no use.

"Go and see Lydia, Miriam. You young girls, you need to learn to be there for one another. Friendship is about more than Sunday socials."

"Shouldn't I know what I'm walking into, though? Wouldn't it be better if I understood the situation and what Lydia's needs are?"

"If there's anything Lydia wants you to know, she'll tell you. But if she's on your heart, child, there's a reason *Gotte* has put her there."

⫷ *Chapter 6* ⫸

A aron ended up taking Lydia's buggy because she insisted.
He didn't want to, but he needed to make his trip to see
his *onkel*'s widow as quickly as possible. There was much
work to do at the cabins, and he didn't wish to extend his stay in Wisconsin any longer than was necessary.

Tin Star gazed at him distrustfully as Aaron harnessed him to
the rig and turned him onto the blacktop road. Lydia had at least
told him that raisins were the secret. Raisins! He'd heard of spoiling
horses—he'd been guilty of it a time or two himself—but he'd never
considered raisins.

As he followed the road away from town, he focused on what he
would say to Elizabeth. He hadn't seen her in many years. He'd been
a young boy then and uninterested in *onkels*, *aentis*, or family time.
His main concern had been when he could be back outside. It didn't
matter if he was playing baseball or working in the fields. Even at the
age of twelve, when his *onkel* Ervin had moved away, he'd felt a desperate need to be outdoors.

That much he remembered clearly. Probably because it hadn't
changed much over the years.

He hadn't a clue what his *aenti* was like. There had been letters,
of course, but he hadn't read them. Sometimes in the evenings his

mother had read them aloud to the family. He hadn't paid much attention. He'd been focused on scouring the *Budget* for animals to add to their stock or reading the weather forecast, trying to determine how it would affect their crops. He had much to learn, much to catch up on in regard to farming and livestock. His father and grandfather knew a lot, but he was interested in the newer methods—not necessarily *Englisch* methods, but new Amish methods.

It had chafed against his nature that he had to wait through eight years of schooling to be able to study the subject that most interested him. Once he was free of the schoolhouse, he'd thrown himself into learning all he could about farming and being successful at it.

Now he was twenty-three, things were finally going very well at the farm in Indiana, and where was he? Stuck in Wisconsin. The injustice of it rankled him.

He was so busy brooding over his situation that he nearly missed the lane Lydia had warned him would be hard to see.

Yanking abruptly on Tin Star's reins, he turned the buggy south and across Pebble Creek. The house that sat back and to the right was not his *onkel*'s. Lydia had been adamant about that. This first house had fertile land, and Aaron considered for a moment how productive the crops would be once the fields dried out from the recent flooding.

With a shake of his head, he pushed those thoughts away.

He wasn't staying, and if he were, he wouldn't be farming. He'd be stuck maintaining the cabins, which he had no desire to do.

Behind the river and the farm was another homestead.

This one reminded him of the cabins. As his heart settled into a sense of disappointment he was quickly growing accustomed to, he realized the rambling house with little land was his *onkel*'s home. On closer inspection he saw that the home wasn't in as bad a state of disrepair as the cabins—the yard was neat, the fences were maintained, and the small barn looked to be in good condition.

It was only that the area was very small. There was no room for crops, and Aaron couldn't understand being satisfied with such a place. Had his *onkel*'s heart been given over completely to the cabins? Was that why he could live on a place with such little space around it?

There was a small garden area to the west side of the home for growing vegetables, and a pasture area to the east for the horses. Ervin had anticipated what he would need for his family and purchased exactly that. What he hadn't predicted was the size of his family—the house looked as if he had added on to it at least twice, building toward the back each time.

The moment Aaron pulled up in front of the house, a woman walked out on to the porch. Peeking out from behind her dress was a little girl in a black prayer *kapp*.

Aaron tied Tin Star to the fence surrounding the small garden area, under the shade of a tall maple tree, before walking over to the porch.

"*Gudemariye*. You probably don't remember me, but—"

"Of course I do, Aaron. It's *gut* to see you. Come in, please." Elizabeth was younger than he expected. Probably in her early forties and somewhat on the plump side. She was pretty in the way of healthy Amish women. He'd heard his parents talking of the fact that she would have no problem remarrying after waiting the appropriate year. It occurred to him, as he followed her into the house, that their assessment was probably true.

"*Danki* for coming. It's a long trip from Indiana."

"Of course I'd come, Elizabeth. We wouldn't leave you to take care of things alone." He glanced around the sitting room. It looked the same as his parents' home, simply furnished and clean.

"Come into the kitchen. I have some *kaffi* on the stove."

"Sure. That would be *gut*. It's still cold here even though it's May."

"June is beautiful, though."

She poured some *kaffi* into a mug waiting on the counter before refreshing her own mug. It was almost as if she had been expecting him. But how was that possible? He'd told no one he was coming by today. It didn't seem she could have known he had arrived in town just yesterday.

Then again, women seemed to have their own form of communication, almost like the *Englischers* telephone system.

"I'm sure summers here are very nice." He almost added that he wouldn't be around to see it, but remembered his parents' warning not to be rude. So instead he gulped his *kaffi*, which was boiling hot. Wincing, he tried to think of how best to begin.

"Ervin, he..." Elizabeth stared down at her hands.

When she glanced up with tears sliding down her cheeks, Aaron searched his mind for what to say. His father had given him a final talk about money, traveling, and interacting with the *Englisch*, but he hadn't mentioned emotional women.

His mother had reminded him to watch his manners and to remember the *Ordnung*. As far as he knew, that set of rules didn't cover this situation.

Elizabeth sniffled and swiped at her cheeks.

"*Was iss letz?*" The young girl was immediately at her mother's side, holding an Amish doll fixed up in a black *kapp* and apron like her own.

"Nothing's wrong."

"Why are you crying?" She slid the doll onto her mother's lap. "Do you want to play with my *boppli*? She always makes me feel better."

"*Danki*, Beth." She whispered something else to the girl, who ran off to the sitting room and began to draw. "I'm sorry, Aaron. You're going to think I'm a mess."

"No. Of course not." He searched his mind for what else to say. "I'm sure this is difficult for you."

"It is. Yes. Ervin was a hard worker and wasn't sick at all, so his passing was a..." Her voice started to wobble, and she swiped at her cheeks. "It was a..."

"Surprise?" He jumped in before she had time to begin crying again.

"*Ya.*" She glanced up, the hint of a smile replacing the grief on her face. "So you understand."

In truth, he had understood nothing since landing in Cashton or Pebble Creek or wherever he was, but he nodded. Elizabeth went on to explain about Ervin's heart attack and how he hadn't suffered because it had been so sudden. She added that *Gotte* had been merciful in taking him quickly.

Agreeing with her seemed to calm her and stop the flow of tears.

How did men do this? Why did they marry if it meant dealing with emotions and tempers and who knows what that he hadn't seen yet.

Elizabeth stirred cream into her *kaffi*. "It was such a surprise. The night before we were talking about our spring garden and how the rains were heavier this year. He went out to tend to the horses, and he never…"

This time Aaron let the silence stretch between them.

Finally, Elizabeth repeated what he'd heard his parents pronounce when they had read the letter notifying them of Ervin's passing. "It was *Gotte's wille* that he pass, though he was only fifty-two."

"*Ya*. I suppose it was." Aaron finished his *kaffi* and wondered how long it was proper to wait before he turned the subject to the real reason he'd stopped by. He needed to finish here and head back to the cabins. Already the sun was high in the sky, and the list of repairs in his pocket was long.

Beth ran into the room, but instead of going to her mother's side, she stopped a few feet shy of Aaron.

"I believe she has something for you," Elizabeth murmured.

Written across the top of the page in lopsided German script was his name. Her name was signed at the bottom. She'd colored a picture of him standing in the field with tall stalks of corn growing all around him. In the page's bottom corner was one her father's cabins.

"*Danki*, Beth. This is very nice." He didn't mention that in the picture his arms reached nearly to the ground and his head was the size of a large melon. "May I keep it?"

The little girl smiled and nodded.

Aaron said, "I see the family resemblance."

"Ervin often said so."

Beth stepped closer and pointed to the picture. "My *mamm* told me you like to work in the fields."

"*Ya*, I do."

"That's why I drew the corn."

"It's beautiful corn."

Beth ran a finger along the picture, tracing a blue line across the bottom of the page he hadn't noticed before. When she reached the corner of the drawing where she'd sketched the cabin, she said, "But now you're going to stay here in Pebble Creek instead and help us. 'Cause *dat's* gone."

Aaron glanced up and caught Elizabeth studying him.

"Go pick up your crayons now, Beth. We've chores to do in a few minutes."

When the little girl had left the room, Aaron cleared his throat and tackled the subject he'd been avoiding. "When was the last time you were out to visit the cabins?"

"It's been a while. I offered to help, but Ervin hired Lydia and said there was no need. Mostly I handled things here at the house and worked in the garden, and Ervin and Lydia took care of matters at the cabins."

Aaron nodded as if that made sense.

"I know business has been slow, Aaron. We were hoping that once Amish Anthem opened, more tourists would visit the Cashton area."

"What is Amish Anthem?"

"It's the large hotel in town. Well, it's not actually a hotel now. It was many years ago before it closed and fell into disrepair. An *Englisch* developer purchased it and remodeled it into a tourist attraction."

"We have similar places in Indiana."

"It turned out to be much better for our area than what was first planned, though the owner is not a particularly pleasant man. That's all a long story that you probably don't have time for, but the point is that Gabe Miller stepped in and things changed."

"Gabe?"

"Yes. Do you know him?"

"He gave me a ride yesterday."

"There are two Plain districts in the Cashton area. Gabe lives on the more conservative side, but he convinced both districts to become involved, and because of that the establishment downtown is better than it would have been, in my opinion."

"But it still hasn't helped business at the cabins."

"I suspected as much, though Ervin didn't speak about it. He brought home what we needed for me and the *kinner*." Elizabeth ran her thumb around the top of her *kaffi* cup. "Ervin felt strongly that *Gotte* led him to open the cabins, that he was to offer a place of solitude and peace for people to come to—a place where folks could rest and draw closer to *Gotte*. Along the banks of Pebble Creek seemed the perfect place to do so."

Beth sang as she picked up her drawing supplies in the sitting room.

And Aaron felt, maybe for the first time, the full weight and responsibility of being an adult.

"Perhaps it hasn't been long enough," he suggested.

"Amish Anthem opened three months ago."

Aaron stood, pulled the list out of his pocket, and stared at it. Finally he raised his gaze to Elizabeth's.

"How bad is it?" she asked quietly. There was something in her eyes, something in spite of her earlier tears that convinced Aaron she had the strength to hear the truth.

"It's not *gut*." He pushed the piece of paper across the table. Waiting, he looked beyond her to the neighbor's farmland that stood in water. Farmland he knew must be fertile, lying so close to the river, lying in this valley where there was such abundance.

"I'm not a carpenter, Elizabeth. I'm a farmer, and I don't have to tell you how young I am." He reached for his hat and pushed it back on his head. "But a business is a business. If we can make the repairs listed on that sheet, and get the word out that the cabins have been upgraded...There's a chance things will turn around."

"How long will this take?" Elizabeth handed the sheet back. "And where will we get the money? We were earning enough, but barely. The other *kinner*, they're all four still in school. They can't work yet unless I ask them to quit."

Aaron thought back to his childhood and how he would have jumped at the chance to be out of the classroom. He was learning things were different here, though, and he had been the odd kid even then. Most students had enjoyed their eight years in the schoolhouse.

"Let me worry about it," he said. Even as the words came out, he wondered why he said them and what he would do to ease the concern in her eyes.

He glanced back down at Beth's drawing, at the ridiculous picture of him towering over the stalks of corn with his long arms and giant head. Perhaps in her five-year-old eyes he seemed enormous, but Aaron was realizing his limitations.

As Beth and Elizabeth walked him out to Lydia's buggy, he knew he couldn't let those limitations stop him.

For their sake, for Ervin's family—who was also his family—he needed to find a way around the problems.

For his sake, he needed to do it quickly.

≈ Chapter 7 ≈

G abe had finished caring for his animals by noon.

He wanted to be out in the fields, planting. But his field was soaked from last week's rains. Trying to plow it would do nothing more than aggravate him and tire his horses. Instead of frustrating them both, he left a note on the counter for Miriam.

David had asked him to stop by when he had a chance, and he figured this afternoon was as good a time as any. David King was Miriam's middle brother, sandwiched between Noah, the oldest, and Simon, who came after Miriam. Though Gabe had grown close to the entire family since moving to Wisconsin, he had the most in common with David.

He'd been helpful in giving advice on ways to improve what was planted and where to plant it last year. Gabe had some new ideas this year he wanted to run by him, and he needed his opinion before he began planting.

He scratched at his beard as he allowed Chance to settle into a somewhat fast trot. The horse wasn't used as much as he had been before Gabe married, and he needed to burn up some energy nearly as much as Gabe did.

Now, why did David want to see him? He couldn't remember. No matter. He would find out soon enough. David managed to stay busy, even when the fields were flooded. Between the farm and the toy business he had on the side, he and his wife, Anna, made ends meet. He had confessed that some years were hard. Other years they had bonus crops. Such was the way in Wisconsin.

Gabe had told him it was the same in Indiana.

Perhaps it was the same all over.

Gabe's mind drifted back to Indiana and the farming he'd done there. There were days he missed it, but more and more that life seemed as if it belonged to another man. This was his life now, and he couldn't imagine going back. He was still grateful he had met and married Hope, Grace's mother. Still thankful for the time they'd had together. Her death from cancer hurt less and less, though, which was nothing short of a miracle.

As Grace grew older she was becoming her own person, but there were times, when she was studying a problem, or gazing out at a sunset, that she reminded him very much of her mother. Hope lived on through Grace.

But he couldn't imagine his life without Miriam. God had given him a peace about that. He knew it was best for him to move on and best for his daughter. And now he had Rachel. Who could say? Perhaps one day he'd have a boy as well, though he wouldn't be like those fathers who went on and on wishing for a son to walk in their footsteps.

He started daydreaming about a boy, about teaching him how to plow and work with horses. Maybe he'd even take an interest in woodwork. Gabe was so caught up in wondering how old the boy should be before he began working with the woodworking tools that he drove right past David's lane and had to turn the buggy around.

Honest mistake. Anyone could make it. It wasn't as though he was preoccupied with the idea of another child. Could be years yet. Rachel was still an infant.

Chance trotted down the lane and past the house toward David's barn. Because it was after lunch, Gabe knew David would be working in the portion he'd turned into a toy shop.

Before he had pulled to a stop, Seth, David's oldest son, stepped out of the barn. Staring at the ground as he trudged toward Gabe's horse, hands plunged into his pockets, he was the walking image of a discontented teenager. At five foot ten with sandy brown hair and a thin build, he was also a mirror image of his father. Perhaps somewhat thinner and smaller, but he'd grow into him, and he'd grow out of the surliness. As Gabe climbed down from the buggy, he almost laughed but swallowed it back. They were hard years—the ones between a child and a man—and no laughing matter. But what could cause such an expression of misery?

"Good afternoon, Seth."

"If you say so."

"I do. Would you say otherwise?"

"I'm stuck working in this barn. *Ya*, I guess I would." Seth glanced up, daring Gabe to argue.

Gabe put his own hands in his pockets and considered what Seth had said, listening for the real problem behind the words. "I suppose if I didn't want to be in the barn, it wouldn't be a very *gut* day."

Seth's expression turned from surly to hopeful. "Could you tell my *dat* that? He doesn't seem to understand that I don't want to work with his cattle or plow his fields."

"Have you told him?"

Seth ran the toe of his work boot across the pebbled lane. "Not in so many words," he mumbled.

"Huh." Gabe ran his hand down Chance's neck. He was truly a beautiful gelding—a quarter horse more than fifteen hands high, a dark bay with white tips. "Guess he's not picking up on your hints."

"No." Seth followed his lead and began paying attention to the horse. "This is a beautiful animal, Gabe. This is what I want to do. Work with animals, but not in a field."

Gabe glanced up to meet the boy's gaze. "Explain that to your *dat*. I'm sure Bishop Beiler would be willing to take you as an apprentice."

Seth returned his attention to Chance. "I've heard his rules are harsh."

"*Ya*. Things are different on our side of Pebble Creek. You know that from visiting your *grossdaddi*."

"I wouldn't be living there, though. Only working."

"True enough."

"But I've also heard he doesn't abide any...stepping outside the rules." Seth glanced up from the horse.

David had mentioned he thought the boy was experimenting with his *rumspringa*. It would seem from his comments that perhaps he was caught deep in its throes.

"I believe I've heard the same." Gabe patted Chance once more. "I need to visit with your *dat* for about an hour. Would you see that Chance has some water?"

"Sure thing. He's a handsome animal."

Seth seemed a shade less petulant as he walked back into the barn. Gabe didn't envy the age. It was a time he hadn't struggled with as much as some, but he was glad when he was married and it was over. Those years reminded him of Pebble Creek when it was swollen and moving fast, as it was now. He preferred the calmer, slower days of summer same as he preferred the more contented years of married life.

Walking into David's toy shop and looking at shelves lined with playthings for babies up through Grace's age, Gabe realized he was completely satisfied being a husband and father. He was glad the confusion of teenage years was behind him.

"Gabe. I wasn't sure you would make it today." David walked in from the back room. He was a big man, nearly as tall as Gabe's six foot two, which made it all the more strange to see him holding a doll cradle in his hands.

"*Ya*. Can't plow, so I had some extra time."

"*Gut*. I'm glad you stopped by. Did Seth see to your horse?"

"He did."

Something in Gabe's tone must have alerted David, or perhaps he caught Gabe's glance out the workshop's window, his look toward the boy. "I won't abide him showing bad manners to customers or *freinden*. Tell me he wasn't rude."

"No, he wasn't bad mannered at all." Gabe perched on a stool that sat next to a counter. David had done a nice job of turning this portion of the barn into a real shop. What was it like to have strangers traipsing on and off your property, though?

"But..."

Picking up a truck carved out of maple, Gabe rolled it across the counter before glancing up and grinning. "Nice wheels."

"Uh-huh. You're avoiding the conversation about my firstborn."

"He seems to be having a hard time, is all."

"He seems to be having an attitude, and I'll have none of it."

Gabe studied David. A saying his *mamm* often quoted darted into his mind. "Don't argue with a fool—people watching may not be able to tell the difference." He remembered the proverb and decided to keep it to himself.

David was no fool, but where his son was concerned, he might be somewhat blinded. Regardless, who was he to tell the man how to raise a seventeen-year-old boy? He'd never raised a teenager himself. He had his hands full with an infant and a nine-year-old girl.

"Why was it you wanted me to stop by?"

"I received some of that new seed we were talking about, and it came with literature I thought you would want to look over."

They spent the next hour weighing the benefits of planting oats versus spelt and wheat. Both men were growing restless with waiting on the ground to be ready. Their conversation became so animated they took it outside. Soon they were talking about the advantages of rotational grazing, something Gabe had studied over the winter and wanted to try.

"You're going to put your cattle in your fields."

"I am, come fall."

"It's foolish," David said, scowling.

"No, it's not." Gabe shook his head. "I believe it will increase my yield."

"I believe it will increase your work."

"And I believe you two need to find something else to do until the land dries." Anna had joined them at the fence without either one of them noticing. Shorter than Miriam and expecting their sixth child, she had recently entered the final month of her pregnancy.

Miriam had shared that the baby's size was making sleeping hard for Anna, and when Anna didn't sleep he supposed David didn't sleep. The next month wouldn't be easy for his brother-in-law or sister-in-law. He needed to remember to stop by more often and offer to help however he could.

"Can't you find any work?" Anna asked. "You're frightening the goats with your arguing."

"What would you have us do? My shop's shelves are full of toys. There's a limit to how much woodwork a man can do in one day." David smiled at his wife, but Gabe could sense the nervous energy in him.

It was the same energy he felt in himself. They were both used to working long hours all year. The winter work was finished, though, and they couldn't begin the spring's work yet. It was frustrating for everyone.

"Maybe you could..." her hands came out and fluttered toward the road. "Run an errand or something."

"It sounds as if she's trying to get rid of me."

"*Ya.* It does." Gabe grinned at the two of them.

"What are you smiling about? Miriam probably sent you over here to get you out from underfoot." David tested the top board of the fence. It was sturdy. He'd knocked the entire place into tip-top shape. Either that, or he'd had Seth working on it to keep the kid busy.

"No, Miriam's at your parents'." Anna placed her hand at the small of her back.

"She told you that?" Gabe asked.

"She didn't have to. She goes there every Friday."

"Women share everything," Gabe muttered.

"Not everything, but many things. Now, isn't there somewhere you two can go? And take Seth with you."

"Why would we do that?" David's scowl returned.

"Count it as a favor. He just came banging through the house. I'm worried about him, David. He seems so unhappy."

"What does he have to be unhappy about?"

"Do it for me. It would be a big help."

"Speaking of help..." Their worry over Seth had reminded Gabe of Aaron. "I met someone yesterday who could probably use a hand."

He related meeting Ervin's nephew, taking him by the cabins, and Aaron's confrontational meeting with Lydia. David and Anna exchanged knowing glances as he neared the end of his story.

"Might be a *gut* idea for us to go by there," David admitted.

"David's tried to help before, but Ervin always said he could take care of things himself."

"The place looked as if it needed repairs. I'm not sure Aaron can do it alone, at least not quickly."

"Why should he?" David asked. "My *fraa* wants us out from underfoot, and young Seth apparently has some energy to burn off."

"Sounds like a *gut* reason to stop by."

"Ride with me or take your own buggy?"

"I'd better take my own. The cabins are on my way home."

Fifteen minutes later they were underway. Gabe wasn't sure they would be welcome, but he was glad they were going by to check on Aaron Troyer. Something told him they should at least offer to help. After all, it was the Amish way.

He wasn't sure how the cabins had fallen into such a sad state of repairs, or what the look between David and Anna meant, but he wouldn't be able to plant his fields before next week even if the sun came out and started shining this very minute. Pushing his hat back, he stared up at the low-lying clouds. At least they had stopped pouring rain down onto the ground. He would have to be grateful for that and trust God knew what He was doing regarding the weather.

As far as he could reason, it didn't seem as though he had much choice other than fussing about the rain, which was a useless way to spend his days.

Now, would Aaron allow them to lend a hand?

They would find out soon enough.

~ *Chapter 8* ~

G race sat on the swings with Sadie and Lily during their after-noon recess. Sadie was her very best friend. She had been almost since the first November day Grace had walked into the one-room schoolhouse beside Pebble Creek. She was nearly like Grace in every way, except Grace was sure Sadie was prettier.

That was something she wasn't supposed to think about. Bishop Jacob had spoken about humility again just last Sunday. It was a hard idea for Grace to put her arms around. She understood modesty and the emphasis on it, but her eye naturally looked for the beauty in things. Her mind found those things and focused on them. Those were the objects she liked to draw.

It wasn't that she didn't like herself when she checked her reflection in the small mirror beside her bed before leaving in the morning, but when she looked at her *freinden* she noticed small details worth draw-ing. A few moments ago she came across Sadie helping Lily with her prayer *kapp*, and her fingers itched to draw the two of them, with Sadie scrunching her nose as she focused on refastening Lily's hair-pins, Lily biting down on her bottom lip as she held perfectly still, and the light bouncing off their black *kapps*. They made a picture like the ones Grace had seen on the shelves in the *Englisch* store.

Sadie and Grace were similar in size and height. Lily was smaller and younger. She was also a little chubby, probably because she liked her mother's sweets so much. Lily's mother cooked wonderful cookies and pies. Most days Lily brought extra helpings to school and shared them.

Every day they ate their lunches together. After they ate, they usually played tag or sat on the swings.

"Why do you think the boys would try to play baseball in the mud?" Sadie asked.

"Because they're boys," Grace said, leaning forward in the swing to catch a glimpse of the game going on around the other side of the school yard. The sun was breaking through the clouds in spots, and it was a little warmer, but the thought of all that mud on her clothes made her shake her head.

"What is it, Grace? Whatcha thinking about?" Lily stopped a few feet shy of the other swing.

They had the area to themselves. Some of the girls had stayed inside, and the rest had gone over to watch the baseball game.

"Are you thinking about playing ball?" Lily cocked her head, reminding Grace of Hunter and causing her to laugh.

"*Nein.* I was thinking of the washing I'd have to do if I played ball."

"You're right. It wouldn't be worth the extra chores." Lily hitched up her dress, stepped carefully over a puddle of water, and plopped into the swing beside Grace.

Sadie moved around behind them and began to push Lily's swing. She had to reach out with her arms so that she wouldn't step into the water that had gathered under Lily's seat. Grace satisfied herself with sitting in the swing and rocking it back and forth.

"I'm surprised Hannah and Miss Bena allowed us to come outside at all." Sadie stared at the schoolhouse as she pushed Lily again.

"Hannah must have talked her into it," Grace said. "She seemed eager to have the boys out from underfoot."

"But Miss Bena—" The way Sadie whispered their teacher's name pretty much summed up their confusion about their new teacher.

She'd been their teacher only since January.

Several replacements had been tried since Grace's stepmother had married and stopped teaching. None had worked out particularly well. They had tried a nice Mennonite woman, but the pay was too low and the distance too far from her home. They had also tried an Amish man, but he'd left when he purchased a large farm to the north.

For more than a month a round of substitutes had marched through the classroom each day—her classmates' mothers, fathers, and even grandparents. That was fun, at first, but it quickly grew old.

Then Miss Bena had appeared.

"I sure hope those boys don't get muddy," Lily said.

"She'll never let them back in the schoolroom." Sadie slowed the swing Lily was in, as if she suddenly feared the girl would fly out and topple into the muddy water.

"She'd probably give them a bucket and have them scrub off outside." Grace started laughing as she pictured that. It would make a great drawing.

Suddenly they all heard a cheer go up from around the corner of the school yard, followed by clapping, and the three girls glanced at each other.

Grace turned toward the ball game.

Sadie took two steps away from the swings so she could see better.

And Lily leaned back in the swing.

When she did, she slid farther down into the seat, and then the thing that wasn't supposed to happen, happened.

Lily, Sadie, and Grace stood outside the doorway to the schoolhouse. They didn't dare step inside.

Miss Bena stood inside the doorway, arms crossed and mouth scrunched up as though she'd swallowed something sour. Grace had seen that look before. It wasn't good. Hannah stood behind Miss Bena, her right hand over her mouth and her eyes open wide.

"You are dripping, Lily Gingerich." The words came out of Miss Bena's mouth quietly and slowly.

Grace wondered if she thought that by speaking slowly she could change the scene in front of her. Miss Bena hated dirt of any kind, and she especially detested mud. She'd used that exact word last week. "I *detest* mud in my classroom." Grace hadn't heard the word "detest" before Miss Bena had stood in front of Luke and Adam Lapp and proclaimed her dislike for mud.

Sometimes Grace questioned if teaching was the best job for their new teacher, as kids did tend to be dirty at times.

After Miss Bena proclaimed, "You are dripping, Lily Gingerich," Lily only nodded.

"She fell out of the swing," Sadie explained. "Into the puddle."

"I told you to stay inside if you couldn't be careful." Miss Bena was still speaking slowly, as if they had trouble understanding. Grace knew about that too. Back when she had lost her voice, people would talk that way to her sometimes, as if her mind was lost as well as her voice.

Lily glanced up at Grace, her eyes *pleading* for help.

Grace wanted to say something that would erase the expression of shock off Miss Bena's face, but the words in her mind seemed to catch and stick in her throat.

Memories of the years she couldn't speak crowded in on her, kind of like the other school children crowding in behind them. Now everyone was interested in what they were doing. Usually no one noticed them because they were quiet and small.

Grace turned to look at the other kids.

The boys weren't exactly clean.

Adam and Luke both had mud stains on the knees of their pants. As if they knew what she was thinking, they ducked to the back of the crowd. No one looked like Lily, though. Dirty brown water was still dripping onto the top step of the schoolhouse.

Lily's eyes crinkled up and her mouth turned down at the corners, and Grace knew what was going to happen next. Once Lily started crying, it usually lasted at least fifteen minutes.

She needed to speak up, now, or things were headed toward an even bigger disaster. "It was our fault—mine and Sadie's."

Sadie's eyes popped open wide as quarters.

"Sadie was pushing her in the swing, and I was sitting beside her. I guess we weren't being careful enough." Grace reached out to clasp Lily's hand. She was relieved when Sadie did the same. "We'll take her to the girls' room and wash her up, Miss Bena. When we bring her back, she'll be real clean."

Sadie nodded her head and Lily sniffled, but at least she didn't start bawling like the calf in the sad barn when it wanted its mom.

"Any lesson you miss will be made up at home. Hannah, see if you can find Lily some extra clothes from upstairs."

Hannah winked at the girls from behind Miss Bena's shoulders before she turned and hurried upstairs to the apartment over the schoolroom. It was where Miriam and Esther used to live, but now Miss Bena lived there alone. Hannah still lived with her parents because their farm was very close to the schoolhouse—or maybe because she would rather live at home than with Miss Bena. You would have to be awfully clean if you lived with their teacher.

The three girls turned around and walked back down the steps. When they did, the other children spread into two groups, making a wide path for them.

"Guess no one else wants to get muddy," Lily said.

"You'd think we had the chicken pox or something," Sadie muttered once they were through the small crowd.

"They just don't want Miss Bena to be mad at them." Grace put a little distance between Lily and herself, though she continued to hold the younger girl's hand. She didn't need any of the mud on her dress. They had enough extra washing at home with Rachel's dirty clothes and their regular washing.

"She's awfully mad." Lily looked up at Grace as they all tried to fit inside the outhouse.

"She wasn't happy, but it's hard to tell with Miss Bena. I'm not sure she's a happy kind of person."

"I'm not sure I'm going to fit in there with you two," Sadie said. She stood in the doorway as Grace studied Lily.

"I'll get her out of these clothes and you can bag them up. We'll need some water too, and the clean clothes from Hannah."

"Sure. I can do that."

Grace did her best to stay clean, but some of the mud found its way on to her clothes anyway. By the time they were finished, she had to use another rag to wipe off her own apron.

"*Danki*, Grace." Lily looked exhausted but cleaner in clothes several sizes too large.

"*Gem gschehne.*" Grace hugged the younger girl and turned her toward the classroom. Sadie had slipped inside ahead of them and was already working.

Grace had missed almost half an hour of the afternoon lessons. She would need to make them up tonight after chores.

What she wanted to do, though, was go home and draw the three of them standing on the schoolhouse step, a puddle of muddy water growing around them. At the time she'd been terrified of being in trouble, but now that the crisis had passed, she thought it was kind of funny. How they must have looked had captured her imagination.

She even knew how she'd cut off the top of the drawing. She'd draw their backs and the tops of their heads covered by their prayer *kapps*. She'd also draw Miss Bena's crossed arms, but not her expression. There was no need for anyone else to experience that.

At times, the woman was actually frightening.

⚏ Chapter 9 ⚏

Lydia had been working cleaning cabins all morning. They had three weekend reservations, and she wanted things to be in tip-top shape. She was in cabin six, dusting the furniture, when Aaron returned from visiting Elizabeth. If anything he appeared to be in a worse mood, though she hadn't thought that was possible.

He didn't pause to speak with her at all.

Instead, he'd unharnessed Tin Star and then banged around in the barn for thirty minutes. When she saw him next, he was attacking the shrubs and vines in front of the nearest cabin. "Attack" was certainly the best word for what he was doing with Ervin's gardening tools. Aaron was apparently working his way away from the parking lot toward the back of the property, butchering anything that was green and touching a cabin wall.

After a while he climbed up on the old wooden ladder Ervin kept for repairs in order to brutalize the top limbs of a lovely white ash tree. Unfortunately, he set the ladder in the mud—everywhere the ground was slick with mud—and the bottom of the ladder slipped. It all happened quickly, leaving him hanging from the tree limb with both hands, his handsaw having fallen to the ground below him.

Lydia had almost gone to help, but before she'd made it out the door of cabin five, he'd swung his leg over the limb and shimmied his way down the tree.

Humph.

Ervin wouldn't have been able to do that, but then Ervin wouldn't have been trimming ash trees in May when the ground was too soft from rain to properly hold the ladder.

Truth was, Ervin hadn't trimmed a tree since Lydia had come to work for him, but that wasn't the point. The giant white ash was beyond beautiful, especially in the fall when its leaves turned golden. Had Aaron Troyer thought of that when he took his saw to it?

Doubtful.

He was too busy taking his frustration out on every living thing in his path. He'd made it to cabin three when Lydia dropped her mop and marched over to where he stood with his garden shears.

"Don't even think about cutting down that speckled alder."

"It's taken over the entire east wall. You can't see out the window at all."

"Birds nest there."

"I'm more concerned that guests nest inside the cabin than whether birds nest in this bush. Guests won't if they walk up to a cabin that looks like this because they can barely find the door with all the shrubs, vines, and tree branches covering the place."

Lydia moved in front of the seven-foot shrub and shook her cleaning rag at him, forgetting for a moment he was her boss and she needed her job. "You chopped down almost all of the juniper in front of cabin two. There won't be an eastern bluebird or cedar waxwing in it now."

"Move out of my way, Lydia."

"I won't."

Aaron shook his head, removed his hat, and wiped at the sweat beading on his forehead. When he replaced his hat he was smiling, but there was nothing pleasant about it. In fact, his expression was absolutely grim.

She'd last seen that sort of look on the baseball field, and it was indicative of a dare if she remembered correctly.

"I thought Amish women were submissive."

"I thought Amish men were levelheaded." She refused to look away from his dark brown eyes. So what if they reminded her of one of the pups her father used to raise? He apparently had no more sense than the beagles did.

"It's only a bush." He waved the garden shears at her.

"They're all only bushes, but together they make up the riverbank and the area where the animals come." Lydia took a step toward him, her hands coming out and encompassing the entire plot of land as if she could fold it into her apron and hold it to herself. As if she could protect it somehow.

"Together they make up this little haven Ervin loved. If you mow them all down we're just another motel like the *Englischers* own."

"But maybe a profitable one!" Aaron's voice rose in some effort to overcome her reasoning. "Maybe one that has automobiles in the parking lot and paying customers!"

Lydia opened her mouth to answer him. She had the perfect retort ready, but she snapped it back just in time. She finally noticed Gabe, David, and Seth approaching. No doubt they had heard Aaron shouting.

How much had they seen and heard? She and Aaron remained less than a foot from each other. Aaron had been hollering and waving his garden shears. Lydia was still red faced with her hands on her hips.

"Sorry. We didn't mean to interrupt." David nodded at them both.

"Guess we didn't hear you drive up," Aaron muttered.

Gabe shrugged, combing his beard down with his fingers. To Lydia he looked as if he were trying to comb a smile off his face. She wondered if he somehow thought this was funny, because it wasn't. Destroying an animal's habitat was a serious offense.

"Aaron, this is David King, my wife's *bruder*, and his son Seth."

"Pleased to meet you." Aaron's face was still red, but Lydia noticed he'd loosened his grip on the garden shears.

"I suppose you both know Lydia?"

"*Ya*," David nodded. "How are you?"

"*Gut*." The word slipped from Lydia's lips before she realized what a lie it was. She was actually horrible! Her apron was filthy from cleaning, and she could feel her hair slipping loose beneath her *kapp*. Young Seth was looking at her as if she had crawled out from under one of the cabins.

All of that didn't matter as much as working around Aaron Troyer. He was making her *narrisch*! Maybe they could take him back to the bus stop, where he could catch a ride all the way back to Indiana.

Instead of asking if they would be willing to return her boss, she yanked her apron down straight, tugged her *kapp* into place, and folded her arms. Best to glare at the river. Better than meet Aaron's gaze.

"We thought we'd stop by to see if we could lend a hand," David said. "Gabe explained you'd come to see to Ervin's things."

"True, but I believe we have it under control."

Lydia didn't even try to keep the exasperated expression from crossing her face. Seth must have seen it because he snorted. When his father gave him a pointed look, he crammed his hands into his pockets. Gabe seemed to be the one person enjoying himself.

"*Ya*, I can see that." David said, glancing back at the branches and leaves littering the walkway between the first three cabins.

Gabe stepped forward, reached up and pulled at a branch of the speckled alder that was caught in the roof's eave. "Truth is, we can't plant our crops yet. The ground's still too muddy. I came to town looking for something to do."

"And my *fraa* decided we were underfoot." David hooked a thumb under his suspenders. "We were planning on offering to help anyway, but she sort of..."

"Sent us over today." Seth finished up for his father, a smile crossing his face for the first time since they had arrived.

Aaron glanced from Gabe to David. "You're saying I'd be doing you a favor to let you stay and work the rest of the day?"

"*Ya*. Pretty much, that's true." David actually sounded eager. "All the work around my place is done."

"Same at mine," Gabe admitted.

"How are you at trimming shrubs?"

Lydia didn't wait to hear their answer. One stubborn Amish man she might be able to outlast, but three men and a boy with an attitude? Not a chance. She trudged back toward the cabin she'd been mopping and satisfied herself with saying a prayer for the birds who would need to find new lodgings once their habitat had been chopped to the ground.

Aaron was more than a little surprised when Gabe showed up, and with friends! Of course, he had seen his share of barn raisings in his life, even helped in quite a few.

But he wasn't working on barns. He was working on cabins.

And they didn't need raising. If anything, they could use leveling.

That was exhaustion and frustration talking. He knew the cabins weren't as bad as he was making them out to be. As they chopped away Lydia's precious speckled alder, plus Virginia creeper, trumpet honeysuckle, and poison ivy—yes, poison ivy—he could see that the cabins were well constructed.

The shutters might be falling off, but he supposed Wisconsin winters could do that to a window shutter.

No, the reason for his foul mood could be traced back to two females. One didn't quite reach his waist and had eyes that looked at him with such trust. He still had the picture she'd drawn in his pocket. The other he barely knew, but she was family nonetheless. What fouled his mood was the knowledge that he was responsible for them both, for them and for the other four girls in Ervin's family.

He had thought he could show up, settle his *onkel*'s things, and return to his own life unchanged.

He had thought it would take only a few days.

Aaron was finding that life was not following the plan he had envisioned. Life was unpredictable, and he was not pleased about it. That his young cousin thought he had arms big enough to solve the problems and a head large enough to hold the answers did nothing to ease his worries.

So he attacked the winterberry vines which had grown up to entangle itself along the wall of cabin ten.

"Might want to leave some of that." Gabe eased himself onto the porch steps. "The grapes will attract all sorts of waterfowl this summer and even game birds come winter."

Aaron breathed a silent prayer for patience, sighed, and joined Gabe on the step. He stared at both of his palms.

"I've been working fulltime in the fields since I escaped the schoolhouse. I never had blisters like this before."

"It's different work than plowing," Gabe acknowledged.

"I prefer the plowing."

Gabe didn't speak immediately. Aaron had known the man less than twenty-four hours, but he was already learning his ways. Apparently slow, measured responses and a healthy sense of humor were two of them.

"*Ya*. I can tell."

"Why would my *onkel* allow this place to become so overgrown? He might as well have called them the Plain Cabins in the Jungle. How would he have expected *Englischers* to want to stay here? Why would they want to stay here?" The questions which had circled round and round in his mind exploded out like a fireworks display during a Fourth of July celebration.

Instead of attempting to answer them, Gabe turned so that his back rested against the square post of the porch and studied him.

"Even I can see why the cabins weren't making money, and I know nothing about running a business." Aaron busted open the blister in the middle of his palm, frowning as he probed the raw skin beneath.

"So you plan on staying long enough to turn the cabins around?"

"Do I have a choice?"

"Sure. Everyone has a choice."

Aaron thought on that, staring out over the grounds. The sun was heading westward. Seth was dragging all that they had cut toward the far end of the property, making a large brush pile. David was standing near the water's edge, talking to Lydia. It was the first time he'd seen her when she wasn't working or hollering at him.

She cared about the cabins, that much was plain. No doubt she cared about his *onkel*'s family as well.

And there was the rub. He wasn't without feelings, but he didn't want to carry the weight of so many on his shoulders. He wanted to go back to the acreage he had already bought seed for, back to fields he had already planned and marked out how he was going to plant. Half of the job was already finished because they hadn't had the rains Wisconsin had endured.

If he stayed here, chances were he wouldn't see those crops harvested, because what needed to be done...

What needed to be done and be done properly would take several months, at least.

But the alternative would be to let his *aenti* and his nieces depend on the charity of the church. Which was fine if they needed it.

His father had sent him so they wouldn't need it.

He stared at the raw center of his hand, at the place that would be sore for a week now. He should have left it alone instead of picking at it. So many times he knew what to do, but he chose wrong. Maybe this once, he would choose right.

So he looked sideways at Gabe and nodded. "*Ya*, I'm staying."

"Let's go talk to David and Lydia, if you're ready to lay out what you have in mind." Gabe stood and stretched. "Because as soon as our fields dry out, you're going to lose most of your day labor."

Aaron and Gabe walked back toward the office in the late

afternoon sunshine. Clouds were still covering a fair amount of the sky. They would have more rain before morning, but Aaron was optimistic for the first time since he'd arrived. Maybe it was knowing he wasn't working alone. Or maybe it was knowing he'd finally made a decision.

His *grossdaddi* was fond of saying, "No dream comes true until you wake up and go to work." The cabins along Pebble Creek weren't his dream, but they were his *onkel*'s. Perhaps by respecting them, by making them profitable again, he would be able to move through this part of his life—move back to where he belonged. And the best way back was to "wake up and go to work."

Already the restlessness worrying his insides was beginning to ease. The answer was in the work. It always had been.

Work hard, turn a profit, and then he could go home.

Chapter 10

Miriam had readily agreed to Gabe's plan to go back to the cabins on Saturday. Grace wasn't so keen on the idea.

"I usually stay home and play with Hunter on Saturdays." Grace shifted from foot to foot, staring at the buggy.

"You can stay if you want." Gabe winked at his wife over the top of Grace's head.

"Stay?" Her voice squeaked up a notch. "Couldn't we take Hunter with us?"

"Could, I suppose, but a pup might go chasing after something along the riverbank and become lost."

Grace clutched her bag with drawing supplies closer. "Probably he won't miss me."

She glanced back toward the barn.

"There's always tomorrow, Grace. You'll have time to spend with him then." Miriam remembered being a young girl, loving Saturdays, and having a dozen different ways she wanted to spend them.

"No church tomorrow!" Her daughter's eyes lit up—and she did think of Grace as her daughter, every bit as much as Rachel. One by circumstances, the other by birth. Both were precious to her.

Grace bit back her smile. "'Course, I miss the church meeting on days there is no service."

"I'm sure you do." Miriam placed Rachel's carrier on the back-seat of the buggy. "We'll be going to my parents' for lunch. You can play with Hunter in the morning, after our Bible study, and you can see Pepper in the afternoon."

"That settles it. I'm going." Grace scooted into the back of the buggy.

Gabe held out his hand to help Miriam up. "Nice logic. Just like a schoolmarm."

He squeezed her hand lightly before he let go and walked around the buggy to climb in on his side.

Miriam marveled at how Gabe's touch still sent fireflies spinning through her stomach. She'd thought when they married that such feelings would pass with time, but so far they hadn't.

And that was one less worry.

Gabe pulled down on his hat, smiled at her as if he could read her mind, and called out to Chance. The quarter horse set off at a steady trot down the lane.

The day was cool and beautiful. Though another half inch of rain had fallen during the night, the sun was shining brightly this morning.

"Think you'll be able to plant next week?" Miriam asked.

"Maybe by midweek. If the sun will stay out."

"The *Budget* says we'll have dry weather soon," Grace piped up.

"Oh, you're reading the *Budget* now, are you?"

"I finished the book Miss Bena loaned me, and we're only allowed one per week."

Miriam tightened her lips over the retort that rose too easily to her mind. Gabe also remained silent.

Eventually the steady clopping of Chance calmed her anger, though she still couldn't fathom why the teacher would want to limit a child's reading to a single book a week. She needed to talk to Gabe about their signing up for a library card at the Cashton library. She'd never needed one before, but now it would be the best way to supplement Grace's need for additional reading material. They certainly didn't have any extra income for purchasing books—not this year with all the repairs they had done around the farm.

The library, though. She should have thought of that sooner, especially as she was a teacher.

By the time they had reached the new development in Cashton with a large sign proclaiming Amish Anthem, she'd put her irritation toward Miss Bena behind her. The downtown area was surprisingly busy, but then it wasn't often that they came into town on a Saturday.

"Lots of folks," Grace said, peering out of the buggy.

"You stay close, Gracie. Wouldn't want you getting lost."

"Seriously, *dat?* There are like two roads. You can see from one end to the other."

"Good point." He continued to the end of the street and parked the buggy in the farthest lot, then tied Chance to a hitching post under the shade of a cottonwood tree.

"It was nice of Mr. Drake to provide so much parking for buggies," Miriam said, waving at a few Amish families she knew who were also entering the lot.

"The way I heard it, Drake only wanted to have paved lots with small spaces for the *Englisch* cars." Gabe pulled Rachel out of her carrier and handed her to Miriam, and then he reached back into the buggy for the quilted diaper bag.

Miriam nearly laughed when she didn't have to remind him to bring it. They had all quickly learned not to take Rachel anywhere without spare clothes and supplies. She had a way of causing havoc before smiling her sweet smile.

"Did Mrs. Goodland insist on this lot?" Miriam asked. "The shade is *wunderbaar* for the horses, and the fact that it's not paved is *gut* too."

"Our village president had a hand in it as much as she could, or so the papers have reported," Gabe said, guiding his family across the busy street. "I have a feeling the fact that the papers have followed the development so closely also helped. The front page coverage did much to persuade Drake to be sensitive to local needs."

"By 'papers,' do you mean—"

"*Ya.* Rae Caperton."

"She never mentioned it to me. She rarely brings the paper when she stops by, unless there's an article on crafting or teaching or farming she thinks we'd like to see." Miriam reached up to tuck a stray hair into her *kapp.* "Rae is a special person, Gabe."

"That she is. *Gotte* sent her to us, it seems."

Miriam's mind drifted back to the first time she'd met the young woman who was a news reporter for the *Lacrosse Tribune.* Her connection to the Amish was a strong one, and though her past included tragedy, God has used it to build a strong bridge to them. "I can't believe we haven't been here yet."

"Why would we? Amish Anthem has only been open a few months."

"And it isn't as if we ever did plan on shopping here—it's such a tourist attraction. I still can't believe he actually built it, right in the middle of Cashton."

They walked up the steps of what was once their town's only hotel, though now it had been refurbished into a collection of specialty shops. Miriam couldn't help being surprised. The work had been going on for more than a year. She'd been in the initial group from their district that had met with Byron Drake and tried to convince him to modify his plans to build Amish Abbey.

Amish Abbey indeed. The thought still made her shake her head. The man had known nothing of their culture or their faith, and he hadn't cared to learn. He'd been focused on making a dollar, making it quickly, and making it multiply.

His ideas had been misguided at best and harmful at worst. He would have plunged ahead too, if it hadn't been for Rae Caperton and her news stories.

The woman had become a close friend, and that also amazed

Miriam. She'd known many *Englischers*, but she'd never had one she'd taken into her confidence before. Now a week rarely passed when she and Rae didn't share a cup of tea and have a long chat together.

And they had talked about Amish Anthem (not Amish Abbey—the name had been changed along with much of Drake's original plan). Discussing it was one thing. Seeing it was completely different.

As Miriam was finding out.

Gabe had driven by the hotel while they were doing the remodel. Possibly he could have picked up a few extra dollars helping with the carpentry work, but he didn't need employment so badly. He and Miriam were making ends meet all right.

After the short talk with Aaron yesterday afternoon and hearing his plan, they had all agreed to meet at the hotel and take a closer look.

"Aaron and David are over by Amish Artwork." He noticed his wife cringe at the alliteration, and he couldn't stop the smile spreading across his face.

"Gabe Miller, I believe you're laughing at me."

"I am not. Do you hear me laughing?"

"Inside you are."

"You can't blame a man for laughing on the inside."

Rachel began to squirm in Miriam's arms, and Grace reached up and tugged at his hand as customers coming in from outside jostled up against him and his family. The place was actually quite crowded.

"Can I go look around on my own?"

"Sure thing, but remember we'll only be here a little while."

"How long?"

Gabe shrugged. "Half an hour, maybe."

"To go through the entire building?" Miriam moved Rachel to her shoulder and stared at Gabe in disbelief.

"I suppose."

"There are two floors!"

Understanding dawned slowly. After all, he'd been married to her only a little over a year. "Make it an hour, Grace. I believe someone has a hankering to shop while she's here."

"I'll meet you on the front porch in one hour."

His daughter was gone before he could remind her to be careful. The thought crossed his mind that she was growing up too fast, but before he could fret over it, Lydia joined them.

"Remind me why we're here."

"Lydia, *gudemariye*." Miriam beamed at the younger woman, who instantly softened.

"*Gudemariye*. I've already been through Amish Accents and Amish Accessories. I don't know what we're supposed to be looking for." Stepping closer to Miriam and the baby, she added, "How's Rachel?"

"*Gut*. I'd love to have a peek at the baby things."

"They're probably over in the Amish Angels section."

"He has to run out of A's eventually," Gabe muttered. "I'm joining the men. You two have fun."

"I don't know what to look for, either," Miriam admitted, calling after him.

Gabe didn't answer, but he waved in acknowledgment as he made his way through the crowd.

He certainly didn't understand what they were doing in Drake's establishment. He wasn't going to pretend he did, so he couldn't very well explain their morning errand to his wife. Aaron had said that if they wanted the cabins to be successful, they needed to pattern themselves after other successful businesses. From the size of the crowd, he was right about one thing—Drake was certainly drawing in plenty of people.

"You made it." Aaron glanced up when Gabe entered a room full of furniture. A look of relief washed over his face, and Gabe was reminded again of how young his new friend was. The cabins would be a large responsibility at any age.

"I said I'd be here."

"From what David has told me, those animals on your place don't always allow for the things you schedule."

Gabe glanced at his brother-in-law, but he only shrugged and pushed his thumbs under his suspenders. "It's true. Sometimes they put me behind more than I'd like."

The three men moved off to the side, next to a display of Amish rockers, and studied the crowd of people.

David finally spoke. "What are we looking for?"

"I'm not sure," Aaron confessed. He frowned as people jostled up against one another, making their way through the packed room. "First of all, where are all these people staying?"

"I suppose some drive in from neighboring towns." Gabe combed his fingers through his beard. "And some live here."

"Seems to be about half Amish, half *Englisch*," David noted.

"All right. If even a quarter of them are from out of town, those are folks who could be staying at our cabins."

Gabe noticed he used the word "our" but didn't call him on it. If the young man was starting to take ownership in his *onkel*'s place, that was a good sign. "So you know you have potential customers if you can get them to the cabins."

"I saw a rack for brochures near the front door." David stepped out of the way of an *Englisch* woman who was carrying a huge purse.

It occurred to Gabe that Rachel would have easily fit inside the bag.

Aaron looked thoughtful. "Seems I heard anyone could place their flyers there."

"Do you have any flyers?" Gabe asked.

"Not yet, but we could make some." Aaron took his hat off and ran his fingers through his hair. Glancing down at the rockers, he noticed the tag hanging off the arm.

Gabe noticed where his eyes were directed and reached down to flip it over.

"A little pricey." Aaron leaned closer to double check the hand-written tag. "Do all your craftsmen charge this much?"

"Nathan Glick makes these," David said. "But he doesn't normally price his items so high."

"Probably Drake upped the charge," Gabe suggested.

The three stared at each other.

"Man has to make a profit," David admitted.

"How much does Nathan Glick usually sell these for?" Aaron asked.

"I never bought one myself, but if I was to guess I'd say probably half that."

"So why would folks buy one here if they could buy one at Nathan's place for half the price?"

"Well, let me think." David watched an *Englisch* couple walk over and sit down in two of the rockers at the end of the row. The man ran his hand over the chair's arm and said something to his wife about the quality of the woodwork. "Nathan lives pretty far off the main road. He has a sign out in front of his place, but I'm guessing that not many people see it. Just a handmade sign, like most folks have."

Gabe pointed to the man and woman who had removed one of the price tags from the chair and were walking toward the register. "Maybe these people don't realize Nathan sells the same thing for less."

Aaron pulled a small pad of paper out of his pocket and made a note. "Let's walk around."

"What are we looking for?"

"More ideas."

Gabe still had no clue as to what they were doing, but he rather enjoyed watching Aaron take notes. The lad seemed to have more in mind than simply offering rooms to travelers.

He jotted down notes when they walked into a room filled with wooden toys. When David mentioned that he had a workshop full of the same things, Aaron scribbled another line and kept walking. They literally bumped into Miriam and Lydia. Aaron glanced at them before referring back to his notes.

"Could you two look at quilts?"

"Quilts?" Lydia squeaked.

"*Ya*. See how many are on display, how reasonable the prices are, and whether or not any customers are actually purchasing them."

Lydia put her hands on her hips. "Why would we—"

"My *aenti* has some quilts here. Let's see if we can find them." Miriam hooked her arm through Lydia's and pulled her away from the men.

Aaron nodded toward the grocery shop. When they made their way toward that area, though, they found they could barely squeeze into the large room designed to look like an Amish kitchen—the sign over the door proclaimed Amish Cupboard.

"He ran out of A's," Gabe mumbled.

"Is there a reason they've put a root cellar in the corner of the kitchen floor?" David asked.

"I'm surprised they've given it a floor. Rae Caperton told us Drake wanted a dirt floor so it would look more rustic, but the council told him he couldn't sell food in a room with a dirt floor."

"Who is this Drake fellow?" Aaron asked.

"Owner," Gabe explained.

"And developer." David shook his head as two *Englisch* boys took turns going up and down the small ladder leading into the make-believe root cellar.

It was a three-foot drop, but Gabe was still amused to see Drake had actually put it in the room. He would have thought the possibility of someone falling and getting hurt would have dissuaded him. But then again, he did have that group of lawyers Gabe had seen at the information meetings held in town. They followed him around wherever he went. No doubt he could fight or pay off any legal suits from *Englischers*. Besides, it was common knowledge that Amish folk wouldn't sue.

"Does he actually believe our kitchens look like this?" Aaron was watching the customers file into the kitchen. Straw brooms were gathered in one corner. They looked like something one would use on a dirt floor. The walls were made to look like a log cabin. A hand-cranked water pump was situated over a washbasin, and a black stove large enough to satisfy a blacksmith took up the entire back wall. Fortunately, it didn't have fire in it or they would have all been overheating.

Where did he find a monstrosity like that?

Every surface of the stove was covered with ceramic dishes and iron skillets for sale. The countertops and cabinets were full of goods as well.

Most of the customers held a shopping basket over their arm, which they were filling up with canned goods from the shelves. Local cheese and sausage were stored in electric coolers made to look like old-fashioned iceboxes, and fresh baked breads were set out on the counters under warmers.

"He's thought of everything," Aaron said. "Everything except what our kitchens actually look like."

"I doubt he's ever stepped inside one." Gabe knew Drake better than he would have liked to. "He doesn't care at all if the portrayal of Amish folk is accurate. He only cares if he sells a lot of goods."

Aaron watched a minute longer, and then he pulled out his notebook and added a few more lines.

By the time they walked back outside to the front porch, Grace was already there, sitting in a rocker. She looked as if she had been waiting for a few minutes.

Gabe stepped to the edge of the porch, happy to have the sun on his face. The crowds had been too much for his comfort level. David and Aaron followed directly behind him.

Miriam and Lydia came out within a few minutes, with Rachel screaming at the top of her lungs.

"Is she all right?" Aaron asked.

"*Ya.*" Gabe smiled at his wife. "That's her midmorning snack howl. You get used to it pretty fast."

"I could use a snack myself," David said.

"I have some of my *mamm*'s cinnamon cake in the buggy." Lydia glanced around, and shrugged when Gabe raised his eyebrows in question. "She'd already made it before last night's guests canceled."

Aaron walked down the steps, knocking his hat against his leg before replacing it on his head. "We might as well drive back to the cabins, if you all have time. I have some ideas, and I'd like to hear your opinions."

"I like ideas," David said over Rachel's hollers. "Especially when they're served with cake."

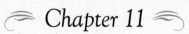

Chapter 11

Grace loved her little sister. When she thought about it, she loved her more than Stanley and Hunter combined. But that child could scream louder than Lily when she started crying. How could such sounds come out of such a small baby? And why? Didn't she understand that they were headed to the buggy as fast as they could walk?

What puzzled her even more was that her father and Miriam seemed amused by it. They both kept smiling at each other, practically laughing.

It was no laughing matter in Grace's opinion. People were starting to stare, and Grace's ears felt as if they might start bleeding at any moment.

Blessed silence filled the buggy as soon as Rachel began to nurse.

"Whew. That was close. I was afraid she was going to shout the *kapp* right off her head." Grace sank against the back of the buggy seat as her dad called out to Chance.

"Worried, were you?" He glanced back at her.

"*Ya.* Weren't you?"

"No. I remember you crying the same way."

"Me? You're saying I was that loud?" Grace leaned forward, staring from her father to Rachel, contentedly nursing at Miriam's breast. Her face was peaceful now, almost angelic. One hand was resting against Miriam's dress. "I couldn't have been that loud. Half the town must have heard her."

"I believe you were. Rachel must have inherited it from our side of the family."

"Makes sense," Miriam said. "We had quiet babies. My *mamm* says even my *bruders* were quiet. But our Rachel has healthy lungs."

They continued that way for a few miles, Rachel nursing and Grace trying to remember. Had she ever been like that? Was it possible? Finally Miriam sat the baby up, supporting her in the front with one hand and rubbing her back gently with the other.

A loud burp filled the buggy.

Grace giggled so hard she fell back against the seat.

"That she also gets from me," Gabe boasted.

They traveled in peace on the road out of town, leaving the crowds behind them.

"What did you think of the shops, Grace?" Miriam resettled Rachel at her other breast.

"I thought they were awfully crowded. I didn't know we had so many people in Pebble Creek."

"Technically in Cashton." Gabe pulled gently on Chance's reins to direct him to the right side of the road so that an *Englisch* car could pass.

"*Ya*. I know it is Cashton, but I think of it by our name—Pebble Creek."

"Well, Pebble Creek is the river's name. Amish refer to the area as Pebble Creek because we're not all in the city limits."

Her dad had explained this before. It seemed the older he got, the more he repeated himself. She decided it would be rude to point that out. "*Ya*. I like the name Pebble Creek better than Cashton, though. It's softer."

"Could be you like rivers more than towns."

"That too."

"So what did you think of Amish Anthem?" This time Miriam

raised Rachel to her shoulder to burp her. The sound that came out was more girlish, but it still made Grace giggle. She liked the way her sister smiled at her over Miriam's shoulder.

"Some of the things they sold were nice enough, but it was much too crowded. I enjoyed the porch more than the store."

Gabe pulled his beard thoughtfully. "I was wondering if you two would like to have a kitchen like the one Drake designed. We could rip ours out and redo it."

Grace knew her dad was making a joke. He might be old but he wasn't crazy. If he'd been serious, she would have asked Miriam to take him to see Doc Hanson. Miriam knew he was kidding too.

"*Ya.* I'd like that root cellar in the kitchen. How about you, Grace? Then we wouldn't have to use the pantry."

Narrisch. Possibly both of her parents were *narrisch.* She'd heard that falling *in lieb* could make you that way, and it seemed to have happened.

She'd talk to Joshua and Abigail about it the next day. Her new grandparents were good at explaining things to her. They were the best. They were *wise.* The word sounded exactly right in her head. When she said it, pictures of Joshua and Abigail always popped up in her mind. She enjoyed Sundays at their home. Sometimes her whole family went over to the Kings' on Saturday afternoon, and she was allowed to stay and spend the night there.

Those nights were the very best—filled with hot chocolate, games of checkers, and *daddi* Joshua's stories. He would tell her tales of when he was a young man, when he'd fish along the banks of Pebble Creek, when there was no noise from cars along the roads and panthers could be seen along the opposite bank.

Remembering those stories made her fingers itch to draw her *grossdaddi*'s memories.

They arrived at the cabins in no time at all. As soon as they pulled into the parking area, Grace remembered why she'd wanted to come along with her family.

The cabins still appeared tired and lonely sitting among the trees, though someone had recently given the trees a cutting. Instead of making things look improved, to Grace it seemed as though all that had been accomplished was allowing a visitor to better see what still needed to be done.

But as she climbed down from the buggy, her eyes were seeing something else as well, and her fingers were tapping against her book bag.

"Are you sure you don't want to come inside for a bite to eat? You're bound to be hungry." Miriam reached out to pull back the strings of Grace's prayer *kapp*. It was something Grace had seen mothers do for their daughters a hundred times, but she hadn't thought anyone would ever do it for her.

She smiled at Miriam, shook her head, and then she threw her arms around her waist and gave her a tight hug.

"All right, then. *Danki* for that."

"I'm going to draw at the river." Grace turned and began to run down toward the bank.

"Be careful," Miriam called.

"I will!"

She heard her father talking to the other men, and Miriam had been right—her stomach was growling even now. But her hunger pains would wait. The sun was slanting through the trees just so, splashing on top of the water as it sloshed and splattered past the cabins. Another hour and she'd miss what was left of the morning shadows.

Sitting with her back against a red cedar tree, she pulled out her pad and pencil, and she began to draw.

Directly in front of her was the water, and to the right was the corner of one of the cabins. Chokeberry covered the cabin's side, and though someone had cut much of it down, bluebirds were searching among the branches for early fruit. She knew they wouldn't find any, but perhaps there was something else they could eat there. She'd have to ask Miss Bena. Although the woman was severe, she knew more about birds than anyone else Grace had ever met.

A fish splashed in the river at the exact same moment a red-tailed hawk dove, just barely missing the fish.

Grace paused, thinking of the circle of life, of how the fish had narrowly escaped and how the hawk would continue searching or go hungry.

She bent back over her tablet and continued to sketch.

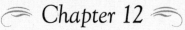

Chapter 12

Aaron met the stares of the group of folks sitting around the table in the cabin's office. His *onkel* Ervin had set the room up to resemble a comfortable Amish kitchen and sitting room—a real Amish home. In other words, it looked nothing like Amish Anthem.

He stared down at his notes and cleared his throat.

It didn't help that he'd known these people only two days. Or maybe it did.

They had no expectations of him. So what if his plan didn't work? He'd pack up Elizabeth and children, put them on the bus to Indiana, and take them back home.

His arm brushed against Beth's picture, still in his pants pocket, still weighing on his mind. The young girl would probably prefer to stay here, as Elizabeth most likely would. If he could help them to do so, it would be better for everyone. Of that he'd convinced himself last night.

Lydia waited impatiently, watching him.

Miriam held her baby as she sat next to Gabe, who was reaching for a second piece of cake. David seemed in no hurry. The man appeared to have one speed—measured and deliberate. Seth hadn't shown up this morning, but Aaron would need him as well.

"I know you're wondering why I asked you to go to town with me today."

"Seemed to be a waste of time," Lydia muttered.

Instead of ignoring her comment and her bad attitude, Aaron turned toward her and forced his voice to be calm and reasonable. He would need Lydia on his side most of all. He couldn't run the cabins without her, though he would rather. The last thing he wanted was a front desk attendant with a sullen manner.

She hadn't been rude to the guests last night, though. He'd watched her as she'd tried to convince them to stay. Lydia was good with *Englischers*.

No, the problem and the cause for her bad attitude lay elsewhere.

"Why did it seem to be a waste of time?"

Lydia looked surprised that he'd asked her and all but speechless that he was waiting for an answer. They had worked so hard around the cabins the day before that she'd gone home looking as if she'd crawled underneath them. Today she was wearing a clean dress and a crisp apron. The light brown hair that tended to escape at will was tucked neatly under a fresh *kapp*, and her face didn't bear a single smudge of dirt. It occurred to him that she was of marrying age, and he wouldn't have her as an employee for long. The thought annoyed him more than it should have, so he pushed it away.

Lydia glanced first at Miriam, and he thought she wouldn't answer, but finally she sat up straighter and began ticking points off on her fingers. "We aren't centered in the middle of town. We aren't a retail store. We don't have Drake's resources. And we wouldn't operate the way he does even if we did."

"Excellent points, especially the last one."

"So why did we go?"

"Because he has customers and we don't."

"If that's what we have to do, I'm not interested."

"Are you interested in having a job?"

Lydia opened her mouth to protest, but then she clamped it shut again. Instead of responding, she folded her arms tightly across her chest and glared at him.

Gabe cleared his throat but waited for Aaron's nod before he spoke up. "Lydia is right that there's little about the man to admire.

Miriam and I were on the committee assigned to work with him before Amish Anthem was built. He's incorrigible."

"And yet he's successful." Aaron reached for his *kaffi*.

"Apparently," Gabe conceded.

"It's obvious he is whether we like it or not." David stopped eating and sank into a chair. "We might not agree with his methods, but customers weren't standing around with their hands in their pockets. They were handing over money as fast as Drake's minions could put it in the register."

"How does this affect us?" Lydia's voice was as sharp and brittle as the small rocks layering the parking lot outside the window. "How does his store, which is disgusting and a disgrace to all we call being Plain, help us in any way?"

Aaron was still standing near the end of the table. He put down his *kaffi* and stuck his hands in his pockets. The notes in front of him said it all, but he didn't need to look at the notes. All he'd needed to know was if his plan was possible, the plan that had first rooted in his heart when Elizabeth had handed him the badly drawn picture.

Seeing Drake's store had confirmed that his ideas, and what had been done previously in his hometown in Indiana, could be transferred here to Wisconsin. But he couldn't do it alone. He'd need help.

How did he explain it all to them? And why did he suddenly care so much?

Miriam was the one who opened the door for him. "You weren't looking at what Drake was doing. You were looking at his consumer base."

"*Ya*. Partly. Mainly."

"I still don't understand," Lydia said.

"Good students listen and learn, like you did in class, Lydia." Miriam was smiling now as she handed Rachel to Gabe and stood to cut a piece of the breakfast cake. "We went to Amish Anthem today to learn if it was possible to be successful commercially, with the *Englisch*, in this area."

Aaron nodded again. He thought of interrupting her, but he decided it might be better if his plan came from her rather than from him.

"But we operate cabins," Lydia pointed out. "A place for people to stay."

"And yet they are empty." David glanced out at the vacant parking lot.

Silence filled the room as they all considered the truth of his statement.

"In our meetings, Drake bellowed on and on about the Amish experience—how he wanted to allow people to live the Plain life. It was ludicrous, because he stepped from his private jet straight into the downtown Cashton council room, never straying to the dirt road of a farm." Gabe leaned back, Rachel cradled in the crook of his arm. "Maybe he was onto something, though."

Miriam turned toward her husband. "And even with the details wrong—"

"Like a cellar in the kitchen." Lydia wrinkled her nose in distaste.

"*Ya.*" David drank from his *kaffi* mug before continuing. "Even with major points wrong, he was still selling items as quickly as customers could pluck them off the shelf."

Lydia clutched the side of her chair. "If our single goal is to make a profit, we might as well ride the busses and work in the city. That wasn't what Ervin wanted. He wanted to offer a place of solitude."

"What if we could be successful and still honor Ervin's dream? Maybe there's a way to replicate Drake's success and get the details right." It was the first time Aaron had spoken in five minutes. "What if we could offer a genuine Plain experience, but still give visitors the canned foods to purchase—"

"And the fresh baked breads and pies." Miriam's smile widened.

"Even put rockers on the front porches for sale." David slapped his knee. He stood and walked around the room, looking at the space as if he were seeing it with new eyes. "We could build shelves in here and fill them with toys. Toys visitors would want to purchase for their children, who might just happen to be bored without their video games and computers."

"Are we to sell them the quilts off the bed as well?" Lydia's mouth was set in a grim line, and Aaron's heart took a dive. While everyone else had been catching on to his vision, Lydia had been setting her feet against it like a stubborn mule.

Why was he disappointed? Why was he surprised? He'd suspected she would be the hardest to convince. Some people disliked change, and he was asking her to make major adjustments. Of course, he could do it without her. She didn't own the cabins. He did, or rather his aunt did. Still, he would have liked to have had her help.

A silence had settled over the room, and Aaron realized the others were waiting for him to answer Lydia.

"Of course we won't sell the quilts off the bed. For one thing, our beds are covered in old blankets." He spoke quietly, reasonably, as if he were trying to calm a colt. "Offering quilts isn't a bad idea, though. Amish women are admired across the country for their quilting talent, but we will strive to not be like Drake in any way. There's no need to put a price tag on every item in every cabin."

"Are you quite sure?" She hopped up now and began collecting dishes. Aaron jumped when she dropped them back on the table with a clatter. "Because it sounds to me like we'll be a miniature Amish Anthem, and that's not somewhere I care to work, Aaron Troyer."

"I suppose you'd rather barely work at all."

"What?"

"There's certainly not much to do when there are no customers."

"If you're saying I haven't earned my pay—"

"I'm saying maybe it's easier to leave things the way they are. You don't strike me as someone afraid of a challenge, but perhaps I was wrong. Perhaps you are afraid that you couldn't keep up if all the cabins were full."

Her face had turned red, but she wasn't backing down.

"Have they ever been full, Lydia? Have they ever been even half full?"

Instead of answering, she turned and ran from the office, the screen door slapping shut behind her.

Silence filled the room, broken finally by David, reaching for more *kaffi*. "I thought it was a *gut* idea."

"Maybe she'll come around, Aaron." Gabe stood and began pacing with Rachel, who had started to fuss.

"Would you like me to go and speak with her?" Miriam offered. Her eyes were kind and sympathetic.

Aaron was tempted to send her.

The last thing he wanted to do was deal with an emotional employee. Why couldn't he be home in Indiana, tending the fields?

But he wasn't home. He was here, and he needed to see to this.

He needed to resolve it now. As much as he would like to send Miriam out to smooth over the differences that had been brewing between him and Lydia since he'd arrived, he knew the answer had to lie between them.

"I'll do it." He grabbed his hat off the peg by the door and rammed it down on his head. "If I'm not back in fifteen minutes, send out a search party. That woman seems to have quite the temper."

Lydia didn't need to turn around to know Aaron was standing behind her. Whenever he was within shouting distance, her skin felt as though a hundred ants were crawling over it. No, that was wrong. It felt as if a hundred butterflies were rubbing against her skin at the same moment.

Maybe that was why she was overreacting. And she did realize she was overreacting.

Yet she didn't respond when he cleared his throat. Instead, she continued staring at Pebble Creek, hoping the sight of the water rushing downstream would calm her nerves. They felt as taut as her brother's kite string when she used to hold it for him as he ran in the fields back behind their house—their old house.

Before her dad got sick.

Before they lost the farm.

"Tell me what's bothering you," Aaron said. He didn't walk any closer. Instead, he moved toward a large flat rock on her right and sat on it, studying the river as if he were trying to see what she saw.

Lydia shook her head.

There was no way she could explain to someone she'd known for only a few days all of the emotions tangled in her heart.

"Help me see what's wrong with making this place profitable."

"Maybe nothing," Lydia admitted. "Maybe it's simply that I don't belong here anymore."

He turned to study her as he'd been studying the river. She didn't want to look into his eyes—eyes that were the color of molasses. Lydia was certain she'd see pity and condescension there. She didn't want to look, but she could no more resist than the water could decide not to flow downriver.

When she did she saw only curiosity and maybe a speck of pleading, and behind all of that the same stubbornness she saw in her own eyes when she checked the small mirror in the bathroom each morning before leaving for work.

"Why would you not belong here, Lydia? My *onkel* trusted you. He needed you, and I need you too."

"I doubt that." She heard the bitterness in her voice and cleared her throat. When had it lodged there? How long ago?

"You've probably noticed I don't have the best tact, but I'm not one to lie. I do need you, and we both know it. I could hire someone else, but they don't know this place like you do. I don't know this place like you do."

Lydia glanced downstream.

She shouldn't throw away this job. There was no way she could go home today, face her parents, and tell them she'd lost the small amount of income the cabins provided their family. What did she hope to accomplish by arguing with Aaron?

"So many changes..." Her voice died like the breeze in the trees around them.

"If we don't make some changes, this place will close. You're an intelligent woman. I know you can see that."

"Our faith holds fast to the old ways. We set ourselves apart."

"Let's show that to the *Englischers* who come here." Now he smiled slightly, and Lydia's heart actually tripped in its rhythm. She recognized that she faced more danger from her feelings than she did from the change in the cabins or a great crowd of tourists.

She didn't need to be caught up in those eyes and that smile. Aaron Troyer was not here to stay, and she did not need that sort of heartbreak in her life.

So she stared at the river and frowned.

"We can offer that place of rest and solitude my *onkel* wanted to provide. We can be an example to the *Englischers* of what it truly means to be Plain. It's not what Drake is showing them."

"No. It's not."

"We'll present something different. An authentic experience."

She stole a peek at him.

"Let's clean up the cabins and give this place a face-lift. Invest some of my *dat*'s money. I even have a little of my own."

"Why would you do that?" The words were out of her mouth before she could reel them in where they belonged.

She thought he would tell her it was none of her business. Instead, he brushed at the pocket of his pants.

"Because Elizabeth and her children want to stay here." He stood, walked over to where she was, and stopped in front of her.

She could smell the soap he'd used that morning, see a small rip on the shoulder seam of his shirt that needed mending, and then she was looking again into his eyes.

"I had no desire to travel here, Lydia. I wanted to be in Indiana, working the fields. But I am here. Apparently *Gotte* wants me to be in this place at this time. So I should do the best I can, *ya*?"

"*Ya*." The word cost her dearly.

"I've seen the way you are with the customers. You're *gut* with them. But the cabins..." He glanced away, back toward the buildings, and when his gaze was off her she felt her stomach plummet. She knew at that moment that it was already too late. Already her heart was falling for Aaron Troyer, even though her head knew better.

"The cabins aren't much as they are now, but you're right about the river. The river is special, especially here where it bends. I suspect Ervin knew that. We can make the river the focus of the property. When I look at this place, I can almost see how it was meant to be. Like when I look at a field in the winter, and I can see what it will look like before the fall harvest." He waited for her to nod that she understood. "If we improve the property, it will help your community too. The *Englisch*, they like to purchase things. We'll give them things to buy, which will help families who need income in your district, *ya*?"

"*Ya*." She sounded like a parrot in a story she'd read as a child.

"I can do it without you, but it will be harder...much harder. Truth is, I need your help." He pulled in a deep breath, glanced at the ground, and when his eyes met hers again she thought a blush stained his cheeks. "And Elizabeth does too. Elizabeth and the girls. Will you stay and work? Stay and help us make the changes?"

Lydia thought of her parents and siblings—all the people counting on her. Now she was going to add another family to that number?

She thought of all the things she could say to Aaron, all the ways she could answer him, but only one word came out.

"*Ya*."

It must have been enough, because a smile spread across his smoothly shaven face—the first genuine smile she'd seen.

"Let's go back to the others. We have a lot of work to do, and they sounded as if they would be eager to get started. Plus, if we don't hurry, David will have eaten all the *kaffi* cake. Did you even have some?"

Lydia wanted to laugh as she walked back to the office with him. She'd always been self-conscious about her weight, not that she was big. Certainly she wasn't tiny like her sister Clara. She liked to think of herself as hardy, which was important when working long difficult hours. Each year she looked more like her mother—whether or not that was a good thing. Aaron's question, though, had put the icing on a bizarre morning.

It might have been the first time anyone had asked her if she'd had a piece of cake.

Chapter 13

Lydia woke to the smell of bacon frying and knew before she opened her eyes that she'd slept longer than she'd intended. Then she heard two of her younger sisters arguing in the small bathroom next door.

What time was it? If Clara was up—up and arguing—it was later than it should be. Clara always slept in until the very last minute, especially on Sundays they didn't have church.

Lydia forced one eye open and peeked out of the covers. The room was light, so she stuck her entire head out from under the quilt. The sky outside the single small window was a pearly gray.

The other two beds in her room were empty but unmade.

And the fight next door was escalating.

She pulled on her robe and slippers and hurried from the room.

"I'm not done in here. You'll have to wait." Clara's voice rang out from inside the bathroom.

"You've been in there for ten minutes. Hurry or I'm going to have an accident." Sally Ann, the youngest of the Fisher family, continued to turn the doorknob back and forth.

"Girls," Lydia's mother called from the kitchen. "Settle down out there or I'll come take care of it."

"Problem, Sally Ann?" Lydia squatted down beside her little sister.

"I have to goooo..." she allowed the word to drag out as she hopped from foot to foot. "And Clara won't come out of the bathroom."

"I told you. I'm not...finished...yet." With the last word, Clara yanked the door open at the same moment Sally Ann let go of it, sending Clara sprawling across the bathroom floor and on to her backside.

All three girls looked at each other in surprise.

Before anyone could say a word, Sally Ann sprinted past them to use the toilet.

"You did that on purpose." Clara spat the words at her as she pulled herself up off the linoleum and smoothed her dress down over her boyish figure. "And you!" She turned on Lydia. "You probably put her up to it. You're jealous because I'm going to the singing tonight and you're not."

Lydia felt her right eyebrow arch. "You're getting ready now? For something that's twelve hours away?"

"Humph. At least I have something to look forward to, unlike some people around here." Clara brushed past her and into the kitchen.

"I'm here, *mamm*," she declared, her voice suddenly all sugar and sunshine. "What can I do to help while Lydia and Sally Ann dawdle in the bathroom?"

Sally Ann washed her hands and reached for the towel. "Why's she so mean, Lydia? Were you that way at sixteen? Am I going to be that way?"

"Clara's having a difficult time right now."

"Why?"

"Because being sixteen is hard."

"You were sixteen once. I don't remember you being so terrible. What do you mean—hard? Like math is hard?"

Had she been sixteen once? She could barely remember. Sixteen years old. That had been six years ago. An eternity ago. Before her father became sick. "Don't worry about Clara. You go change your clothes, and then I'll help you with your hair."

Ten minutes later they were all at the breakfast table—all six of the Fisher children. Lydia had recently turned twenty-two and was beginning to feel like an old maid. Clara was sixteen and should be working now, but jobs had been hard to find. Martha and Amanda were the middle girls at eleven and ten. Last of the girls was Sally Ann, who was eight and small for her age. The only boy, Stephen, was fourteen and in his last year of school.

Menno and Ella sat together at the end of the table. Her mother always sat near her father so she could help him eat. The place at the other end was left for Lydia. She put the bowl of fried potatoes on the table, sat, and bowed her head.

The moments of grace often left her confused.

There was much she was grateful for, and she had no problem offering up those words to Gotte. They had a home in the community in which she was raised. Her brother and sisters were healthy. Her mother was a constant source of strength. Her father had not died from the terrible disease that could have taken him years ago.

Her father...

Sitting with her family surrounding her, with her dad at the end, so often unable to even eat the food they put in front of him, she often found herself wondering about Gotte's provision. Then she would reprimand herself, and the clatter of dishes would bring her out of her prayer.

More times than not, she'd find Stephen studying her when she raised her eyes. Were his thoughts the same as hers? Did he struggle as she did? Surely the burden on him would be even greater than the one she carried.

"I heard you were at Amish Anthem yesterday," Stephen said, reaching for the potatoes.

Lydia nodded as she helped the younger girls fill their plates.

"It's still the talk of the town, even though it's been open a while now." Her *mamm* smiled as she helped her *dat* with his food.

"I thought you were working, Lydia." Clara pushed the strings of her prayer *kapp* behind her shoulders. "I'm sure we all would have enjoyed a shopping trip yesterday, but the rest of us were here cleaning the house."

Four sets of eyes turned and stared at her. All the girls—Clara, Martha, Amanda, and even Sally Ann. Her mother, father, and brother continued eating.

After a moment, Ella stood and walked to the counter. "If Lydia was at the new place in town, I'm sure there was a reason." She came back with a bowl and put Menno's potatoes, eggs, and sausage in it, which she began mashing all together.

Menno looked at Lydia and winked.

"Was it, Lydia? Was it for *work*?" Clara emphasized the last word as if it might be a foreign idea to everyone else.

Or maybe Lydia was imagining that. One thing was certain, working for Aaron Troyer sounded better and better each moment she had to spend with Clara.

"Yes, it was for work. Aaron—"

"Who?"

"Aaron. Aaron Troyer, Ervin and Elizabeth's nephew."

"Oh, yes. Elizabeth told me he's a very nice young man. Came all the way from Indiana to help run the cabins." Ella spooned some of the mush into Menno's mouth. He dutifully chewed it but waved her away when she tried to feed him more.

"Young? And from Indiana?" Clara perked up considerably. "So that's why you've been spending such long hours at the cabins. Could it be my older sister is finally interested in a man?"

Lydia didn't rise to the bait, though she did send her sister what she hoped was a scathing look. All she received back was a smile that could have curdled milk. What was with Clara this morning? Maybe she was spending too much time at home. For all their sakes, Lydia hoped she found a job and soon.

The morning settled into the quiet rhythm of spoons on plates and raindrops on the roof.

"I'm finished," Stephen suddenly declared. "Think I'll be heading back out to look after Tin Star."

"Oh, no, you won't." Ella shook her head. "It's still Sunday morning, whether we have church today or not. You'll stay in here and study with us."

"*Mamm*, Lydia was gone with him all day yesterday. I need to check his hooves and give him a *gut* brushing."

"That horse will wait, Stephen Fisher. You'll stay right here with your family. Now help your *dat* into the living room while we clean up these dishes."

Stephen didn't argue any further. When he helped Menno to stand and slipped his father's arm over his shoulder, Lydia saw such a mixture of emotions on his face that she had to look away.

She began gathering dishes while Ella made sure the younger girls washed their hands.

"So what gives, sis? What's with the new boss? And shopping? And keeping secrets?" Clara dipped the first dish into the water, careful not to splash any soap onto the sleeves of her dress.

"No secrets."

"Then why won't you talk about it?"

"You've never been interested in my work before."

"Why would I be interested in what old Ervin Troyer was doing? How old is this Aaron?"

"Too old for you, I suspect." Ella walked up beside them and picked up a dish towel. "Do you like working for him, Lydia?"

Lydia thought of his eyes, the one bright smile he'd shared with her, and the way he had of taking over a place all of a sudden. She shook her head. "Doesn't matter if I like it or not. He's the boss now, and he's making big changes."

She started to rinse a plate, but then she noticed it still had egg on it and handed it back to Clara.

"What kind of changes?" Ella asked.

Lydia gave them a brief outline of what Aaron had in mind.

"Sounds *gut* for our community." Ella slipped a dried plate into the cabinet. "Most families could use more income. Nearly everyone makes things at home they could sell, and word is that they can't expect to earn much from Drake."

"I'm not surprised, based on what Miriam and Gabe said of their meetings with the man." Lydia elbowed her sister, who had stopped washing and was gazing out the window.

"Ouch."

"Dishes!"

Clara rolled her eyes but resumed washing.

"If we can get the business Aaron thinks we will, I'm going to have more work than I can handle. Between cleaning cabins, selling goods, and reordering items, we'll need more help."

"More help?" Clara's voice climbed a notch.

"Don't even think—"

"Why not? I'm a *gut* worker."

"Since when? You're washing those dishes with your fingertips when you do them at all."

"*Mamm*, tell her."

"Your *schweschder* does need a job."

"But—"

"It would be a *gut* way for her to mature."

"Yes, but—"

"And bring in some extra income, which *Gotte* knows we could use."

"But, *mamm*—"

"*Danki* for thinking of her, Lydia." Ella reached forward and kissed her on the forehead. She walked around to Clara and kissed her as well. "Clara, *danki* for offering. Does my heart *gut* to see you two girls work together. Isn't it amazing how *Gotte* provides?"

Lydia's mind scrambled for a way out of the approaching predicament. "It's not certain there will even be another job, *mamm*."

"I understand. But we'll make it a matter of prayer. I have a feeling this Aaron Troyer knows what he's doing, and *Gotte* has a plan. Never forget that. Now I think I'll go check on your *dat*. You girls finish up here and come join us for our Bible study."

Clara waited until Ella was out of sight before she collapsed onto one of the kitchen chairs.

"What are you doing? We're not finished."

"I am. My hands look like prunes. Disgusting." She held them up for Lydia to examine, but Lydia didn't bother. She closed her eyes, wondering if she could go to bed and start this day over. Maybe she could somehow leave out telling her family about the changes at the cabins.

If she could replay the morning, there would be no risk of having to work beside Clara all day, every day.

The mere thought of it caused her shoulders to tense up and a headache to form at the base of her neck. Clara? At the Plain Cabins?

She silently finished the breakfast dishes, and then they walked together into the sitting room. It was nowhere near as big as their old sitting room in their old house out on their old farm. She might be the only one of the children who could remember that. Maybe Stephen remembered. Maybe that was the reason for the anger and sadness in his eyes from time to time.

Maybe he understood what they had lost.

Somehow all six of the Fisher children, Ella, and Menno fit into the small sitting area. They gathered round.

Menno didn't have enough strength in his lungs to read the Scripture. Farmer's lung had robbed him of that as it had robbed them of many things. But he was able to open his Bible, run his finger down the page, and find the Scripture he wanted read.

Lydia sat there watching her father's hands, spotted with age, and thinner now—much thinner. In that moment, a dozen memories passed through her mind and traveled over her heart. Her father holding her hand as he walked her into the schoolhouse the first day, helping her up into the buggy, handing her a Christmas present. His hands as they dealt cards for Dutch Blitz or helped to birth a calf or smoothed the blankets on her bed.

Her father's hands had always represented strength to her, but looking at them now—with the strength gone—she realized that, more than strength, they represented love and patience.

Menno leaned forward and set the Bible on the table. He reached for Stephen with his right hand and Ella with his left. Slowly, each family member reached out to the person beside them, until they formed a circle, unbroken.

Wordlessly, they all bowed their heads.

This time when she prayed, Lydia had no problem being grateful. She forgot about being irritated with Clara or worrying about the cabins. She didn't think to question God's decisions or fret over what was to come. She closed her eyes, nestled in the warmth of her family, and thanked the Lord that for the moment at least, the circle remained intact.

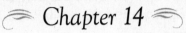 Chapter 14

Miriam frowned at her father.

"She's old enough," Joshua said, "and you know it."

The fact that he was right didn't settle the feeling in her stomach.

"You were a year younger. Now let her have some fun." Joshua smiled at her and brushed his fingers over his beard.

"I'll be careful. I promise. Please." In the end it was the hopeful look on Grace's face that convinced her, that and the knowledge that she wouldn't do it if Miriam had said no.

"All right, but absolutely no trotting. Do you promise?"

"We promise!" Grace ran to the other side of the pasture fence, where one of Joshua's older mares stood patiently waiting.

"She'll be fine." Abigail stood next to her, a shawl wrapped around her shoulders even though the Sunday afternoon was turning warm. The rain had stopped early in the morning, and the sun had finally made an appearance. Abigail was holding Rachel in her arms and smiling. "You loved learning to ride in a saddle."

"I haven't done it in years. The horse looks so large and Grace looks so small."

"You're looking at it as a mother instead of as an adventure."

"I guess you're right. Are you cold, *mamm?*"

"Maybe a tad."

"Do you want to go inside?" Miriam studied her mother. Had she lost more weight? It occurred to her again that Abigail had grown thinner as she moved into the latter half of her fifties. She didn't have any extra weight to lose.

"No. The shawl is *gut*. I want to hold Rachel and watch Gracie ride. Now, quit worrying and do stop staring at me that way."

"Should I be worrying?"

"You sound like your father."

"He's worried too?"

Instead of answering, Abigail nodded to the commotion on the other side. "She's in the saddle."

And indeed she was. Wearing a pair of her cousin's britches under her dress, Grace had climbed on to the old mare and was sitting pretty. She clutched the saddle horn as if it had the power to save her from any disaster and broke into laughter when the mare started to move.

Joshua led the horse by a rope, and before they had gone the length of the pasture, Gabe had walked out of the barn to watch. He climbed up on the fence across from them and waved, and then he proceeded to cheer Grace on as if she were in a buggy race.

Grace released one hand from the saddle as she passed their side of the pasture so that she could wave. "I'm doing it! I'm riding."

"Be careful," Miriam called.

"I will, *mamm*. But look! I'm doing it."

The word was said so simply, so casually, and it was followed by another peal of laughter. Miriam knew Grace wasn't aware she'd even said it. She brushed at the tear on her cheek, wondering if her hormones were still out of whack because of the baby.

"First time?" Abigail asked.

"*Ya*. Well, it's the first time she hasn't backtracked and corrected herself, calling me Miriam instead."

Abigail nodded and smiled. "She's a *gut* girl, and she's been through a lot in the last few years. The Lord is healing her heart, in the same way He healed her voice."

"He is." Miriam exhaled a big breath as Grace began a second lap around the pasture. Closing her eyes, she placed both hands on the cedar post fence, relishing in the warmth of the wood. It would be nice if she could stop this day, slow it down a little, and keep Rachel and Grace the age they each were right now.

"How are things with you and Gabe?"

Miriam's eyes flew open. "*Gut.* Why do you ask?"

"Sometimes things are...difficult after a baby."

Placing her chin on her hands, Miriam stared across at her husband, who had taken to calling out at his daughter as if he were an *Englisch* rodeo clown. "He's patient with me, especially when I'm emotional. And he helps with the *boppli.*"

"Perfect man, huh?"

"Maybe not perfect. He learned some bad habits while he was a bachelor—like tracking mud into the kitchen and leaving dirty socks all over the house. I found one on the front porch the other day and its mate in the sink. Why in the world—"

"If that's the worst he does, I'm thinking you can live with it, Miriam."

Grace passed them again, and Miriam heard herself shout, "Hold on, honey!"

After a moment she added, "*Ya.* It's only socks. I can learn to live with a little messiness. You're right."

"Of course I'm right."

Rachel began to cry and Miriam took her *boppli* back in her arms.

"I think I smell something terrible." She laughed. "I better take this girl inside."

Glancing toward the pasture once more, she saw that Grace was where she'd started and Joshua was helping her off the mare. Gabe had hopped off the fence and was showing her how to unsaddle the horse.

"She's so small," Miriam murmured as they turned and walked toward the house.

"Yes, but it's all the more reason to prepare her." Abigail shivered slightly and pulled the shawl more tightly around her shoulders. When she did, Miriam noticed her mother's hands, noticed and thought immediately of old folks suffering from the Parkinson's disease.

"*Mamm*, are you all right?" Miriam's heart surged into a double beat.

"Don't worry, dear."

"I am worried. You're shaking."

Abigail stared down at her hand, held it out in front of her in the sunlight, as if it were a fault in a blanket she were knitting.

"You don't have to keep things from me. I'd rather know."

"It started a few days ago," Abigail said, no real alarm in her voice. "It's the most curious thing. Comes and goes."

She tucked her hand back in her shawl.

"Are you ill?"

As usual, Abigail took her time answering. "I don't think I am, Miriam. But your father's concerned."

"Why? Why is he concerned?" Miriam's mind searched for anything he might have said, and landed on the day she'd stopped by when she'd asked how her mother was feeling and he'd said, "*Gut*. Today is a *gut* day." Did that mean she had bad days? How bad?

"Why is he concerned, *mamm*?"

"Because I've lost more weight."

"We've all noticed that." Miriam tried to keep her voice low and quiet, though she felt anything but calm. Suddenly it seemed that her mother might collapse right in front of her eyes as they walked back toward the house. "Do you have any other symptoms?"

"*Nein*."

"There's the shaking."

"Which just started," Abigail pointed out. She sighed in frustration. "I've tried several of my herbs, including yerba mate, which is proven to reduce fatigue."

Miriam could feel her teeth grinding together.

"It doesn't seem to be helping, though. I still tire more easily than I should, but we have to remember I am older now."

"*Mamm!* You're not even sixty."

"No. I'm not." Abigail chose her words carefully as they walked into the sitting room.

Miriam laid Rachel on the couch and began the process of changing her diaper.

"I have an appointment to see the doctor on Tuesday," Abigail admitted.

"Doc Hanson?"

"Yes."

Miriam cleaned up Rachel, grateful she'd put disposable diapers on her for the trip. "What do you think is wrong?"

"I don't know, honey. Whatever it is, if it's anything, God won't be surprised by it. We don't have to be worried. And maybe it's nothing."

Once she was changed, Rachel began rooting, so Miriam settled her at her breast. Nursing her always brought a sense of calm, and it did so now. As she watched, her mother picked up her quilting and began the top stitching on a crib quilt. The quilt was for the baby her sister-in-law Anna was expecting. The familiar routine further quieted her worries.

They remained that way for some time, until Joshua and Gabe and Grace came in, bringing their laughter with them. Soon they were joined by her younger brother Simon and his new wife, Emma. It occurred to Miriam that they would probably be adding more grandchildren to the family in the next year or so. Grace and Rachel would have more cousins to play with, and Abigail and Joshua would have another *boppli* around.

Like many Amish families, theirs was a large one and growing larger daily, it seemed, but they all drew strength and comfort from one another.

Surely whatever was wrong with Abigail, they could face as a family. Watching her brother hold Rachel, she thanked God for the people around her.

It didn't erase the worry that had taken root in Miriam's heart, but it helped that they were together, surrounded by one another, her *mamm*'s soft humming of a Sunday hymn easing her fears.

Chapter 15

Gabe would have liked to work behind his plow Monday morning. The sun actually broke through the clouds, which had him clomping around the southern section of the farm, caking mud on his boots and generally wasting time.

"How long until you can begin to work in the fields?" Miriam asked when she brought him a thermos of hot *kaffi* to the barn.

"Two more days, maybe three." Gabe frowned as he ignored the *kaffi* and whacked his hammer against a two-by-four. Gus had managed to escape his enclosure next to Snickers, Gabe's workhorse. Sometime during the night, he'd caused quite a ruckus in the barn, turning over benches, getting into feed, and finally butting his head through one of the older stall doors Gabe had been intending to replace.

"Miriam, do you think you could find a recipe for donkey stew?"

Gus brayed loudly from outside the barn, where he'd been put in a time-out.

"Hmm. I might have to ask Rae to look that one up on the Internet. Don't believe my *mamm's* cookbooks have donkey stew."

"They would if she'd ever had a donkey like Gus!" Gabe slammed the hammer down harder than necessary, and the wall vibrated from the force of the blow.

Miriam cocked her head and studied him.

Gabe had seen that look before, and he chose to ignore it. The last thing he needed was analyzing by a woman. He knew when he was acting like a fool. He didn't need someone else reminding him. This blasted weather was making him crazy.

He needed to plant his corn. He had stacks of seed waiting to go into the ground, a bright sunny day, and here he was stuck mending walls in the barn.

Pulling the hammer back, he slammed it into the barn partition one more time. When metal met wood, it sent a satisfying jolt up his arm. Wasn't quite as good as field work, but apparently for today it would have to do.

Glancing up, he realized Miriam was still waiting.

"Was there something else you needed?"

"*Nein.* Nothing else I needed."

He nodded. She wasn't one to hang about the barn. Rachel had been fine that morning. Grace was off to school.

"Something someone else needed?"

"Oh, I don't know."

She turned over a pail and plopped down on it, reminding him of a schoolgirl, bringing his first smile of the day. He was fortunate to have such a beautiful *fraa.*

"I was thinking of our new friends," she said. "You've done more than is necessary to help Aaron. You probably don't have another day to spend hitching up Chance and driving the buggy around on errands. I'd go myself, but I have wash on the line, and I couldn't load the items Aaron needs anyway."

Gabe glanced up and looked out the barn door to where the sky was blue. If he couldn't be in the fields, at least he could be out of the barn. He studied his wife. "I don't know what you have in mind, but if it gets me out of this barn, I'm for it."

"*Ya?*"

"*Ya.* I believe I've fastened this well enough to hold Gus tonight."

They both turned to look at the enclosure Gabe had hammered

together. He'd doubled-layered the two-by-fours, first one direction, then the other.

"I believe that would hold Clemens Schmucker's biggest bull," Miriam said.

Laughter broke out of Gabe at that. There had been a time when Clemens Schmucker had tried to warn him away from Miriam. Though the man was Amish, he wasn't exactly humble. He was one of the most prosperous farmers in the Cashton area, and he didn't mind other folks knowing about it. He'd apparently hoped his son Aden and Miriam would one day marry, and though the father often rubbed Gabe the wrong way, Aden had been instrumental in helping to find Grace when she was lost in a winter storm the year before.

Aden now lived in a more liberal neighboring district. He and Gabe had actually become *gut freinden*.

"I suppose it might hold Clemens' prize bull." Gabe stood and stretched. "Now tell me about this errand of yours, woman."

Miriam's plan was a good one, and something he should have thought of himself. Something he probably would have thought of, except he was too busy focusing on what he couldn't accomplish that day.

Thirty minutes later, Chance was hitched to the buggy, and Gabe was on his way to the first of five stops, Miriam's list in his pocket.

The meeting with Aaron on Saturday had ended with the decision to offer Amish-made goods at the cabins, but they hadn't come up with a more detailed plan beyond that. Aaron had given them all leeway to begin collecting goods to sell at the cabins. He'd even instructed them on how many of each item he'd need. He was going into town to wire for additional money to reimburse everyone, and they would meet back at the cabins throughout the week. In the meantime, Aaron would continue working on repairs.

Miriam had given Gabe a list of five homes between their farm and the cabins where the families made and sold items.

She'd also put a star by the three families on the list who were currently selling items at Drake's Amish Anthem. How his wife knew that, he had no idea. Maybe she remembered details better than he did. Or maybe he'd been too busy gawking at what Byron Drake had done.

Gabe knew all of the families on the list, some better than others, and he had no problem finding the name Miriam had written at the top of the paper. The farm was located three miles down the road. A hand-lettered sign proclaiming "Rugs for Sale" hung out by the roadside. Two older girls were hanging fresh laundry—sheets that stretched down the length of the clothesline.

Floyd walked out of the barn to meet him as he pulled up, and raised a hand in greeting. "Your fields too wet to work?"

"*Ya.* Nearly lost my boots in them trying to walk from end to end."

Staring out at his fields, Floyd pulled on his beard, worry coloring his voice. "We're counting on this year's crop to be a *gut* one. Wouldn't mind it if things would dry out real quick."

Gabe considered that a moment. He didn't know a lot about the Hershbergers. Their only son was some years older than Grace. Several girls were already out of school and close to marrying age.

"Miriam sent me over," Gabe explained. "I wanted to talk to you about the rugs you sell if you and Barbara have a minute."

Shrugging his shoulders, Floyd turned toward the house. "Suppose we do. Barbara and the girls are doing laundry. I'm hiding out in the barn trying to stay out of the way."

It was a sentiment Gabe understood too well. Spring turning to summer was his favorite time of year, but it was a time meant for work. When they were hindered by weather, it made everyone jumpy. The list of what needed to be done grew longer, and the time to accomplish it shortened.

Perhaps it was *Gotte's* way of teaching them patience. As Gabe followed Floyd into the steamy kitchen, he hoped any divine lesson would be a short one. He was ready to get on with the planting.

Someone had cracked open the window over the sink to allow in the morning breeze. Large pots of water boiled on the stove, and another of Floyd's daughters had just picked one up, holding it carefully away from her dress, and was carrying it into the washing room.

"*Gudemariye,*" she said in surprise as she moved past him into the adjacent room.

He heard the splash of water into a machine. The soft sound of women's voices was interrupted by the yank of someone pulling on a starting cord. Then the familiar sound of a gasoline engine caused a washer to hum, and Barbara Hershberger walked into the kitchen.

Her face flushed from the laundry work, she patted at the sweat beading on her forehead with a dish towel. Gabe almost envied her that. Perhaps men should take up housework. At least they wouldn't be interrupted by the whims of nature.

"Gabe. How are you?"

"*Gut.*"

"Can I pour you some *kaffi?*"

"*Ya.* If it's no trouble. *Danki.*"

Barbara poured three mugs of *kaffi* and walked over to the table.

Floyd pulled out a chair and sat, but he didn't relax. Instead, he drummed his fingers against the tabletop. "He came to speak to you about the rugs."

"Oh. Does Miriam need something?"

"No. No, not exactly."

Floyd was tall and thin, reminding Gabe of the pictures in the schoolbooks of President Lincoln. Barbara, though, was quite the opposite. Shorter and plumper, she had the look of a contented housewife. They seemed like opposites in many ways.

Even now, she sat down opposite him, relaxed and patient, while her husband continued to tap his fingers in an impatient rhythm.

"You might have heard that Aaron Troyer has come to help at the cabins since his *onkel* died."

Barbara pushed cream and sugar across the table, and then she asked one of the girls to bring over some breakfast rolls. Gabe knew Miriam would tell him he shouldn't, that he needed to watch his waistline. He didn't want to appear rude, though, so he accepted one.

"*Ya*, I think Floyd may have passed Aaron on the road and said hello."

"I did."

"Aaron is trying to make the cabins more profitable so that Elizabeth will have a better income for herself and the girls."

"Sounds like the boy has a *gut* business mind." Barbara studied him as she drank her *kaffi*. "We all care about Elizabeth, and we'll help her however we can."

"That's why I'm here."

Floyd finally stopped drumming his fingers.

"Aaron would like to sell Amish goods at the cabins. Offer items to the guests who stay there."

"Barbara sells her rugs here." Floyd scrubbed a hand over his face.

In the adjoining room, the washer had stopped, and the wringer had started. Gabe's mind flashed back to when he'd done his and Grace's clothes, to when Miriam wasn't a part of their lives. It had been a lonely time, a hard time, and for more reasons than laundry. He gulped his *kaffi* and pushed on.

"Do you have lots of folks stop in? They see your sign by the road?"

"*Gotte* sends those we're meant to sell to," Floyd insisted stubbornly.

"*Ya*. That's true." Gabe stared down at the near empty mug in his hands and resisted stating the obvious. Instead, he waited for Barbara to do that.

"Could be He also sent Aaron to us, and if we're helping Elizabeth..." She stood and rinsed out her cup in the sink. "What sort of arrangement can he offer, Gabe?"

"He's offering an eighty/twenty split."

"We get a hundred percent here." Floyd shook his head and began drumming again.

"A hundred percent of nothing isn't helping us, husband. I've more rugs stacked in the sewing room than we'll sell all this coming summer if last year is any indication."

For the first time a smile twitched at the corner of Floyd's lips. "*Ya*, Barbara weaves faster than you or I can plant a row. It's a sight to behold."

"That's not all," Gabe said, having withheld the best for last. "He'll purchase five up front. Once business picks up, he'll purchase more as he's able."

Floyd and Barbara both stared at him in disbelief. "The lad is setting up house?" Floyd finally asked.

"No, I don't believe so." Gabe drained his cup. "His idea is to place some of each product in the cabins. When guests see—and use—the items...maybe they'll come to the office seeking to buy."

"It's a *gut* plan," Barbara said, moving to the washroom to check on the girls.

"We've finished, *mamm.*"

"*Ya*, and with no missing fingers. Only clothes went through the wringer." The girls giggled as they walked out in front of their mother each carrying a basket. As they crossed the room and stepped out into the warming day to hang more clothes on the line, Gabe wondered what that would be like.

What would he feel like when his girls were that age?

And would he ever have a family large enough to require a full morning's laundry work?

If so, he'd need to expand the washroom and extend the lines where Miriam hung their clothes.

"Let's go and fetch you some rugs," Barbara said.

Gabe wasn't sure what he expected when they walked into Barbara's sewing room. It was obviously a newer addition Floyd had built onto the side of the house. Maybe at one point it had been a woodshed or mudroom, but now it was finished nicely into a sewing room.

What surprised him was the size of the loom, and the fact that every square inch of the room was filled with thread, rags, and rugs.

"Have you seen a loom before?" she asked, her eyes twinkling.

"Maybe when I was a *kind*, but I don't remember it being so large."

"Three hundred and sixty spools of thread." Her hand lingered over the spools that were a variety of colors. "No doubt it works much like the one you saw. Weaving is one of the things that has remained constant for us. I learned from my *mamm*, who learned from hers."

Barbara pushed up a horizontal wooden bar, sent a shuttle across—from right to left, and pulled the bar back down.

Gabe grinned. "My *dochder* would love to see this. Maybe I could bring her by sometime?"

"Of course, Gabe. I'd be happy for Grace to visit. Floyd repairs the loom when I manage to break it, though mostly it's a low-maintenance operation."

"The *Englischers* love her work, but you're right..." Floyd stared out the single window of the room. "We don't see much traffic here."

"One of Drake's men came by before their store opened." Barbara moved away from the loom, walked to a stack of completed rugs, and began thumbing through them. "He offered us a fifty/fifty split. We told him we'd take our chances with road traffic."

Barbara selected a dozen rugs of different sizes and colors for Floyd to carry to Gabe's buggy.

"He can only purchase five—"

"You tell Aaron he can pay when he sells them. We have plenty more, and we will pray *Gotte* smiles on his efforts. It would be *gut* to sell the rugs, but it's even more important that Elizabeth be able to keep the girls here if possible. I know that weighs heavily on her heart."

Gabe thanked her and climbed into his buggy. As he drove away, the girls were walking back toward the house, having hung the last of the trousers, shirts, and aprons on the line. Floyd was walking back into the shadow of the barn, and Barbara was standing on the porch, watching over her family like a mother hen.

It occurred to him then how they were like the rugs she wove. They were dependent on each other, much like those many strands of thread. He felt foolish for his earlier frustration over a muddy field...as if he could understand *Gotte*'s ways, *Gotte*'s plans.

What he could do was trust and persist in doing what he knew was the right thing.

As he continued toward the next family on Miriam's list, he knew with certainty that those two things would be enough.

☙ Chapter 16 ☙

Grace stared up at her teacher.

As usual when she was with Miss Bena, she felt confused. One part of her wanted to run outside and enjoy the rest of the lunch recess with Sadie and Lily. That part of her could barely wait for the school term to be over and summer to start.

But another part of her wanted to stay right beside Miss Bena and hear what she was about to say, even though she was afraid it might be criticism, which it probably was. After all, her face was scrunched up as though she'd just tasted some of Doc Hanson's worst cough syrup. But then Miss Bena's face usually looked that way, so her expression might mean nothing at all.

Grace started to tap her foot, but she stopped when Miss Bena raised her eyebrows in a pointed look. Miss Bena did not abide fidgeting.

"Grace, this was supposed to be your end-of-the-year report on our history unit."

"Yes, Miss Bena."

"And you chose to focus on Jakob Ammann."

"Yes, Miss Bena."

Her teacher tapped the page where Grace had erased a word and replaced it—the word was "fought" and she'd replaced it with "struggled." She liked struggled better. It seemed to describe what Ammann had gone through. Fighting was what boys did behind the outhouse sometimes. It was childish and against what they stood for as Amish people. She'd heard enough preaching in her nine years to know that word didn't feel right. It couldn't possibly describe Ammann's part of their history.

But "struggled," that word slipped into her sentence like her foot slipped into her well-worn shoes. Ammann had struggled—with others in his church, with his own beliefs and feelings, and with the things he had done.

Miss Bena tapped the spot with the end of her pen and moved on to the next page. "This was supposed to be a two-page report."

She frowned at the second page. "You wrote half a page here, but you filled the rest of the paper with your drawing."

Grace squirmed in her seat. She'd wondered about that, but in the end she'd had no choice.

"Did you not understand the assignment?"

"I understood." Grace's words came out small, like before, when she was first finding her voice again.

Miss Bena removed her glasses and rubbed them with the hem of her apron. When she placed them back on the edge of her nose she cleared her voice. "I'd like an explanation."

"You said we couldn't go over two pages, and I wanted to tell the whole story of Jakob Ammann. I didn't want to leave anything out."

Instead of saying she understood or correcting her, Miss Bena waited. Miss Bena could outwait Gus, she was that stubborn.

"Sometimes I feel I can say a lot more with my drawing than I can with words."

They both stared down at the picture. It covered every available space on the bottom half of the page. Grace had never drawn anything like it before. All of her other sketches made sense. You could look at them and identify the place or the person.

The drawing on the bottom half of the paper looked like a crazy patchwork quilt of Ammann's life, struggles, and kindnesses. At least that was what she had aimed to draw. Jakob was in the bottom right-hand corner, washing the feet of one of the men in his congregation. Hans Reist and the other Mennonites in Switzerland whom Jakob had put under the ban stood behind him, a look of disapproval on their face, and the snowcapped Swiss Alps towered over them.

Stretching toward the left of Jakob was a long line of Amish folk, leading the way to America. The line stretched across the ocean and to Pennsylvania. Above this portion of the picture was a light outline of their Bible, their German Bible. Grace had hoped the half-page sketch would show the connection between their present and their past.

The story of Jakob Ammann had captivated her, and she'd tried to include all she'd heard, all she'd learned on that half sheet of paper. She'd worked hard to pencil it into the five-by-eight-inch space. She wasn't sure if she'd done well or made a mess of things.

It had never occurred to her that she should have written that last half page.

Miss Bena sighed and closed the folder holding their reports. "You may go."

"Yes, Miss Bena."

Grace fled to the playground.

Sadie and Lily jumped from the swings to meet her.

"Were you in trouble?" Sadie pulled her out into the sunshine.

"Did she holler?" Lily's eyes widened in horror.

"Miss Bena never hollers." Sadie plopped down in the grass. "She doesn't need to holler. She stares at you, with those eyes, until you feel like a field mouse caught in a cat's paws."

"She didn't holler, and she didn't stare overly much." Grace crossed her legs so that her dress made a tent over her lap, then she fell back into the grass. The sun felt warm and yellow on her face. It felt like honey, and baby Rachel, and Hunter all in one.

"What'd she say, then?" Sadie reached over and tickled her nose with a blade of grass. "No sleeping. Tell us what happened."

Grace opened her eyes and stared up at her *freinden*. "She

questioned me about my paper, about why I drew part of it instead of writing—"

"Is that when she hollered?" Lily's light eyebrows shot up.

"No. She frowned more—"

"More?"

"And then she stuck the paper back into her folder. Maybe I'll still pass."

"Maybe you won't." Sadie looked worried.

"Maybe you should offer to rewrite it." Lily tried to catch a butterfly in her hand. "I'd rather rewrite it than fail. If I didn't pass, my *dat* would have me doing extra chores all summer. The chores I have are bad enough."

Grace wondered what her *mamm* and *dat* would do if she received a poor grade. Of course, she wouldn't fail the year, only the paper. Her grades were *gut* and could survive one failing paper. Plus, she had the sneaking feeling her parents didn't approve of Miss Bena, though they had never actually said anything out loud to make her think that.

It was more the looks they exchanged when they thought she wasn't looking.

Sadie reached a hand out and tapped her, calling "Tag, you're it" before darting off across the school yard.

Grace would have been happy lying in the sun, but she did not like being "it," so she stood, dusted the grass off her dress, and took off running after her *freind*. Soon everyone not playing baseball was playing tag, which ended up being at least a dozen kids. By the time Miss Bena rang the bell, Grace was out of breath but ready to go back inside and sit until the afternoon break.

She walked past Miss Bena's disapproving gaze, careful to put her hand over the grass stain on her apron. But Miss Bena's attention was on the boys who were late lining up to return for lessons.

One student's misfortune was sometimes another student's good luck. That wasn't a morning proverb, but it could be.

As Grace slid into her desk and stared out the window, she

noticed that Pebble Creek was still running quickly, but the water level seemed to be going down. Maybe Lydia and Aaron had been able to make progress at the cabins.

She hoped so. She wanted to go back to draw them when there were lots of people sitting on the porches and playing on the lawn. Maybe she'd even see someone fly-fishing. She and her *dat* had been riding into Cashton last year when they had seen a man doing that very thing along the river. They had pulled over and stopped to watch for a few minutes, but she hadn't had her drawing tablet with her.

The way the man had flicked his wrist and sent the line into the air in an *S* curve had amazed her. The sunlight had sparkled off the water, and the fish had practically jumped on to his hook. Oh, how she'd like to draw a picture of that.

"Grace Miller, are you going to complete your math, or are you going to stare out the window this afternoon?"

Luke Lapp snickered behind her, but he kept his head down.

Grace pulled out her tablet and quickly began copying down the arithmetic problems from the board. When her *mamm* had been teacher, they'd had story time after lunch, but Miss Bena had switched that along with a lot of other things.

Arithmetic on a full stomach wasn't a smart idea in Grace's opinion, but then no one was paying her to teach a classroom full of students. *Gut* thing too, or she'd probably stick to the three *D*'s— Drawing, Doodling, and Daydreaming.

The idea at least helped her to smile as she worked out the math problems and fought hard not to squirm under Miss Bena's occasional glare.

Chapter 17

Aaron was perched precariously on top of the roof of cabin four when he glanced over the edge and saw Gabe pulling into the parking area of the Plain Cabins.

Looking down brought on the dizziness, but seeing Gabe added relief to the nausea.

The morning had gone all right. He'd left first thing and gone to town to receive the money transfer his father had sent. Yesterday they had talked on the phone, though he'd had to call the phone shack in Indiana three times to catch his *dat*. Aaron was relieved when his *dat* agreed that he'd made the right decision and that the money they were investing would be well spent. If the cabins became more successful, Elizabeth and the girls would be able to stay. If they didn't draw more customers, the updates would make the property more attractive to a prospective buyer.

Everything had been moving along at a great clip until about an hour ago, until he'd decided to tackle the roof repairs. Now he was trying to patch the area where the roof was leaking, and he had no idea what he was doing.

Add to that his current predicament—a fear of heights. As if he didn't have enough to contend with this morning.

Gabe draped Chance's reins around a hitching post and walked over to stare up at him.

"Do you know what you're doing up there?"

"*Nein.*"

"Could you use a hand?"

"I could use two."

Gabe climbed the ladder and immediately began laughing. "You've everything up here but the kitchen sink."

"I couldn't carry the kitchen sink."

"Never repaired a roof before?"

"I'm a farmer."

"Farmers live in homes too." Gabe climbed easily over the top of the ladder, as if they weren't dangerously high off the ground, and walked across the roof toward him.

"Is there a reason you're sitting in the middle of the roof, when the damage seems to be over in that corner?"

Aaron licked his lips, placed both hands beside him against the warm shingles, and reminded himself *not* to look down. "Could be I'm somewhat afraid of heights."

Gabe's laughter rang out so good-naturedly, Aaron couldn't for a minute believe there was an ounce of malice in it. Besides, he was too ill to care.

"Haven't I seen you climbing ladders to trim those trees?" Gabe dropped down beside him.

"*Ya*, suppose so."

"How did you manage that?"

"Trees don't bother me. They seem firmer. Grounded somehow. Plus if I'm angry, sometimes I forget to be afraid for a moment." He peered over the edge and sweat popped out on his forehead like grease on a hot skillet. "The day you're remembering, I was so upset about the condition of this place, I didn't think at first. Once I'd reached the top of the ladder, I realized how high up I was. That's when the ladder tilted and I grabbed for the tree."

He stared down at his hands, slick with sweat. "Makes me nervous all over, thinking about it."

Gabe stood and stretched in the sun, reminding Aaron of Pumpkin—a mouser they had recently inherited at the office. "Look on the bright side. This roof isn't so tall. If you fell off, I doubt you'd do much more than break a leg."

Accepting the hammer Aaron offered him, he snagged the correct box of nails and reached for the roofing shingles. "You're a boy no longer, Aaron. Roofing is part of being a man. Part of owning a home."

"I'm twenty-three and unmarried, in case you haven't noticed. I live with my parents."

"Not anymore you don't." Gabe's hammering halted all conversation, and in fifteen minutes the patch was complete. Though Gabe did most of the work, Aaron handed him supplies. He was surprised to find that while they were working there was a time that he forgot to be worried about falling. His stomach didn't even roll until they began gathering the supplies to carry down.

"How'd you bring all this up here?"

"Wasn't easy."

"Why did you bring all this up here?"

"Didn't know what I'd need."

They both turned and studied the roof patch. Aaron's previous attempt looked like something a child would have done. Gabe's shingles were laid down like stitches Aaron's mother might have sewn on a quilt—even, uniform, and without a pucker.

"Snug. Shouldn't leak now."

"Say, can I hire you to be my roof man? If you're free..."

Gabe slid the hammer and nails into the toolbox, squinted out across the property, and then nodded. "Today I am. You have other cabins that are leaking?"

"Cabins one and seven."

"Got it. While I'm doing that, you might want to unload my buggy. Miriam thought we should get started on picking up the Amish-made goods you wanted."

"Did you have any success?"

"Put it this way. You might want to ask Lydia to help you."

Lydia began a list of the items as Aaron brought them into the office. She was stunned by all Gabe had been able to collect and still unable to envision Aaron's plan for what they were going to do with it. Where would these items go? They couldn't leave them in the office. She wouldn't be able to move around to do her work.

By the time Gabe was finished repairing the other two roofs, Aaron had unloaded everything and set the items on the table or stacked them along the wall. He was returning from feeding and watering Chance when Gabe scraped off his boots and walked into the office.

Lydia continued to stare down at her tablet, tapping her pen against the paper.

"This is a *gut* start, Gabe. You had a busy morning." She moved to pour him a glass of tea, which he accepted gratefully. He also eyed the peanut butter cookies she'd filled up the glass jar with, but when she moved to offer him one, he shook his head no.

"If I come home weighing more than when I left, Miriam won't let me leave again." He laughed and patted his stomach, which Lydia didn't think needed watching.

She supposed it was natural for married couples to look out for each other. Better early than after one had gained twenty or thirty pounds. She glanced at Aaron, and then she quickly looked back down at her pad.

"Each family was satisfied with your terms of eighty/twenty. And they all had plenty more already made up should you need it. Some weekends are *gut* and some aren't, so there's no continuity to their sales."

"And do any of them offer their goods at Drake's?"

"Only Irene Gingerich and Nathan Glick." Gabe picked up a walking stick and ran his hand down the smooth finish. "You ought to go by and see all he has in his woodshop. I couldn't bring the larger things in my buggy, and I wouldn't have purchased them if I could. Those are big items you need to decide on yourself."

"Blanket chests?"

"*Ya*, and rockers that would look *gut* on the porches."

"I'll want directions to his place."

"Sure. Or Lydia knows the way. It's not far from here."

Lydia felt the heat rise in her cheeks. The thought of riding in the buggy with Aaron unsettled her, though she knew it would be for business purposes and not for pleasure.

Waving her hand over the abundance of goods, she tried not to sound whiney. "Where are we going to put all of these things, Aaron? They can't all stay here. There will be no place to serve breakfast, assuming we have customers who need serving, and I pray we do."

"Gabe, you purchased five of each item, right?"

"*Ya*. Like you said." Gabe emptied his glass and carried it to the sink. "I told them you would bring around the money in the next week. Some people insisted on sending more than five. They claimed to have extra stock lying around and said it might as well sit here where someone might see and purchase it."

"Looks like we have Gabe's walnut bowls—nicely done—plus quilts, walking sticks, canned jams, rugs, dolls, and bonnets." Lydia stopped and walked over to the pile on the table. "Do you honestly think *Englischers* will purchase hand-sewn bonnets?"

"I do," Aaron said. "And I plan on ordering straw hats as well from the same factory Drake orders them."

"Why would *Englischers* want straw hats and cloth bonnets?" Lydia asked. "They're not Plain."

"The straw hats are for the children and the adults—folks protecting themselves from the sun. The bonnets, now those are for the young *kinner*." Aaron reached for a cookie as he explained. "Didn't you notice how many were purchasing them at Drake's?"

"I did not."

"Probably he's right, Lydia. Irene Gingerich sews those. She's Lily's mom, and Lily is Grace's *freind*."

Lydia wasn't convinced, and it must have showed on her face, for Gabe pushed on. "She's the one house I stopped at who was making *gut* money at Drake's. Said he'd actually raised the price from what she set it at because they sold out of the first bundle she sent—both the dolls and the bonnets. But she said she'd rather sell things here with you. She said not only would she make more, but she'd sleep better at night."

"What about Miriam's *bruder* David? He's going to bring some of his toys, right?"

"*Ya*, I think so." Gabe caved in and reached for one of the cookies as well. "Lydia, don't forget to offer your *mamm*'s baked goods. I know they will sell."

Lydia was momentarily distracted by the thought of extra income for her family and by the knowledge of how it would help, but then her eyes refocused on the pile of stuff in front of her. "This isn't a large room, Aaron. When we have a few families here and I'm serving breakfast, it becomes full quickly. Add in a general store, and we'll be tripping over each other. Or maybe you're thinking of building a store on the property?"

"That's not a bad idea, actually. Write that down for phase two, would you?"

"Phase two? I was kidding!"

"It's a *gut* idea, though," Gabe said. "You're lucky to have her around, Aaron."

"Don't I know it."

Lydia sighed. "You two aren't listening to me. We offer a place for people to sleep and then we provide them breakfast. Where are you going to put all of this?"

Both men stopped chewing long enough to stare around the office. It was well constructed, like the cabins.

And it was Plain.

"David suggested building shelves." Aaron stood and walked to the far wall. It was bare, without pictures or a window. "We'll put them here, floor to ceiling."

"And all of this is going on the shelves?" Lydia tried to envision it and then scolded herself for being such a pessimist.

"No. I want you to go to work on cabins two, seven, and eight. They have the best view of the river. Those will be our three *new* Plain cabins..."

"New because..." Lydia felt Gabe's eyes on them, watching, enjoying the tug as Aaron pulled her over to his vision.

"Because we have to start somewhere. Our guests want a home away from home, and we're going to give them one—a simple, clean, Plain one." He walked around the table, collecting a quilt, a walking stick, some rugs, a walnut bowl, and a doll, and then he placed them all into her arms. "You start on cabin two while Gabe and I fetch wood for shelving."

"Sure, boss. It's not like we have any customers I need to get ready for."

"Well, you will have. I'm also picking up some office supplies. You're about to start a letter-writing campaign."

What was a letter-writing campaign?

Not that she should complain. She needed this job, and with empty cabins, she realized Aaron couldn't pay her to sit around in the office chair. So she'd tote new quilts into cabins near the river and she'd write letters.

Sure. She could do that.

It didn't bother her so much that she wouldn't do it.

She squared her shoulders as she traipsed down the trail toward the river. Hard work had never bothered her.

What did worry her maybe a smidgen was Aaron Troyer. As he had fetched his hat off the hook by the door, she thought she heard him whistling. She was sure she saw a grin on Gabe's face. The two of them together might manage to patch a leaky roof and build shelves. They might complete a lot of work that needed to be done, but there was also the potential for trouble—same as when two boys sitting at the back of the classroom took to whispering.

Trouble.

She could smell it, like rain in the air.

Chapter 18

Miriam was ready to leave for her mother's house Tuesday morning as soon as Grace had climbed into Eli's buggy. Their old *freind* smiled and lifted a hand as he pulled away, his vehicle filled with his children bundled and eager for school. A familiar pang sliced into Miriam's heart as she thought about the schoolhouse and the days she'd spent teaching there, but she pushed the memory down. Today she needed to focus on her family. There was no time to look toward the past.

"We could drive Grace to school ourselves now," she said to her husband.

"And deny her the chance to ride with Sadie? It would break both of their hearts, not to mention hurting Eli's feelings." Gabe finished harnessing Belle.

"I didn't want to bring it up in front of Grace, but what did you think of the grade she received on her report?"

"The *B*? I was happy with it."

"Yes, but Gabe, it was a fine paper. There were no errors in spelling or grammar."

Gabe stopped fiddling with the horse, stepped closer, and cupped her face in his hands. Kissing her softly on the lips, he whispered, "You're a *gut mamm*. You know that, right?"

"Yes, but—" Miriam tried to put her thoughts back into order.

"Grace explained about the grade and about the meeting with Miss Bena."

Miss Bena, that's what she'd meant to talk to him about before he'd kissed her, before he'd distracted her.

"The drawing is the best she's ever done," she said.

"And I think the bishop will appreciate seeing it."

"So you believe the grade to be fair?"

Gabe leaned forward and kissed her again—this time his lips like the brush of a breeze against hers. "I think it would do more harm than good to argue over it. Grace knows we are proud of her."

Miriam nodded. Every teacher graded differently—some more harshly than others. Perhaps it wouldn't be beneficial to confront Miss Bena over the paper.

"Want me to keep the *boppli*? She might be small, but she's a *gut* helper in the barn."

"Gabe Miller. Rachel is not even three months old and already you are trying to get her more used to the smells of the barn than the kitchen."

Gabe smiled but didn't deny it.

"I'd rather take her along. It will be *gut* to have her with us. She can cheer *mamm* up some."

"Maybe it's you that needs cheering."

"*Ya*, maybe so."

As Gabe handed her up, Rachel reached out, swatting at Miriam's *kapp* strings. Miriam kissed her once, closing her eyes and breathing in her sweet powdery baby scent. Then she tucked her into the carrier on the floor of the buggy.

"I'll come with you if you like."

"Of course not. There's little worse than a man in a doctor's waiting room."

Gabe pulled on his beard. "I believe I should feel insulted, but I don't."

"*Gut*. I expect to be home after lunch."

"I'll be watching for you. If the sun stays out, I could be in the west field by then." He handed her the reins to Belle, and they set off at a nice easy trot.

An hour later, her mother was in the buggy beside her, baby Rachel tucked in the carrier at her feet, and they were headed toward town.

"You know your *dat* would have been happy to take me."

"Would you rather have ridden with him?"

"No. He's like a bull in an unfamiliar pen when he's inside the doc's office. He never knows whether he should wait out in the visitors' area or come into the exam room with me. It's all very awkward."

"Then I'm glad I came."

"Afterward, I'd like you to take me by to see Lydia at the cabins." Abigail pulled her shawl more tightly around her shoulders, though the day was warm. "I'd like to see what they are doing. Everyone's talking about the improvements."

"Maybe we should wait and see whether you're up to it. We should listen to what Doc Hanson says."

Abigail gave her *the look*, and Miriam wanted to laugh but she couldn't...not with the stone of fear tumbling around in her stomach.

"Miriam Miller. Regardless what Dr. Hanson says, I believe I know when I feel *gut* enough to visit neighbors, and visiting is what I plan on doing later this morning."

"Yes, *mamm*. It's only that—"

"Miriam."

"Yes, Mother."

The soothing *clip-clop* of Belle's hooves filled the morning. A bird called from its perch in the woods. And the sound of Pebble Creek provided a pleasant harmony behind it all.

"Rachel is smiling at me."

"Is she?"

"I believe she heard me scolding you."

"Perhaps she did." Now Miriam was smiling, along with her mother and her daughter. The worry hadn't left her stomach, but it had been wrapped in something she was familiar with—the constant reminder that she should appreciate this moment, this day.

It wasn't in her nature to worry. When she did, when she gave into it, she felt almost as if she had a terrible stomachache. Like when she used to eat too much of her *aenti*'s pie or when she stayed up too late reading with the aid of a flashlight hidden under her blankets. In the first case, the sugar went to work on her, leaving her stomach roiling. In the second, it was guilt, pure and simple—knowing she was disobeying the rules and also realizing she would be very tired the next day.

Worrying was much the same. It seemed like it went against her system, and it also felt like she was disobeying.

Rachel chortled.

"Now she's blowing bubbles." Abigail seemed satisfied with her granddaughter's progress.

Belle trotted down the road, and an *Englisch* car slowed as the passenger snapped a picture of their buggy. Miriam knew they meant no harm. She understood that her black mare made a pretty sight indeed this summer morning.

By the time they pulled into the doctor's office, a sharp smell was coming from the baby carrier and Rachel had begun to fuss.

"She's wet through and through," Abigail said.

"I'll take care of her while you check in."

The waiting room was filled with Amish and *Englisch*, aged preschool to elderly. By the time Miriam returned from the ladies' room, Abigail was deep in conversation with the wife of one of the *Englisch* pastors. Abigail had seen her in town before but couldn't remember the woman's name or what congregation her husband guided.

They were talking about a benefit for a child with cancer that was to be held at the hospital in Eau Claire. Miriam caught bits and pieces of the conversation as she settled into the chair with Rachel. She couldn't hear what her mother promised to do, but she did hear the pastor's wife say, "I'll stop by your home next week to pick them up."

Before she could ask what the woman was going to pick up, the doctor's nurse appeared at the door and called "Abigail King."

Miriam's heart rate kicked up a notch, which was ridiculous. Why did doctors make her *naerfich*?

Dr. Hanson had always treated them kindly. Still, her palms began to sweat as she gathered Rachel's things and stood.

Then the thought occurred to her that perhaps her mother would rather go inside alone. She stood there, indecisive and sweating, as Abigail made her way toward the nurse.

"Do you want us to wait here or come with you?" Miriam realized too late that she sounded like her father.

Abigail paused and turned her head like a small bird listening for something important in the breeze. "Better to come. Then I won't have to explain to you what he says, and you can be the one to tell it over again to your *bruders*. That will save me a lot of trouble."

Ever the practical one, Miriam thought, following in her mother's wake as she proceeded around the chairs, through the doorway, and into the inner room. A moment later the nurse was holding her mother's shawl and weighing her.

Virginia had been Dr. Hanson's nurse for the past three years. She was almost as round as she was tall, and she was short by any measure. A very motherly type, she put patients at ease immediately. Miriam judged her to be in her mid-thirties, but it was hard to tell with *Englischers*. Her skin was a beautiful ivory white and her hair, tumbling free down the back of her scrubs, was a bright red.

The scrubs featured Dalmatian puppies. They frolicked about completely unaware of how serious this visit might be.

"Let me check that one more time, sweetie." Frowning, Virginia motioned for Abigail to step up onto the scale again. When she had, the nurse tapped the number into a device the size of a book.

"What happened to my chart?" Abigail asked.

"We've gone digital. Everything's on computers now. This way if you go to the hospital, they'll have access to your records."

"I don't plan on going to the hospital."

"Patients rarely do. That's why it's helpful to have the data transfer automatically." Virginia glanced up, caught sight of Rachel, and beamed. "We haven't seen this one yet."

"No, she's a little young for Doc Hanson."

"True. We'll have to wait a few years, I suppose." She stepped closer as they moved toward the examining room, reached out, and cupped her hand around the back of Rachel's head. "Did you birth her at home?"

"I did. At my *mamm's*, actually."

"Oh, Abigail. You helped to deliver her?"

"Most natural thing in the world, and you know that, Virginia. Didn't I hear that you've been assisting our midwife in your off-hours?"

A smile crept across Virginia's face as she directed Abigail to sit on the examining table and motioned Miriam toward the extra chair. Slipping the blood pressure cuff on Abigail's arm, she admitted, "I'm working on my master's degree."

All conversation halted as she took Abigail's blood pressure and noted it on the small computer. "For one of my projects this semester, I was studying home births among the Amish."

"*Ya*, and what did you learn?" Abigail asked.

Virginia's expression turned suddenly serious. "Five of the six births I attended went off without a hitch. I learned that childbirth is, as you say, a very natural thing. One birth though, had complications. We had to call in an ambulance. If the emergency medical personnel hadn't arrived in time, I'm not sure the baby would have lived."

"I know the family you mean, and the woman should have seen a doctor beforehand. Several of us visited her and tried to talk her into going, but she refused."

"And yet they let me attend the birth."

"It's hard to understand people sometimes, whether they are Amish or *Englisch*."

Miriam listened to this exchange as she held Rachel to her

shoulder, rubbing tiny circles along her back. Her mother was so caught up in the conversation that she seemed to have forgotten why she was in Doc Hanson's office. Or perhaps her mother was so involved in all of the lives around her that she often dismissed her own problems.

"Doc will be in soon."

Then it was only the three of them, waiting.

Abigail didn't even pretend to read the magazines next to the bed. Instead, she opened her handbag, pulled out her knitting, and set to work. Miriam continued to lull Rachel to sleep as she stared at drawings done by young patients and tacked to the doctor's wall. In most of them his head was quite disproportionate to his body. In many of them, probably the ones drawn by Amish children, his *Englisch* car was in the background. In all of them he had his stethoscope around his neck, had bushy eyebrows, and was smiling.

The door opened, and for a fraction of a second Miriam's and Abigail's eyes met.

"Hello, Abigail. Miriam. And this must be Rachel." Doc's hand brushed the curly brown hair at the top of her *boppli*'s head. Like Gabe, he had big hands. Miriam's father often said if Doc had been born Amish, he'd have made a fine farmer with those hands.

Virginia walked in behind him and shut the door. She was still carrying the small computer and set it on the counter where the other medical supplies were.

Doc sat down on the stool with the wheels, and then he took the knitting from Abigail and placed it on top of her bag. He cocked his head, looked at her, and waited.

"Joshua insisted I come see you," she finally admitted.

"Ahh." Doc Hanson scrubbed a hand down his jaw line. "What's got him worried?"

"I'm still losing weight."

"How much since last time, Virginia?"

"Eleven pounds," she said softly.

Miriam felt the stone within her stomach grow.

"Don't suppose you're dieting."

"*Nein*. I don't believe in such silliness unless someone has a health issue, and you know I have no diabetes."

"Do you have any appetite? Do you eat?"

Abigail's hands came out in front of her, as if she were blind and searching for her way. "*Ya*. I think so. At least I am hungry at first, but then...then when I sit down to dinner not so much. That's probably normal for my age, though."

"Maybe. Why don't you lay back for me. I'd like to check your stomach."

Virginia took Abigail's shawl as she stretched out on the table. "Nice shawl, but it's a warm day. Do you find you're cold a lot?"

"Oh, *ya*. I guess that's the *change*."

Doc glanced over at Virginia, and she shook her head no. "You went through the change already, Abigail. That's a one-way road. Don't have to go down it twice."

The doctor continued to touch her stomach gently. Miriam tried to watch his hands, his expression, Virginia's response, and her mother's reaction all at the same time.

"Feeling any pain when I do that?"

"*Nein*."

"How about here?"

"Still no. Joshua, he worries more now that he's old."

Doc Hanson smiled as he rolled his stool to the other side of the exam table, then he looked up and winked at Miriam. The stone in her stomach shrank a little.

"Do you worry?"

"*Gotte's wille* is fine with me, Grady Lee Hanson. It's not my place to be questioning what His plans are for this old woman."

He smiled at the use of his full name, which Miriam had never even heard. "Uh-huh. You can sit up now. How long has your hand been shaking?"

"Started a while ago. It comes and goes."

After asking her a few questions about her diet and activities, he stood behind her and felt her throat. "Could be thyroid or any number of things, Abigail. I'll be honest with you. I can't tell you why you're losing weight, but I'm concerned. When you combine the weight loss with the hair loss and the tremors, it suggests an aggressive change of some sort."

Sitting again, he rolled the stool back in front of her and placed his hands on his knees.

"I'm glad you came in. Glad you listened to Joshua. I respect your beliefs about *Gotte's wille*." He pronounced it with an Amish accent, pausing until he saw the smile on her face he was waiting for, and then he pushed on. "But I happen to believe that *Gotte* brought me to this community for a reason, and one of those reasons was to look after fine folk like yourself."

"Humph. That's a fancy way of saying what?"

"I want to do some blood tests, and I'd like you back in here next week."

Abigail clasped her hands together in her lap. It was rare that Miriam had ever seen her mother's hands still—at church perhaps, but then they were usually holding the Bible or were held together in prayer. Folded there, in the light coming through the single window, Abigail seemed her full fifty-five years. Miriam could make out the blue veins and the delicate bones even from where she sat, and they reminded her of a small bird. But more than that, they reminded her of all the times her mother had tended her—made meals, applied bandages, cut herbs for teas she did not want to drink, canned food, and wrapped Rachel in a blanket.

Miriam blinked away her tears and tried to focus on what her mother was saying.

"Why blood tests? What are we looking for, Doctor?"

The list was long and included most of the fears Miriam had wrestled with since Sunday—cancer, diabetes, Parkinson's, and hyperthyroidism. Some she hadn't even heard of, like Hodgkin's, and Addison's disease.

"Do you have any other questions?" Doc asked.

"Are these treatable? Because if they're not, I see no point in knowing. You understand I won't abide long vigils in a hospital. I've been clear how I feel about that topic."

How did he know how she felt about the topic of hospital stays and long vigils? When had they ever talked about it before?

"I know. I haven't forgotten, but you're placing the buggy well in front of the horse in this case. Let me run the tests, and then we'll talk again."

Abigail nodded and rolled up her sleeve so Virginia could take the blood samples she needed. Doc Hanson stood and left the room without another word, but Miriam thought he looked more concerned than when he had walked in. She thought the entire day had changed in the last ten minutes, and it had changed for the worse.

⸻ Chapter 19 ⸻

Aaron once again borrowed Lydia's horse and buggy. He didn't want to purchase his own transportation. He still didn't believe he'd be in Wisconsin long enough to justify the expense, plus he'd have to deal with selling both buggy and horse when he left. He'd rather borrow Lydia's and pay her a little more each week for their use. Today he was on an errand to sign up some extra labor, and the person he had in mind didn't have a phone.

As he drove Tin Star into David King's yard, the shouting was at full volume.

Seth and his father stood a few feet outside the barn, nose to nose. It wasn't the first time Aaron had seen such confrontations between fathers and sons. There had been a few in his own family—not with his father, who wouldn't stand for hollering. No, Ethan Troyer stated how things were and allowed you to stew or work yourself into submission or exhaustion.

The hollering in the Troyer family came from his *onkels* and their sons.

Folks tended to think Amish were always peaceful and quiet—peaceful, yes, but there were times of discord within their families as in any life. One such situation was playing out right in front of him at the moment. He dropped the reins to Tin Star and sat back to watch.

He'd place his money on David if he were a betting man, though of course Amish didn't bet any more often than they hollered.

"You know I will not abide you speaking to me or your *mamm* in such a manner!"

"And what will you abide? Can you tell me that?"

"I'll thank you to close your mouth at the moment. That would be the best thing for you to do, and if you have any brains in your head, you'll prove it right now."

"I'm not a *kind*, you know."

"Then stop acting like one!"

"You seem to forget that I'm seventeen—"

"How can I forget when you remind me of it every day?"

They might have gone on like that for some time, and Aaron thought it was more interesting than an *Englisch* picture show. David, forty years old, had an abundance of energy and muscle. He hadn't been able to use enough of it recently, what with the rains, and so now his hands were working overtime, punctuating every third word by flinging an arm out—first toward the barn, then the house, then the pasture.

Seth was a mirror image of his dad. One day they would probably work side by side in the fields, contentedly. Odds were certainly on their side because most Amish youth did stay within the Plain community. But at the moment, Seth was still struggling emotionally and physically with his place in the community and the family. All of that was evident in the way he squared his shoulders, rammed his hands into the pockets of his pants, and glowered at his father.

He reminded Aaron of a pup with extra skin he hadn't quite grown into yet.

The two of them made quite a pair—a young frustrated pup and a bull with too much energy.

Ya. Spring on an Amish farm was full of entertainment.

"Are you going to stay in your buggy, sitting there and grinning at us?" David demanded.

"Wasn't sure it was safe to come out yet."

"It's safe, all right. Not sure it's worth your time, but it's safe." David turned and stalked into his barn.

Seth moved closer to Tin Star.

When the horse nudged him, Aaron thought he had better offer a warning. "Lydia's spoiled that gelding. I'd be careful unless you have—"

Pulling a handful of raisins from his pocket, Seth offered them to Tin Star, who ate them greedily as if he hadn't been fed earlier at the cabins.

"That horse is incorrigible," Aaron muttered, wondering if everyone in Pebble Creek spoiled their animals or if Seth knew Lydia better than he realized. The boy was old enough to court a girl, but Lydia was too old for him.

The thought caught in his throat, and he nearly choked. Was she courting? He'd never thought to ask. It wasn't his business to ask.

"Word's going around," Seth grumbled.

"What word?"

"Incorrigible. My *dat* called me that earlier, before you arrived. Before the shouting started."

Aaron hopped out of the buggy. "Are you?"

"I don't know. I didn't pay that much attention in school. Couldn't wait for eighth grade to be done so I could be free. And for what? So I could get bossed around by him instead of by a schoolmarm."

"Incorrigible means incurable or hopeless, and I doubt your *dat* feels that way about you, Seth. Sometimes people say things they don't mean when they're frustrated, and no man is perfect, not even your father."

"Tell him that."

"I'm sure he knows."

Seth rubbed Tin Star's neck as he thought on that a minute. Finally he shrugged his shoulders. "I need to get off this farm before I go completely *narrisch*."

"Would the cabins be far enough? I came by to see if your *dat* could do without you half days the rest of the week. I need some help building shelves in the office...if you know how."

"I can build shelves. He's made me learn to make everything from shelves to those stupid toys he has stacked up in his workshop. I've done enough woodwork in the last six weeks to make me wish I'd never seen a saw."

"So you're not interested?" Aaron asked.

"Yes, I'm interested."

"I also need you to drive me over to the east side of Pebble Creek."

When Seth started to ask why, Aaron held up his hand. "There will be other errands and more busywork around the property. Nothing fancy, but I can pay you minimum wage four hours a day."

Seth glanced over at his father, who had led two of the horses out of the barn to turn them loose in the pasture. "It's a deal. If I stay here I'll be cleaning out horse stalls all day."

"Let's go talk to your dad, then." Aaron didn't mention Seth would probably still be cleaning out those stalls. He would just have to finish it in the morning hours before he came to work at the cabins.

Aaron needed the boy's help, and apparently David and Seth could use a little time apart.

He remembered those years well enough. It hadn't been that long ago that he'd determined to buy his own fields, tired of working on his father's place. Tired of doing everything his father's way.

He'd found a small piece of land easily enough, but he hadn't been able to purchase it right away. His dreams hadn't come true overnight. He'd had to put in his time on the family farm and work extra hours as a hired hand at the neighbors' places. The money he'd earned had been carefully tucked away and saved. While others his age had taken bus trips and bought new mares, Aaron had continued to watch the account grow until he had enough to buy the small section down the road from his parents' farm.

Walking toward David, he recognized the irony in the situation. By the time he'd earned enough money to purchase land that was all his own, by the time that land had become productive and was finally turning a profit, he'd no longer felt the need to have distance between himself and his *dat*.

Which was when the call had come that his *onkel* Ervin had passed. He'd had to leave his land and his family behind.

Now his land was being tended by his younger brothers. As the oldest nephew, it had fallen to him to come to Wisconsin and see to Elizabeth and the girls.

Those days of struggling against his father seemed far off as he watched a similar situation play out between David and Seth.

After talking with David and coming to an agreement regarding Seth's hours, choosing lumber for the shelves, and picking up toys to sell, Aaron climbed into Lydia's buggy and headed back to the cabins.

The sun was starting to move toward the horizon, but he felt he had accomplished a lot in one day. Aaron was pleased. Each day more was done. Each evening he was a day closer to stepping aboard the bus and returning to his piece of land in Indiana. He might miss this year's planting, but surely he would be there in time for the harvest.

Gabe hadn't expected Miriam to be home in time for lunch, and he didn't begin worrying when she still hadn't returned by the time he took a midafternoon break. He'd been able to work in the fields, finally, though the going was slow in the wet ground. He didn't mind too much. It was good to be out on his land again.

Concern began to gnaw at the back of his mind when she still hadn't returned by late afternoon, when he met Grace at the end of the lane. As they walked toward the house, he listened to her chatter about her day at school. She'd come in second in the spelling bee. She reminded him again about the school picnic on Friday. Could Sadie come over to play afterward and stay the night?

He heard her and he was paying attention with one part of his mind, but his thoughts were wandering.

What was keeping his *fraa*?

Had Doc Hanson found something seriously wrong with Abigail? Had he sent her on to the hospital? But if that were the case, Miriam would have found a way to send word to him.

"*Dat*. Are you listening?"

"Sure. *Ya*, of course I am."

Grace stepped in front of him, her lunch pail in one hand and the books she insisted on carrying herself in the other.

"You are?"

"Yes." Gabe ran his thumbs under his suspenders, as he glanced back up the road.

"What did I say?"

"You came in second in the spelling bee."

"Uh-huh. Go on."

"School picnic's Friday."

"And then?"

"You want Sadie to stay over on Friday. Sounds *gut*, but let's ask your *mamm*."

She squinted at him. "What else?"

"There was more?"

Grace trudged ahead and flopped on the front porch steps. "I knew you didn't hear me. I told you all about Adam Lapp and how he keeps following us around. Not following us, exactly, but popping up at odd times. And that's not all. One minute he'll be nice to me, and the next minute I'll ask him something and he'll ignore me completely. I don't know what to make of it."

Something in his daughter's voice caught his attention, his complete attention, and for a moment he forgot everything but the little person right in front of him.

"How old are you?"

"*Dat*." Grace began to giggle, and then she fell over on to her back, staring up at the porch ceiling. "I'm nine—"

The word stretched out between them.

He sat on the porch next to her. On impulse he lay back too, staring up at the unpainted wood boards of the porch roof. A few cobwebs were in one corner, and a mud dauber's nest from last summer was in the other. "I remember nine."

"Must have been a long time ago."

"*Ya*, but nine isn't something you forget."

"Really?"

"Sure. It's the last of your single digit years. It's important."

A bee buzzed over them before flying off in search of sweeter pickings.

"This Adam, he used to bother you when we first moved here."

"True, but that was a long time ago, way back before our first Christmas. Since then we became *freinden*. Now he acts a little strange. I don't know what to make of it."

Something in Gabe's heart twisted, and he thought of Hope. He closed his eyes, shutting out the sight of the old porch boards, and recalled her sweet face, how much he had loved her. He adored Miriam and was grateful for his new life, but how he wished that Hope could have had this talk with Grace.

Pulling in a deep breath, he began the conversation he most certainly wasn't ready to have.

"You know that boys and girls sometimes feel sweet on each other."

Grace popped up and placed a hand on his chest, right where the pain had been a moment earlier. She stared down into his face, her brown eyes wide and serious.

"I'm a kid, *dat*. I'm *nine*."

"*Ya*. True. But even at your age—"

"Adam's a year older."

"Oh."

"Double digit." Grace lay back down, but this time she twined the fingers of her left hand with his right.

"Right. Well, that's probably the age boys start thinking how pretty young girls are. Maybe Adam is confused by his feelings."

Silence stretched between them. Gabe heard Gus braying out in the pasture, followed by the sound of Chance neighing in response. The rhythms and sounds of farm life had a soothing effect on his father's heart.

As did the rapidly changing moods of his daughter.

"I guess I'll go see Hunter now." Grace jumped up, dusted off her dress and hopped down the steps. Humming to herself, she stacked her lunch pail and books. Gone were her worries, or so it seemed. She turned away from him without another word.

"Don't forget your chores," he called after her.

She never even slowed down, only waved as she skipped toward the barn.

He stood and stretched, which was when he saw Belle pulling Miriam's buggy down the lane. His heart skipped in the same way Grace had, and he realized he'd been more than a little worried. But she was home now. Everything was fine with his family.

Or so he thought, until he reached the buggy and saw the expression on his *fraa*'s face. If he had to put a name to it, he would say it was exhaustion wrapped in fear.

⇜ *Chapter 20* ⇝

G race had never been shy about her drawing.

She'd actually never thought about others' opinions of what she did that much. Drawing what she saw, what caught her eye, was something she loved doing when her chores were done, when school was out, and when her baby sister was asleep. Why would she be shy about it?

Her *dat* wasn't bashful about his farming. Her *mamm* wasn't timid about proclaiming the newest thing Rachel had done, but neither did it seem as though she was boasting. Rachel was the most beautiful thing Grace had ever seen. *Mammi* wasn't shy about her quilting. She said *Gotte* expected everyone to use their gifts.

So when her *mamm* brought up the subject of her drawing at breakfast Saturday morning, Grace wasn't quite sure what to think about it.

"I want to take you over to the cabins today, Grace. Lydia and Aaron would like you to draw a picture for them—a picture they can put on postcards."

"They said so?"

"Yes. When your *mammi* and I stopped by earlier in the week. I told them you couldn't do it before today because of school."

Grace glanced at Sadie, who shrugged and reached for her glass of milk. They'd had a lot of fun the night before, playing ball with Hunter, making new furniture for Stanley's box, and taking her cat, Stormy, into the barn and watching him chase mice.

"Can Sadie go?"

"Sadie's *mamm* said to have her home before ten. I believe she has chores."

Sadie nodded, her milk mustache causing Grace to dissolve into giggles.

"Seems to me you need some Danish muffins to go with that milk," Gabe said, passing her the plate of warm sweet bread.

"I have chores too."

"I'll take care of those today, Gracie." Gabe broke a muffin in half and slipped a pat of butter on one side. He aimed for more, but Miriam moved the dish out of his reach.

"Aaron and Lydia need your help." Miriam refilled Gabe's *kaffi* cup, and then she walked out of the room to tend to Rachel, who was letting the whole world know she was awake.

"They need my help drawing?" No one had ever *asked* her to draw before.

"Seems so." Her *dat* smiled and reached for more butter before her *mamm* returned.

"I don't understand why they want me to draw a picture for their postcards," Grace said. They had dropped Sadie off at her home and were almost at the cabins.

"They need to advertise, and the best way to convince people to spend a night there would be with a picture."

"A picture I'm supposed to draw?"

Miriam smiled and patted her hand. "Lydia and Aaron have seen your drawing. They think it's very *gut*."

"They could hire someone."

"Yes, but that would cost more money, and they're trying to save money to help Elizabeth and her girls."

"Because the girls' *dat* died."

"Yes."

"Like my *mamm*—my first *mamm*."

"Yes."

Grace considered that a moment, as Belle trotted down the road. She certainly wanted to help however she could. She was only nine, so it was a little surprising that anyone thought she could help.

"Do I know Elizabeth or her *dochdern*?"

"You might have seen the family in town or at one of the benefit auctions, but they go to the church on the west side of the district."

"Bishop Atlee's church."

"Correct."

Grace reached down and handed Rachel one of her baby toys, one of the rattles Rae had given them. They were curious toys, but Rachel seemed to like them. This one was soft and quilted with a pig's head. The pig was smiling and had a pink polka dot body. Rachel shook it twice, attempted to put it in her mouth, and dropped it.

"Of course I'll help, but I'm not sure what they want."

"Aaron will tell you." Miriam reached over and patted her knee. "I think you're going to be surprised when you see the cabins."

"Has he cut down more bushes?" Grace frowned. She had rather liked the overgrown look.

"Everyone's worked hard all week. Even your *mammi* has become involved."

"How—"

"It's a long story."

"I thought she was sick."

"*Ya.* But there's no stopping my mother when she sets her mind to something—"

"*Mamm.*" Grace sat up straighter in her seat as they neared the parking area of the cabins, trying to see over Belle's ears, which were ridiculously tall.

"Hmm?"

"There are *Englisch* cars here."

"Of course there are cars. The idea is to rent the cabins, and they're usually rented to *Englischers* who drive cars."

"But there are four of them. Have they rented out four of the cabins?"

"They have now, and they hope with your drawing and the post-cards they'll be mailing that they'll soon rent out all of them."

Grace was more than a little surprised at all of the changes. The office didn't even look like the same place. It looked like a real store! Shelves lined one wall and were filled with all types of baskets, assorted jams and jellies, packages of homemade noodles, and baked goods from Lydia's mother. There were also Amish dresses and *kapps* for young girls and babies. Why would *Englischers* want to buy those?

She had to step around two small *Englisch* children and their mother to see the items in the toy section, which were stunning. The items lined up on the shelves included dolls, beginner sewing items, and plenty of wooden horses, buggies, and animals.

Quilted items of every sort took up another part of the shelves—everything from table runners to hot pads. Then there were the quilts—bed quilts, lap quilts, and baby quilts. She also recognized *mammi* Abigail's knitted blankets among the baby items. A *gross-mammi* who reminded her of her *mammi* Erma back in Indiana was holding one of the blankets.

"Do you know how to knit?" the gray-headed woman asked, peering over her small glasses.

"*Nein*, but I can quilt a little. I'm not very *gut* yet." She stepped closer and touched the blue-and-yellow knitted blanket the woman was holding. "My *mammi* made that."

"She did?" The woman reached out wrinkled fingers and patted her hand. "Please tell her she did a very nice job. I used to knit, but now arthritis makes my hands cramp too badly. This will make a lovely gift for my great-grandchild."

Grace nodded, glancing over at Lydia, who was wrapping up someone's purchase. The place was certainly busy—nothing like what she'd seen on her first visit.

Careful not to knock anything over, Grace made her way out of the crowded room to the front porch of the office.

The front porch.

It had been a vacant, lonely porch, but now it was covered with places to sit. An old man lounged in a bent hickory rocking chair. He was probably waiting on the *grossmammi* inside. While he waited, he was trying to coax an orange cat over to his side, but the cat was having nothing to do with him.

Lydia had said the cat's name was Pumpkin. He was a stray that had shown up after the rains stopped and certainly looked as if he needed a home. His right ear was nicked off at the top, and his tail took a sharp turn before it reached the end.

Pumpkin sat winking at them both, feet tucked underneath, a look of utter contentment on his face.

The porch reached all the way across the front of the office building. Grace had barely noticed it before, but she noticed it now. It was filled with all different types of places to sit—large rocking chairs, double rocking chairs, small children's rocking chairs, and a "Welcome Friends" bench. In between the chairs were baskets with flowers in them.

Grace walked slowly up and down the length of the porch, but she didn't stay. She needed to move off a ways. She needed to find some distance.

Stepping into the sunshine, Grace barely heard what Aaron said to her. Something about letting him know if she needed anything. When she'd first arrived, he'd offered her a cold drink, and he'd given her a blank postcard so she'd know what size to make the drawing. She carried the blank card on top of her drawing supplies, clutched to her chest as she stepped off the front porch.

Aaron was carrying lumber over to a shed they were building. Grace thought it was a good idea, and she hoped it didn't take him and Seth very long to finish. If they put one more item for sale in the office, Lydia and the customers would have to stand outside.

With some effort she pushed the inside of the office out of her mind. She didn't need any of the things in there.

All she needed was a little time and the right light. She'd already found the picture she wanted to draw.

When she glanced up, the *grossdaddi* was beginning to doze in the rocker and Pumpkin hadn't moved at all. She could just make out the waters of Pebble Creek, hurrying by in the background. Everything was right where it should be.

≈ Chapter 21 ≈

Lydia stepped outside, looking for Grace, about an hour later. The check-out rush had finally ended and the check-in rush hadn't yet begun. She was surprised she recognized what a crowd looked like. It had been several years since they'd had four of the cabins occupied at once. Several years since they'd had four reservations and the people had actually stayed.

How had people heard? How had word spread so quickly?

She glanced over to where Aaron and Seth had framed the Plain Shop. It looked good. Aaron had good ideas, including sprucing up cabins two, seven, and eight. She'd had to hurry to prepare cabin four when the last-minute reservation had called in. Luckily, they'd had plenty of extra goods in the shop to put a new quilt on the bed, a new rug on the floor, and a rocking chair on the porch.

Now, as she dropped down into the grass beside Grace and looked around, she forced herself to let go of some of the resentment she'd been harboring against Aaron. Change was hard for her, but the changes he'd made had worked for the cabins, and they would produce income for Elizabeth and her children.

"Do you like having so many people here?" Grace didn't look up but merely kept drawing.

"I suppose there are *gut* and bad sides to that."

"The bad..."

"Is that there is more work and less time for me to enjoy the quiet and peacefulness of the creek."

"And the *gut*?"

"We can pay our bills, stay open, and I still have a job." There was more to it than that, but Lydia wasn't sure she could explain it to a nine-year-old. She wasn't sure she could have explained it to herself. It had to do with the sense that *Gotte* wanted her to share this place with others—Amish and *Englisch*. Hadn't that been Ervin's dream? Deep inside her heart she understood that this little tranquil corner along Pebble Creek was a special place, and it would be wrong to keep it private, no matter how tempting that idea was.

Grace put her pencil back in her box and closed her tablet. "It's nice having sweet old couples on the porch, and seeing *kinner* running on the grass. They make the place look less lost, but I also liked it how it was before, all overgrown and wild looking."

"*Ya.* There was a certain charm to that."

"Wild is nice because you never know what will pop out from behind a bush. Maybe a black bear—"

"Very unlikely."

"Or a coyote."

"More frequent in the northern part of the state."

Grace turned and stared at her, causing Lydia to smile. She'd never thought much about having kids. A house, yes. She longed for her own home, but she'd always been surrounded by so many siblings that children had never been on the top of her list. Grace had a way of creeping into her heart, though, making her reconsider.

"How do you know so much about animals?"

"My *dat* taught me a lot before he became so sick with farmer's lung. And with business being slow here lately, I've had plenty of time to read and watch."

"The creek passes through our place too, but the fields go right down to it. Here it's different. What kind of animals did you see in the woods and along the creek, before Aaron trimmed everything back?"

"Oh, I've seen quite a few bats, which are *gut* for eating insects.

You can see those right before dark when they go hunting for food. Also plenty of deer, but I'm sure you have those on your land."

"A few, but they frighten easily."

"If you're quiet, if you move slowly, they'll let you watch them. Also you might catch sight of a red or gray fox."

"I've heard you have mink, muskrat, and opossum as well." Aaron settled into the grass beside Grace, and Seth sat between Aaron and Lydia, making a circle of sorts.

"*Ya.* All of those," Seth said. "We don't have the creek on our place, but it goes through the spot where our school is built. I've also seen rabbits, raccoons, skunks, and flying squirrels."

"Squirrels don't fly," Grace said, shaking her head until her *kapp* strings looked as if they might take off.

"They glide from tree to tree," Seth explained. "Rather like a kite."

"Do you think the animals will all go away now that you have guests?" Grace asked Aaron.

"Of course not." He leaned back in the grass. "The woods stretch out around this place and across the river. As long as we respect their habitat, there's no reason for them to leave."

Lydia couldn't help returning Aaron's smile. Grace had looked so worried, but now relief washed over her face like sunshine blessing a field first thing in the morning.

"I finished your drawing." Grace popped up as she pulled the piece of drawing paper from her tablet and dropped it in Aaron's hands. "Will that work?"

Lydia scooted over into Grace's spot next to Aaron. They both stared down at the four-by-five drawing of the front porch of the office.

Raising their heads to glance back over their shoulders at the actual porch, their eyes met. A delicious shiver crept down Lydia's spine, but she ignored it and focused again on the drawing.

Seth let out a whistle. "Nice doodling, Grace. Where did you learn to do that?"

"I'm not sure." Grace shuffled from one foot to another. "Do you need another?"

"No, Grace. This will work fine. *Danki*. You did a *wunderbaar* job."

"*Gut*. If my *mamm* comes looking for me, I'll be down at the river, watching for flying squirrels." She took off skipping, tablet and pencils tucked in her arms, never bothering to look back.

Aaron handed the postcard to Miriam as she walked up and joined them. "Do you think she has any idea how *gut* this is?"

"No," Miriam said. "She's a child, doing what she enjoys."

Seth stood and stretched. "I think Lydia is going to be writing out a lot of postcards. If you're done working me like a mule, I'll be headed home to finish my chores there."

He stuck his hands in his pockets and strolled over to the barn, in a much better mood than he had been when he'd first shown up, grumbling and unloading lumber so loudly Lydia had thought she was going to have to take her broom after him.

"It's better than I expected," Aaron confessed.

"She even included Pumpkin." Lydia took the drawing from Miriam, holding it up so she could scrutinize the details more closely.

Miriam settled in the grass beside her, Rachel in her arms. They studied the drawing together.

Grace had captured more than the front porch of the office. She'd included the rockers, the bench, and even the old man dozing, though you couldn't make out his face because he was in the shadows. What you could make out was his hand, aged worn and resting on the arm of the hickory rocker. Pumpkin sat in the sun, watching him. The words "Plain Cabins at Pebble Creek" stretched over the top of the porch. Running along the back bottom corner, sparkling as if the sun was glinting off it, was the water of Pebble Creek.

How had she done that with only her pencils?

Lydia felt proud of Grace, and she knew pride was something she was to avoid. The girl's work was good, though. God had blessed her with a special ability. One look at Miriam's face and Aaron's expression told her they realized it too.

This drawing could help them.

If they followed Aaron's plan and had it printed on the front of note cards, and sent it out among the *Englisch*, it could possibly work.

She would certainly visit the place Grace had drawn.

It looked like a place where she could curl up and rest, a place that could restore your soul. It looked like a place of grace.

Gabe stepped into the sitting room, looking for Miriam. The fire was banked in the stove and a lantern was lit on the table, but no wife.

Both Grace and Rachel were asleep.

Everyone had finished with their baths and were ready for Sunday service the next morning. He'd rocked Rachel after Miriam had finished nursing the babe so she could have a few moments of rest alone.

Where was she?

He stood in the middle of the room, circling like a pony attached to a rope. The house wasn't so large that he couldn't see into the kitchen, which was empty, or down the hall, which was dark. Finally he noticed that the front door was cracked.

He pulled a lap quilt off the couch and grabbed a plate of cookies from the kitchen. What was he forgetting? Milk! Cookies without milk were no good at all. He snuck back into the kitchen, poured a tall glass they could share, and moved back across the sitting room as quietly as possible. Waking Rachel up at this point would be a disaster. His arms full, he nudged the door wide open with his toe.

There she was.

His Miriam, standing with her back to him, a shawl wrapped around her shoulders, gazing up at the stars.

He pushed through the screen door, a witty remark on his tongue, just as she turned toward him, and his romantic plans came to a screeching halt.

Even in the little amount of light that came from the front room he could see the redness around her eyes and that her nose was still running a bit from her crying.

"I found you," he said softly.

"You found me." Her voice sounded as if it had been rubbed with the sandpaper David used on his toys.

"Come and sit in the swing. I have a blanket—"

"It's a quilt."

"And cookies—"

"Oh, Gabe. Those were for church tomorrow."

"No one will miss these cookies at church. We'll only eat a few. And I also have milk to ease your throat."

She sipped the milk before pushing it back into his hands, but she did curl up into the crook of his arm as they sank back against the old wood and he set the swing into motion.

"Still worried about your *mamm?*"

Miriam nodded as she rubbed her nose against his shirt. "There was no message from Doc Hanson at the phone shack. I checked on the way back from the cabins."

"Ah. So that's the reason for your tears."

"Shouldn't we have heard by now?"

"I don't know, *mi lieb.* I don't understand much about doctors and tests and such."

Miriam picked at the quilt he'd wrapped around their shoulders. The night was pleasant, but a quilt was always good for snuggling or settling a woman when she was weeping.

"But you have been through this, when Hope was sick."

His wife's body felt almost foreign next to him—all tense muscle and bone. All fear. He rubbed her arm and kissed the top of her head. "*Ya.* I do remember that. Would it help you if I told you about it?"

"You wouldn't mind?"

Gabe understood this was one of those turning points in a man's marriage. How he knew it, he wasn't sure. Maybe it was the way he felt Miriam peering up at him in the dark.

"Of course I don't mind. We can speak of anything, Miriam. If it will help your fears, I want to talk about it."

"But if remembering hurts you…"

"There was a time when it did. Now it's almost as if the pain happened to someone else, though the *gut* memories are still mine."

For the next hour, he told her how quickly the ovarian cancer had claimed his first wife. How her menstrual cycle had changed and she'd finally become concerned and gone to the doctor. He'd found the mass in her ovaries. By the time they did the surgery to biopsy it, the cancer had spread.

"I'm sorry you and Grace had to go through that."

"Miriam, it was *Gotte's wille*."

She was silent for a moment, clutching the quilt more tightly. Finally, her voice no more than a whisper, she asked, "Do you believe that?"

"I do, though I'll admit I struggled against it for a long time. Each person's life is written, our number of days are known to *Gotte*—"

"I know the Scripture."

"And I would have chosen that Hope's years reached far into her nineties, that she became a *grossmammi* with gray hair and wrinkled skin." He pushed the swing with his foot. "But my ways aren't *Gotte's* ways."

"And now you have me."

"I have you and I have Rachel. Maybe we will have more children and maybe we won't." His plans for the night certainly weren't panning out, but he didn't think now was a good time to bring the matter to her attention.

Miriam sighed. "I understand what you're saying. I do, but this is my *mamm*, and I love her. I don't want her to hurt, and I don't want her to go. I'm not ready."

"We're never ready, *lieb*, and perhaps now isn't her time. Don't be rushing Abigail off. If there's one thing I've learned about her, it's that she's a strong woman."

The night grew quiet around them, the single sound the squeaking of the swing.

"You may have a cookie now."

"Oh, I may?"

"One. No, two."

Gabe laughed as he removed the dish towel and reached for two of the peanut butter cookies. He handed one to Miriam.

"There's a little milk left," he said.

"I love milk and peanut butter."

"Then I'll share."

The evening took on a pleasant, peaceful rhythm. It wasn't a silent night, but the sounds he heard were ones familiar to him, ones that brought peace to any troubled spaces in his heart. The talk of Hope hadn't bothered him.

What it had done was remind him again of those years alone with Grace. He would have survived them if that had been his future.

But this? It was better. Life with Miriam in his arms, Grace growing strong, and Rachel in her crib was *gut*. It was a future rich and bright. If it meant that he had more to risk losing, then so be it. He could trust all he had to a wise and loving *Gotte*. Already he had been more blessed than any man had a right to be.

How could he explain those things to Miriam?

Or were those truths that each man and each woman had to learn for themselves?

He didn't realize immediately that Miriam had fallen asleep. He nudged her gently, but there was no response. Before she could wake enough to argue that he was too old for such foolishness and would surely throw out his back, he picked her up in his arms and carried her to bed.

Chapter 22

Sunday morning Miriam sat on the hard wooden bench, Grace to her right side, Rachel in her lap, and her *mamm* on her left. She wished she could stop the tears streaming down her cheeks. It wasn't that she minded crying during church services. She understood that worshipping *Gotte* meant laying aside all pretense and coming before Him honestly—baring her fears and her worries.

But this ache in her heart, it hurt like a physical pain.

After talking to Gabe the night before, she had managed to bury her worries. This morning she'd managed to put on her Sunday clothes and act normal as they all prepared for church, same as she'd acted normal all week, every day since the visit to Doc Hanson's. She'd kept herself busy and pushed away all the things that might be wrong with her mother.

But now as she sat worshipping, all those words the doctor had said came crashing back into her mind, pushing pressure against her heart—eleven pounds lost, possibly cancer, diabetes, hyperthyroidism, Hodgkin's, Parkinson's, or Addison's disease.

One look at her mother this morning had stirred her fears to life. Seeing the way her father was with her, how he'd helped her carefully out of the buggy as if he were protecting the most precious thing in his life—and perhaps he was.

As they turned to go into Esther and Joseph's home, Miriam saw that Abigail seemed to have lost even more weight since Tuesday. Was that even possible?

Miriam had rushed forward and tried to talk to her about it, but her *mamm* had only patted her arm. She hadn't said a word to her! Instead she'd stooped to ask Grace how school had been.

As soon as the singing had started, Miriam's tears began to fall. Music always had that effect on her during worship. While the spoken word touched her mind, the voices raised together in worship never failed to tap her heart.

Grace moved closer within the circle of her arm.

Abigail passed her a handkerchief, though she had one in her own pocket.

As they began to sing the last verse of the *Loblied* song, the *Praise Song*, Miriam wanted to run from the morning service, or at least scamper to the other side of the room and into Gabe's arms. Could she praise God even as her mother stood beside her weak, frail, and hurting?

Thine only be the Glory, Lord,
Likewise all might and power.
Praise thee in our assembly, and
Feel grateful every hour.

How was she to feel grateful every hour? Would God's might and power heal her mother?

She didn't understand.

Why hadn't Doc Hanson called? Why hadn't God intervened? Her mother was wasting away before her eyes, and there didn't seem to be anything she could do about it.

Was this *Gotte's wille*? Miriam had heard the phrase all her life. Until this very moment, she had thought she understood it, but now her heart was breaking and she realized she didn't understand anything.

The song ended and they all sat.

Grace twined their fingers together, sitting as close as she could.

Miriam wanted to assure her that everything would be all right, but would it? The child had lost one woman in her life. Was it fair that she lose another so soon?

She resettled Rachel on her lap. The baby slept on, blissfully unaware of the worries plaguing her *mamm*.

But Miriam's questions piled up as the sermon began. She tried to focus, but the preaching seemed like words, just words—empty, hollow, meaningless. Soon they were reading Matthew's admonition to pray sincerely. "When you pray, do not be like the hypocrites."

Was that what she'd become? A hypocrite? Miriam felt like a fraud for doubting, for questioning God. "But when you pray, go into your room, close the door and pray to your Father, who is unseen. Then your Father, who sees what is done in secret, will reward you. And when you pray, do not keep on babbling like pagans, for they think they will be heard because of their many words. Do not be like them, for your Father knows what you need before you ask him."

What did that mean?

"Your Father knows what you need before you ask him." The words circled in her mind and sank into her heart.

Was it acceptable to cry out with her heart? Did God understand her pain? Had He heard her prayers? Would He answer her cry to save her mother?

The service finally ended.

Miriam felt more exhausted than if she'd cleaned her home from top to bottom. She turned to her mother, ready to explain her tears. She reached for her, tried to snag the sleeve of her dark blue dress, but Abigail was already moving off to help in the kitchen.

Miriam felt small hands pulling on her arm.

"Are you all right, *mamm?*"

"Yes, dear."

"You were crying."

"I was feeling a little emotional."

"*Dat* says I'll understand when I'm a few years older. He says all girls, all women, go through such times."

"Your *dat* is a pretty smart guy."

"I know." Grace stood on tiptoe and kissed Miriam's cheek before planting another on her sister, who had begun to squirm and rub at her eyes. "I'm going to find Sadie now, if you and Rachel don't need me."

"We're fine. *Danki* for asking."

But she didn't feel fine. She felt like a liar for saying such a thing, even if she had said it so her nine-year-old wouldn't worry. Rachel's squirming turned into fussing, followed by howls of hunger, and Miriam sighed in relief. At least she had an excuse to be alone. She hurried from the main room of Esther's home.

Esther Bontreger, previously Esther Schrocks, had been Miriam's assistant at the schoolhouse until she'd married. Now she had a *boppli* of her own. Miriam missed their times together—mornings readying the schoolroom, afternoons sharing a lunch, and evenings in front of the fire in their upstairs apartment. She meant to stop by and visit, but she seldom did.

What had her mother said? *"You young girls, you need to learn to be there for one another. Friendship is about more than Sunday socials."*

Here she was, on a Sunday, regretting she hadn't visited earlier.

Moving down the hall, she knocked on a bedroom door, and when she heard a soft "Come in," there was Esther, nursing her own infant, who was a month older than Rachel.

"Miriam. Do they need me in the kitchen?"

"No. At least a dozen women are in there. Everything is fine." Miriam glanced around the tidy little space that had been turned into a room for the baby. A crib was against one wall, a twin bed against the other, and a rocker—where Esther was nursing—was snug in a corner.

"I had to leave the service early. Jake wouldn't wait. He woke early, so his feeding time is off a little."

"I don't mean to disturb you."

"Don't be silly. We're done. Sit here in the rocker. I need to stand and walk with him or he'll never burp."

Miriam settled in the chair with Rachel and tried not to notice Esther studying her.

"Difficult service?" Esther asked finally.

"*Ya.*"

"Because of your *mamm?*"

Miriam nodded, afraid her tears would start again if she spoke.

"We're all praying for her. You know that, right?"

Rachel patted her mother's *kapp* strings as she settled, content and nursing. Miriam's tears did start then, and Esther gave her a clean cloth diaper to wipe them with.

"Doc will have the tests back Tuesday?"

"*Ya.* I thought they'd call earlier, but there have been no messages at the phone shack. I've checked every day."

"He would have driven out if he'd heard anything. You know Doc Hanson."

Miriam nodded, not trusting her voice.

Esther pulled a lap quilt off the side of the crib and placed it over the quilt on the twin bed. Laying Jake on it, she began to change him. Even at four months, the boy was a spitting image of his *dat*—long, thin, with a mop of brown hair and a lopsided grin.

"I want to ask your forgiveness, Miriam."

"Whatever for?" Miriam looked at the younger woman in surprise. Even after they had birthed their children, and even though they had seen little of each other in the last year, still it was like looking into a mirror. Other than the color of their hair—Miriam's black and Esther's the color of wheat—they could have been sisters.

"I should have come by to see you and Rachel."

"And we should have come to see you—"

"*Nein.* Your hands have been very full. You married into a family, Miriam. One daughter already, a husband, Rachel's birth, and now your *mamm* is sick. I should have been by, and I meant to come. I wanted to, but every day it seems I have more work than the day before."

"I understand. My days aren't so busy. They aren't as busy as the days at the schoolhouse—"

"Who can forget those?"

"But still they do seem to hurry by..." Miriam stared out the window. Children were running between the tables as the food was placed out and men helped with the carrying of dishes and seating.

"I meant to come and see you as well. My *mamm*..." Fear lodged in Miriam's throat, but she pushed on. "My *mamm* says we haven't learned how to be *freinden* yet. That we haven't learned how to be supportive of one another."

Esther finished changing Jake and handed him a quilted toy. "Even on a farm, it seems time won't slow down."

Smiling, Miriam raised Rachel to her shoulder. "An *Englisch* woman at the cabins yesterday was saying how nice it would be to live the Plain life, because we don't have to worry about time moving so fast."

"Probably she has never milked a cow or done laundry the old way. Those things tend to steal hours from your day."

"I wouldn't change it, though. Would you, Esther?" Miriam cocked her head, wanting a truthful answer from her friend.

"No. I enjoy our life, and I appreciate the continuity of it. There are days when I wish I could feel less tired so that I could appreciate it more."

There was a knock on the door, and Esther's niece opened it. "*Mammi* says you'll miss all of the food if you don't get out here, and also she wants to see baby Jake before the meal is over. She says she can't eat without holding her newest *grandkinner* in her lap."

"Tell her I'll be right there."

Miriam rose too after readjusting her dress. The pain from the service was still in her heart, but she felt better from her time with Esther. How had she forgotten that she wasn't alone? Others understood and knew what they were going through. They were praying, and their prayers counted.

Whatever Doc Hanson's tests revealed, at least they wouldn't have to face it alone.

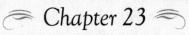

Chapter 23

Aaron stood when he saw Elizabeth heading toward his table. "Is everything all right?"

"Yes. I wanted to make sure you don't need a ride back to the cabins."

"*Nein*. David or Seth will drop me. You're leaving already?"

Elizabeth's laughter eased some of the worry in Aaron's heart. "We've been eating for nearly two hours."

"Oh. True, but I thought the girls would stay and play longer. I promised Beth I'd go with her to see some calves or something...I didn't quite understand what she was asking."

"You're a *wunderbaar* cousin. Beth will run you ragged if you let her, and she's already been to see the newborn calves." Elizabeth attempted a smile, but it trembled a little and finally fell away. "We tend to go home early on Sunday afternoons so the girls have plenty of time to rest in the afternoon."

Her gaze dropped to the ground and back up, darting over the group of family and friends from their church. Aaron was reminded that this must all be very hard for her. She was used to enjoying the meetings and picnics with Ervin.

"Thank you again for all you've done at the cabins."

"It's a start, Elizabeth, but we still have a long way to go."

Her smile this time was genuine. "Ervin would be proud, and I appreciate your hard work. I should go. Maybe I'll see you later in the week."

Aaron watched the girls run up and join her as she left. Beth turned and walked backward, waving at him as the group moved toward the buggies.

He almost forgot about the other people at his table as he grew drowsy sitting in the warm afternoon sun. He wanted one more piece of apple pie, but he knew from experience it would make his stomach hurt to stuff himself.

Then again, if he went to the dessert table, he'd be able to talk to Lydia. He hadn't had a private word with her all day. She was surrounded by people every time he glanced her way. First it had been women and children during the service, and then it had been teenaged boys and men since the meal had begun.

He had thought to sit by her when she took a break to eat her own meal, but he hadn't yet seen that happen. How was a man supposed to speak the things that were on his mind when she was never alone? It had been that way since the four families of *Englischers* had shown up at the cabins. He almost longed for the days when the cabins were empty, which was crazy.

Busy was good. Good for business. Good for Elizabeth, and good for getting him back home to Indiana.

Finally, the crowd at the table where Lydia was serving disappeared.

"Where are you headed?" David asked. The man looked as if he were about to fall asleep in his ham salad. His wife had gone into labor on Friday night, but it had been a false alarm. Good thing too, as the baby still had three weeks before it was officially due to arrive.

"Thought I'd have a look over at the desserts."

"My wife made the apple pie," Nathan Glick said. "You should have some. She makes the sweetest pies in Pebble Creek." The man grinned. Plainly he was still crazy in love, though he'd told Aaron they had been married for more than ten years and had three children.

Aaron glanced at the table again and tried to focus, though the fried chicken was settling and he was beginning to feel even sleepier. Lydia was wearing a dark green dress today. It was exactly the opening line he needed.

He stood and started away from the table.

"Wait," David called. "Bring me back some of my *fraa*'s oatmeal cookies if there are any left, would you? They don't last more than a few minutes at my house the way my five *kinner* eat."

"Soon to be six," Nathan reminded him.

"*Ya*." David slumped forward on the table.

"Might want to bring him some *kaffi* as well."

Aaron nodded and carried his plate over to the dish tubs outside the kitchen door. Setting his utensils in one tub and his plate in the other, he wiped his hands on his pants before moving down the line to where Lydia stood.

She looked up in surprise when he approached her table.

"Hello, Lydia." He tried to remember what he had decided to say to her, but suddenly his mind went blank. Something about pie and how she looked. "You're looking as *gut* as that apple pie today."

Lydia smoothed her apron over her dark green dress, looked left and then right, and finally stared at him as if he'd stepped into Nathan's fields and splattered mud all over his Sunday clothing.

"That is...what I meant to say was...uh...nice dress."

"Oh." Lydia gazed down at the table as her cheeks turned a rosy pink. "*Danki*."

As if she finally understood why he was standing in front of her table, she added, "Did you want some of the apple pie?"

"*Nein*. I already had dessert—twice, while you were refilling drinks." He patted his stomach uncomfortably. "Couldn't fit another bite."

She pulled her *kapp* strings to the front, her brow furrowed, and finally asked, "Then why are you here?"

"*Ya*, well, David wanted me to pick him up some coal...I mean, cookies." He glanced down at the cookie plate, which held only crumbs, and shook his head.

This wasn't going well. Why did he feel so awkward? They worked well together at the cabins, but now he was tripping over words and forgetting what he meant to say. "Also...I was wondering if you'd like to go for a walk and see Nathan's new calves."

He thought she would say no. She was still gawking at him as if he'd sprouted red hair, but at that moment her mother walked up. "What a *gut* suggestion, Aaron. I was just saying to Lydia that she should get away from this table. She even stood here as she ate her lunch. A little exercise would be a *wunderbaar* idea."

Lydia stared at them both in disbelief, but she didn't argue with Ella Fisher. Aaron smiled his thanks as they walked off toward the pasture behind Nathan's barn.

"I apologize if I embarrassed you in front of your *mamm*. I thought it would be nice to talk, you know...when we're away from work."

"It's okay. *Mamm* jumps at any chance to throw me into a buggy ride with an eligible Amish male. You'll have to be careful around her, or she'll be having you over for dinner and plying you with shoofly pie."

"I wouldn't mind that. I love shoofly pie, and pumpkin pie, and even peach cream pie. I have something of a weakness for dessert—or dinner, for that matter. Truth is, I've been missing my *mamm*'s cooking since I've been here."

"Don't say yes if she invites you over to eat. It would be better if I smuggled you food. Coming to dinner would encourage her matchmaking tendencies. She'll think you're interested, and that's a road you don't want to start down with her."

Aaron laughed out loud, causing some of the young *kinner* to turn and stare at them. "Your *mamm* loves you. She's no different than any other parent."

"Is that how you see it?" Lydia threw her arms over the fence and stared down at the week-old spotted calves.

"*Ya*. How do you see it?"

Lydia took her time answering, focusing instead on choosing the right weed to pull from the grasses growing by the fence.

"Lydia?"

"It's not as if I think they want to be rid of me. It's only that..." She turned away from the calves, leaned back against the metal fencing, and wrapped her arms around her stomach as she studied the group of adults still assembled under the stand of trees. "They worry I'll be an old maid."

"How old are you?"

"Twenty-two, but you know how it is with Plain folk. Don't pretend you don't understand." She pierced him with those brown eyes he thought about first thing when he woke each morning, and while he was chopping wood for the cabins, and after she'd gone home at night.

"Ya. I know what you mean, but your parents seem reasonable."

"They are, but my family situation is—different."

"Because of your daed."

She frowned, turned around, and began to walk the length of the pasture, as if she was suddenly interested in following the calves, who were following the cows. "I don't believe you know much about my family situation, Aaron Troyer."

"I met your father before the service this morning. I can tell that people respect him and like him." When Lydia didn't say anything, only crouched so that she could put her hand through the fence railing and reach to pet one of the calves, Aaron squatted with her. "Why didn't you tell me, Lydia? Why didn't you explain to me that he's ill?"

She jumped up faster than a bull bolting when he'd been spooked by a snake. "I don't need your pity, Aaron. If that's why you asked me to take a walk, you can go back to your table and back to your apple pie."

He hesitated, and then he allowed a smile to slowly spread across his face. "I told you. I asked you because you look pretty in that dress...pretty as apple pie."

Lydia rolled her eyes, but her anger evaporated. "Ya. If I remember right you also asked for some coal—"

"Cookies."

"Whatever."

She turned her back to him and continued walking down the fence line, but not before he saw a smile tugging at the corner of her lips. He couldn't leave it like that, though, with the barest hint of a smile. He wanted to chase that worried look completely off Lydia's face. He enjoyed making her happy. Enjoyed it more than apple or shoofly pie.

"I know you don't need my pity, Lydia. I'm *not* offering pity, but you're practically the first person I met when I came here. We work together every day. I'm trying to figure why you never mentioned that your father is so ill he's not able to work. Why did you never mention that you're having to carry the burden of helping to bring home the money to raise four other children?"

"Five."

"There are five?"

Lydia ticked them off on her fingers. "Clara, Martha, Amanda, Sally Ann, and Stephen."

"I missed Stephen. Hard to keep all these Amish kids straight. They all look the same."

Lydia threw the handful of weeds she'd pulled at him, but Aaron dodged right and most of them dropped to the ground.

"Got you."

"You did?"

"*Ya.*" She stepped closer, reached up and pulled a piece of timothy grass from his hair.

Aaron thought to touch her face. He was about to raise his hand and tuck the strings to her prayer *kapp* back out of the way when she turned. "We should go back. My *dat* will be tired and needing to go home."

He put his hands in his pockets and fell into step beside her.

On the way back they talked of Menno's condition. Aaron had heard of farmer's lung, but he'd never known anyone who actually had it. Lydia spoke matter-of-factly, as if she were describing the breakfast of muffins and fruit she'd left in the cabins for their guests.

He wasn't fooled, though. He'd seen the way she'd stared at her father during the church service. Her expression of concern had drawn his attention from the sermon, or maybe it had focused him more on the pastor's words. "Let no debt remain outstanding, except the continuing debt to love one another, for whoever loves others has fulfilled the law." The words from the book of Romans were barely out of the pastor's mouth when Aaron had noticed the worry on Lydia's face and seen her eyes locked on Menno.

Aaron didn't owe anyone anything, so that part of the Scripture he'd followed, but had he loved others as the Bible taught? He wasn't so sure.

And what of Lydia?

She kept herself apart, and he wanted to know why.

As she explained about her father's condition, he began to understand some. Who had time to socialize when she was working a job, taking care of her siblings, and caring for her parents?

And to think he'd popped out of bed that morning, patting himself on the back for what he'd accomplished.

Lydia's problems outweighed his by more than a bushel. Not that he didn't have problems of his own. His hands were full taking care of Elizabeth and all his cousins.

Still, he and Lydia were friends, and friends loved one another.

Not to mention, she did look pretty in that dress.

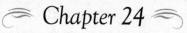 Chapter 24

L ydia could tell right away that Tuesday morning was not going to
go as smoothly as Monday had.

On Monday morning the last of their guests had left after
promising to encourage their friends to come and visit the new
and improved cabins along the banks of Pebble Creek. Aaron had
agreed to continue with Ervin's policy of not accepting reservations
on Monday evening. This allowed them time to do any repairs to
cabins and also gave everyone a break from tripping over *Englischers*.

Lydia had spent the day cleaning the four cabins while Aaron and
Seth finished the Plain Shop. The day had been quiet and productive. Finally their work had found a steady, easy rhythm.

And then Aaron had asked her if Clara could come in to work
for a few days. He was probably trying to be helpful. Or perhaps her
mother had mentioned it to him on Sunday.

Regardless how the topic came to his attention, Lydia couldn't
actually lie about it, not that she would have. So she went home Monday night with the blessed news. Her sister had jumped at the chance,
and so Lydia's quiet morning ride to work had been ruined. That was
the first thing to go wrong on Tuesday. Things didn't improve once
they were settled in the office.

"I have to write the same thing on every card?" Clara stared at the boxes stacked next to her chair. "There must be thousands of them."

"Two thousand five hundred to be exact. And Aaron isn't paying you to stare at them, so get started." Lydia was already twenty minutes later than she liked to be, thanks to Clara's need to primp in front of their one mirror. You'd think she was going to a singing instead of to work.

"How did he have these printed so fast?" Clara ran her finger over the penciled drawing of the office on the front of the card. "I thought Grace drew it on Saturday."

"*Ya*, she did. There's a place in Cashton that is open on Sunday. Aaron dropped it off on Saturday before they closed, and it was ready yesterday afternoon. They call it their forty-eight-hour guarantee."

"But why didn't he have both sides printed?"

"Because it would have cost twice as much," Aaron said, stepping inside the office. "Also, I think a handwritten note is a nice personal touch. Don't you, Lydia?"

"Nice touch if it gets done."

"What a *wunderbaar* idea, Aaron." Clara stood and ran her hand down the length of her apron. "I wish my *schweschder* had taken the time to explain your reasoning to me. I totally understand what you want now."

"You don't need to understand your employer's reasoning." Lydia whacked at a fly with a rolled-up piece of newspaper. "What you need to do is your assigned work."

Lydia could have sworn she saw Aaron hide a laugh as he stuffed a piece of her *mamm*'s raisin bread into his mouth.

"I'll hang more bags of water to draw the flies out to the porch. Seth will be here at lunch, and we're going to begin working on a fishing pier."

"Seth King?" Clara had written the first postcard. At the sound of Seth's name, her pen slid across the note.

"*Ya*, Clara. Seth King, and you'll be owing Aaron ten cents out of your pay for that card you ruined."

Clara glanced down at the postcard and frowned, as if it had offended her in some way. Sighing dramatically, she dropped it into the wastebasket.

"If you need me, I'll be spending the morning working on the path along the river." Aaron picked up two Ziploc bags and filled them with water, added a few drops of oil, sealed them shut, and started for the front porch. Remembering what else he needed, he turned and snagged another piece of bread before he walked outside into the morning sunshine.

There was the sound of a hammer on a tack as he nailed the bags of water to the tops of the windowsills on the porch.

"Does that actually work to keep the flies away?" Clara asked her sister.

"Better than a newspaper. Not to mention I have other things to do."

"Helping me with postcards?"

"Nope. I'm stocking the Plain Shop."

"That sounds fun!" Clara practically bounced out of her seat.

"*Nein.* If we don't have guests staying here, no one will be purchasing the goods I'm moving over to the shop."

"I thought you said we had reservations every night."

Lydia had to smile at the pout, which reminded her of the young sister she once walked to school. Clara's use of the word "we" also amused her. After all, she'd been on the job less than an hour.

"True. We do have reservations every night, but only a few, and we need the cabins to be full, or so Aaron says. I have no idea how we'll handle so many *Englischers* and their *kinner.*" Lydia filled her arms with quilts, leaving one—the best one, in her opinion—on the quilt rack. They had decided to leave one item of everything for sale in the office, with a sign pointing to the Plain Shop.

"Where did you find this many addresses?"

"Ervin never threw away anything. We have records of guest information going back to the day he opened the cabins."

"Great. I imagine you have enough for all of these cards."

"At least." Lydia could barely see over the stack of quilts in her arms. "Look at it this way. As long as there are cards, you have a job."

Clara squirreled up her nose. "Can I have a break after I do fifty?"

"Sure. By that time I'll need help sweeping porches for tonight's guests."

Lydia should have felt some guilt for the way she was treating Clara. She didn't, but she experienced a twang of remorse that she didn't, which had to count for something.

Carrying the quilts to the shop, she inhaled deeply as soon as she stepped inside. The smell of fresh-cut lumber had always held a certain appeal to her. Maybe because it spoke to those dreams of a home of her own.

Which was silly.

Most young Amish couples did not move into a brand-new house. They usually moved into a rented house in the beginning, or sometimes into a home that a relative no longer needed. Occasionally, the young man had saved up enough to purchase a place, but in those cases it was rarely a new place.

As Lydia shook out the quilts and displayed them on the dowels Aaron and Seth had fastened to the wall the day before, she allowed herself to take a side trip down the daydream trail she usually avoided—the one where she had been courted by a boy, they'd planned their wedding, and they were moving into a home of their own.

Any home would do. A place where any decisions made would be theirs.

One close to family, but with a measure of privacy. Perhaps it would have enough room for children—a few. They would have to add on eventually. She would have a garden out back which she would dote over in the spring and sweat over in the summer. But the fall? The fall would be the time of harvest.

Standing back, she gave the quilts on the dowels a once-over. Quilts on a wall looked strange to her, but these did display well—the simple patterns and green, blue, and black fabric stood out nicely against the unadorned walls.

The quilts she'd sewn, the ones at home in the blanket chest in her room, might not compare in workmanship, but in dreams stitched within their seams? Prayers quilted within their layers?

Ya. She thought her quilts compared nicely.

By the time Clara joined her in the Plain Shop, Lydia had moved over all of the hand-sewn and treadle-sewn items, the toys David had made, and half of the canned preserves.

"You didn't bring anything with you?"

"I wasn't sure I could hold anything. My hands are cramping after writing fifty cards." Clara held out her right forefinger for inspection. "Look! A blister—"

"Tsk, tsk. I thought you were made of tougher stuff, *schweschder.* Band-Aids are in my desk drawer. Let's go fetch you one."

"I like the way this shop looks. It's hard to believe they built it so quickly. And only Aaron and Seth worked on it?" Clara walked around the room, running her hand along the shelves.

"*Ya.* They worked on it Saturday and yesterday. I suppose they have both participated in enough barn raisings to know how to put up a single room quickly."

Lydia started toward the door, but Clara wasn't finished. She sat in one of the rockers Aaron had placed in a corner of the small room. "I know Seth King, but I don't know him well. He's about my age, right?"

"*Ya.*"

"Remind me what he looks like." There was a twinkle in her sister's eye that suggested she knew very well what Seth King looked like. Seth was a year older, and therefore had been out of school a year longer than Clara. Maybe she'd forgotten what he looked like, but that was doubtful. No doubt Clara saw him at the church services and even at the evening singings, unless Seth didn't attend those. Maybe Seth was a loner. Clara seemed to enjoy the various activities the group of young people found to do.

Young people? Four, five, maybe six years younger than she was. The way she thought of them made her feel as if she were ready for a *grossmammi* house.

"Well, what does he look like?" Clara asked.

Lydia decided to play along.

"Let me see. 'Bout this high." Lydia reached above her head four inches or so, until she thought she'd reached around five foot, ten inches. "Sandy brown hair and thin. He's David's son, and David is Miriam's *bruder*. Bad attitude at least half the time."

"Hmm. Bad attitude could describe several of the boys I know. They usually grow out of it. I'm still having trouble placing him."

"I bet you saw him at the singing you went to the other night."

"*Nein*. Seth doesn't go to singings." Clara clapped her hand over her mouth as if she'd given herself away.

"Don't remember him, huh?"

Clara shook her head, as if something didn't make sense.

"Question?"

"Why is he doing this? Helping out here?"

"I think he's working afternoons to get some time away from his father. Like you, he's going through his *rumspringa*."

"I am not!" Clara's face blushed a bright red.

"What about that cell phone you keep in the barn?"

"Lydia!"

"Thought I didn't know, huh?" Lydia turned and started out of the shop.

"I hardly ever use it. Only to call the girls but never boys. And I don't bring it in the house." In Clara's rush to catch up with Lydia, she bumped into the back of her sister.

"Don't worry. Your secret is safe with me." Lydia was staring toward the river at their boss. She needed to talk with him. "If the injury to your finger can wait, let's walk down to the creek and see who's speaking with Aaron. Unless you'd rather get back to your postcards."

Clara's answer was to tuck her arm through Lydia's.

It was rare that Lydia felt close to her sister, but she did in that moment. Or maybe it was that she was worried about the *Englischer* standing next to Aaron. Something about the man bothered her, even from a distance, but she couldn't put her finger on exactly what.

Better they go and confront him together.

Chapter 25

Grace sat on an overturned milk pail as her *daddi* Joshua added feed to the buckets in the horse stalls. Usually she followed along behind him, stroking the buggy horses on the nose and standing on a stool to touch the big workhorses. She'd even feed each one a treat—some raisins or a slice of apple. She couldn't do it today, though. Today she felt all *trembly*.

So instead she sat on the milk pail, whacking the floor with a stick.

When her *daddi* was done with the feeding, he returned to the front of the barn. Pepper trotted behind him, close on his heels. *Daddi* sat down beside her on an old crate and picked up a sanding block. He didn't say a word. Instead, he went to work on a large square piece of wood. It was bigger than his lap, and he kept having to turn it to work on it. Pepper dropped to the ground between them, close enough that Grace could reach out and touch his ears, which she had to do.

Who could resist Pepper? The German shorthaired pointer was black with little patches of white and brown. Grace thought Pepper was the closest thing to perfect she'd ever seen. Maybe more perfect than her own dog, Hunter—though it would be hard to choose. She adored those animals, and tonight Pepper almost had the power to make her heart ache a little less.

"Remember when Pepper found me in that snow cave?" Grace asked. Unable to resist the look in the old dog's eyes, she slipped off her pail to the floor, moved closer so she sat right up against him, and buried her face in his soft, silky coat.

"Sure I remember. That was something."

"It was a miracle."

"Suppose it was."

"*Gotte* was watching out for me."

"That He was, Gracie."

"And He sent Pepper."

Daddi smiled at her, and then he resumed sanding the piece of wood.

"Do you believe He sent Doc Hanson to watch over *mammi*?"

"Could be. Doc seems to be doing a *gut* job."

Grace felt better while she was holding on to Pepper. Her stomach stopped flipping, but she still felt *trembly*, like the leaves in the fall. Like she might blow away.

She might as well ask. *Daddi* had never lied to her before.

"What if the medicine doesn't work? What if *mammi* gets worse? What will we do?"

Daddi set aside the block of wood and joined her on the floor of the barn, on the other side of Pepper, who seemed happy with all the attention. "You know the Bible tells us that *Gotte* has a plan for each of our lives."

"*Ya*, I know that."

"And He has a *gut* plan for Abigail's life."

"Does it include her getting sick?"

"I don't know. I hope it includes her getting well. I'm trusting in *Gotte's gut* plan. You can always trust in His word, and in His promises. That's what it says in Jeremiah."

"*Ya*. I memorized that verse."

"Can you say it to me?"

"'For I know the plans I have for you,' declares the LORD, 'plans to prosper you and not to harm you, plans to give you hope and a future.'"

"*Gut!*" *Daddi* stood. When he did his knees popped. He looked at her and winked, which made Grace laugh. "My knees sound like the popping corn in the pan. That happens when you're old."

Sitting back on the wooden crate, he returned to working on the piece of wood. Grace had no idea what it was going to be. It didn't look like a bowl because it was square. She couldn't see what was on top.

"The verses that follow the one you quoted are important too. You're growing old enough to learn to study the Bible and not just memorize what a teacher gives you."

"I'm nine." Grace sat up straighter. *Daddi* knew how old she was. He'd hired a driver and taken them all to the top of Wildcat Mountain State Park for her birthday. They'd had a picnic and walked the trails. She'd seen wild deer and trees taller than any she'd ever imagined. *Daddi* had not forgotten her ninth birthday.

"The verses that come directly after the one you quoted from Joshua speak to *Gotte's* desire for us. They say, 'Then you will call on me and come and pray to me, and I will listen to you. You will seek me and find me when you seek me with all your heart.'"

Grace stared at Pepper, who didn't seem perturbed at all.

"Does that mean His plan won't work if we don't pray enough?"

"*Nein*, child. I wouldn't say that. But we might not understand it if we don't pray enough."

"*Ya*. There's a lot I don't understand."

"Have you been praying much?"

"I try." Grace stood and followed him as he put away his sandpaper and closed up the barn for the evening. "Sometimes, though, in the middle of my prayers, my mind wanders. I start thinking of school or drawing. Half the time I fall asleep. And the other half I go off worrying about things."

She was beginning to feel worse again.

If *mammi's* health was depending on her prayer life, they were in big trouble.

Daddi stopped at the pasture fence and pointed toward one of the calves that was trying to nurse. The big brown heifer tolerated it for a moment before she walked away.

"See how that cow treated her calf?"

"Kind of rude."

Daddi's laugh rang out across the field. "She's teaching it. The calf has to learn to eat other things than milk. It won't grow strong enough on milk alone."

"Okay..." She drew the word out as she ran the stick along the pasture fence. Pepper ran a few feet in front of them, sniffing for ground birds, but he always circled back.

"*Gotte* is always teaching us, Grace. Same as that heifer is teaching that calf."

"I feel like a calf sometimes."

"Is that right?"

"Sure. I don't like it when things are hard. Look how the calf is running after its *mamm*. That's me. Running after Miriam." She laughed in spite of her misery. The calf did look funny. He wasn't quite skilled on his four legs yet, and the heifer was once again allowing him to nurse.

Daddi put his hand on her back. "*Gotte* doesn't mind your attempts at prayer, even when they fall short. You keep trying. He loves you, Gracie, more than that heifer loves that calf—much more. He'll take care of you and me and your *mammi* as well."

"But there's no promise she'll get well."

"Nope. We don't get that kind of promise in this life. The promise we get is that He loves us. You can count on that one."

Grace threw her arms around his waist. He smelled of barns and wood and calves. He smelled like *grossdaddi*.

More than anything, that sent the trembles away and calmed her stomach.

As they climbed the porch steps, she was greeted by the smell of oatmeal cookies. Someone had felt well enough to cook.

"Cookies, milk, and checkers sound *gut*?" *Daddi* held up the piece of wood, and she saw that it was a new checkerboard.

"It's beautiful." Grace took it from his hands and ran her fingers over the pattern of light wood against dark. "When did you have time to make this?"

"A few minutes here and there are easy to find. I sent the last board with your youngest cousin—he needs the practice. I know how this family loves a *gut* game, so I made another."

Grace thought the evening was one of their best ever. She still didn't understand exactly what her *grossmammi* was suffering from—though now she knew the name of it was a disease called hyperthyroidism. Her *mamm* had explained it to her on the ride over, but Grace couldn't imagine how a thing in your neck, a thing you couldn't even feel, could make you so sick. Your heart? Yes. She could put her hand to her chest and feel her heart beat. But something in your neck? That was hard to imagine.

The important thing was that Doc Hanson would give *mammi* the medicine she needed on Friday—something radioactive, which sounded horrible.

If it worked, they would all be grateful for the medicine. If it made her well, she supposed horrible was fine.

Until they knew for sure, Grace would pray.

~ *Chapter 26* ~

abe was happy to be laboring in his fields. The sun was shining on his back, the workhorses were hitched to his plow,
and his arms ached from the effort of hours of work.

Finally the restlessness that had plagued him for weeks disappeared. If it meant he fell asleep the moment he dropped into bed,
that wasn't a problem. His *fraa* smiled and said she understood.
What did concern him was that he woke with more aches than he'd
ever had before.

When he first stood in the morning, he feared his legs might
buckle. That was what months of working in the barn did to a man—
softened him and added an extra five pounds where he didn't need
it. Gabe refused to accept that it could be his age. He was only thirty-
four, which was not an old man. Men across the community, men far
older than he, were in the fields today. However, there was no denying that his knees hurt. His legs ached. His abdomen felt as if their
donkey Gus had run into him at top speed.

Yet in spite of the soreness, working in the fields improved Gabe's
mood. It would also toughen him up, which apparently he needed.
Next winter he would find a way to stay in better shape. Perhaps he
would have sons to follow his two *dochdern*. He wanted to still be able
to plow a field by the time they were able to work beside him.

That thought—of sons—brought a smile to his face and helped him push past the muscle fatigue. He plowed for another hour, his mind focused on the horses, the rows, and the crops that would grow. The four Belgian draft horses were powerful, hardworking animals. Three sorrels and a red, they were handsome geldings. Young and healthy, they stood between seventeen and eighteen hands high. They were too large to ride comfortably, but Gabe hadn't bought them for riding...he'd bought them for plowing.

The animals seemed to recognize that.

They pulled the plow in unison, responding to Gabe's direction easily. The thought crossed his mind that perhaps they were as relieved to be working as he was. The labor was *gut*. It was what they had waited the winter for. With the fields finally dry enough to be worked, he was eager to allow it to exhaust him. He might have continued through lunch, but by the time he saw Miriam step outside the back door, placing food on the table under the shade tree, he was dripping with sweat and as needful as the horses for a break.

"Out here is a *gut* idea for lunch," he said, as he washed off at the pump. "I believe I smell bad. You wouldn't want me inside."

Miriam smiled, but it didn't quite reach her eyes.

"Rachel asleep?"

"*Ya.* I cracked the window a little so I could hear if she wakes up."

They bowed their heads, and as they prayed silently over the noon meal, Gabe asked for wisdom. He knew his *fraa*'s heart was heavy, and he suspected he knew why, but how was he to help her? How was he to ease the pain she was experiencing?

He knew from his own past that sometimes waiting was the worst, and Abigail wasn't scheduled to go to the medical center in Eau Claire until Friday.

What comfort could he offer?

They had both taken the first bite of their sandwiches when Rachel let out a howl which could be heard quite easily through the open window—could probably be heard across the field to where he'd left the horses.

Miriam closed her eyes, chewing her food as Rachel's cry picked up steam.

"Would you like me to fetch her?"

"I would not," she said, glancing under the table to stare at his work boots, caked in mud.

"What I hear you saying is that I might be more trouble than I'm worth."

Instead of answering, Miriam took one more bite of her sandwich, this one so large she had trouble chewing and wagged her finger at him. "Don't eat my sandwich."

The words were barely discernible, but the fact that he saw a hint of humor in her eyes eased a little of his own worry.

She returned with a red-faced Rachel, rubbing her eyes and hiccupping now that she was being held by her *mamm*.

"Teething?" Gabe asked.

Miriam rubbed her finger along Rachel's bottom front gum. "I don't think so. Honestly I don't know what's wrong with her. No fever. No runny nose. And no teething."

Sitting back down at the table, she took another bite of her sandwich, misery etched on her face.

"Maybe she has cabin fever," Gabe offered.

Miriam gave him what he'd taken to calling her teacher look. "We don't live in a cabin."

"True, but I imagine the same condition could claim a person regardless where they live or who they are—*boppli* or *mamm*."

Jerking her gaze up, Miriam sat perfectly still for five seconds. Finally she shrugged. "I can't go to my parents'. *Mamm* says I worry over her like a bird over newly hatched eggs. She's practically banned me until I ride with them on Friday to Eau Claire. I don't much feel like visiting with Esther or Lydia. I'm not exactly in a visiting mood."

"Hmm...that is a predicament." Gabe stood and walked around the table. He took Rachel from her arms and laughed when she smiled at him.

"You won't laugh if she's doing what I think she's doing."

"Did you hear that, Rachel? She says you're making a mess."

Rachel grunted and confirmed Miriam's suspicion. The odor that followed overpowered even Gabe's bad smell.

"Back into the house for us," Miriam said wearily.

"How about you clean up this little one, and then you two come out into the fields with me?"

"Fields?"

"Sure. I seem to remember someone used to like sitting outside while I plowed, back last year before this bundle of joy was born."

"The carefree days." Miriam sighed.

"Clean her up, *mamm*. Pack a blanket, some toys, and a book you've been meaning to read. I'll walk you two to the far side of the field and leave you under your favorite stand of trees."

"Gabriel Miller. You're suggesting I forget my housework and go sit under a tree while you plow?"

Gabe stepped closer and traced her face—brow to chin—with his fingertips, and then he slipped his hand to her shoulder and massaged the tight muscle there. "That's exactly what I'm suggesting. It wouldn't hurt for you to take a few hours off, and I believe it would help me to plow a straighter row if I had two beautiful gals at the far end."

Miriam shook her head at his teasing, but he noticed a light blush in her cheeks. She also glanced toward the far grove of trees, as if they were beckoning her.

"You've worked extra, helping at your *mamm*'s home, helping with the cabins, and the work here. A few hours watching Rachel and sitting in the shade isn't a sin, Miriam. It will ease your mind. And I suspect your work in the house is done anyway."

"I finished an hour ago."

"*Wunderbaar.*"

"It would be nice to do some sewing outside."

"It would."

She took their daughter from his arms and started toward the house, but she stopped, turned back, stood on her tiptoes, and kissed him on the lips. "*Danki*, Gabe."

Before he could think how to respond, she went inside to change Rachel.

A few hours outside wouldn't solve all her problems. He didn't have the ability to do that, but he was glad the note of despair had left her voice. He was satisfied with that for the moment. Tomorrow they would deal with the problems that came with it—and they would deal with them together.

Miriam should have realized that some time outside would remedy the blues she had been feeling. Maybe she hadn't understood how much the house had closed in on her lately. Maybe she didn't appreciate how much a different perspective could help.

She was sitting under her favorite grove of trees—the same grove she'd sat under last October and watched as Gabe had harvested the crops, watched while she'd thought about the babe growing inside her. Somehow in her mind, this shady spot had become their special place. Even Rachel seemed to realize it. She played with the rattle from Rae—this one blue-and-yellow triangles with a cow's head. It was the silliest-looking thing.

Rae was coming for lunch tomorrow. Miriam missed seeing her, and she couldn't wait to hear all about the latest news story she was chasing—something about a string of robberies in the next district.

She spent an hour sewing, and Rachel soon fell asleep on the blanket. Miriam found the sense of peace she'd been chasing all week. She hadn't found it while praying, and she certainly hadn't found it while she'd done the chores inside. Perhaps she needed to be outside, out where God's world had opened to summer's bloom.

As she ran the needle and thread through an apron she was hemming for Grace, it occurred to her how silly she'd been. She could have gone outside and worked in her garden. In fact, she had worked there one afternoon when Grace had come home from school. And before that, last Saturday, she'd worked outside at the cabins.

The shaded spot under the trees was special, though—it was a balm to her heart. She would remember it next time she felt pressed down and out of sorts. It wasn't as if she couldn't walk out here anytime she wanted to come, though carrying Rachel and all their things so far might be a challenge. She'd need a wagon. Her baby girl was growing every day.

She did like watching the big horses and Gabe working behind them. One of the sorrels had a white stripe down his forehead. Grace had named him Gideon. The other two sorrels she'd named Big and Billy. The red might have been Miriam's favorite. He was a velvety color, and Grace called him Prince. In the fall, Gabe hooked up the wagon behind the giant horses and they gathered the crops. She'd helped some, and it reminded her of when she was a child and in the fields with her father.

Remembering when she was a young girl, thinking back to the previous year, those things brought a lightness to her heart. When she'd first married Gabe, it had been so exciting just to walk by his side. Being in the fields with him again reminded her of who she had been. It helped her feel rooted, and it made her feel carefree once more.

She continued to sew, even found herself humming one of the hymns from Sunday's service, and her worries slipped away with the light summer breeze.

The afternoon passed more quickly than she would have thought possible. She was surprised when Gabe pulled the horses to a stop and jumped down to join her.

"Rachel looks happy."

"*Ya.* I guess the fresh air agrees with her."

"Looks like it agrees with you too."

Miriam tucked her sewing into the basket she'd brought, and then she gave her full attention to her husband. "*Danki* for sitting on the ground, Gabe."

"Are you saying I'm too dirty to sit on your blanket?"

They both looked down at his pants, which had started out black but were now a solid brown. He began laughing before she did, but soon Miriam found she couldn't catch her breath. Their laughter felt good.

"You were right. I needed to get out of the house. The breeze, it feels nice. I think it blew some of my fears away."

When he reached for her, he kissed her lightly at first, but it quickly grew in intensity until she found herself wishing they had more time and he wasn't quite so dirty.

"It's the sweat," he said, jumping to his feet, reaching down, and pulling her up. "Makes me irresistible."

"Is that so?"

"You watch. Tonight, you'll fill Grace up with extra dessert so she'll fall asleep early, and you won't have any sewing because you finished it here. Rachel will sleep well, and then I'll be proven correct." He held Rachel as she folded the blanket. "You won't be able to resist me."

"So you're promising to stay awake."

"If you'll make me a pot of strong *kaffi* with dinner—*ya!* I promise I can stay awake."

He draped the blanket over his left arm and switched Rachel to that side. She squirmed but didn't waken. "Mind if I walk you back?" he asked, snagging her hand.

"Mind?" Miriam picked up her sewing basket, feeling like the character in *Little Red Riding Hood.*

"We don't even need to rush. We've several minutes before Grace comes, and the horses can use the rest. It will give us time to talk."

So she told him about the thoughts she'd been chasing round and round in her mind, about how the radioactive iodine Abigail would be taking worked best with patients whose symptoms were mild. To her, Abigail's symptoms seemed severe.

They spoke of his hopes for the summer crops, and how their donkey, Gus, had settled down—temporarily, at least.

Both expressed how happy they were that business at the cabins had picked up.

"Which reminds me." Miriam stopped walking. "I meant to tell you about the *Englischer* who was there."

"*Englischers* are supposed to be at the cabins. Hopefully more than one."

She nudged him with her hip. He slipped an arm around her waist as they resumed walking up the back porch steps and sat looking out over the fields.

"It seems he's bought some property nearby, and he wants to learn how to farm."

"So?"

"He wants to learn how to farm the Amish way."

"Huh." Gabe leaned back against the porch post and closed his eyes.

"Don't you think that's rather odd?"

"What's that?"

"Gabe?"

"*Ya?*"

Miriam nudged him with her foot. When he didn't respond, she reached over and took Rachel from his arms.

"Why did you do that?"

"Because you were sleeping, and you were going to drop her."

"I'd never drop her. What kind of *dat* do you think I am?"

Miriam stood and walked toward the back door. "A very tired one, and one who probably will not be able to keep his eyes open past dinner."

"That's why I need a small rest now."

"Uh-huh."

"Miriam?"

"Yes, Gabe?"

"Did the *Englischer* worry you?"

Now he was wide awake and studying her. Miriam realized that once again she'd misjudged her husband. When would she learn not to do that? It was a good thing he was a patient man. Even now, he watched her, waiting for an answer.

"It seemed odd, and when I walked up—at the same time that Lydia and Clara walked up—he stopped talking at all, which seemed even more suspicious. Clammed right up. Why do you suppose he would do that?"

"Could be he didn't know what to say to three Amish women."

"Maybe. Or maybe he was up to no good and actually has no intention of farming like Plain folk. Seemed an unlikely story to me."

"I'll speak with Aaron about it next time I see him."

Miriam nodded and went into the house as Gabe stood and walked off to fetch his team and finish his day's work in the fields.

She did feel better for her afternoon outside. The hours there had helped in more ways than one. They'd helped to uncover the little thing that had been bothering her memory—the strange visitor at the cabins and his odd request.

Farming the Amish way, indeed.

She wasn't one to think badly of people, but she suspected that man was up to no good.

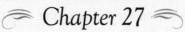

Chapter 27

A aron frowned at the growing crowd of *Englisch* vehicles in the parking lot of the cabins.

"It's *gut*, Aaron. It's what we wanted. What we needed." Lydia stood beside him, a broom in one hand and a dust cloth in the other. She had a smudge of dirt across her right cheek from cleaning up his cabin—his cabin that a guest needed. He'd be sleeping somewhere else tonight.

Aaron realized it was *gut*, but he was not feeling happy.

He wanted to reach out and wipe the smudge off her cheek. He wanted to tell Lydia that she smelled of fresh-baked bread and the flowers growing by Pebble Creek. He wanted to ask her to the singing Sunday night—he'd heard it was going to be held in the bishop's barn. But he had no business doing that. He wasn't staying, and he had no business pretending he was.

So instead he hollered about the cars. "At this rate we're going to need to expand the parking lot. Did you see the folks in cabin two? Three people—parents and one child, but they brought two cars. Where is the sense in that?"

"Yes, but—"

"It's wasteful."

"Actually, they explained—"

"Makes me *narrisch*."

"You are acting a little—"

"I'm going to work in the barn." He stomped off before he was tempted to peer into her beautiful brown eyes. Those eyes were going to trip him up and make him forget his fields and his family back in Indiana.

He needed to stay focused.

"What about the extra shelves you were adding in the shop?"

Aaron shook his head but didn't turn around. The last thing he needed was to spend more time in the shop—it was full of *Englischers* and Clara.

They had moved Clara there and set up a small desk for her to work at. She'd be filling out postcards for at least another week, probably longer since she had to keep stopping to ring up sales for customers.

That wasn't the reason he was avoiding Lydia's younger sister. Wherever Clara was, Aaron was sure to find Seth. Those two seemed to think that the month was February instead of late May. Hearts practically popped up in the air around them. Normally Aaron would laugh about such things, but currently he wasn't in the mood.

He'd caught Lydia staring at her sister during one of Clara and Seth's moments of playful teasing. The expression on Lydia's face had scraped across his heart like splinters across his hands.

Why the look of envy? Why the expression of sadness?

Did Lydia not realize how beautiful she was, how lucky any man would be to have her for a wife?

He opened the door to the first horse stall and began mucking it out. The work was smelly, tiring, and exactly what he needed.

His shirt was drenched in sweat and the stall was cleaned when he heard someone enter the barn.

"Hello? Aaron?"

Laying aside the apple picker, he stepped out and saw his neighbor, Tim Elliott. In his early forties, the man was probably five foot eight and wore coveralls. He was balding and without facial hair—though he'd mentioned a wife and children. His blue eyes twinkled as he stepped forward and shook hands.

"Tim. How are you?"

"Good. Fine." Tim looked around the barn, his eyes assessing what he saw.

Aaron wanted to laugh, but he pushed it down. Did the man expect that an Amish barn would look so different from an *Englisch* one?

"Actually, I'm not fine," he admitted. "That's why I came looking for you. The tilling isn't going so well."

"Huh. Suppose not if you took the time to drive over here."

"Any chance you could come take a look?"

Aaron glanced toward the next horse stall and out of the front door of the barn. Suddenly, staying in the barn on such a gorgeous May day seemed foolish. He was, after all, a farmer. Perhaps a few hours at Tim's place would improve his mood.

"Sure. I'll just put Seth to work on these stalls."

Seth wasn't too happy with the assignment, but he'd taken to complaining less and working harder since he'd become enamored with Clara. He'd been using a push mower to cut grass around the office and shop. When Aaron told him to finish cleaning the stalls, he frowned, shrugged, turned the mower around, and moved slowly toward the barn.

"Boy moves at the identical pace of my teenage son."

"*Ya.* Some attitudes are the same whether they're Amish or *Englisch.*"

When Aaron stopped in the office to tell Lydia where he was going, she was on the phone taking more reservations. He was relieved he didn't have to explain. She'd questioned him once already about Tim. What made women so suspicious?

Five minutes later they were in Tim's truck, headed toward his farm. They could have walked, but Aaron didn't point that out. Tim would learn if he was intent on living the Amish way.

Only one piece of property separated Tim's farm from the cabins. The walk would have been less than a mile.

"Who owns that home?" He'd passed the two-story farmhouse to the south of the cabins several times since coming to Wisconsin, but he'd never paid it any mind. The property appeared almost deserted. Today, the laundry hanging on the line seemed to indicate otherwise.

"Julia Beechy. You haven't met her?"

"Possibly at our church service. There were a lot of new names to remember."

"But you haven't stopped by to introduce yourself?"

"*Nein*. The river divides our property from hers, the way it twists and turns here."

"And you've been busy."

"True, I have." Aaron stared out the window. "I've been here for weeks, though. I should have taken the time to meet our neighbors, but—"

Tim waited, and the sound of the asphalt against the tires as they turned into his place hummed, reminding Aaron of the bus he'd ridden, of the trip he needed to be taking home.

"But I'm not staying. Meeting neighbors has been low on my list of things to do." Aaron shook away the questions that seemed to plague him with every thought. "So Julia must be who you bought your place from."

"Yes. This land was part of her property. I don't think the fields have been farmed in years. I learned a little about her situation when we completed the sell. Apparently, she's not married and cares for her parents, who are elderly and in poor health. I'm not sure what this smaller second house was used for." Tim pulled up to a one-story frame home. It probably had three bedrooms, and Aaron could see the standard wraparound porch stretching across the front and disappearing around the side.

"This would have been the children's home," Aaron explained.

"In Amish families, when the oldest son decides to marry, often he will build a home on his *dat*'s property, especially if there is land that needs working."

"And the parents stay in the big house? The one Julia is in?"

"*Ya*, until the son and his wife start having *kinner* and running out of room. Then they change places. At some point this house would have become a *grossdaddi* house."

They both stared out over the fields that had filled with weeds. Tim's two workhorses stood resting in the shade. Three bicycles lay discarded beside the barn—from the sizes, Aaron would guess one teenager and two smaller children.

"Let's have a look," Aaron said, unbuckling his seat belt. As soon as he'd stepped out of the truck and slammed the door shut, Tim's wife walked out onto the porch.

Shorter than Tim, she was very thin and wore her red hair in a short cut. She walked down the steps, and Aaron saw she had on blue jeans and her top was also denim, with bird houses stitched into the material.

"You must be Aaron. My husband told me about you. I'm Jeanette."

"Pleased to meet you." Aaron stuck his hands in his pockets. Sometimes *Englisch* women liked to shake hands, but he never felt comfortable with the gesture.

"Thank you for coming over. I guess you think we're crazy for moving here and trying—" Her hands came out and waved toward the fields and the barn. "This."

He noticed she wore only one ring, a wedding ring, and her nails weren't painted. Her eyes crinkled into a smile behind purple glasses.

"*Nein*. Folks have reasons for what they do."

Jeanette glanced at her husband. "Yes. Yes, I suppose that's a good way to put it. Can I offer you a glass of iced tea or something else to drink?"

"I'm good, but *danki*."

"All right. I'll go back to my work while you two do your farming thing."

As they moved toward the fields, Tim explained, "Jeanette's a blogger."

"Logger?"

"Blogger. She blogs on the Internet."

"I know what the Internet is, though we don't use the computer often—maybe occasionally when we stop by the public library to research something. There are a few businesses that have exemptions from the bishop. At least in Indiana they do. Here, I'm not sure. What is blogging?"

Tim stopped beside the plow, which he'd incorrectly harnessed to the draft horses. "It's similar to writing news articles. Instead of appearing in newspapers, though, her writing appears on people's webpages on the Internet."

"And she gets paid for this?"

"Yeah. Pays pretty well once you've established a name. She hopes to write a novel one day, but that's a hard thing to break into."

Aaron stepped up to one of the big horses and placed his hand on the animal's neck. "Can't say that I pick up a lot of novels. I read a few in school. Now I mostly read the *Budget* if I can keep my eyes open at night."

"I've seen that in town."

"You might want to snag a copy whenever you have a chance. You'll see where Amish folks will be selling animals, farm tools, and all sorts of things that you could use around here." He took a long, slow look around the farm. "You're going to want to keep an eye out for good deals."

"Yeah." Tim's voice dipped as he ran his hand over the top of his head.

Aaron spent the next hour showing him how to properly hitch the Belgians to the plow. He stayed and watched him work the first few rows, making sure he could properly guide the animals. Seeing him in the fields intensified the desire in Aaron to be home, back on his own place in Indiana.

But that wasn't quite right, either. When he glanced up, past Tim's fields, and saw Pebble Creek in the distance, he felt something very close to desire. This was rich land. It was *gut* land, though some of it—like Tim's—would require many months of backbreaking work because it had been neglected.

And what was he to do with those feelings?

He didn't belong here, not for any amount of time. But he wasn't sure he belonged back home any longer, either.

When he felt that Tim had the hang of it, he raised a hand to slow him. "I'm walking back. You're *gut* now."

"Don't you want me to drive you?"

"*Nein*. It's a mile. I can walk it. But if you have an emergency, I'll be at David King's home tonight—the cabins are full."

"You're welcome to stay here."

"*Danki*. I might take you up on that sometime."

Tim nodded as he called out to the team and continued plowing in the noonday sun.

With a smile, Aaron turned and headed back away from the fields.

Jeanette walked out of the house as he was leaving.

"I wanted to give you these to take back to the cabins."

He looked down at the plate of M&M cookies.

"Is it okay? Do you eat M&M candies?"

"*Ya*. I love them," he assured her with a smile. "I may not even share them with anyone else."

Jeanette cocked her head, unsure how to take his joke. "Maybe I should make a bigger batch next time. We appreciate your help very much."

"No problem. Farming is a *gut* thing to do." As an afterthought, for no reason other than he could remember his *dat* saying it, he added, "If you tickle the earth with your hoe, she will laugh with a harvest."

Instead of smiling, Jeanette sat down on the top step of the porch. "I'm not sure about that. I think my husband may be having a midlife crisis. He could have a heart attack out there. Where I come from, in Oklahoma, we use tractors to do this sort of thing."

"*Ya*. Some *Englischers* here use tractors."

"But not Amish?"

"*Nein*. Amish don't."

"Why is that?" Jeanette took off her glasses and rubbed them gently with the hem of her blouse.

"Plowing this way, the way your husband is learning, it's tried and true. Many in the world still farm this way."

Jeanette replaced her glasses and peered through them across the fields before finally looking back at him. "Why? I understand you have religious reasons. I've researched that. But why would Tim want to?"

"I can't explain his heart," Aaron said softly. "I can tell you that plowing this way makes the soil more receptive to water. In Indiana we offer classes for university students to come and study our methods."

Jeanette sat up straighter. "I didn't realize..."

"*Ya*. Some, like your husband, are turning back to the old ways. Go walk out there. See how it exposes the soil to nutrients—"

"Fertilizer."

Aaron laughed. "We use everything on the farm. Saves money and makes *gut* sense."

"Thank you, Aaron." Jeanette stood. "Tim's had his share of struggles. All of my family have. Problems that we hope a change of lifestyle will help. I'm praying this will...this will be what we need."

Aaron nodded, thanked her again for the plate of cookies, and walked home. He felt better for having spent a few hours away from the cabins. After all, he wasn't an innkeeper, at least not permanently.

Miriam walked Rae out onto the front porch. "Are you sure you can't stay any longer?"

"I wish I could. Our visits always go by too fast." Her shoulder-length hair was pulled back into a pony tail, and she had a dark tan, even though the weather was just now warm enough to spend the day outside.

Miriam could hardly believe they were the same age. In some ways Rae appeared so carefree—no husband, no babies, no home to tend. In other ways, though, her job with the newspaper was far more demanding than what Miriam had to handle each day.

"It seems we've known each other for years," she said as they continued towards Rae's small car. "Hard to believe we met over Drake's project."

Rae opened the car door and tossed her purse into the passenger seat. "At least one good thing came of his plowing through town."

"You still don't like him."

"I don't. Now he's moved farther north, and he's attempting to do the same thing—only those communities aren't standing up to him. They're trying to ignore him, and we both know that won't work."

Miriam reached forward and straightened the collar on Rae's blue jean jacket. "You worry about our communities, but each district has to make their own decisions. All you can do is make gentle suggestions and report the news for your paper."

"I know. You'd think after all these years I would have picked up on some of your *glassenheet*."

"*Gelassenheit*." Miriam covered her mouth so she wouldn't laugh at her friend.

"Isn't that what I said?"

"*Nein*."

"You need to teach me, Miriam. Soon Rachel will speak better Pennsylvania Dutch than I do."

Rae was in the car and buckled when Miriam remembered to ask her about the local assignment covering burglaries.

"Don't worry about that. There's been nothing close to Cashton."

"What's being stolen?"

"Anything they can sell, apparently. They tend to hit places without surveillance."

"Which is—"

"Video cameras, security, that sort of thing."

"Sounds as if Amish places could be a target."

"A few have been." Rae stared out through the front window of her car and seemed about to say something. She shook her head, as if she could shake the worries away. "Whoever is doing this has hit a few churches—different denominations and even a couple of the small outlying schools. The police aren't saying if the incidents are connected at this point, but my instincts tell me they are."

"You'll be careful?"

"I will."

As she drove away, Miriam realized how grateful she was for her *Englisch* friend. She'd printed out several articles on Abigail's disease, which Miriam could read through later this afternoon. And she'd offered to pray for her.

Rae's faith wasn't so different from her own. They might attend different churches, but they prayed to the same God. They believed the same truths, and they would often laugh when one or the other brought up a verse from Scripture—because it was familiar. It was as if their spiritual roots were the same.

Certainly, God had brought Rae Caperton into her life.

Miriam would pray for Rae's safety as she went about her daily chores. Rae's job was important to the Plain community, though they preferred to think they didn't need representation in the *Englisch* paper—and perhaps they didn't. But Rae had convinced her Amish communities were going to be dealt with on the printed page whether they wanted to or not. At least with Rae and others like her on their side, they had a chance of being dealt with fairly.

Rae also said she'd try to stop by the cabins in the next few days and see if she could do an article on the improvements Aaron and

Lydia had done. It wouldn't hurt to give them a little publicity. First, though, she had to run down her lead on the burglary piece.

As Miriam cleaned up their lunch dishes, she prayed that God would keep Rae Caperton out of harm's way. She prayed the person doing this terrible thing would be stopped, and she prayed that God would find a way to use the work of their hands.

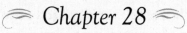 *Chapter 28*

Lydia set out for work earlier than usual Friday morning in spite of Clara's complaining. Aaron had spent the night with David because all of the cabins were rented. He'd be riding into work with Seth. She wanted to arrive before her normal time so that she could open the office and have *kaffi* and breakfast prepared for any of the guests who were early risers.

Everything was off this morning.

Clara was crankier than usual, and Stephen hadn't been himself at all.

The sun had barely lightened the horizon when her brother pulled Tin Star out of the barn, hitched to the buggy. Stephen had dark circles under his eyes and hay stuck to his hair from sleeping in the hayloft. Why had he slept in the barn? Stephen had only shrugged when she thanked him. He had frowned at the ground and walked away without a word.

"Do you think Stephen is doing all right? He seems somewhat sullen."

"Who wouldn't be at this hour of the day? You're getting him up earlier than he would have to be for his normal chores."

"But I didn't get him up." Lydia pulled her shawl tighter around her shoulders. Though it was late May, the morning temperatures were still brisk. "This morning I went to his room and knocked on the door, but there was no answer. So I dressed quickly and went to the barn to see to Tin Star myself. I found Stephen there, asleep in the loft."

"Maybe he was tired of sleeping in a house full of girls." Clara curled into the corner of the buggy, yawning and trying to make a pillow of her arm.

"Why would he prefer a scratchy bed of hay? That makes no sense." Lydia reached over and shook Clara's arm.

"What? Are we there already?"

"Do you think Stephen's in trouble?"

"How would I know? I barely know where I am. One minute I'm sleeping, the next you're waking me. It seems to be your mission in life to wake me whether I'm in bed or in a buggy!"

"You shouldn't be sleeping in a buggy. It's not proper. Where did Stephen go after dinner last night?"

Instead of answering, Clara sat up straighter and focused on straightening her *kapp*, smoothing out her apron, and checking that their lunches hadn't tipped over on the floor of the buggy.

"You know something," Lydia said.

"Why would I know something?"

"Because you didn't say that you don't know something."

"That's the worst logic I've ever heard."

"Tell me you don't know where Stephen was last night."

"You're the one who said he was in the hayloft." Clara became suddenly interested in the passing scenery.

"You know I mean before that, Clara. I'm sure he was late coming in because when I went to fetch Martha, Amanda, and Sally Ann from playing on the porch, the barn door was still open and Tin Star was still gone. Do you know where he was?"

"It's not my job to keep up with our *bruder*." Now she studied her fingers, holding them out in front of her in the early morning light. "I was busy using some of the lotion I bought to try to smooth over the rough spots on my hands. Don't you think Aaron should reimburse me for that expense?"

Lydia didn't bother responding.

Where had her brother been so late the night before? If her mother had noticed, she hadn't said anything about his behavior. Perhaps because she'd been busy herself. It had been a rough night for Lydia's father—Menno's condition often worsened when the days grew warmer, perhaps because so much pollen was in the air. Last night her mother was busy making a herbal plaster for Menno's chest. Lydia had cooked dinner, but Stephen had never shown up to eat it.

"He definitely slept in the barn last night. You saw the hay in his hair, and he was still wearing yesterday's clothing. He didn't look very happy, either."

Clara sighed heavily, as if explaining things to her older sister was a burden far too heavy to bear. "I suspect he was unhappy because he needed another hour of sleep. Our *bruder* is on his *rumspringa*, Lydia dear. You probably don't remember what that's like because you never had one."

How could she have indulged in a time of running around? There had been no bridge between childhood and adulthood for Lydia. No, she'd gone to sleep one night a child and woken the next day an adult. She knew what day it had been too—the day her father had been diagnosed with farmer's lung. Soon after that the farm had been sold. Her mother had become his nurse, and she had become a mother to her brothers and sisters.

Lydia swallowed the answer Clara would never understand. Instead, she focused on the road that Tin Star trotted down. She barely needed to guide him at all. He knew the way so well, and there was little traffic this early in the day. The sound of Pebble Creek, running beside the road, soothed her nerves from the morning, but she couldn't completely lose the feeling that something was wrong. Something *else* was wrong.

Why would that be?

Her *dat* was dying.

Her sister complained constantly, except when she was flirting with Seth, who was the worst example of a godly young man Lydia could imagine.

Her own brother was suddenly evasive and had a haunted look in his eyes.

And Aaron was avoiding her as if she had been proclaimed contagious.

Yet all of that wasn't enough. It was a beautiful summer morning, but she had the strongest feeling that something *else* was wrong.

They were hurrying toward the cabins, which were all occupied— every single one, and she didn't feel at all happy about it.

Why was that?

What was the matter with her? Perhaps she did need a *rumspringa*.

Clara sat cornered on her side of the buggy, head cradled once more against her arm, eyes closed. Resting awkwardly, even she looked more content than Lydia felt.

Lydia allowed her some peace as they traveled the last of the way to the cabins. Pulling into the parking lot, as Tin Star began to slow, she reached over and nudged Clara.

"Wake up."

"What do you want?"

"You'll have to take care of Tin Star."

"Me?"

"*Ya*, you. I need to start breakfast for the guests."

"Why me?" Clara sat up, patting her *kapp* into place. "Aaron always takes care of our horse."

"Aaron stayed with David last night. Remember? Now take care of Tin—" The words fell away as she caught site of the front door of the office.

"I don't see why I have to do it. I can cook as well as you can. I believe you enjoy bossing me around, Lydia, and it's not fair—"

"Stop talking."

"What?"

"Hold these." Lydia tossed the reins at her sister and jumped out of the buggy. She could hear Clara still complaining, questioning her, but as soon as her feet touched the ground, she raised the hem of her dress and began to run toward the front porch of the office.

Grace hurried from her room, through the sitting room, and into the kitchen. She slipped into her chair at the table without making a sound.

Today was the day—the day *mammi* was going to the medical center in Eau Claire. She had remembered the moment her eyes had popped open, remembered and said a prayer for her safety and healing. It was an important day for their family.

But *mammi* wasn't what had caused her to dress hurriedly and make a beeline to the kitchen. No, she'd finally made peace in her prayers over her grandmother, her illness, and what was to happen today.

Daddi Joshua had been right. A little more time studying her Bible had helped. *Gotte* would take care of her grandmother. She could trust Him. Grace would still be glad when this day was over, glad when Doc Hanson said the meds had worked—if they worked. She sure hoped and prayed they would, but as *daddi* had said—God loved them more than that heifer loved its calf. She didn't need to be afraid. He would take care of her and *daddi* and *mammi*.

What had sent her hurrying down the hall was the dream which had plagued her all night long. It seemed as if she had dreamed it again and again, like a song from church stuck in her head—except this was a picture, something she'd seen and tried to draw.

She needed to fix the drawing she'd started last Saturday. If she fixed it, maybe the dream would leave her alone. She flipped through her sketchbook as she sat in her usual place at the breakfast table. This one picture had been bothering her.

It was unfinished.

Finding the picture that was on her mind, she bent over the page. Pencil in hand, she set to work adding the details from her dream before she forgot them, shading in the trees that crowded the banks along Pebble Creek between the cabins and the river.

Miriam walked into the room, baby Rachel in her arms. "You're up early this morning."

"*Ya*. I woke up thinking about something I'd seen."

"Is that so?" Miriam moved toward the stove, where she'd already heated *kaffi* for Gabe. Grace had smelled it as soon as she'd walked into the kitchen. The room was warm and cozy even though it was big. It also smelled nice—not so much because of the *kaffi*, but because of the hot biscuits in the oven.

Things like that were better since Miriam had married her *dat*— less burned food, for instance. Lots of things were *gut* again. Grace sure was glad Miriam had said yes when her *dat* had put the Valentine's Day note in her teacher's lunch box. She loved her first mother, but she also loved her new mother. She remembered how it felt not to have one. It felt bad, and for more reasons than the ruined meals.

Not having a *mamm* felt lonely. Was Miriam worried about that now?

Grace put her pencil down, twisted around in her chair, and studied Miriam.

"Are you okay?"

Miriam turned from the stove, Rachel crooked in her left arm. "I'm *gut*, Grace. *Danki*."

"You're not sad or worried about *mammi*?"

"I was, but I'm better now. Still a little nervous, maybe. But I'm glad today is the day."

"*Ya*. I want her to start feeling better."

"Me too."

Grace ran her hand over the back of the chair. "When do you leave?"

"They've hired a driver. She'll pick up your grandparents first and come by for me about nine."

"And you'll take Rachel? Because I could stay home and watch her."

"I think Rachel will be a good distraction for your *mammi*, but it's sweet of you to offer." Miriam walked over to the cradle she kept in the kitchen and placed Rachel in it.

Grace peeked at her sister, who smiled back at her. She seemed content to lie there, sucking on her fingers. "Will *mammi* have to stay overnight?"

"*Nein*. We'll be home by the time you're out of school."

Grace nodded, satisfied that things were finally moving along. She turned back around in her chair and focused again on her drawing, on the forest, and on what she'd seen there.

"I only need to make hot cereal for breakfast. We still have a few minutes before your *dat* will be here. Would you like some juice or milk to drink?"

Grace held the drawing at arms' length, and then she bent to add more darkness to the woods.

"Honey..."

"*Ya?*"

"Juice or milk?"

"Oh." Grace glanced around the kitchen, confused at first by the question. Of course she'd heard Miriam talking about breakfast, but it had been like the sound of the wind in the trees—background sound. "Milk would be *gut*."

She returned to her drawing.

"You're focusing awfully hard."

"*Ya*. I had a dream about this picture. Do you think that's odd, *mamm*? To have a dream about a picture?"

"I don't know. I used to have dreams about teaching, or sometimes about a novel we were reading. I suppose it's not so unusual."

"That's a relief. I was worried maybe I was becoming *narrisch*."

At that moment Gabe clomped into the mudroom. "Did I hear someone in my home is acting *narrisch* again?"

Miriam smiled and moved to the stove to heat their oatmeal.

"He has some gray in his beard, but he still hears well," Grace murmured.

"I heard that!" her *dat* hollered.

Some of her tension from the dream drained away—some, but not all of it. What had troubled her so much? It wasn't as if anything from the woods could reach her here. She was safe at home, and besides, she was no longer a baby who should be frightened by a dream.

But there had been something threatening, something dark—

"What a beautiful sight this May morning. Three lovely gals in the kitchen and the smell of hot *kaffi* and fresh biscuits." Gabe walked to the stove, poured a cup of *kaffi*, and kissed her *mamm*.

Grace knew not all parents were as affectionate as hers. She'd asked Lily and Sadie. Lily never saw her parents kiss, and Sadie had only walked into a room and surprised hers once or twice. Grace's parents kissed often.

Maybe it was because they hadn't been married very long. She thought that could mean she would have another brother or sister soon, but she wasn't sure. She needed to ask more questions about exactly how that happened. She kept meaning to, but then she would become distracted by something else.

She glanced down again at the picture she was drawing and ran her finger along the edge of the page.

"Whatcha working on Gracie?"

"A picture."

"Huh." Gabe sat down beside her. "Don't usually see you drawing before school."

"Grace said she had a dream about this picture. Said this one was bothering her, so she wanted to get up early and finish it." Miriam brought the cereal to the table and set out brown sugar and raisins along with the bowls.

But she didn't sit down. Instead, she stood behind Grace's chair, studying the drawing that Gabe and Grace were both looking at.

Grace had done her best to put everything on the page that had disturbed her, but she wasn't sure she had caught it all. She wasn't sure how to put into words the dream she couldn't quite remember—it danced and teased at the edge of her memory.

But Grace was focused on the picture as a whole, not the smaller details. The details to her were like stitches in a quilt...she was concerned about getting the overall scene correct, and she wasn't sure she had.

It was her *dat* who placed his finger on the important detail. He set his *kaffi* mug down, leaned forward, and tapped the sheet. "Grace, who is this person in the woods?"

"I'm not sure."

"You drew this on Saturday?"

"*Ya.* When we were there helping. After I'd done the drawing Aaron chose for the postcard. I'd run off to watch the river, to look for flying squirrels...and that was when the light and the shadows in the woods caught my attention. I decided to draw one more scene, but I didn't like this one. It was too..."

"Spooky?" Miriam asked.

"I guess."

"Could this be Aaron?" Gabe now pulled the drawing in front of him and studied it more closely.

"*Nein,*" Miriam said. "I walked up as soon as Grace skipped away. They were talking about how much they liked the porch drawing, and then Aaron went back to work on the shed. He continued working on it until we went home."

"Seth?" Gabe asked.

"He left right after Grace went down to the river," Miriam said softly. "We were talking about how the drawing of the porch would work nicely for the postcard. He said he needed to be home to finish his chores."

Grace again leaned forward and touched the drawing. "For a few minutes I walked along the path Aaron is making. It runs next to the river. This person I saw was peering out from the woods. Kind of watching us."

"Why didn't you tell anyone, Grace?" Miriam reached for Rachel, who had begun to fuss.

"I was going to, but then he disappeared."

She felt more than saw her parents exchange a look of concern. Instead of frightening her, it made her feel better. Maybe she wasn't *narrisch* after all. Maybe her dream had been a warning.

"Can you describe him, Grace?" Gabe handed the tablet back. "All I can tell from this is that it was an Amish male. Could have been a boy or a man."

"I couldn't tell much, either. He didn't have a beard...I don't think. But he was too far in the woods to see much more. I don't even know if he was Amish. I didn't see him that well. That's why you only see his eyes looking out from the trees."

"Okay. Probably it's nothing, but we should let Aaron know that he might have someone watching the cabins. I'll drive over there after breakfast. Do you mind if I take your tablet?"

Grace shook her head. She'd actually be happy to tear that picture out. She didn't want it anymore. Breakfast tasted *gut* now that she'd shared her worries with her family. Maybe the day would go better than her dream seemed to suggest.

≈ Chapter 29 ≈

Lydia knew, positively knew, what she would find when she ran up the steps of the office. Her heart was thundering in her chest, and her palms were sweaty. It never occurred to her that whoever had done this thing might still be there.

When she first saw the chaos and emptiness, she wanted to sit down and weep. Shock, followed quickly by anger, surged through her heart. As her gaze swept the room, she longed to pick up the few items that were left and hurl them through the window. But she didn't. Instead she walked back out the door and moved slowly toward the Plain Shop, which had been open less than a week.

Clara caught up to her before she'd covered half the distance.

"Lydia, what is it? Why was the door open? What did you see?"

Instead of answering, Lydia kept walking. Like the pulling off of a Band-Aid, she wanted to be done with it. When they stepped inside, they were holding hands the way they had done as small girls, for somewhere along those last few yards Clara had gripped her hand tightly and apparently had no intention of letting go.

Clara cried out, and in that moment, Lydia saw that nearly all the things they had stocked in the shop were gone...taken.

Just like in the office.

"Why did they leave the rocking chairs?" Clara whispered.

"Probably too heavy or too bulky to steal." Lydia pulled her hand from her sister's and walked over to the shelves of canned food, which also remained. "And I suppose there isn't a quick market for vegetables or fruit."

She sat down in one of the rockers, cradling a jar of preserved peaches in her lap. Suddenly she was tired, extremely tired. Through the window of the little shop she could see that the morning's light had reached Pebble Creek, but it didn't bring her the hope it usually did.

Too much was wrong. Too much work had been stripped away from them.

"This is not right," Clara declared, her hands on her hips. "We can't...can't stand here and do nothing!"

She turned and stormed out of the shop.

When Lydia saw her sister stomp off, heading down the path toward the creek, she realized Clara's temper might have the upper hand over her good sense. She set the jar of peaches on the floor next to the chair and took off after her.

"Clara, where are you going? What are you doing?"

"I'm looking for the culprit. What do you think I'm doing?"

"You can't go stomping through the woods—"

Clara disappeared around the bend down by the water, and Lydia had to jog to keep up with her. "Come back here!"

Running down the path, she made the curve and nearly bumped into her sister. Clara had stopped where the river turned, stopped and was standing frozen with her hand at her neck. Lydia practically plowed right over her like the children running bases when they played baseball behind the schoolhouse. She reached out to stop herself, put both hands in front of her, and stumbled into Clara. They managed to stay standing as they watched the everyday miracle in front of them.

A doe and two spotted fawns stood lapping at the clear running water of the creek. The doe eyed them as she drank, but she didn't run. One of the fawns stepped closer to the doe, nudged her, and began nursing. The doe allowed it for a moment, and then she walked away, slowly at first, before loping into the woods. The fawns followed closely behind, running in a lopsided fashion.

"They were beautiful." Clara's voice filled with wonder. She didn't move but stared after the deer, as if they might reappear.

"*Ya,* they were."

Clara shook her head as she turned and allowed her sister to place her arms around her. How long had it been since they had hugged? They spent all of their time arguing and struggling against each other.

"Why would anyone steal all of our things, Lydia? I don't understand."

"I don't either, but there's one thing I know for sure."

Clara glanced up at her, wiping at the tears that had escaped down her cheeks.

"In the next thirty minutes we're going to have twelve hungry families, regardless of the burglary. We need to head over and start breakfast."

"*Ya.* I suppose you're right."

They walked back toward the cabins at a more measured pace.

"I wonder if whoever did this knew Aaron was gone last night."

"Maybe." Lydia had been thinking the same thing. "They must have worked quietly for the guests not to have heard them."

"The office and the shop are set to the side a little. They're not exactly located in the middle of the cabins."

"True."

"If whoever did this came in the middle of the night, while everyone was sleeping—"

Lydia stopped in the path and tugged on her sister's sleeve. "What were you going to do if you found the burglar in the woods?"

"I don't know. Demand he gives us our stuff back?"

"Just walk up to him and—"

"I might. Walk up and say, 'Hand it over. That isn't yours!'"

"Okay. Well, promise me you won't go alone to confront burglars anymore."

Clara straightened her apron before looking up with a smile. "I promise."

By the time Clara had taken care of Tin Star, Lydia had used the phone in the office to call the police and report the burglary. After that she started preparing breakfast. The police dispatcher had told her Officer Tate would be out along with a crime tech, who would need to dust for fingerprints, so she prepared breakfast outside.

Not counting the break-in, it was a beautiful May morning. The picnic tables Aaron and Seth had made provided plenty of eating space under the trees. All that was left was to make *kaffi* and pour it into thermoses, which she kept for emergencies. The three cinnamon cakes she'd made the night before were fine served unheated. It was a good thing Aaron was paying her for the baked goods she brought—soon she'd need her sisters Martha and Amanda to help with the extra baking. She had plenty of fruit to put out. They also had milk, juice, and cold cereal. It would have to do for an impromptu breakfast picnic.

Her heart ached over the work Aaron had done, over his loss—after all, the success or failure of the cabins was ultimately most important to him and his *aenti* Elizabeth. Lydia realized she was only an employee, and one part of her knew she could find a job someplace else. But for Aaron—success here meant he could return home.

She focused on making customers happy and assuring them all was well as they came to breakfast under the trees.

And that's where Aaron found her when he arrived half an hour later with Seth. By then he'd already heard about the break-in. The Amish grapevine was alive and well in Pebble Creek. The police had called a neighbor, who had stopped by David's and alerted Aaron.

And Aaron's response surprised Lydia. He made her smile for the first time all day. Even though she was surrounded by *Englisch* moms and dads and children, she felt some of the heaviness in her heart lift. In spite of the fact that two police officers were traipsing dirt through her office, she forgot the extra work.

Aaron's response the moment he arrived wiped all of those concerns away.

His first matter of business made her heart sing like the birds in the trees.

He didn't go to the office.

He didn't hurry to the shop to see how much merchandise was missing.

He walked through the growing crowd of guests, walked past Clara, and walked straight up to her. Putting his hands on her shoulders, he focused completely on her.

"Are you okay, Lydia?"

"*Ya*, of course."

"You weren't here when—"

"No."

"I was worried that maybe…" He never finished the sentence, but he did touch her face, look deeply in her eyes, and it seemed as though everyone else disappeared and it was only the two of them standing near the banks of Pebble Creek.

It didn't last long.

Soon one of the children began crying, and a guest asked for more juice. Lydia heard Clara complaining that she couldn't possibly work if she had to write her postcards outside where the bugs kept landing on her supplies. Seth was grumbling as he pulled the mower from the shed and moved to cut the grass that had begun growing out by the road. He had to stop when the officers told him he could be destroying evidence. Either way that boy was unhappy.

Every single one of those sounds joined together like the voices singing a hymn at church meeting—they blended together almost in harmony.

All of it gave her the impression that somehow things would return to normal, but the memory of Aaron's concern, that gave her hope that perhaps her dreams could come true.

Aaron had risen early at David's house. It would have been difficult not to, what with the five children and the arguing that continued between David and Seth. He thought it might have eased some with the boy working at the cabins, but apparently it hadn't.

Anna, David's wife, was in her last month of pregnancy and had her hands full with the other children and maintaining the house. When the arguing carried into the kitchen, she glanced at Aaron, shrugged, and asked him if he wanted cream with his *kaffi.*

David and Seth had carried their disagreement back outside.

While Anna was reaching for the cream out of the ice box, she'd stopped to rub at her lower back, closing her eyes and blowing out slowly.

Aaron had thanked Anna and told her he'd help with the chores in the barn. The three of them—Aaron, David, and Seth were walking back toward the house when David's neighbor hurried over across the field. He'd heard from his *Englisch* neighbor that there had been a break-in at the cabins. Apparently, the *Englisch* neighbor's wife was the dispatcher at the police station. She'd taken the call from Lydia. A slight adjustment to the Amish grapevine, but it worked nonetheless.

It wasn't the fact that there had been a burglary that caused Aaron's stomach to clench tighter than a man's hand around a hammer. Nor was it the thought of all the merchandise they might have lost. David's neighbor was very clear about who had made the call. It had been Lydia. She had been the first on the scene—the one to make the discovery.

No one had been arrested, but had she been hurt?

Had the burglar or burglars seen her?

Seth and David's bickering stopped as quickly as it had started, though the boy appeared as pale as Aaron felt. "I'll hitch up the buggy now," he said, and without waiting for an answer he was gone.

"Do you want me to go with you?" David asked.

"*Nein*. Stay with Anna. I believe she might be having pains. She could need you to be here to fetch the midwife."

"She had pains twice this week already—"

"And this time it could be the real thing." Aaron scrubbed his face with both hands. "When I was in the kitchen with her just now she had a spell, and it took me back. My *mamm* did the same thing with my youngest *bruder*. She had the same look on her face, the same way of closing her eyes and counting slowly. When she finally did go into labor, he was born within an hour. Stay here, David."

Moments later Seth had driven the buggy up beside him and they were on their way to the cabins. Aaron realized later that he remembered nothing of the ride, only that he was aggravated with Seth for driving so slowly. When he mentioned it to him, the boy only glowered—much like the look he often threw at his *dat*—and urged the horse into a faster trot.

Aaron was out of the buggy before they had completely stopped it in the parking lot, which was full by the time they had reached it. The *Englischers'* cars all belonged to the guests, and two police cars from the Cashton Police Department were in the lot as well.

He didn't go to the office, though he could see that officers were working inside.

He didn't go to the shop to see how much merchandise was missing.

He walked to the picnic tables, where the girls were serving breakfast. Aaron walked through the small crowd of guests, walked past Clara, and walked straight up to Lydia. He put his hands on her shoulders, and stared into her beautiful eyes.

Seeing her there, working efficiently as she did every morning, his heart finally slowed in its wild hammering, but he'd come this far at a madcap pace. No stopping now until he was sure. "Are you okay, Lydia?"

"*Ya*, of course."

"You weren't here when—"

"No."

"I was worried that maybe..." He never finished the sentence, but he did touch her face. Her skin was even softer than he'd imagined. Her eyes widened in surprise, and he felt a small amount of guilt that he'd been avoiding her lately. For the briefest of moments, it seemed as though the small crowd of guests vanished. He could imagine what it would be like, just the two of them standing along the banks of Pebble Creek.

It didn't last long.

Soon a child began crying—he wanted chocolate milk instead of plain. Another guest asked for more juice. Clara complained about the bugs landing on her stack of postcards. Even Seth grumbled in his normal fashion as he first pulled the lawn mower out, but he froze in place when an officer called out to him. Aaron glanced up and caught Seth as he asked no one in particular if he was expected to work without eating breakfast now—but there was something else in the lad's eyes, some new worry. He needed to talk to the boy privately.

The entire group under the trees brought relief to Aaron's heart. The cabins continued to run smoothly. Merchandise could be replaced—people couldn't.

He'd speak with Seth in a moment.

First, he needed to sit and pull in a few deep breaths and watch Lydia as she moved among their guests, occasionally throwing him a questioning glance.

What if she had been there when the burglar had ransacked the buildings? What if she had been hurt? What would he have done?

The questions circled and collided in his mind so that he couldn't possibly join in the breakfast that she had set out so prettily under the trees on the picnic tables they had only recently finished. Their guests were talking among themselves about the break-in, but Aaron assured them that everything was under control.

"So you've caught the person who did it?" This from an older *Englischer* who was tall and thin. "We rather enjoy it here and were thinking of coming back with our grandchildren."

"Rest assured. It will not happen again if I have to sleep on the floor of the office every night the cabins are full."

But he didn't plan on doing that. He planned on getting to the bottom of this matter and soon.

He couldn't go back to Indiana as long as the cabins' success was in jeopardy, and he certainly couldn't leave Lydia if there was any danger to her or her sister. As he walked toward the office to speak to the police, he vowed he would make this right, and part of doing so meant speaking to Lydia's parents and assuring them that Lydia and Clara would not be in harm's way.

He would take care of that tonight.

≈ Chapter 30 ≈

Gabe arrived at the cabins as the police cars were leaving. The parking lot was incredibly full—not only with *Englisch* cars from the guests but with buggies as well.

"What's happened?" he asked Seth as he tied Chance to the hitching rail.

"Burglarized." Seth rammed his hands into his pants pockets and glared across the cabin area toward the river.

"Is everyone okay?"

"*Ya*. The girls arrived and found the office door open." Seth looked as if he were going to add more, but then he shook his head and clammed up.

"Do they have any idea who did it?"

"I heard Officer Tate say there had been some burglaries on the other side of the county. They might be able to match the prints..." Seth shrugged, as if the situation were hopeless.

Gabe thought it wasn't completely impossible. There was a chance they could catch the person responsible.

Seth added, "Now the newspaper woman is here."

Looking over toward the office, Gabe caught sight of Rae. "Excellent!"

"Since when do you like folks who put our business in the paper?"

Pulling in a deep breath, Gabe reminded himself to be patient. Seth was only seventeen, and he didn't know Rae Caperton's history, how she was an advocate for Amish communities, how she had lost a very close friend who was Amish. Few people knew those details, but they were the things that had convinced Gabe and Miriam to trust her.

"I do if the person is Rae Caperton. Few burdens are heavy if everyone lifts. Rae is one of those persons who helps to lift burdens."

Seth shook his head, unconvinced. "What do you have there?"

Gabe glanced down at Grace's drawing. It wasn't much, but it could be a clue. At least it proved that the person might be someone they knew. "Something I want Aaron to see. Where is he?" He held up the piece of drawing paper. "This might help catch whoever robbed us."

Seth's eyes narrowed. "How—"

"Let's find Aaron, and then I'll only have to explain once."

But Aaron was busy.

While Lydia was checking out guests, or attempting to, and Clara had moved from writing cards to cleaning the cabins as they prepared for the next group of guests, Aaron was left to deal with restocking the shed. Filling the shelves with a new collection of Amish goods was proving to be quite a chore.

The buggies Gabe had seen in the parking lot belonged to the line of folks waiting outside the Plain Shop. Many of them were the same people Gabe had visited not so long ago. They were from the whole Pebble Creek community—both the east side and the west side. The line stretched from the front door of the shop, down the steps, and out along the path.

The gathering of Plain folk was causing the guests to stop and stare, which in turn was making Lydia's job of checking anyone out difficult.

"What's going on here?" Gabe asked Clara, who was standing and leaning against the broom she was supposed to be using to sweep off the porch of cabin two.

"You heard about the burglary?"

"*Ya.*"

"Apparently they did too."

Gabe recognized nearly everyone in line. Many were from families who attended his church on the east side of Pebble Creek, and everyone else seemed to be from the west side—families David and Lydia and Aaron would know. The men tended to be older gentlemen who Gabe knew didn't have fields to plant because their sons would be doing that this morning. His own fields were ready for the seed, but he needed to take Grace's drawing to Aaron if he could get past the crowd.

"Everyone just showed up?" he asked.

"*Ya.*"

"All of them are bringing more goods to sell?"

"Looks that way. Aaron explained he didn't know when he'd be able to pay them for what had been stolen. They only nodded and said it wasn't a problem."

"So they're replenishing his stock."

"For free."

Now Gabe understood why the *Englisch* guests were standing and watching. By now they all knew about the burglary, but what they hadn't seen before was what many in the Amish community took for granted—the way each person fell in and helped one another when adversity struck. The guests probably were not aware that Aaron didn't have insurance. They might not understand that business owners often didn't purchase insurance because Amish considered insurance a form of gambling. Rather, they depended on one another.

The line continued to grow in front of the small building with the sign reading Plain Shop. The people patiently waiting for their turn to help were proof of a system that worked. In their community, showing up to lend a hand when someone was struggling was as natural as rain or accidents or hard times. It was the biblical way, and to Gabe's way of thinking, it was the Plain way.

As Gabe watched he saw Rae making her way down the line. She'd told Miriam she planned on doing a story about the cabins, and it looked as if she'd found the perfect opportunity.

"I'm going to help Aaron," Gabe said to Seth. "When the line is gone, I want you to join us. There's something we need to talk about."

It was an hour later before he was able to sit down with Aaron, Lydia, and Clara at one of the picnic tables and show them Grace's drawing. He asked Rae to join them as well. Seth had either forgotten or become too busy.

"Grace drew this last Saturday?" Lydia asked.

"*Ya.* It doesn't prove anything," Gabe admitted. "It might not even be related to the burglary."

"Seems too big of a coincidence." Aaron gazed off toward the woods. "If someone were watching us—"

"Casing your place," Rae said. "I've been following this string of burglaries, and though they seem to be amateurs, they are taking some precautions. They only hit when the place is empty. They choose places with no video surveillance, and they're getting sloppier—like with the footprints in the mud."

"If they were casing us..." Aaron tapped the drawing, "Why did they wait until last night?"

"Or this morning." Clara moved closer to Lydia on the picnic bench.

Aaron nodded. "Could have been this morning. Why did they wait nearly a week to break in?"

"Because they knew you wouldn't be here, Aaron." Lydia turned the drawing so she could study it better. "Whoever this is, he knew you weren't staying at the cabins last night. He waited for the perfect opportunity."

Gabe combed his fingers through his beard. "All right. So it probably wasn't one of your guests unless you announced you weren't going to be here."

"*Nein.* I checked in on every cabin last night and planned on being back before they were up this morning. Plus, if it was someone who has been watching us, it couldn't have been a guest. None of them were here last week."

"Could we make a list of possible suspects?" Rae asked.

Lydia held up her right hand. "The number of men who know Aaron's comings and goings are few—you, Gabe, but we know you were with your family last night, and we trust you wouldn't do this."

"*Danki.*"

Lydia ticked off her first finger. "David."

"He was home all night. Remember? I stayed there."

"What about Seth?"

"Lydia!"

Ignoring her sister, Lydia looked at Aaron. He shifted on the bench before admitting, "I don't know where he was last night. He snuck out after I went to bed and came in late."

"Same as Stephen." Lydia held up another finger.

"You're suggesting our own *bruder* might have done this?"

"He knew no one was here. We mentioned it while we were preparing dinner. And he was also out last night, remember? I went to speak with him and couldn't find him."

"Anyone else?" Gabe asked. "I hate to point fingers at our youth. It could have been anyone."

"It could have been the *Englischer* you've been teaching farming to," Lydia said, looking at Aaron.

"Tim Elliott? He's harmless. Why would you suspect him?" Aaron crossed his arms over his chest.

"Did you mention to him that you were staying at David's?"

Aaron stared at the table, his head bobbing up and down in agreement. "*Ya.* I told him if he had trouble with the plow, I'd be staying with David for the night."

"So he knew," she said.

"He did, but he also offered to let me sleep over at his place. Would he have done that if he were going to rob me? We shouldn't distrust a man merely because he's an *Englischer.*"

Lydia crossed her arms. "*Gut* point, but you also mentioned he has a teenager. Perhaps he mentioned to his son..."

Silence fell around them as they considered their list of suspects.

"I'll run the story in the paper tonight," Rae said. "If anyone saw something, maybe they'll come forward. As far as the drawing, I think it could point to your being watched. I'd certainly be more careful, and perhaps you should mention it to Officer Tate."

Gabe hated that Grace's drawing was arousing suspicions, but he also didn't like the thought of someone being hurt by whoever had done this. "Let's pray about this, and speak with the bishop before we turn names over to Tate. We don't have any real proof."

"*Gut* idea." Aaron slapped the table with his hand and stood. "In the meantime, we don't leave the cabins unprotected."

"How are we supposed to do that?" Clara asked.

"Seth and I will take shifts."

"But if Seth is the one—" Lydia frowned, staring at the drawing which still sat in the middle of the table.

"Think about it, Lydia. If I leave him in charge, a burglary can't happen on his shift."

"I suppose not—"

"It doesn't matter. I'll be here most of the time. I have one errand tonight. After that, I plan to be here until we catch whoever is responsible."

Gabe left Grace's drawing with Aaron. It wasn't proof of anything, but at least they were working together toward resolving the crime. And from the comments he heard from the *Englischers* as he was leaving, instead of scaring guests away, what they had seen had only raised their curiosity. He had the distinct feeling the cabins were going to be busier than ever. If all of them continued to remain full, Aaron was quickly going to need a room to sleep in off the office. Until that could happen, his plan was to sleep on a cot in the Plain Shop.

Miriam sat in the hospital's waiting room. Her *dat* was holding Rachel, and she was working on a crochet project. The problem was that she kept dropping stitches, which meant pulling out the row and starting over. She'd added very little to the baby blanket she was making when the door to the back room opened and her mother walked out, followed by the radiation tech.

Abigail wasn't smiling, but she held her head high, and there was a determination in her step. Or was Miriam imagining that? Was she seeing what she wanted to see?

"I'm Roger, and I've been assigned to take care of Abigail."

Roger didn't look old enough to take care of anyone, in Miriam's opinion, but she held her tongue. He had short spiky hair and dark glasses. He waited until Abigail had sat down, leaving two empty chairs between herself and everyone else.

Everyone introduced themselves, and then Roger leaned forward. "I'd like to explain what we did today, what we still need to do, and what some of the symptoms might be."

Miriam pushed her crochet work into her bag and sat forward on the edge of her chair. Reaching for Rachel, she nodded as her father said, "*Ya.* We want to know how to help."

"That's good. Not everyone has family to support them. I'm glad Abigail will have people with her. I've given her typed instructions of everything I'm going to tell you."

Miriam met Abigail's glance and then both of them looked down to the sheets of paper clutched in Abigail's hand. Her *mamm* had yet to say a word, but she seemed fairly relaxed considering the worst part was over. At least Miriam hoped the worst part was behind them.

"I like to verbally explain the instructions in case patients have questions, especially when my patients are Amish. I realize you have access to phones, but it's not always convenient for you to use them. So let's see if there is any confusion we can clear away from the beginning."

Roger started to explain what would happen after Abigail swallowed the single dose of radioactive iodine.

"You mean she hasn't already taken it?" Miriam looked from her mother back to Roger. "I thought that's what we came here for."

Roger made eye contact with Abigail, who nodded slightly. "The plan was to take the dosage while she was here, but because she has a long car ride back, and because you came along, Miriam, with the baby, we decided it would be best to wait until she's at home."

"I don't understand."

"Once Abigail takes the iodine, she shouldn't sit in a car next to someone for more than an hour. It's a two-hour drive back, at best. Abigail didn't want to put her driver at risk or either of you. Miriam, since you're still nursing, you especially should not be in close, confined proximity to Abigail for the next week, and she shouldn't be with the baby at all."

Miriam stared at Roger. She thought she was prepared for a lot of things, but not this. Rae's printouts had discussed the side effects and the success rates, but not these precautions.

"Another option would have been to have an ambulance transport Abigail back home—"

"*Nein.* I won't be needing an ambulance. I can take a pill on my own."

"Should Doc Hanson come out and check on her?" Joshua asked.

"Yes, and his nurse, Virginia, will be there when she takes the dosage this afternoon. Please don't feel that your visit today was a waste. I still needed to conduct some tests, and I needed to see Abigail before I could release the dosage to her. Abigail technically has Graves' disease, a type of hyperthyroidism. This is why her doctor has recommended treating her with the radioactive iodine."

"But not surgery?" Miriam asked.

"Surgery is rarely recommended in these cases."

He went on to explain that the medicine would in theory destroy part of her thyroid gland without harming any other parts of her body. The list of side effects was long, but Doc Hanson had already warned them of those, so there was nothing alarming there. If neck tenderness, nausea, and swollen glands was the worst Abigail had to deal with, and the result was she eventually would be her old healthy self again, they were all for it.

More alarming were the precautions they would have to take for the next week.

"So she can't see Rachel at all?" Miriam asked.

"It's better that she isn't near any children or anyone who is nursing or might be pregnant." Roger waited until Abigail met his gaze. "We've talked about this at length. I realize you all have a large family and this will be difficult for her, but it's only for a week, and I know she doesn't want to make anyone else sick."

"I have plenty of sewing to do," Abigail said.

"*Ya.* She likes to sew." Joshua ran his right thumb under his suspenders. "The *grandkinner*, they can write her letters for a week. It will be all right. What else?"

"The rest is fairly straightforward. She needs to sleep alone, use separate towels and eating utensils—"

"Sounds like a shunning, *ya?*" Joshua looked at Miriam and winked.

"And she can't prepare your food."

A hint of a smile appeared on Abigail's face. "I'm grateful it's only for a week, Joshua. Otherwise you might starve."

Roger talked about the follow-up exam she would have in four weeks and reminded Abigail that in most cases one treatment was sufficient. By the time they were finished, Miriam was sorry she had questioned his youth. There was no doubt he knew all about hyperthyroidism and how to care for his patients.

Abigail stood. "*Danki*, Roger. You've been very helpful."

"If you have any questions at all, or if you have any side effects that aren't listed on this sheet, call myself, Dr. Hanson, or nine-one-one from the closest phone."

She nodded, or it could have been that she waved him away.

"Abigail, I do want you to contact Dr. Hanson at the first signs of inflammation, and be sure to go in for your follow-up visit. In rare cases, we need to administer a second dose—but it's important in those cases that we do so in a timely fashion."

"You made that clear before. I understand."

"I know you do, and I appreciate your patience with me. I'm used to repeating myself." Roger stood and shook hands with Joshua. He squatted down so that he was on eye level with Rachel.

"You have a beautiful *boppli*," he said.

His use of the Amish term surprised her. Miriam couldn't help laughing when Rachel smiled at him. "*Danki.*"

"Safe travels on your way back to Cashton. If you need a telephone to call your driver, there's one at the information desk for your use."

They waited until he'd gone behind the door marked "No Admittance" before they started talking.

"He's used to working with Amish folk," Miriam said as she stood and gathered her things.

"Roger's grandmother was Mennonite. He grew up in the Mennonite church but is now Presbyterian." Abigail glanced at Rachel but did not move any closer.

"You can hold her now, *ya*?"

"I suppose, but why chance it? No telling what I touched back there. I will be very grateful when this week is up and I can hold that sweet baby again. I miss her already."

Miriam glanced over Abigail's head and saw the way her father's eyes took in his wife and his granddaughter. Her too, she supposed.

Three generations joined together.

Life was fragile, there was no doubt about it, but love was strong. She was so grateful they were together, that they could follow Roger's directions and care for Abigail—that odds were that Abigail would recover just fine.

More importantly, as they walked from the hospital out into the May sunshine, Miriam felt the strength coming from the understanding that their family had a history both tall and wide. It was a history filled with others who would stand in and offer their hands to help, their hearts to love, and their voices to lift up prayers on their behalf.

Her fears relieved, she followed behind her parents, as she held her baby because her mother couldn't or wouldn't. She finally had a peace in knowing that whatever the outcome, God's grace would be sufficient.

≈ Chapter 31 ≈

Lydia stared out over the front of Tin Star as she drove her buggy next to Seth's. It wasn't odd for Seth to leave at the same time she and Clara did, but it was odd for Aaron to be climbing up into Seth's buggy alone. What was even more shocking was what he had just said.

"You're doing what?" she asked. She'd heard him, clear as day, but she was hoping his answer might change if he repeated it.

"I'm following you home."

"I don't understand."

Aaron studied her a minute before securing the reins to his horse and hopping out of the buggy. When he was standing beside hers, he said, "I should have talked to you earlier, but today was—"

"Brutal, *narrisch*, exhausting?"

"All of those things, so I didn't have the chance." He looked past her, over her shoulder to Clara—who was making no attempt to hide the fact that she was listening to every word. "Lydia, I need to speak with your parents."

"What?" Lydia's heart thundered in her chest so loudly she feared Tin Star would hear it and grow spooked. The day had been draining on so many different levels. Her emotions had run in too many different directions from the moment she'd discovered the burglary

245

through Aaron showing up, walking up to her, and showing such concern, to Gabe bringing Grace's drawing. Now Aaron wanted to go to her home?

She wasn't ready for this. Not today.

"You can't."

"Lydia—" Clara leaned forward.

"Stay out of our conversation." Lydia pushed her sister back to her side of the buggy and then she returned her attention to Aaron. "My parents...well, there are things I'm not ready to explain. Tonight wouldn't be *gut*."

Aaron stepped closer and lowered his voice. "I won't stay long, but I will see your *mamm* and *dat* tonight. I've borrowed Seth's buggy, and I'm following you home, so it's best we start and get this over with."

Lydia felt her temper spike at Aaron's words. What right did he have? She hadn't invited him. She didn't want him in her house, and she couldn't tell him why. So he knew about her *dat*'s illness. He didn't know about their poverty. He didn't know how they lived—a family of eight in a home built for four. He didn't know about all they'd lost and how they had adjusted. He didn't know and she couldn't explain it to him today of all days.

Instead, she forced all emotion from her voice and wiped all expression from her face. "Fine."

"Fine."

"I hope you won't be expecting supper."

Rather than grow angry with her, she thought he was going to reach up and touch her. What was with him today? "Of course not. I wouldn't invite myself to dinner, Lydia."

She nodded but didn't move. She just sat there and waited for him to walk away from Tin Star. When he finally did, she set her gelding to a trot.

"Why were you so rude to him?"

"Because he's never been to our home. He doesn't realize how truly sick *dat* is. He's seen him at church meeting, but never when he's very ill, and he hasn't seen where we live—how we live."

"Are you embarrassed of our home?"

"The last thing I need is his pity!" The confession released some of the pressure from her chest. As they traveled down the road, Lydia allowed the motion of the buggy to calm her. Clara wisely remained quiet, waiting until they were well on their way before chirping up.

"Do you think he wants to talk to *dat* about our *bruder?*"

"I couldn't begin to guess what he wants to say to our parents, but if you know anything about where Stephen was last night, it's best you tell me now."

Clara chewed on her thumbnail and stared out of the buggy for the space of a dozen heart beats.

"Clara?"

"I don't know for sure."

"But you have an idea."

"He runs with the older boys sometimes."

"Which older boys?"

Clara reeled off a few names, including Seth's. Some of them were Amish, some *Englisch*. A few of them Lydia knew, but many of them she didn't.

"Some of those boys have taken to drinking, *ya?* And I think I heard one or two of them have even been caught using drugs."

"I think those are rumors, Lydia. Stephen would never be involved in such a thing."

"Let's hope so. For our *bruder*'s sake, let's hope so."

When they reached the house, Lydia was relieved to see that Stephen was home to take care of Tin Star. Aaron said he'd only be staying a little while, and left Seth's horse and buggy in the shade.

Lydia found her parents where they always were in the late afternoon—in the sitting room, her mother near her father in case he needed her. Menno had the *Budget* open across his lap and Ella had her sewing basket near her, completing some darning in the last of the afternoon's light coming through the large window. Her younger sisters were attending to chores outside, though they peeked around the corner, giggling, when they saw Aaron.

Her parents had met Aaron at the last church gathering, and he quickly apologized for showing up uninvited.

"It's no problem at all," Ella said. "Please, stay and eat with us."

"I can't. Seth will be waiting for his buggy."

"All right. Clara, I've started dinner. Would you be a dear and see to finishing it?"

Clara would have never done this if Lydia had asked, not at home, and not after working at the cabins all day. But she smiled sweetly in Aaron's direction and left the room.

Menno passed the newspaper to his wife, who folded it and set it aside.

"The reason I stopped by today is that I assumed you both would have heard what happened at the cabins."

"You mean about the burglary," Ella murmured. "A terrible thing."

"Yes, and that Lydia and Clara were the first ones to find this out." Aaron's eyes sought and found Lydia's. She wondered again what he was thinking and why he was here. At that moment Amanda and Martha ran past one of the windows, chasing a squealing piglet that had escaped from its pen.

Lydia wanted to curl up and die.

As if it wasn't bad enough for Aaron to see how small her house was, to understand how poor they had become since her father's illness, now he had to see her sisters chasing swine!

Aaron smiled—maybe his first genuine, relaxed smile all day—and continued. "I want to assure you, Mr. Fisher—"

"Call me Menno." Her father's voice was strained as he attempted to pull in a deep breath.

Aaron didn't even flinch. "Menno, I wanted to assure you, you and Lydia's *mamm*, that what happened today will never happen again. I can't promise the cabins won't be robbed. We hope not, and the police are working to catch who did this." He ran his hand over his hair, having removed his hat when he walked in the house. "What I can promise is that from this point forward there will always be a man on the property."

He stared down at the floor for a moment, and the only sounds were Clara in the kitchen, the girls on the porch, and off in the distance, a heifer calling to its calf.

"I should have been there, but I wasn't. If either of your *dochdern* had been hurt, it would have been my fault. I'm sorry."

"Forgiven." Menno's hand waved away any supposed sin.

"Starting tonight, I'll sleep at the cabins, even if they're full. When I have to leave, for any reason, I'll be sure Seth or David or Gabe are on the property." He turned to Lydia. "I'm sorry, Lydia. I'm sorry if you were in any danger this morning."

She couldn't have answered him if she wanted to. Her heart was beating such a rapid rhythm that she could barely hear his words, though he was sitting next to her on the couch. So instead she nodded, like someone who was mute, and stared down at her hands.

"I should be going," he said, standing and reaching for his hat.

"*Danki*, for coming by." Ella stood as well. "I have some fresh-baked cookies in the kitchen. Let me wrap up a few for you."

As she left the room, Menno pulled in another ragged breath. "It was *Gotte* who brought you here, Aaron."

Glancing at Lydia, Aaron turned his hat round and round in his hands. "Yes. I believe you're right."

Lydia followed him back outside, carrying the plate of cookies her *mamm* had wrapped in a dishcloth.

"I'm sorry I was so upset about your following me home."

When Aaron only studied her and waited, she added, "I didn't want you to see…all of this." Her hand encompassed the small house, the meager yard, and the tiny barn with the ragged enclosure for the few animals they could afford.

"You're ashamed of where you live?"

"*Nein*. It's not that." Lydia looked past their home, to the next property. A fence separated the two. "See that home? The creek runs through both places, but that home has pastures, a large barn, and fields to cultivate. If we had that home, my *bruder* could learn to be a farmer, like my *dat* was a farmer and his *dat*. But we don't live on that side of the fence. We live on this side, and I suppose I'm okay with that."

"But—"

"But I'm not sure others understand. We're happy our *dat* is alive. Happy for every day we have with him, though it has come at a cost. The farm we once had, we sold and bought this smaller place with the money. Now there isn't any hope of going back to that life."

Aaron reached out and touched her chin, raising her eyes to his. "There's always hope, Lydia."

She didn't know how to answer that, so she stepped back and waited until he had climbed into Seth's buggy and driven away. Slowly she walked over to the fence and watched the last of the sun's rays spread across the water of Pebble Creek.

The property next door was for sale—its sign sitting next to the road proclaiming it available. BUY NOW. GREAT PRICE. FINANCING AVAILABLE. The words pricked her heart each time she read them. Someone would purchase the pastures, barn, and home. Maybe they would be Amish or maybe they would be *Englisch*—like the man Timothy Elliott. It didn't matter. She knew it was wrong to covet what wasn't theirs.

It wasn't the property she longed for, though. It was a home her heart desired. A home to raise her own family in.

A home where her sisters could visit and her brother could learn the trade of his father—the father who now struggled for his health each day.

A home was what Lydia longed for, and she understood it was something you couldn't purchase.

Chapter 32

Gabe accepted Rachel from Miriam.

"Are you sure you won't come in with us?" Miriam asked him as they stood outside the town library.

"It's a beautiful June day. Think I'll sit outside with this girl and watch the Friday afternoon traffic go by."

"We'll only be a minute. Grace needs to return her books and check out more, and I wanted to see if they have any new ones with knitting patterns—"

When his *fraa* stopped midsentence, Gabe glanced up to see what had stolen her attention. His entire family pulled in a deep breath as Miss Bena strode down the sidewalk toward them.

"Hello, Sylvia."

"Miriam. Gabe." Miss Bena didn't smile, but she did stop. It would have been impolite to brush past them. She seemed to realize that at least, though she appeared to be at something of a loss as to what to say next.

"Nice day to visit the library," Gabe offered.

"Indeed. It's *gut* to see you, Grace."

Grace nodded and stepped closer to her *mamm.*

"Well, *gut* day to you." Miss Bena turned to walk into the library and had opened the door when Miriam called out to her.

"Sylvia, would you like to come to dinner Sunday afternoon?"

Miss Bena's features froze, reminding Gabe so much of a frightened rabbit that he almost laughed out loud.

He didn't laugh, though, because another part of him remembered when he'd first come to Wisconsin. He'd built walls around his life, tall sturdy walls. He had been so afraid someone might breech them, that they might find a way into the safe, private life he'd built for himself and Grace. He would often search for ways to avoid such dinners.

Was Sylvia Bena doing the same?

Miriam pushed on. "My mother is so much better. We're having a small celebration. We'd be pleased if you'd join us."

"We have a nest of birds down by the creek. Ones I haven't been able to identify." It was the first Grace had spoken since her teacher had walked up. "If you came, maybe you could help me. I've looked in the books, but I still haven't been able to figure them out, and I'd like to draw them."

Miss Bena's lips softened into something that might one day resemble a smile. "I usually stay home on Sundays we don't have church, but I suppose I could make an exception."

"Do you need directions?" Gabe asked.

"No. I can find it." She turned and entered the library.

"That was odd," Grace whispered. "She almost smiled."

"You noticed too, huh?" Gabe bounced Rachel on his knee, causing her to cackle and blow bubbles.

"How did you know her name was Sylvia, *mamm*?"

"Everyone has a first name, Grace. You didn't think we all call her Miss Bena, did you?"

"None of the students ever called you Miss Miriam, but Miss Bena is, well she's different. She's a bit more..." Grace glanced up at her *mamm* as if she were searching for a word.

"Formal?" Miriam asked.

"*Ya*. That's it. Formal and serious."

As his *fraa* and *dochder* walked into the library, Gabe leaned back against the street bench. It was turning into a fine summer. Crops were in the ground, and it looked as if they would have a good harvest in spite of the heavy spring rains and late start.

Elizabeth Troyer drove by, her buggy full of girls, and he raised a hand in greeting. The cabins were doing well. He expected to hear any day that Aaron was headed back to Indiana. He would miss his new friend. The boy seemed to belong here, though he didn't realize it yet. At least there had been no more break-ins in Pebble Creek. Rae had stopped at the house and told them a similar burglary had occurred near where she lived.

The important thing was that the cabins were now busy on a regular basis. Elizabeth had shared with Miriam that they would definitely be able to stay in the Cashton area.

She would need to find someone to take over the running of the cabins when Aaron left, but Gabe had no doubt there would be plenty of interested applicants. Lots of dependable Amish folk in the area who would be interested in a steady income.

As for himself, he was content farming.

Grace thought Sunday's luncheon was the best picnic they'd ever had. Even having Miss Bena there worked out well.

The nest of birds had stumped Miss Bena, who suggested they meet at the library again next week to try to figure out what the little guys were. "You draw well, Grace. Spend some time down here this week, if you can. Bring your tablet to the library, and we'll compare what you've drawn to the reference books."

Grace wasn't sure she'd ever received a compliment from Miss Bena before. More important than that, her teacher seemed as interested as she was in learning the identity of the tiny birds before they flew. Grace had caught sight of the mother bird only once.

"Some moms are shy," Miss Bena had said. "And sometimes they learn to hide so they won't be hurt." A shadow had crossed over her face when she said that, but when Grace asked her *mamm* why, Miriam only told her to run and play.

So she did. She played with Sadie, whose family had come because they lived so close. Together they visited Gus and Hunter and Stanley. They even tried to lure Stormy into playing, but he was lying in the sun, and that sleepy cat wouldn't so much as chase a ball of yarn.

When they were tired of running around, she asked, "Wanna see my new cousin?"

"Sure. How new?"

"Less than a month. We can't hold her. She's tiny and her skin is still wrinkled."

They found Anna inside changing baby Abigail's diaper.

"You named her after Grace's *mammi?*" Sadie asked, touching the baby carefully with one finger.

"We did. Baby Abigail's *grossmammi* gave us quite a scare." Anna smiled as she snugged a blanket around the infant.

"She's better now." Grace proclaimed. "She's even knitting again, and this summer she's showing me how to do all sorts of things like knit and crochet and quilt better."

"I'm a terrible quilter." Sadie ran her hand along the porch railing as they walked down the steps.

"*Mammi* says we have lots of time to get better."

"I guess." Sadie looked back through the front screen door. "Think you'll have another baby in your family?"

"*Ya.* I expect to get the news any day now." Grace started giggling. "They still kiss a lot!"

Sadie plopped down on the front step. "I think my family's done and I'm glad. No more room."

"I wonder how many kids I'll have when I'm grown. How many will you have? Do you want a lot?" Grace asked.

"Ew! I don't want to do all that kissing."

"Well...maybe it's not so bad once you get older."

"That's what my *mamm* said about broccoli, but I still don't like it."

"True. I saw more cookies on the dessert table. Wanna go and get some?"

"*Ya.* Race you." Sadie was off and running before Grace could blink.

The problem was that Grace was always thinking about the way things looked, like Sadie running across the green grass in her blue dress. That combination made for a nice picture she could draw.

So she stopped and she pulled out her tablet and sketched the outline of what she saw. By the time she caught up with Sadie, her favorite cookies, the oatmeal ones, were gone. Which taught her that if she dawdled, or if she doodled, there was sometimes a price to pay. Might be worth it though—the sketch of Sadie running toward the tables was going to be a good one.

When she finished it. There were still the details and shading to add. Maybe she'd have time later this afternoon. That was one good thing about summer. There was more extra time. She did miss school already, though. She missed seeing her friends, and she even missed class a little.

She selected one of the peanut butter cookies and caught up with Sadie. Peanut butter was all right. They were her second favorites, and sometimes art called for sacrifice.

Chapter 33

Aaron should have known things had been going too well. Reservations were holding strong and the cabins were booked up into the fall. His three employees were managing to get along—and yes, he still needed Clara and Seth as well as Lydia. But something told him the burglaries weren't over, something more than Rae Caperton's occasional visit to check on them.

He suspected that if the culprit attacked again, it would be on a Monday night. He was tired of waiting, so he'd planted a story that he'd be gone—only Lydia and Clara were supposed to have left already. Apparently, the girls had caught wind of his plan.

He reached forward and pulled both of them back into the shadow of the roof overhang of cabin three, his heart racing to match the patter of the rain. Though the last month had been warm and sunny, it seemed to him in that moment as if it had been raining since the day he'd stepped off the bus in Cashton, Wisconsin.

"Where do you think you're going?" he hissed.

"I'm going to catch whoever is doing this." Lydia tried to shake off his hand, which still firmly clutched her arm.

"And I'm going with her. You don't think I'd let her go alone, do you?"

"Neither one of you is going alone. In fact, neither one of you is going." The light summer rain, rain that was sure to bless Gabe's and David's crops, covered the sound of their voices.

Aaron could just make out Lydia's expression in the glow of the battery-operated night-light they had installed on the porch. Though he didn't need good lighting to picture what she looked like. He knew her well enough to envision the irritation and stubbornness. Her eyes were squinted, eyebrows were pulled together, and lips were drawn in a straight light.

He'd never known a woman as willful as Lydia Fisher.

Which only increased his desire to take care of her. The ones who didn't know they needed protecting were often the ones who trudged out into danger.

He could see it in her pose. She was ready to slosh across the wet grass and demand a confession from whoever was in their office.

And her little sister would tag along behind her.

"Let's go, Lydia. He can't keep us both here." Clara tossed her head, sending her *kapp* strings flying. The girl had more sass than he would have thought possible in a young Amish woman. He didn't envy the man who fell for that one.

"I might not be able to keep you both here, but you do both know I'm right. Confronting whoever is in the office right now would be foolish."

"Are we going to allow them to take the last toy off the shelf and the last quilt off the wall?"

"Not to mention the last dollar out of the drawer?" Lydia moved the branches of the speckled alder, the same bush he'd tried to cut back to oblivion in May. It had leafed out quite nicely again since that day, providing them good cover. "They've been in our office for five minutes, and apparently had no problem getting through our new lock. How is that possible?"

"I don't know, but we need to go for help, not rush in like three fools."

"Go for help?" They both turned toward him, but it was Clara who spoke. Lydia reserved her condemnation to a stare and a sad shake of her head. "How would you even make it to the barn without them seeing you? And by the time you got back, they'd be gone!"

"Clara's right. This doesn't sound like you, anyway, Aaron." Now Lydia put her hands on her hips, and he felt his throat go dry. He did not need a confrontation with her right now.

"You've fought awfully hard to bring these cabins back from near ruin." Lydia ran her fingers over her lips, as if she could bring forth the words that would reveal his secrets. "Now you're just going to let them get away with this? I don't think so. Not when we're finally turning a profit."

She turned and stepped off the front porch.

Aaron knew in that moment that he had no choice. He had to act.

Lydia thought she was a big girl. He heard the disparaging comments she sometimes made about herself. But he thought she was beautiful and precious, and he knew she weighed hardly more than Clara—maybe just another ten or fifteen pounds.

He reached forward and grabbed her around the waist, picking her up with no problem. With his free hand he opened the door of cabin three. He shoved her inside in one fluid motion and grasped Clara's hand, Clara who was staring at him as if he'd lost his mind—and maybe he had. He pushed her in as well.

Pulling the door shut, he grabbed the master key out of his pocket and overrode the inside lock.

"Aaron! Aaron, what are you doing?" Lydia's voice was startled, and he almost smiled. He'd finally done something that surprised her.

"He locked us inside." Clara rattled the door, her tone clearly insulted.

"Aaron, let us out right now!"

"Keep your voices down. We don't know if they're armed." He rested both hands against the door. They might raise the window and crawl out, but it was a good drop to the ground. They would risk turning an ankle—and they would have to pry off the window screen first. He didn't think Lydia would actually damage property in order to escape the cabin. Surely they wouldn't resort to that. He prayed they wouldn't.

"I'll hurry and see if I can catch a glimpse of them and identify who it is. As soon as I do I'll go after Officer Tate."

The girls had stopped arguing with him, but someone continued to rattle the doorknob.

"Wait here, please."

He prayed once more that *Gotte* would keep them safe, and then he turned and crept out into the rain.

Lydia kicked the door, and then she realized mud covered the toes of her shoes. She'd be cleaning that off later—more work! Exactly what she did not need.

"Why would he do that?" Clara smacked the door with her hand. "He's so rude, so arrogant, and so mean!"

Lydia turned on her sister with a vengeance, yanking her away from the door. "He was trying to protect us!"

Clara pulled back, rubbed at her arms. "What is it with you two? You're worse than *mamm* and *dat*. It's not as if I'm a child, and you're not, either. And it's not as if *dat* could protect us anyway."

Maybe it was the rain, her frustration, or being locked in a room with Clara, but for the first time in a long time, Lydia listened past her sister's words. She listened to the hurt lurking beneath.

"It doesn't always take strength to protect someone. *Dat* protects us with his prayers and his words. He guides us in many ways, even though he's physically weak."

Clara plopped onto the bed, a sigh escaping her lips. "Do you believe that?"

"I do."

"That sounds like something *mamm* would say."

"Should I apologize for that?" Lydia sat beside her on the bed.

"I guess not." Silence enveloped them until Lydia became aware of the sound of rain dripping on the roof of the cabin.

Clara plucked at the quilt top, her voice softening and merging with the sounds of the night. "Everyone thinks I don't remember *dat* being strong, but I do. Sally Ann, Amanda, and Martha might not remember, but I do. He used to pick me up as though I weighed no more than a loaf of bread."

Lydia thought of interrupting, but instead she waited as she listened for the bark of a rifle shot or the rumble of an *Englisch* car starting.

What was Aaron doing now? Should they try to escape the cabin and go after him?

"When I see how he's changed, it makes me sad, Lydia. It breaks my heart."

"It's not a sin to feel heartache over what has happened to him." Lydia reached out in the darkness and covered Clara's hand with her own.

"But you still believe it's *Gotte's wille?*"

"I believe *Gotte* has a plan for *dat.*" She searched her heart and added, "I don't understand it, but I trust Him. It's only hard sometimes to know how we're supposed to meet the needs of our family..."

Clara turned her hand over underneath Lydia's and laced their fingers together. "Sometimes I think if I were to marry soon, it would be one less worry."

Lydia snorted. "Is that why you go to the singings every week? *Dat* would not want you to marry for any reason other than that you had met the person *Gotte* meant for you."

"How will I know?"

Were they actually having this conversation right now? Lydia's mind turned to Aaron, who could be confronting the burglars even while she talked to Clara about courting. "You'll know. If you're not sure, wait."

"I'm not *gut* at waiting," Clara admitted.

"Runs in the family."

"Seems as though we could be doing something to help Aaron right now."

"I agree."

"Are you *in lieb* with him, Lydia?"

"What?" Lydia's voice jumped a notch, and she released Clara's hand.

"It's confusing watching you two. You argue about almost everything, but then you'll laugh at the same moment. And you often blush when he looks your way. I don't understand."

"Let's focus on tonight's problem."

"Maybe we could think of a way out of this cabin if we worked together instead of fighting all the time."

Lydia didn't answer.

Had her sister received a bump on the head when Aaron had pushed them inside?

Why had she even agreed to come back and check on him? They should have gone home. They should be making dinner right now. Why was Clara suddenly talking like a reasonable young woman instead of her bratty little sister? Why the change in attitude?

And why was she pulling her off the bed toward the window?

"Aaron told us to stay here," Lydia reminded her.

"When did you start minding him?"

"He locked the door from the outside."

"There's a window."

"This is cabin three. There's a slope. The window's built on the high side, and we would be jumping into the wet grass. If one of us turns an ankle—"

"It'll be like when we were *kinner* and playing outside." Clara was already working on the latch. "Find me a flashlight?"

"*Nein*. The burglars might see us." Lydia realized there was no stopping her sister once an idea took root in her mind, and she was tired of waiting. "You open the right latch. I'll open the left. They slide left to right to unlock."

Would she regret agreeing to this?

The summer night air came through the window with a whoosh, and with it the soft rain still falling. "Help me with the screen so it doesn't fall out into the mud."

Clara held the tabs at the bottom while Lydia inched the screen up. It raised enough for her to slide her fingers underneath the frame and pull it into the room.

"I'll go first," Clara said.

"No, you don't. I'll go first, and if it's dangerous, you'll stay here. If I whistle, you'll stay here. Agreed?"

She felt more than saw Clara's nod.

So she climbed over the sill, careful that her dress didn't catch on the window casing. She couldn't tell how much of a drop it would be. She couldn't see anything as she hung there, her feet dangling in the darkness.

So she closed her eyes, pictured the wall of the cabin on the slope, and let go.

Chapter 34

Aaron had no intentions of confronting the two men rifling through the office cabinets.

As he crouched beneath the windows, peeking inside, he tried to get a better look. All he could make out was their clothing—work boots, leaving muddy tracks all over Lydia's clean floor, blue jeans, long-sleeved cotton shirts, and baseball caps.

Both men had brown hair that went below the baseball caps and reached to their collars.

Both men had their backs to him as they searched through the desk and the filing cabinet.

They each carried a duffel bag, which they were dumping things into, apparently anything they found to be of value.

If they would just turn around, Aaron might be able to tell if they were Amish or *Englisch*. He might be able to tell if he knew them.

He'd looked for a car or buggy first, but there was nothing in the parking area. They must have left their ride farther down the road. So again—they could be Amish or *Englisch*.

He'd been hunkered in the rain for ten minutes, watching, water from the roof dripping down the neck of his shirt, when he heard a noise behind him.

Turning, at first he saw only darkness, but then he made out the white prayer *kapps* of Lydia and Clara.

He wanted to rant. He wanted to holler at them for not staying put. But he did not want to alert the robbers, so he kept his mouth shut and motioned them beneath the sill of the window.

They crept closer and peered inside.

At the exact moment Lydia and Clara pressed their faces to the glass pane, the taller of the two burglars turned toward them. Young and clean shaven, the man's face was gaunt, his eyes sunken and bloodshot. Aaron's first thought was that this was a very ill person, someone who must need the money for medical reasons. But if that were the case, and he were Amish, he'd only need to make his need known. He'd only need to ask.

Whatever the situation, he didn't appear to notice them. Unaware of the flashlight in his hand, its beam shining up on the ceiling, he stood there for maybe fifteen seconds. Instead of calling out, or running, he stared past them for a moment, and then he walked across the room and began shoveling David's toys into his duffel bag.

Aaron became aware that Clara was clutching his arm, pulling him down and away from the window. When all three of them were crouched near the ground, huddled in the darkness, she hissed, "I know who that is!"

"What?" Lydia squeaked.

"It's Jerry Beiler!"

"The bishop's nephew?"

"*Ya.*"

"You're sure?"

"Positive."

"Girls, I hate to interrupt, but if you're certain maybe that's all we need to know. We can go to the phone shack and call Officer Tate. As long as you can identify him—"

Aaron never finished his sentence.

Before he had a chance, before he even realized what she was doing, Clara had let go of his arm. Initially he was relieved to have the pinching sensation stop, but then he understood she meant to go inside. She meant to confront this Jerry Beiler.

He reached out for her, but his hand closed around darkness.

Lydia was also gone. She was sprinting after her sister.

And he was running to catch up, following them up the steps of the office, through the front door, and into the midst of the burglary.

As they thundered through the door, the two burglars turned to stare at them, their hands frozen in the middle of pouring more goods into their bags.

Aaron understood two things instantly.

The taller of the two was more than ill. He was off in some other sense, completely disconnected from the reality around him.

And the second burglar? He was not a *he* at all, but rather an Amish girl, no older than Clara.

Lydia skidded to a stop in the middle of the room, bumping into her sister, who had stopped a few feet shy of Jerry Beiler. Maybe she was mistaken. Could the eighteen-year-old in front of her be Jerry? She hadn't seen him in several years. Now that she was closer and saw him in the light of his and Mattie Keim's flashlights, she wasn't absolutely sure.

It was their neighbor Mattie standing beside him, though she wore a man's clothes, with a ball cap covering her hair. She looked pale and scared, but not sick—not like Jerry. Only determined.

"Jerry! Are you *narrisch*? Why are you here? Why are you stealing from us?" Clara threw the words at him, as though they were rocks, and she could make him drop his flashlight and duffel bag and run away.

Instead, Jerry clutched the bag in his hand and glanced first at Mattie, back at them, and then to Mattie again—his eyes widening. He flinched at Clara's words, drawing back into himself, pulling his jacket around his shoulders tighter and looking up at the ceiling. Did he expect more people to jump out at him?

"Clara?" he asked, but he didn't sound certain as he pointed the beam of his flashlight directly at them.

"Of course it's me. I work here. Who else would it be? Me and my *schweschder* and Aaron also." Clara's voice remained loud and angry, like when she was scolding one of the younger girls at home.

Lydia reached out, put her hand on Clara's arm, and pulled her back away from Jerry a few steps. There was something about him that bothered her. Something that wasn't right. His eyes continued to dart about, and he had a hacking cough.

Mattie still hadn't spoken. She had moved closer to Jerry's side of the room.

What was she missing? What was actually going on here?

Aaron seemed to sense it as well. He spoke in calm, even tones. "Jerry, I'm going to light this lantern, the one over the table." He held up his hands, as if to show he had no weapon.

Jerry twitched or maybe he shrugged. He wiped his nose on the sleeve of his jacket. By the time the lantern was lit, he had resumed shoving items from the shelves into his bag.

"Stop!" Clara still hadn't lowered her voice. "Why are you doing that?"

"Because he needs to." It was the first words Mattie had spoken. "Because *we* need to."

They all turned toward her in the soft light of the table lantern. She clicked off her flashlight and slipped it into the pocket of her oversized jeans.

"Mattie, I don't understand." Clara moved toward her, but Mattie raised her hand to stay her off.

"You don't understand. No. Of course you don't. How could you?"

"Did you...did you steal the key from me? Is that how you got into the office? The one I lost? Did you take it from my pocket at church? Why would you do that? I thought you were my *freind*."

"And what do you know of being a *freind*, Clara Fisher? Did you notice Jerry growing sicker each day? Did you notice the way his clothes droop on him like fabric on a scarecrow? Maybe you did and you looked away. Fine! Fine. We don't need you. But don't stare at me that way for taking a key. Leave us alone. We'll get what we came for and then we'll be on our way."

"You will not." Clara stomped her foot. "Aaron won't let you."

Lydia was listening to Mattie, trying to hear what she was saying beneath her words. While the girl was talking to them she never took her eyes off Jerry. She didn't look afraid exactly, but terribly sad and more than a little concerned. Though her words spoke of a deep pain, her voice never rose. She used the same tone Miriam did when Rachel was sleeping. Only Mattie spoke almost as if she was afraid of Jerry, almost as if she wasn't sure what he would do next.

Lydia remembered now that she had heard the two were courting. But were they accomplices? They certainly looked like it, dressed the same, both holding duffel bags filled with stolen goods.

But something was off, other than the fact that they were being burglarized.

Why was Mattie watching Jerry as warily as they were?

The feeling persisted that things were very wrong between these two. Something she didn't yet understand.

Jerry was ignoring them, still stuffing items in his bag. She noticed he worked with jerky movements, and he kept pausing every few seconds to scratch at his arms and his torso. His face was even shinier in the light of the table lamp.

Was he sick? Running a fever, maybe? Why wasn't he concerned about being caught?

And what was going on with Mattie? Why was she supporting him in this burglary?

She had heard rumors about Jerry—that he'd been on his *rumspringa* too long. That Bishop Beiler might send him away to live in a different district, or even send him to live with a Mennonite group. She'd heard about the drinking parties with *Englischers* and even with other Amish boys, but she hadn't witnessed it herself or asked Clara since the night they had caught Stephen staying out late.

Mattie was a good girl, though.

Lydia knew Mattie's family, who lived close to her parents' home. It hadn't been that long since Mattie had been in school with Clara. What could have gone so wrong in only a few years? And why hadn't Lydia noticed it? Had she been so caught up in her own problems that she hadn't taken the time to pay attention to a family who attended church with them?

Guilt and regret washed over her, much like the rain still falling gently outside the window. Mattie and Jerry were a part of their community. This shouldn't be happening. They shouldn't be stealing, and certainly Aaron shouldn't call the *Englisch* police.

Whatever the cause of this problem, they could handle it among themselves.

They could call their parents and talk it over.

While she'd been sorting through her feelings, and studying Mattie, Clara had moved closer to Jerry and was now trying to take the duffel bag from him.

"Give it back. It's not yours."

Jerry pushed her away hard enough to knock her into the pie safe. Dishes rattled and a bowl they used for serving fruit fell off the top shelf, landing on the floor and shattering. Jerry flinched, as if the shattered pottery had somehow pierced his world in a way they hadn't been able to.

Lydia stepped forward, moving toward Clara, ready to step around the table to help her.

Clara had hit the edge of the pie safe, and though she hadn't fallen to the floor, she was off balance. She grabbed the edge of the table as an "Oh" escaped from her lips and her feet nearly came out from under her.

Aaron was closest, and he moved to catch her, to keep her from falling completely between the table and the cabinet.

Everyone was moving too quickly. Later, Lydia realized maybe the problem was the shadows or the abrupt silence left by the absence of Clara's accusations.

Whatever it was, it spooked Jerry.

He turned back toward them suddenly. In one smooth movement, he pulled a knife from his pocket, touching a button on the handle to release the blade. Even in the dim light from the lamp hanging over the table, Lydia could see how sharp and long the edge was when it popped opened.

How deadly.

"Get back," Jerry screamed. "Just get back. Why are you here? Why are you after me? I want you to leave me alone!"

But he moved toward them, jabbing at the air with the tip of the blade, striking the air in front of Clara and Aaron.

No one spoke for several seconds.

Aaron stayed where he was, between the pie safe and the table, Clara half in his arms. And for once, Lydia didn't feel even one ounce of jealousy. She was so grateful they were there, together, and at the same time so frightened that Jerry might harm them.

Why was Jerry doing this? What had happened to him?

The silence was broken by Mattie's voice—quiet and soothing, as if she were speaking to a small child.

"It's all right, Jerry. They didn't mean to startle you. It's only that Clara slipped. Remember last week when we were in my *grossmammi's* house? I slipped in the kitchen because the floor was wet. It's the same. See? The floor is wet where Clara's shoes tracked in the rain and the mud."

They all glanced down at the floor, which was indeed a mess of mud and rainwater. Jerry looked back up and stared at Mattie.

"Hand me the knife, Jerry, so you can finish filling up the duffel. When you do, we'll go and buy you what you need."

His tongue darted out, moistened his lips again, and he swiped at the sweat running down his face.

"I'll hold the knife for you while you finish. I promise I'll give it right back."

He licked his lips once more, coughing as he did. Deftly he switched the knife to his other hand so he could scratch at the insides of his arm, which was when Lydia saw how red his skin was, how raw. He'd scratched the top layer off in places, until there was nothing but sores.

"Something's crawling on me, Mattie."

"I know. I know it is, Jerry." Her voice started to break, but she pushed on. "It'll get better soon. It always gets better."

Jerry switched the knife back, and Lydia saw the burns on the inside of his palms.

"Finish with the bag, and we'll go. The car—it's just down the road. Clear off that shelf." Tears tracked down her cheeks.

"After I do, we'll go?" he asked.

"*Ya.* Sure. We'll go." She was only a foot away from him.

It occurred to Lydia that the girl was both incredibly courageous and unbelievably foolish.

Jerry nodded once, flipped the knife closed in one fluid movement, and dropped it into her hand.

⤳ Chapter 35 ⤳

Aaron didn't wait.

As soon as Mattie closed her hand around the knife, he let go of Clara and launched himself at Jerry.

He wasn't sure what he expected. Maybe some part of his mind thought the guy was desperate enough to put up a fight. The man had certainly been acting erratically.

When he hit Jerry with the full force of his body, knocking him to the floor, he caved like a dry, dusty skeleton.

Aaron actually thought he heard all the air go out of him in a whoosh.

Jerry lay perfectly still.

For one moment, it occurred to Aaron that he might have killed him. The man had looked as if he were standing on death's door. What if he had pushed him through it?

The terrible hacking sound resumed, and everyone began talking at once.

"Get off him. Can't you see he's hurting?" Mattie sounded desperate.

"Hurting?" Clara's voice was shaking with anger and indignation. "He's *hurting*? He had a knife and was going to use it on us!"

"No. He wouldn't have. Please, help him up."

"Mattie, step back," Lydia said, suddenly taking charge. "Give Aaron room. He won't hurt him. I promise. Clara, go and fetch a glass of water for Jerry."

"Fetch him a glass of water? He was robbing us—"

"Please."

Aaron pulled himself up off the floor, dragging Jerry with him. The man was all bones. He jerked when Aaron touched him, but he didn't offer any resistance. The jerking seemed involuntary—almost like the child with Tourette's syndrome Aaron had gone to school with back in Indiana. Jerry's facial muscles twitched, his eye twitched, and he repetitively touched the same spot on the side of his face, his chin, and finally his chest.

The pattern never varied.

Jerry refused to look him in the eye as Aaron pushed him into a chair. Now that the immediate danger was over, Aaron was noticing other things he hadn't seen from across the room. The odor from the guy was sour and overwhelming. Also, he had burns on the inside of his palms. Some had scabbed over but others were raw and red. Though he was almost six feet tall, he couldn't have weighed one hundred and sixty pounds.

Clara returned with the glass of water.

Aaron handed it to Jerry, but he shook his head, waving it away after making eye contact only briefly. He continued to glance toward the open door, the window, Mattie, and back to Aaron. He didn't seem able to focus on any one thing for more than a few seconds. Mattie was crying now, sobbing really. Aaron heard Lydia trying to comfort her.

Clara remained between Jerry and the door, as if he might make a run for it.

"Do you have any other weapons?"

The tics and three touches. "No. Why would I have a weapon?"

"You had the knife."

Jerry shrugged.

Without turning away from him, Aaron asked Mattie, "Does he

have any other weapons, anything he could harm himself or some-one else with?"

"No. He doesn't. I promise he doesn't. Please, just let us go. Let us leave."

"Where would you go, Mattie? You need to stay here and let us help you." Lydia's voice was soft but firm.

"You can't help us. That's why we have to go. We have a plan. We're leaving Pebble Creek. We'll never come here again. I prom-ise you that."

Aaron pulled out another chair, turned it around, and straddled it. "Everyone sit down. No one's leaving until I understand what's going on here. If I'm going to let you rob me not once but twice and not call the bishop or the police, I have to know what has happened, and I have to be sure no one is in danger."

"And why would you do that? Why would you let us walk away?" Jerry's smile followed the grimace, the touch to his face, chin, and chest, but the smile was more of a sneer, and he'd begun scratching again.

"Call it grace. You remember grace, right, Jerry?"

Clara pulled out a chair on the side of the table near the windows and flopped into it. Mattie and Lydia sat down across from her. Mat-tie was still crying, but she seemed calmer at the thought there might be a way out for them.

Aaron turned back to the man sitting in front of him. The man who looked as if he couldn't walk to the end of the parking lot, yet he'd managed to break into their office two times. Had they bro-ken into other places? Had they robbed the list of businesses and churches Rae had shown him?

Jerry continued to jerk, and Aaron's mind went back to Andy, the boy who had transferred into his school in fifth grade. His con-dition had been full blown by the time he'd moved to Indiana. His parents had explained to the church that they had moved to give their son a new start, and also because the grandparents in their old town had trouble accepting the boy with his Tourette's. They thought Andy could control the tics and the words he would throw out when he found himself in a tense situation.

Aaron soon learned just how smart Andy was. He'd even cheated off a paper of his once—something he'd done a month of extra chores for when he'd been caught. Andy had shown up to help, even though it wasn't his fault.

Jerry reminded him of Andy in several ways, but not in every way. There were several things that were off, like the smell and the sores. Those things reminded Aaron of other men he'd seen in Fort Wayne, when he was older. Men he'd walked on the other side of the street to avoid.

"What are you using, Jerry?"

Jerry didn't even look up. "What difference does it make?"

"Maybe it doesn't. But you're not leaving until you answer my questions. Or Clara can take the buggy to go fetch Officer Tate."

"What about the bishop?" Clara asked.

"Bishop Atlee will insist we call the authorities. Drug use is not something he will tolerate in the district." Aaron was playing a hunch that Jerry would not want to deal with Tate. "Atlee is a *gut* man, but his hands will be tied. I think you both know that."

Jerry began scratching again. "I need to go, man. You don't understand."

"Explain it to me."

The laugh was more of a bark, and it brought on a fit of coughing.

"My guess is crack. Is that what it is? Is that why you're stealing?"

"I'm stealing because I lost my job. Me and Mattie. We're leaving." The coughing grew worse, and Jerry doubled over in the chair.

Aaron scooted back. He didn't trust him. The guy looked frail and thin, but drugs could do strange things to people. And someone who was strung out? Desperate for their next high? There was no telling what Jerry was capable of doing if he thought he had a chance of getting away with it.

"Mattie, is that true? You're both leaving?"

"*Ya. Ya*, it is. We're going to the city next week. Jerry has some *freinden* there. We can stay with them until we're married."

Silence filled the room, and Aaron was once again aware of the rain outside, falling softly. Finally, he pulled in a deep breath. "Is that what you told her, Jerry? You need the money to go to where...La Crosse? Or were you headed all the way to Green Bay or Madison?"

When Jerry didn't answer, he pushed further. "Or maybe you were going to keep the money and score a few more highs."

Jerry still didn't speak, but he kept glancing toward the door.

"Who are you purchasing from, Jerry?"

"Different people. Why? Are you interested?"

"Amish or *Englisch*?" Aaron waited, but Jerry didn't answer. "I'm guessing you owe them. I'm guessing you need to leave town for several reasons. It's not hard to score a little, but when your habit owns you, things become complicated. Is that it, Jerry? Maybe you were planning to leave, but you weren't going to take Mattie with you?"

"You can shut your mouth." Jerry had tensed and was clutching the arms of the chair. Waiting in the room and unable to move around with them all watching him was beginning to take its toll.

"I'm guessing you told her that so she'd help. You probably don't even care about her—"

Maybe Aaron's words pushed him over the edge. Maybe it was Mattie's crying.

Aaron recognized too late that his hunch was correct—the man had more muscle left in him than you would think looking at his emaciated form. And his need for the drugs had the ability to push him beyond what he should have been able to do.

He rocketed out of the chair.

Instead of heading toward Aaron, he shot past Clara.

Aaron jumped up.

He darted to the right, but his path was blocked by the back of Mattie's chair and Lydia, who had risen to comfort the girl.

He moved back around to the left past Clara, who had her hand over her mouth and still managed to let out an ear-piercing scream.

Jerry darted through the open door.

Aaron ran after him, down the wet steps, and slipped in the

rain-soaked grass. He caught himself, regained his balance, turned the corner, and tore out after Jerry.

The fool would get himself killed if he actually made it to the car he had hidden. His mind seemed to be operating in starts and stops, worse than an old *Englisch* tractor.

They had both made it across the parking area and to the street, which was pitch dark. Aaron stopped and listened for the sound of Jerry's footsteps. He had gone to the left. He was sure of that. But had he kept to the road or gone off into the brush?

Suddenly a car accelerated around the curve, and Aaron could clearly see Jerry's image in the middle of the road, silhouetted in the headlights of an oncoming vehicle.

Jerry froze.

The car continued approaching.

Three hundred feet.

Two hundred feet.

A hundred feet.

Jerry shielded his eyes, covered his entire face with his arms, but still he didn't step out of the path of the car, which had rolled to a stop only fifty feet from where he stood on the center stripe.

The red and blue lights began to pulse, and an officer stepped out.

Aaron couldn't see him in the backdrop of the lights, but he immediately recognized Officer Tate's voice.

"Son, I want you to put your hands up and turn around for me."

∽ *Chapter 36* ∽

Lydia stared at the female police officer.

The woman had just asked her something, probably had repeated the question twice, but Lydia had no idea what it was.

"Look, Miss Fisher. I understand it's been a long night for you, but we're almost done here."

The Hispanic officer was unlike any woman Lydia could remember meeting before. She wasn't ultrathin like most *Englisch* girls Lydia knew. If anything, she tended toward being on the heavy side, but it seemed to be a muscular weight. She didn't look like someone most criminals would mess with. She was all business, from the way she planted her feet to the uniform she wore—complete with a belt like Officer Tate's, which had all manner of items clipped to it: radio, handcuffs, gun...

Lydia did not question that Officer Mendoza had been well trained to use every item hanging from her belt. The scowl on her face conveyed that she wouldn't hesitate to do what needed to be done to maintain order in her jurisdiction.

There were no doubts in Lydia's mind. This policewoman was as different from her as the crane which visited the river behind them was from the fish that darted in and out of the rocks. They had nothing in common.

She couldn't imagine why anyone would want to cross a law officer. At least Lydia wouldn't, but then she wasn't the one being arrested.

She glanced over at Jerry, who was waiting in Officer Tate's squad car, and to Mattie who waited in Officer Mendoza's car. They should have been able to prevent this from happening.

The lights from the patrol car continued to splay an unnatural pattern of red and blue beams across the parking area. In addition, battery-powered floodlights had been set up in the office, in the shop, and along the path in between.

Crime techs were collecting fingerprints, shoeprints, and taking photographs. With each snap of the camera, Lydia felt herself flinch, and each flinch reminded her of Jerry and Mattie.

Yellow crime scene tape was strung from the speckled alder bush to the parking lot. It seemed to hang everywhere she looked, garish in the *Englisch* lights.

Officer Mendoza clicked her pen. Golden brown skin, long black hair that was pulled back and fastened with a clip, and a Spanish accent did nothing to soften her appearance. Her dark eyes, though, eyes that met Lydia's and didn't blink—they spoke of understanding.

"Is this...all of this...necessary?"

"There have been other burglaries in Cashton and the surrounding villages. We need to be able to confirm whether Mr. Beiler—"

"Jerry wouldn't do that."

Mendoza didn't argue with her. She glanced down at her notes one more time. "Is there anything else you'd like to add to your statement, Miss Fisher?"

"No. That's all I can think of. I appreciate your sending someone out to my parents. They would have been very *naerfich*. I'm so late, and they might have heard there's a problem here. They might have heard from the family who reported Jerry's car." Lydia ran her hand down her dress, attempting to brush off some of the mud caked on it.

It was no use. Some of these stains might not wash out. What had happened tonight, it couldn't be undone.

"It's no problem. Let me check with Officer Tate to be sure he doesn't need anything else from you or your sister. Once he clears you, it should be okay for you both to go. Would you like a patrol car to follow you home? It's late to be on the road."

"That's not necessary. We'll be fine."

"I'll follow them."

She hadn't heard Aaron walk up behind her, and she didn't turn to look at him, but the sound of his voice sent her stomach tumbling. So much had happened, so much she didn't understand. She wanted to talk to him, but she wasn't sure she was ready to hear the answers to the questions circling around in her mind.

"All right. I'll be back with you in just a minute."

Aaron dropped down beside her on the porch steps. From where they were sitting, they could see Clara—Clara, who was already in the buggy waiting, staring straight ahead and looking very much alone.

Lydia didn't know where to start, what to ask first, and she was suddenly so tired she wasn't sure she could drive Tin Star home.

"Are you okay?"

She shook her head as tears slipped down her cheeks.

Why was she crying now?

Instead of asking her about her tears or what he could do to help, Aaron reached over and laced his fingers with hers. Lydia stared down at their hands, and focused on taking deep breaths and pushing the images of the previous three hours away. She slowly became aware of other things—a fish splashing in the creek, the call of a night bird and another's answer, the croaking of a frog, and the breeze in the trees.

When had it stopped raining?

"Gabe will be glad the rain was light and didn't last." Aaron's thoughts mirrored her own.

Did he know her that well? Did he know what she was thinking of now? All that she was worrying over?

She turned to look in his eyes, warm brown eyes she sometimes dreamed about.

Did he know what effect he had on her?

"We'll be all right, Lydia." He reached forward and pushed the hair that had escaped her *kapp* out of her eyes. "And I understand there are some things we need to speak of, but not tonight."

"When?"

"After you rest."

He leaned forward and brushed her lips with his own, sending warmth cascading through her. With a smile, he pulled her to her feet.

They were both covered in mud, but the cabins were safe.

Walking through the maze of crime scene tape, Lydia had the absurd idea she was trying to navigate her way through a dream. She heard the squawk of Officer Tate's radio and saw him bend down to say something to Jerry. They passed within a few feet of the squad car, close enough to see what was going on, but Jerry remained hunched over, unresponsive and defeated.

She glanced back at him. He raised his hand to brush his hair out of his eyes. With that movement, the metal handcuffs around his wrists caught the reflection of the cruiser's flashing lights, and she thought he looked up at her for a moment. She thought they connected. It didn't last long. His head and shoulder twitching slightly, he slumped forward again.

Mattie was in a cruiser parked farther down the lot, and though her face was turned toward them, she didn't blink or acknowledge them in any way.

"We can't let them go, alone..." Lydia's voice felt raw. The words actually hurt as they clawed their way out. She barely knew these two, but seeing them cuffed and about to be driven away was like seeing two animals from a herd cut and separated for slaughter.

"Bishop Atlee has gone to collect their parents. He'll meet them at the station." Aaron rubbed his thumb over the back of her hand. "They won't be alone for long."

They reached her buggy at the same time Officer Mendoza

returned and told them they could leave. Clara still had nothing to say. While Lydia was worried about her, she realized Aaron was right. They all needed rest. Any questions they had, any answers they were searching for, could wait for another day.

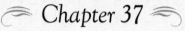 *Chapter 37*

G abe pushed his way in between Aaron and David in the serving line. "You two plan on taking all of that chicken salad?"

Aaron added another spoonful to his plate, the frown on his face deepening. "A man has to eat."

"He doesn't have to eat that much." Gabe took the spoon out of his hand. "Miriam won't make this dish unless it's for church dinners. She claims my waistline is expanding."

"She's right," David said without looking up from the plate of cold meats and cheeses he was helping himself to.

"You're one to talk."

"I need to eat whenever and wherever I have a chance. You're forgetting I have a newborn *boppli* in the house."

"Still waking up in the middle of the night?"

"*Ya.*"

"Once or twice?"

"Three times."

"That's tough. Guess we were lucky with Rachel. She was happy with one middle-of-the-night feeding. Even that only lasted about six weeks."

Aaron gave them a stormy look. "Do you two have to talk about families and *bopplin* while a man's preparing to eat? You'll steal my appetite."

"Why? You planning on getting married?" David laughed and jabbed Gabe in the ribs with his elbow.

Aaron shook his head in disgust and trudged off to the farthest table.

"What did I say?" David looked perplexed.

"I have no idea. Let's go find out." Gabe added a roll on top of his heaping plate, smiled at Miriam, who was shaking her head no to the extra bread he wanted, and hurried off after Aaron.

The first Sunday in July had turned into a perfect day for an after-church meal, especially an outdoors one. The temperature was in the low eighties, the sun was shining, and everything had finally dried out. From where they sat outside Bishop Atlee's barn, Gabe could see fields of hay growing tall. *Gotte* had been faithful to His Word for sure. As the Scripture they had read this morning proclaimed, "For the LORD your God will bless you in all your harvest and in all the work of your hands, and your joy will be complete."

Gabe's joy certainly was complete.

He had a wife and two *dochdern*. His life seemed whole again. He still missed Hope, and he wouldn't trade the years he had shared with her for anything, even if it meant he could bypass the pain of losing her to the cancer.

But now *Gotte* had given him a new life, with new *freinden*, even though some of them seemed a bit out of sorts this fine Lord's Day.

Aaron glanced up when Gabe and David sat down, but he didn't say anything. He only picked at his food, which he now didn't seem very interested in eating.

"Problem with Miriam's casserole?"

"No."

"I didn't think so. Her cooking is *gut*. I should know. Those years as a widower, I nearly starved." Gabe laughed, remembering the first time Miriam had visited his house. He'd been burning bacon and she'd cooked dinner for him and Grace.

"You can stop smiling. That only makes a man feel worse." Aaron tentatively tried a forkful of chicken salad, but he looked as if he were having trouble swallowing it.

"Are you *narrisch* or sick?" David asked, his fork paused an inch from his mouth.

"Maybe I'm neither one."

"Bad mood. That's for sure." Gabe broke the hot roll open and watched the steam escape from it. At that very moment, Lydia happened by.

"Need fresh butter for that, Gabe?"

"*Ya*. That would be *gut*. You have perfect timing." He smiled up at her. He'd realized since helping with the cabins what a fine young woman Lydia was. She'd make someone a *gut fraa* one day...

Lydia set a small dish of butter on their table and hurried away, never smiling and practically walking into Grace and Sadie as they balanced plates and drinks and walked toward a nearby table to sit with Sadie's parents.

Oddly, it seemed as if Lydia hadn't even seen the girls—Lydia who always had a kind word to say to them. Lydia, who always stopped to ask Grace about her drawing or her puppy.

Gabe turned back to Aaron, who was still frowning at his plate. Suddenly, he wasn't so interested in his roll anymore.

"What's happened with you and Lydia?"

Aaron only shook his head and continued to push his food around.

"Girl trouble? Is that what this is about?"

Now Aaron dropped his fork all together. "Would you keep your voice down? You make it sound as if I'm a child still in school. It's not 'girl trouble.' It's worse than that."

Gabe and David exchanged glances, and it was all Gabe could do to hold back a smile. It was obvious that Aaron had lost his heart to the young woman. "Lovesick" was written all over his face.

Either that or he'd taken the stomach flu. Gabe had learned through the years that the two things had similar symptoms. "You might feel better if you talk about it."

"Now, why would you think that? Talking doesn't solve anything. You can see she won't so much as glance my way." Aaron scrubbed his hands over his face, and now Gabe did smile. He couldn't help it.

He could remember that feeling. It was coming back to him with the force of a hard driving rain. He'd solved his problem with a valentine in a lunch box, but that solution probably wouldn't work for Aaron because it was July.

Four more people sat down at their table and started talking about the baseball game the boys had been playing the day before. From bits and pieces of their conversation, apparently the older Lapp boy had a decent pitching arm.

Aaron stopped talking completely when they arrived.

"Let's go have a look at Bishop Atlee's southern hayfield," Gabe suggested.

"Why would we do that?" David stared at him before looking back down at his plate, which was only half empty.

"You can bring it with you. I wanted to show Aaron how Atlee mixes the red clover in more heavily than some do. Makes for an interesting crop."

Aaron pushed his plate away and stood, though he'd eaten very little. David grabbed his plate, some of the extra bread on the table, and his drink.

Ten minutes later they were standing in front of the clover, alsike, alfalfa, and timothy. It was a sight to behold, full of color, birds, and butterflies. But, of course, that wasn't why Gabe had brought Aaron away from the increasingly crowded table.

The boy needed to talk, to share the burdens he was carrying. He was merely giving him a chance to do so.

"So what happened?" Gabe leaned back against an old fence that partially enclosed the field.

"If I knew that, would I be standing out here with you two?"

David continued eating his food and studying them both. Swallowing a large bite, he pointed his fork at Aaron. "I'm a bit sleep deprived, but let me see if I can catch up. You care for Lydia."

"*Ya. Ya,* I do."

He moved the fork toward Gabe. "And you think something's wrong between the two of them. So we're out here to give him some advice."

Gabe shrugged. "He has no family here."

"True."

Aaron folded his arms across the top slat of the fence and stared out over the field. "I don't understand women. Everything seemed fine after the last burglary. We even shared a kiss. I followed her home and—"

"You kissed her?" David finished eating and placed his plate on the ground, finally more interested in Aaron than in his food.

"I did, *ya*. She was tired and maybe a little scared. It had been a long night."

"Is that why you kissed her?" Gabe asked. "Or did you kiss her because you care for her?"

"Well, both, I guess."

"You guess?" David belched. "A man should know why he kisses a woman."

Aaron took off his hat and rubbed his hand over his hair. "Because I care for her. Sure. But I'd been waiting for the right moment."

"And being surrounded by police officers seemed like the right moment." Gabe pulled his fingers through his beard.

"*Ya*. At the time it did."

David made a sound between a laugh and a harrumph. He stretched and then reached over the fence, pulled up a piece of the clover, and commenced to chewing on it.

"Maybe it was. Maybe so. Go on with your story." Gabe made a forward motion with his hand.

"So I saw her home. And the rest of last week we were busy at the cabins, and now she won't speak to me."

David and Gabe stared at each other, and then they turned and looked out over the hay field. Finally, Gabe said, "You're leaving something out. Miriam always tells me I'm leaving something out. She says I've skipped over something—something that doesn't seem important to me but is very important to someone else."

"Huh. I'm lucky to remember where I left my buggy." David yawned. "You're sure Rachel only woke you once a night?"

"*Ya*. Just the once."

Aaron dropped his head between his arms and stared at the ground. "Well. I can't think of anything else. We were going to talk of some things, but we haven't yet...so I figured after she rested she didn't want to talk anymore."

"Oh, never figure that." Gabe shook his head.

"Nope. You're supposed to offer answers," David said, yawning again.

"I am?"

"Yes, you are." David worked the clover to the other side of his mouth.

"Why would I do that?"

"You're supposed to go to her and tell her you're ready to talk," Gabe explained.

"About what?"

"You need to talk about that kiss." David put his hands on the fence, stepped back, and stretched his back, which made a satisfying crack.

"Lydia's a *wunderbaar* girl. I didn't want to move too fast, though. I wanted to give her more time."

Gabe and David exchanged another look.

"Why do you two do that?"

"Do what?" Gabe asked.

"Look at each other that way."

"What way?" David's smile stretched so that his beard reached up nearly to his eyes.

"Oh, never mind."

"Giving a girl more time isn't always best." Gabe tugged his hat down. "Unless she asks for more time."

David said, "Giving her more time can make her think *you* want more time."

"Or that you're having second thoughts about the kiss." Gabe turned and faced back toward Atlee's barn. All this talk about kissing made him think of Miriam. He wondered what she was doing.

"I'm not having second thoughts," Aaron said.

"Have you told her that?" David asked.

"Well, no."

"Sounds to me like you two should talk more." Gabe slapped him on the back.

"That's my problem to begin with. She won't talk to me."

The three considered Aaron's predicament for a moment.

Finally, David said, "I bet they've set out the desserts now."

"Might help us to think better. You know, Aaron, most things look better after a piece of shoofly pie."

"I don't feel much like eating."

Gabe glanced at David and shrugged. "Say, how's your neighbor doing, the *Englischer*?"

"Tim?"

"The guy who's trying to farm our way."

"Tim Elliott. He's *gut*. I checked on him yesterday. He saw a tedder advertised in the *Budget* and purchased it. The man has no idea how to hitch it to his team. If I'm not back by the time his hay has been mowed, would you show him how to use it?"

"Sure, we can do that," David said, yawning again. "Wait. Where are you going to be?"

"I'm going home."

"Indiana?" Gabe asked.

"*Ya.*"

"Kind of sudden, isn't it?" Gabe studied Aaron. "Any problem with your family?"

"*Nein.* It's only that I need to speak with my *dat*, and I didn't want to do it on the phone this time."

Both Gabe and David nodded in understanding.

"I'll check in with Tim to see if he needs any help." David rolled his shoulders, as if he were trying to loosen a kink in his muscles.

"And I'll stop by the cabins," Gabe said. "When do you leave?"

"Tomorrow."

"That soon? I suppose Lydia will have a way to contact you if she runs into anything we can't help with."

"Lydia doesn't know yet."

Gabe and David exchanged a look.

"Don't you think you should tell her?" David asked. "She's bound to wonder what happened when you're not at the cabins."

"I was meaning to talk to her. I just haven't had the chance."

Aaron stuck his hands in his pockets and slouched his shoulders as they walked back over to the picnic tables, but Gabe noticed that he did eat the pie instead of pushing it around his plate.

So maybe their talk had helped a little.

Chapter 38

Miriam caught up with Lydia as she helped to load the last of the dishes into her mother's buggy.

"Are you sure you want to walk, Lydia?" Ella was holding the reins to Tin Star in one hand and reaching behind her with the other to check that the younger Fisher girls had carefully stored the dishes on the floor of the buggy.

"I'll be fine, *mamm*. It's only half a mile and the weather is *wunderbaar* today."

"All right. We'll see you soon."

It wasn't lost on Miriam that Lydia's *dat* didn't speak. His breathing was labored, but his eyes expressed as much as his voice would have. He reached out and patted his daughter's hand, and Lydia stood on the tips of her toes to kiss him on the cheek.

Miriam was so pleased to see that Mr. Fisher was able to attend church. His health had deteriorated considerably since the time when Lydia was her student. But she could see in his expression how much he was still able to care for his family, and that *Gotte* was still using him for things other than farming. He provided for his family even in his weak condition, but in different ways.

"I'm glad you could attend our church service today," Lydia said to her as they walked back toward Bishop Atlee's kitchen.

"It was special for us as well. David has been trying to get us over here, but we haven't had the chance. With the baptism of my nephew Seth, today was the perfect day."

"*Ya*. I was happy to see Seth settling down and committing himself to the church and affirming our beliefs..." Lydia's voice trailed away, like the light summer breeze in the trees.

Miriam guessed she was thinking about Jerry, who hadn't settled down, and about the tragedy of his arrest and pending trial. It hung there between them as they crossed Bishop Atlee's yard.

Miriam looped her arm through Lydia's and pulled her toward the picnic table under the willow tree. Its branches draped the table gracefully, offering them some privacy from the half dozen families who were still milling about.

"You know, Lydia, *Gotte* is still watching over Jerry. He may have a long road back, and it may be a difficult one, but he won't be alone. We'll be here for him."

Lydia nodded as she ran her fingers down the length of the strings of her prayer *kapp*.

"But..."

"But what?"

Lydia waited a moment, and then the questions that had been building for a week came tumbling out of her. "Why did he have to choose that path? Why didn't anyone notice and try to stop him? Why wasn't I aware of the troubles Mattie had? What is she guilty of, other than loving Jerry? Why does she have to suffer so much now? And how did Aaron guess what was wrong with Jerry?"

Miriam didn't answer immediately.

She was thinking of what her mother had told her, back in May, when Aaron had first arrived and she had first gone to the cabins along Pebble Creek. When she had first asked her mother about Lydia's situation. Her mother had said, "You young girls, you need to learn to be there for one another. Friendship, it's about more than Sunday socials."

Now here they were, on a Sunday, and her mother had been

right—again. Friendship was about more than supporting each other on Sundays. It was about carrying each other's burdens all week long. It was about praying for one another and working beside one another.

"You've been struggling with these questions all week?"

Lydia nodded.

"Have you spoken with Mattie or with Aaron? Have you tried to see Jerry?"

Lydia shook her head as her tears began to fall.

Miriam reached forward and claimed the girl's hands in her own.

"It would be difficult to see Jerry today, but we can pray for him, Lydia. And we can hire a driver to go see him next week. Or we can write him a letter. I think he would like that." She waited for Lydia to nod, and then she continued. "Mattie has already left for her home. She didn't even stay for dinner, but I think she would like to hear from you. I think she could use a *gut freind* right now."

Reaching in the pocket of her apron, she handed Lydia a fresh handkerchief she kept there for just such emergencies.

"I tried to speak with her, but she walked away, and it's no better with Clara."

Miriam wondered if she should share the other reason she'd attended the service today. She waited a few moments, prayed silently, and finally decided it was something Lydia would need to know anyway. "The bishop and Mattie's parents have asked me to try to help."

"In what way?" Lydia glanced up, her eyes darting around the yard, looking for the bishop.

"Only to help Mattie to feel more comfortable in the community again. Also they're concerned, as are your parents, that perhaps Clara is blaming herself for some of what happened."

"Have you spoken to my parents?"

"For a few moments. I'm going to pick Mattie up tomorrow and bring her to the cabins for lunch. Would you mind preparing something for us?"

"Not at all, but what makes you think she'll come?"

"Her parents will insist that she come, and I don't think she'll say no to me. I'll give her my most serious teacher look."

Lydia smiled, but then she shook her head. "Everything has been off since that night. I don't understand. Things were finally going well."

"Are we still talking about the girls?"

A slight blush stained Lydia's cheeks.

"Ahh. So we're talking about the cabins."

Lydia smiled, though she still seemed to be fighting it. "You tease more now than you did when you were a teacher."

"It's Gabe's fault. Do you want to talk about it?"

"I don't know how. I don't understand what I feel or how Aaron's acting. I'm completely confused and miserable...and stop smiling! This is serious, Miriam."

"Of course it is. It's only that I don't think you're alone in your misery. Aaron has been looking more unhappy than Gus does when left alone in our back field." Miriam peeked out through the featherlike leaves of the willow. "In fact, I see he's standing over there by David's buggy, helping to load the church pews."

Lydia's head jerked up, and she peered in the direction Miriam indicated.

"Why don't you go talk to him?"

"*Nein*. I couldn't."

"Why don't we go together? I imagine he has things he'd like to say to you, but he doesn't know how to begin."

When Lydia raised her eyes, there was such hope there that it took the breath from Miriam's chest. She raised her hand, tucked the girl's hair into her prayer *kapp*, and smiled. Standing, she pulled Lydia to her feet.

"What do you say? We'll stroll over together."

Miriam thought she would refuse, but Lydia pulled in a deep breath, plastered on a smile, and squared her shoulders as if she were going to do battle with a stubborn mule.

Which did describe Aaron on a bad day. Miriam nearly laughed at that thought.

But, of course, young love and breaking hearts were no laughing matter. She remembered that herself. It hadn't been so long since she'd sat in a classroom, watching valentine lunches disappear and wondering why a certain farmer was waiting so long to let his feelings be known. Yes, she remembered all that very well, and it wasn't a time in her life she cared to repeat. So she laced her fingers with Lydia's and walked with her toward the man who could either set things right or tear them apart completely.

❦ Chapter 39 ❦

Grace was sitting on the steps, watching the men load the benches and holding her baby *schweschder* when her *mamm* and Lydia walked up holding hands. The sight made her smile, as did the realization that she'd again thought of Miriam as her mother.

It felt so natural now that she hardly noticed it anymore. She'd recently had a letter from her *mammi* Sarah, back in Indiana. *Mammi* Sarah said that *Gotte* would want her to treat her new mother with respect, which also included loving her the same as her mother who was in heaven. It didn't mean she loved her first mother any less.

She'd known those things before receiving the letter. She was nine years old, after all. She wasn't a *boppli* anymore. Not like Rachel.

She glanced down at the infant nestled across her knees, her thumb tucked in her mouth, her brown eyes staring up at her.

What was Rachel thinking? What would she say if she knew how to speak? And how did she see things? How did the house and the tree and the horses appear to her?

What would her mother, her first mother, think of baby Rachel? Her *dat* had told her they had always planned on a big family. He'd also said that when the midwife had first placed her in her mother's arms, she had called her an "angel" and compared her hair to "the chestnut pony."

Looking down at Rachel, Grace thought her first *mamm* would like her very much, though her hair didn't make her big sister think of Chance or Snickers. The way the afternoon light was falling across the top of her head, her hair color reminded Grace of Gus.

Grace shook her head, causing her *kapp* strings to flap back and forth and Rachel's eyes to follow them. She didn't want to think of Rachel being like Gus in any way. That could be a disaster.

It had been nice to read the words of blessing from her *mammi* Sarah. It had been *refreshing*—that was a new word she'd learned last year from Miss Bena. It wasn't a hard word, but one she hadn't used before. Now she had five pictures drawn in her book, with the word "refreshing" underneath them. All included some portion of Pebble Creek, and the last one included a corner of the letter from *mammi* Sarah laying on top of the big rock out in back of the cabins where Lydia worked.

Right now, Lydia reminded her of Miss Bena when she was addressing the younger boys in the schoolroom. She was not smiling at all. No, that was wrong—she had a small tight smile. It wasn't her real one.

Fortunately, she was headed to the buggy and not toward her or Rachel.

It wasn't as if Rachel could have done anything wrong. Rachel was almost perfect, except when she cried. And most of the time there was a reason for that.

Grace couldn't think of anything she had done wrong.

"Everything *gut* here?" Bishop Atlee strolled over and sat down beside her on the porch step. His beard reached down to his lap when he was sitting, and his skin was very wrinkly—like Rachel's when she'd first been born.

"*Ya.* I was thinking how nearly perfect Rachel is."

"So you like having a baby *schweschder*, do you?"

"I do. I wouldn't mind having more, even maybe a *bruder* one day." Grace glanced up at her parents, who were now standing side by side and smiling at each other. "But we can keep that between us, bishop. There's no rush."

"Oh, right. No rush."

"One baby, a donkey, a puppy, a tom cat, and a mouse are a lot to look after some days."

"You take care of all those things?"

"Not all of them. My *mamm* mostly takes care of Rachel." Grace ran a finger over her *schweschder*'s perfect hand, and her tiny fingers reached out and circled hers, sending a river of delight through her heart. "I only watch her for a few minutes when everyone else is busy. And my *dat* mostly cares for Gus."

"Gus is..."

"The donkey."

Atlee nodded as if everything was making sense to him now.

"I'm not completely sure why *Gotte* made donkeys."

The bishop didn't offer an answer, so Grace pushed on. "At first, I wanted Gus so bad I thought I'd die if I didn't have him. This was at Mrs. Kiems' benefit auction."

"I remember that. Your *dat* won him."

"*Ya*, because I begged him to enter the woodchopping contest, and I still do love Gus. But now, some days, it seems like he's more work than he's worth."

Atlee considered her words for a moment, combing his beard with his fingers. "No one is useless in this world who lightens the burden of it for someone else."

Grace glanced up at him in surprise. "Miss Bena taught us that proverb last year. I thought it was talking about people."

"Could be, I suppose. Or it could be talking about donkeys. You know, Grace, God used donkeys in the Bible as an example for us to learn from—learn humility and service and even obedience."

"There were donkeys in the Bible?"

"Sure. You remember the donkey Mary rode on..."

Grace nodded.

"And the donkey Christ rode into Jerusalem."

"*Ya*."

"There was also Balaam's donkey."

"Who?"

"Balaam's donkey. He saw the angel of the Lord. Numbers twenty-two. You might want to read that chapter. It could give you an entirely different perspective on Gus."

Atlee placed his hand gently on top of her *kapp*, and Grace felt the same way she did when she stood in the sunlight. Gently he reached forward and did the same to Rachel. He didn't say anything, but Grace knew, with a certainty, that he was praying for them.

It reminded her of watching Seth's baptism, which she had questions about. She wanted to ask her parents about the water, and also how old she needed to be. She wanted to ask Seth how he knew for sure when the time was right and if he felt different when the water was pouring down his face.

Smiling, the bishop stood and moved on to speak with David, who was ready to drive off with the church pews. They laughed about something, and her *onkel* climbed up into his buggy.

Grace liked visiting the church on this side of Pebble Creek. Things were certainly different over here—bathrooms inside the house, gas stoves, refrigerators that didn't have blocks of ice in them. They even had different washing machines, which Grace didn't understand, but she'd watched her *aenti* and the process certainly looked like something she could get used to.

The west side of Pebble Creek was different, but it seemed like it was also the same. Church had the same songs. Preaching was the same—long! And families were the same—big. Sometimes grumpy and sometimes happy.

Bishop Atlee moved on from the buggy and stopped to help one of the older couples with their mare. He was a nice man.

He reminded her of her *daddi* Joshua. Next to her *dat*, her grandfather was her favorite person in the whole world. Miriam's *dat* had taught her to ride in a saddle, to play checkers well enough to beat Adam Lapp, and he never said a word when she climbed trees.

Sometimes *Gotte* did take people from your life, like her first *mamm*, Hope.

But sometimes He gave you extra—like Rachel, *daddi* Joshua and *mammi* Abigail, and Miriam.

She'd spent a lot of time worrying about *mammi* this year, and now it seemed as if she was better. Doc Hanson's medicine had worked. Or maybe their prayers had worked. Possibly it took both.

She stared back down at Rachel, who had managed to drool all over the front of her dress. How much drool did one baby have? Why did they have so much? Where did it all come from?

Life was sure hard to understand.

Maybe she didn't need to figure it out. Maybe she needed to keep praying, and going to Doc Hanson if the need arose, and seeing the bishop—both bishops.

That thing about Gus, though. She'd have to think about that. Maybe she would go home and read about Balaam's donkey.

~ Chapter 40 ~

Aaron was relieved when Lydia agreed to allow him to drive her home after the church service. He'd borrowed David's extra buggy again, hoping she would say yes, but he'd been worried she would say no.

He was more than a little nervous. His hands were actually sweating on the reins. He wiped them on his pants and stole a glance in her direction.

She still wasn't talking much. And she had her arms folded around her stomach.

"Did you have enough to eat?"

"*Ya*. No." Lydia sighed and glanced out the side of the buggy. "What I mean is I didn't eat much. I wasn't very hungry."

"*Ya*. Me either."

Lydia studied him a moment, started to say something, but then she stopped herself.

"What is it?"

"Only that I'm wondering why you'd lie about a small thing like eating."

"I wouldn't lie—"

"Aaron Troyer, only an hour ago I saw you eating a giant piece of shoofly pie."

Aaron settled back against the buggy seat. He'd rather have Lydia argue with him than have her silent.

He'd rather have her in the buggy with him than be alone.

The truth of that hit him deep in his heart and settled over him like the sight of a well-plowed field. He took a steadying breath and thought back over the afternoon.

"Ya. I forgot about the shoofly. But who can refuse a piece of your pie?" When Lydia only stared at him, he added, "And I barely ate any dinner at all. That's what I meant when I said I didn't eat much—didn't eat much dinner. I couldn't stomach it."

"But you could stomach something that's made from shortening, flour, sugar, and molasses?"

Switching the reins from his right hand to his left, Aaron ran his hand over his jaw. "I thought there was some nutmeg and cinnamon in there as well."

Lydia rolled her eyes, but a smile tugged at her pretty lips, and that made the ball of tension in his stomach unwind enough to allow him to relax for the first time in several days. Had it been Thursday when it seemed she'd been crying while cleaning cabin five? Why would that have caused her to cry?

"You were supposed to turn down that lane, Aaron."

"Oh, ya." Aaron checked the road behind him as he slowed the mare. "I know the way to your home. I thought maybe we had time to go by the cabins before I took you to your parents'."

Smoothing her dress, Lydia stared down at it. He thought she would say no, and the knot in his stomach tightened again. When she glanced up, her golden brown eyes met his, and she nodded once.

He set the mare to a trot before she had a chance to change her mind.

The cabins looked like something from an *Englisch* storybook.

Bathed in the light from the setting sun, they had a gentle appearance. The white fluffy bank of western clouds helped to paint the perfect scene.

What wasn't to like, though? The hedges were neatly trimmed. The shutters and porches were freshly painted. Only last week they had both worked to lay gravel along the path leading from one cabin to the next.

Pumpkin was curled up on the office steps, winking at them as Aaron pulled the buggy to a stop.

Behind it all lay Pebble Creek.

It was a quieter stream than the one that had greeted him in early May, still moving past the cabins but not in as big of a hurry. Like Aaron, the river seemed content to take its time, to pause and enjoy the bend and the scene, the beauty of the alcove.

Things had changed here since he'd arrived, and he knew that he had Gabe, David, and Lydia to thank for that. Even Seth had proven to be a big help. He couldn't have done it alone. Because of their work, Elizabeth and the girls would be able to stay in Pebble Creek. Their life here was secure. After spending nearly two months getting to know them and their community, he understood better than ever why that was important.

Gotte had plans for them here, and he hoped that maybe *Gotte* had plans for him here too.

The cabins and the stream weren't all that had changed. He was different.

As he took Lydia's hand in his and led her to the swing by the banks of the creek, he realized that he no longer resented being here. It was the thought of *not* being here that frightened him.

"*Was iss letz?*" He asked as they sat in the swing.

He thought she'd wave his question away, or deny that anything was wrong, but instead she stared down at their hands, drew in a deep breath, and haltingly began to speak.

"I'm not sure. Lately, instead of wondering what is wrong, I wonder what is right."

Aaron reached out and touched her face. He didn't stop to think if it was proper. Touching her felt so natural. "Look in front of us, Lydia. Look at the river. How can you wonder what is right? Everything is. It's like the verses from the Psalms the preacher read today. 'How majestic is your name in all the earth.'"

"Psalm eight. I remember."

"I hear those words, read them, and in my mind I picture this spot. *Gotte* has blessed us."

Lydia nodded, covered his hand with hers, and pulled it away from her cheek and into her lap. "I know what you're saying. When I focus on nature, I do feel that everything is *gut*, but then my mind wanders, and everything turns upside down."

Instead of interrupting her, he waited.

"The flooding was bad before you came, Aaron. We never talked about it, but every day I would come and the water would have swept more debris up to the steps. I would clean it away and pray that the river would go down."

He glanced from the peaceful waters in front of him back to her.

"And it did go down, but it left behind more work than I knew how to deal with." She brushed at a tear with her free hand. "You arrived just after..."

"I didn't make a *gut* first impression."

"You saw the work left behind from all that Ervin couldn't do, from all the flooding had left. It was tremendous. If you hadn't come, this—" She turned and looked back toward the cabins. "All of this would still look as it did after the flooding. Probably it would be closed by now."

"I'm glad I came, but surely others would have helped you. The people in your district, they are kind."

"*Ya.* I suppose you're right. It's only that I'd become so used to doing things alone..." Now the tears tracked down her cheeks and he reached out, had to reach out, and brush them away with his thumb. "I forgot how to ask. What if I forget again, after you leave?"

"First of all, these are not your cabins to work alone. They are also Elizabeth's, and though she has a family to raise she will help with any decisions. Ervin should have included her in the decision making as I do now. Any questions you have, you go to her. Okay?"

Lydia nodded.

"Secondly," he paused so she would raise her eyes to meet his, but she didn't—wouldn't—so he continued. "Who says I'm leaving?"

She turned to face him, finally, and he thought he could gaze into those brown eyes every morning. That would be a pleasure. It would be a blessing.

"You haven't said you're staying."

He wanted to ask her that very minute, but he knew she had other questions. Their life together needed to begin on solid footing.

"I promise we'll speak of that before darkness falls, but what other questions have been troubling you?"

"Why didn't I notice the problems Mattie was struggling with?"

"I didn't realize you two were *gut freinden*."

"We weren't, but I should have been there for her. If I had, maybe she wouldn't be in the trouble she's facing."

Aaron stood and pulled Lydia to her feet. They walked along the path that ran beside the river. "You two have something in common—your stubborn nature. She wanted to handle it on her own."

"*Ya.*"

"Perhaps she was determined to hide things from everyone, but now that it's in the open you can be her *freind*. I heard Miriam is bringing her here tomorrow."

Lydia nodded.

"You can't be responsible for what you didn't know, Lydia. It hurts, *ya*. Same as it hurts me that I didn't realize my *onkel* needed our family's help, but he chose not to share that with us."

They walked around a bend in the path and startled a rabbit on the path. It blinked, nose twitching, before hopping into the brush.

"I was too quick to suspect others when the first burglary happened. Your friend Tim...I was sure in my heart it was him."

"Because he's different?"

"I suppose. It's hard for me to believe an *Englischer* would choose to live our way."

"We can't know what's in someone else's heart, Lydia."

"*Ya.* You're right."

"I think you'd like Tim if you took the time to know him, and his wife, Jeanette. She's trying to be a writer."

Lydia nodded and cleared her throat. "The night of the second burglary, you guessed that Jerry was using drugs. How did you know that?"

Aaron laced his fingers with hers. He remembered now that he'd seen a look of alarm on her face that evening, but so much had happened so quickly that he couldn't place what had startled her.

"There were boys in our district in Indiana who became involved with drugs. Several tried it only once—"

"While they were on their *rumspringa?*"

"*Ya.*"

"Did you?"

"I did not. I'll be honest with you, Lydia. I did try alcohol, several times. This was four, no, five years ago when I was eighteen. The alcohol, it wasn't so bad. It made me feel as if I were floating out there on the river. But the next morning, when I had to be out working in the fields, was terrible indeed."

Lydia smiled as they turned in the path and headed back toward the parking area. "Like a stomachache?"

"Worse. I decided that anything capable of taking away my love for what I do...well, I wasn't interested in it."

"And the other boys, the ones who used the drugs?"

"Two tried them only the one time, but one...he had a real problem, like Jerry. He had to go to the rehab center in our area. It was hard for him and his family, but he was improving the last time I saw him."

They walked past the office, and Lydia stopped to give Pumpkin a scratch behind the ears. The orange cat purred like the sound of the *Englisch* automobiles. Both Aaron and Lydia began to laugh until the cat stood, stretched, and stalked away.

Aaron wanted more than anything to lock that image in his memory, of her standing there in the last of the day's light, bending over the orange cat, the cabins behind her, and in back of that the river moving past.

"Before I can tell you I'm staying, I have to go back to Indiana."

Her head snapped up.

"I have to speak with my *dat*, and I want to do it in person. I've made arrangements to leave first thing in the morning."

She nodded, her eyes impossibly round and full of trust.

Stepping forward, Aaron once again brushed his lips against hers—like he had the night of the burglary. And like that night, the kiss confirmed everything he already knew.

He was not going to disappoint Lydia.

He would find a way to make this right, but he had a few questions of his own, questions he didn't have a clue how to answer. Life was incredibly complicated. That was one thing he'd learned in the last few months.

He'd take the bus home and speak with his *dat*. Then he would come back to Pebble Creek.

And when he did, he'd have a question for Lydia.

Chapter 41

Miriam glanced across the buggy at Mattie. The young girl had been through her preliminary hearing, but she was still awaiting her formal trial regarding the drug charges and the burglary. Aaron wanted to drop the burglary charges, but Officer Tate had explained things weren't so simple with the *Englisch* legal system.

Jerry and Mattie were wanted in a string of burglaries. It seemed apparent that Jerry was the main culprit, but Mattie would have to testify against him. Up to this point she'd been unresponsive. The trial had been scheduled. Jerry was in jail, receiving medical care and going through withdrawals. Mattie was released to her family, pending the trial and possible future charges.

The family had asked Miriam to act as a counselor with the girl, actually with both girls. Clara also seemed to be having trouble coping with the events of that evening. Today was their first time to meet.

"I left Rachel with Ida, my brother Noah's wife." When Mattie only continued staring at her lap, Miriam pushed on. "Rachel has been teething, and she can set up a holler louder than schoolchildren at recess. Ida has seven of her own, so she's *gut* with *bopplin.*"

Mattie never looked up, but she did trace the hem stitch on her apron with her index finger. "My *mamm* kept juice in ice trays in the icebox. We'd fetch one and rub it over my *schweschder's* gums when she'd start to fussing."

"*Ya?* Did it work?"

"Sometimes."

"I'll give that a try."

That was the extent of their conversation. When the cabins came into sight, Mattie pulled back into the corner of the buggy as if she could become invisible there. Miriam wanted to reach out and comfort the girl, but she was afraid any touch might make her bolt into the woods.

Lydia stepped out onto the porch of the office before they'd even pulled to a stop, and Seth walked out of the barn to care for Belle.

"Should I unhitch her for you?"

"We'll only be an hour or so."

"I'll put her in the shade and give her a few oats."

"*Danki.*"

She did reach out her hand to steady Mattie at that moment. After they got out of the buggy, the girl stood frozen where they had parked. She showed no intentions of walking toward the office. Clara had joined Lydia on the steps. Because it was a Monday and nearly noon, all of the Sunday guests had left and no one new would be arriving until sometime the next day.

They were alone. They wouldn't be interrupted.

Mattie stared at the office as if a dozen police officers might jump out and arrest her. She crossed her arms and ducked her head, staring at the ground.

"Lydia and Clara are the only ones here, Mattie." Touching her softly on the arm, Miriam turned her attention toward the girls. "Seth is taking care of Belle. It will be just us girls."

Mattie glanced up, though she still didn't move a step forward.

"I made us a light lunch," Lydia called out. "Some sandwiches."

Mattie had begun to shake, and Miriam knew there would be no forcing the girl into the office. She looked out and over the grounds of the cabins. They had appeared so forlorn that first day when she and Gabe and Grace had first driven up with Aaron to see his *onkel*'s place. Now the property had the appearance of a well-tended park. Miriam remembered her days teaching, when the weather would grow warm and the students would become restless. Her cure had been for everyone to take their lunches outside to eat.

"How about we sit at a picnic table?" Miriam suggested.

Lydia shrugged.

"I'll help you carry things. Clara, would you walk Mattie down to the table?" Instead of waiting for an answer, Miriam climbed the steps, patting Clara on the arm as she passed her.

Once in the office, she and Lydia watched out the window as Clara and Mattie made their way down the path. The girls walked with a good foot in between them, neither talking or even acknowledging the other was there.

"How's Clara?"

"How's Mattie?"

The questions were uttered nearly simultaneously. For the first time since picking up the young girl, Miriam felt some of the tension in her shoulders ease.

"Quiet," Miriam said. "She's very quiet. Barely utters a word, and when she does I have to lean forward to make out what she's saying."

"Clara's not much better, and to think there was a day when I wanted her to stop talking."

"These things take time. It was a shock for Mattie, who probably thought they would never be caught. No doubt she envisioned a better ending—the young usually do."

"And what of Clara? I still don't understand her connection. Certainly it was traumatic to be here, but..."

"Perhaps today we'll find out."

"Mattie looks as if she's lost even more weight." Lydia craned her neck to see better out the window. "I believe she could blow away if we have a big wind."

"Your lunch looks *gut*, Lydia. Maybe we can convince her to eat. Maybe the fresh air will help her appetite."

They gathered up the sandwiches, cups, and pitcher of tea.

"Did Aaron get to the bus station okay this morning?" Miriam asked.

"I suppose. He was gone when I arrived."

"When will he be back?"

"He didn't say."

"Oh." Miriam paused, wondering how best to proceed or if she should just drop the subject. Finally she asked, "Were you able to have a talk with him before he left?"

She tried not to smile when Lydia blushed all the way to her prayer *kapp*.

"*Ya*, we did. He answered a lot of my questions, but I still don't understand why he has to go home or why he has to see his parents." Lydia shook her head, frustration creasing her brow. "I miss him already, and he only just left."

"Time apart is difficult."

Lydia thought about that, and then she motioned toward Mattie and Clara. "Do you think these meetings will do any good?"

"I don't know, but we're called to support one another, and that's what we're going to do. It's up to us to be the string that holds this package together. Those two look as if they've each lost their best *freind*."

"Mattie has."

"She's going to have to find another, and I have a feeling the gal sitting beside her is a very good candidate."

"Maybe that's what Clara wants, but she doesn't know how to say so. They certainly don't look like *freinden*. We could put Seth and Aaron in between those two, they're sitting so far apart on that bench..." Lydia's words trailed off as they reached the picnic table.

They didn't have long to wonder about what the girls were thinking. The meal had barely started when the shouting began.

Miriam had bitten into her sandwich, ham-and-Swiss on rye, when Clara threw out the first words. She'd moved across the table from Mattie when she'd stood to help Lydia with the food.

"It's not my fault, so you can stop staring at me that way."

"Did I say it was your fault, Clara Fisher?"

"Maybe your words weren't necessary. Maybe the scowl on your face was sufficient."

Mattie pushed her plate away, though she'd yet to take a single bite. There were two spots of color on her cheeks, and her hands were balled into fists in her lap. Miriam didn't move other than to place her sandwich back on her plate.

She was reminded of the years she'd spent teaching at the Plain School on Pebble Creek, the same creek now slipping peacefully by a few yards in front of them. There was nothing peaceful about their lunch, though. The tension could be sliced with the butter knife Lydia had brought to cut their sandwiches.

But like those teaching days, Miriam realized this time it might be best if she remained quiet—as long as the silverware did not start flying.

"You're going to remain silent? Still? Is this your way of punishing me?" When Mattie didn't speak, Clara smacked the table with the flat of her hand. "It's not my fault Jerry's in jail. You shouldn't have allowed him to continue down that path of destruction—"

"Do you think I didn't try?" Mattie's voice was broken, pouring from her as the tears slid down her cheeks. "Do you honestly believe I watched him and did nothing to turn him back to our ways? But he wouldn't come. He would promise. He would look me in the eyes and tell me that it was...was the last time."

"Why did you believe him?" Clara asked, no longer hollering.

"Because I wanted to." Mattie met her gaze now. "And yes, if there was sin, there was sin in that—sin in seeing what I wanted to see. Sin in hoping where there was no hope to be had."

"There is always hope, Mattie. With *Gotte*, all things are possible."

Miriam didn't move any closer. She didn't want to frighten Mattie off.

"*Ya*. I've read that verse."

"Do you believe it?" Lydia asked.

"I don't know what I believe anymore." Mattie crossed her arms on the table, leaned forward until her white *kapp* met the gray fabric of the sleeve of her dress and her face was completely hidden, but she didn't make any other sound.

Clara stood, walked around the table, and sat on the other side of Mattie. When she put her arms around her, Mattie turned and allowed herself to be enfolded in her embrace. She wept.

Whether she was weeping for Jerry or herself or the dreams that might never take place, Miriam couldn't say.

She could say, with certainty, as they sat in the sunshine, their lunches uneaten and the cabins silent around them, that they were making progress. The fortress Mattie had built around her heart had been breached, and she'd allowed friendship inside.

Together, they could face whatever lay ahead.

≈ Chapter 42 ≈

Gabe tried to stay awake as Miriam caught him up on the day's events. Suddenly, there was something warm, squirming, and a little wet on his stomach.

"How does she learn to pull my beard while she's still so young?" He stared at his daughter in wonder, who smiled back at him and slobbered on his nightshirt.

"It tickles her. Of course she's going to pull on it."

Gabe rolled to his side, placing Rachel on the bed between them. Miriam had the gas lantern turned to low, sitting on her nightstand. She was rubbing lotion onto first one leg and then the other, and he wondered briefly if he could stay awake long enough to apply some to her back. That always earned him extra points in the incredible husband category.

Rachel yawned and he yawned.

Probably he shouldn't have worked the extra hour after dinner. Tomorrow he'd stop early so he'd have more energy in the evening, more energy in the bedroom.

His eyelids felt so heavy, and the bed so good. The sheets smelled fresh, the quilt was just the right weight for a summer evening, and his pillow was perfect for drifting off to sleep.

"Gabe?"

"Hmm?"

"Are you still awake?"

"*Ya*. I'm awake."

"I wanted to talk to you about Mattie and Clara, but I didn't want to bring it up in front of Grace."

Gabe stretched his eyes wide and blinked repeatedly. It had worked when Rachel was first born and Miriam needed sleep. "I'm here for you, *fraa*. Here and wide awake." He covered his mouth with his hand to stifle a yawn.

"I saw that."

"It was Rachel's fault. She yawns and I yawn. It's a natural reaction."

"I'll give you the short version." Miriam placed her lotion on the nightstand and snuggled down under the quilt so they were eye to eye, the top of Rachel's head between them.

Gabe realized again how blessed he was. Grace was down the hall, another year of school behind her. She'd adjusted to their new community, her new *mamm*, and now a new sister. He was lying in bed in a good house, on a productive farm, next to a woman who loved him.

Rachel blew a bubble and waved her fist in the air.

Rachel. She was a miracle beyond what he could even comprehend.

Gabe raised his eyes to Miriam.

God had blessed them, more than he would have ever hoped or dreamed. The thought wakened him more than two cups of strong coffee could have.

"Give me any version you like," he said quietly.

"Mattie told her side of what happened today."

"*Ya?*"

"She didn't suspect Jerry's drug use at first. He promised they would marry. She knew he was on his *rumspringa* and that he was drinking with the other boys. At the time, she didn't share her fears with anyone because she wanted to protect him. She thought love protects."

"Sometimes it does."

"But this time her silence helped him to hide his addiction. Others might have been able to intervene if she hadn't carried the burden alone."

Gabe reached out to touch his wife's beautiful black hair and run his hand down the length of it. "That's a natural enough reaction, though—to protect. She's young and was frightened, I'm sure."

"Jerry used up all his...sources, I think she said. After a few months there was no one else for him to turn to in the area. She kept begging him to stop going with the other boys. One time she even vowed to quit seeing him, but that only lasted a few days. When he showed up at her house asking for her help and promising to change..." Miriam reached out and adjusted Rachel's blanket.

The babe had popped her fist into her mouth and her eyes had drifted shut. She was fighting sleep, her eyes fluttering open occasionally, but Gabe knew the fight wouldn't last long.

"So Mattie took him back."

"*Ya*, and she started helping him again." Miriam stared across the room, out into the night, speaking slowly and carefully as she remembered the girl's confession. "She wasn't in on the first burglaries, only those that occurred the last week. Jerry convinced her they would get enough money to make it to Eau Claire, where he would find a job. He even told her they would eventually send back money for what they stole."

Gabe didn't answer that. He only flipped over on his back, stretched, and then folded his arms under his head.

"Her guilt is so heavy, Gabe, and she's so young. Jerry is the one who persuaded her to do those things."

"And yet by that point she realized he was under the influence of the drugs."

"True."

"She knew he couldn't be trusted."

"Yes, but—"

"And she went along with him anyway."

"You make it sound as if she were the one making the decisions."

Gabe allowed the silence of the summer evening to permeate the troubles and questions disturbing his wife.

Rachel had fallen asleep during Miriam's story, lying peacefully between her parents.

Miriam stood and carried the baby to her crib, which sat in the corner of their room. Soon they would be moving it to her bedroom down the hall. Gabe wasn't quite ready for that, but he knew all things changed. His not being ready wouldn't stop time from steadily pushing them all forward.

When Miriam climbed back into bed, she snuggled up against him. "Love forgives," she whispered.

"*Ya*, and I'm glad it does." He ran his hand up and down her arm.

"You're right, though. Mattie will have to accept responsibility for her actions in this situation. By doing so, by treating her as an adult instead of a victim, perhaps she will grow stronger."

"Our strength comes from the Lord. Mattie is fortunate to have a good community and good *freinden*."

"Once Clara worked past her anger, she admitted she felt guilty for not noticing all that was going on with Jerry and with Mattie, for not intervening earlier. I think those two girls will become very close."

"See? Good *freinden*. They will be fine." Gabe was suddenly wide awake. The eye exercises must have worked.

"For a moment this afternoon, I thought they would throw the food or the dishes at each other."

"That would have been terrible," Gabe said, nuzzling her neck.

"Indeed."

"But with all that experience as a schoolteacher, you'd know what to do."

"It helps me to handle you."

Gabe thought about arguing with her, but it didn't seem like the best time to say anything other than "Yes, dear." A light breeze was coming through the window, Rachel was sound asleep, and he was feeling surprisingly energetic.

Grace couldn't believe it when she woke up the next day—a Tuesday—and her mother asked if she wanted to go to her grandparents'.

"Sure, I do!" She had her chores done and her bag of drawing supplies ready to go quicker than Hunter could tree a squirrel.

"What's the occasion?" she asked as they set off down the lane.

"I thought we could help with *mamm's* garden."

Grace stared down at her lap, and then she decided to ask the question that had popped into her head. She was learning it was better to ask than to let something bounce around inside there for days.

"Is she worse? Is *mammi* sick again?"

"No, honey. She's still getting better."

"Oh, *gut*." Grace let her head fall back against the seat and rubbed her hand against her chest. "My heart actually jumped up and down."

Miriam smiled. "You love your *grossmammi*, don't you?"

"*Ya*, and I'm trying to learn not to worry, but it's hard. When I think I've got the hang of it, I slip up."

"Feed your faith and your doubts will starve to death."

"What does that mean?" Grace allowed the last word to drag out as she turned around in the seat to hand Rachel one of her rattles.

"It means you need to study—"

"My Bible." Grace plopped back on the seat.

"*Ya*, and if you do, eventually you'll worry less."

"Does it work with you?"

Miriam smiled. "I'm still learning."

By the time they reached Abigail and Joshua's, Rachel was tired of the rattle and ready for something to eat. Miriam left to feed the baby while Grace helped unload their gardening gloves and some seed plants they had brought from their own garden.

"How's *mammi*?" she asked her grandfather.

"Go see for yourself. She's in the garden."

"I thought that's why we were here." She held his hand as she skipped beside him.

"Abigail can always use more help. Your *mammi* is a little frustrated that she's moving slower than she did last year, but the medicine has been working *gut*."

They walked around the corner of the house, and Grace spotted her grandmother. She wasn't kneeling in the dirt or working on the rows of vegetables. Instead, she was sitting on a bench in a corner of the garden, a shawl wrapped around her shoulders and a glass of water in her hand.

She also wasn't alone.

Miriam was sitting beside her, cradling Rachel and nursing her. *Aenti* Ida and *aenti* Anna were standing at the front of the rows, directing the children—Grace's cousins.

"Oh, my. It's a gardening party!" Grace let go of her *grossdaddi*'s hand and started to run toward the garden, but then she turned back. He stopped suddenly and she bumped into him. Throwing her hands around his middle, she hugged him tight. "I love you, *daddi*."

"You don't say?"

"I do say!" She took off running, still holding the basket of seedlings.

When she showed Ida the plants, Ida sent her two rows over and half way down. All seven of her children were helping, even the little ones. Some of them were playing in the dirt more than helping. They had little tin pie plates, and they kept filling them up before emptying them out again.

Grace wanted to stop and draw that scene, but she kept on planting. Sometimes work came first and drawing came second.

All of six of *aenti* Anna's children were there too, from the youngest, who was even younger than Rachel, to the oldest—Seth.

"I thought you worked at the cabins," Grace said as he helped her to water the tomato plants she'd carefully planted into her row. She and Miriam had raised them from seed at home, with plastic milk jugs around them to keep the rabbits away. The milk jugs had come from her mother's friend Rae, who always seemed to know what to bring on her visits.

"*Ya*, I do." He moved the bucket of water for her.

She dipped her cup in, dribbled the water out carefully over the next plant.

"Don't they need you today?"

"I made sure it would be okay to take the morning off. I can always stay later tonight if I need to in order to finish my work."

"And Lydia doesn't mind?"

"*Nein.*"

"Is Aaron back?"

"Not yet. I haven't heard when he is coming back." Seth pointed to the plant she was watering. "Don't put too much on that one. It'll fall over. Needs a few days to set."

"Oh, yeah. I forget sometimes. *Danki.*"

"Sure thing. Holler if you need more water." He walked away, off to cart water for someone else.

Grace felt something land on her shoulder and turned to see Ida's middle son with a small pail holding half a dozen grasshoppers. He giggled and tossed another at her. Instead of jumping, which she did want to do, she looked at him the way she imagined her mother would and said, "Wouldn't those be *gut* for fishing?"

"Fishing. I wonder if *daddi* will take us." He darted off, running toward the barn.

Grace finished watering her plants and walked up the aisle toward the grown-ups, who were all sitting now, laughing over something the babies had done.

Mammi was still too skinny, but she did look as though she was feeling better. Grace understood now that she was old. But old wasn't bad. It only meant that someone had been around long enough to grow wise, long enough to grow special.

Rachel was special too.

They all were in some way.

But *mammi*? They had learned this year that she was a precious gift, one not to be taken for granted. Sort of like the bishop of a church. *Mammi* and *daddi* were the head of their family. They knew when to hug, when to bake cookies, and when to go fishing.

Grace set her watering can at the end of the row, near the other supplies. She had meant to draw when she finished with her part of the gardening, but maybe instead she would go and see what everyone was laughing about. Maybe she'd go spend some time just being with *mammi*.

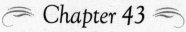 Chapter 43

Downtown Cashton
Thursday afternoon, two weeks later

Aaron stepped off the bus and smiled broadly when he saw there were no large puddles of rainwater to avoid. If anything, the street was somewhat dusty from the combination of cars and buggies traveling down Main Street. Apparently, it hadn't rained since he'd been gone.

No one else was exiting the bus at Cashton, so he didn't have to wait long for the driver to remove his single bag from the storage compartment.

"This it?"

"*Ya. Danki.*"

He had shouldered the duffel when a buggy coming in the opposite direction careened past them. Raising a hand, he waved at Raymond Eicher, who tipped his hat but did not slow down. The boy had not learned to drive any more safely.

The bus driver keyed something into his handheld device before climbing back on board the bus. "Good luck to you, son."

Aaron watched as the bus chugged to life, pulled back on to the road, and headed farther west. There wasn't even one small part of

Aaron that wished he was riding with the group of travelers. There was nothing for him out west.

He glanced back the way they had come. Didn't want to go that way, either. His past was that direction, in Indiana.

His future...he hoped his future waited for him here.

As the afternoon sun warmed his face, he began to walk. Funny how the little town seemed so familiar to him—as if he'd lived there years instead of months. He passed the town hall, tavern, café, general store, feed store, and, of course, Amish Anthem.

Not much to Cashton.

But had it lived up to whatever expectations he'd brought when he'd first stepped off the bus in May? He'd anticipated hard work, and he'd certainly found that. He hadn't thought to find the disaster that was his *onkel*'s cabins. A car signaled to turn in front of him, and he paused to wait on it.

The work at the cabins had shown him that *Gotte* could use his talents in other ways. He glanced down at his hands, still calloused, but from using a saw and hedge clippers instead of a plow.

He preferred the plow.

Whistling he crossed the road.

There had been the burglaries and Jerry's arrest. No, he could not have guessed all that had waited for him when he'd first stepped off the bus and onto the streets of Cashton. If he had guessed, he might have told the bus driver to hold up and let him back on.

Which meant he would never have met Lydia.

The tune he'd been whistling stuck in his throat. He stopped, removed his hat, and wiped the sweat off his forehead with his sleeve. When he started walking again, he was once more whistling, this time the hymn they had sung at his old church in Indiana on Sunday—"Amazing Grace."

Wildcat Mountain rose to the east. What would the trails and ridges look like in the fall? He hoped he would still be there to find out. He hoped he would see snow cover the roads he was crossing now.

Pushing his hat down more firmly on his head, he cinched up the duffel bag and walked resolutely, increasing his pace, when he heard the sound of a buggy slowing behind him.

"Need a ride?" The voice was familiar, as was Gabe's smile.

"I could use one." Aaron tossed his duffel into the backseat, grinning at the man who had become like a brother to him.

Gabe signaled to Chance, and they went at a fast trot out of town. "*Gut* trip?"

"*Ya.*"

"Took you longer than you thought it might."

"It did."

Aaron had almost forgotten how tall his friend was. Even sitting, it was apparent. Gabe's somber brown eyes glanced at the younger man once or twice, but he didn't ask the questions that caused him to tug on his beard.

"How's Miriam?"

"*Gut.*"

"And the girls?"

"Fine. Rachel seems to have grown another size, and Grace has put up some of her drawings for sale at the cabins."

Aaron nodded. They had talked of this before he left, but Grace wasn't sure she wanted to part with any of the sketches. She'd planned to discuss the idea with Miriam's parents and Bishop Atlee, whom the young girl had taken a liking to.

"I'm glad to hear that. She has real talent, something *Gotte* will use to touch people."

Gabe nodded, opting to study the road in front of him instead of answering.

When he pulled up on Chance's reins to turn the horse onto the road where the Plain Cabins sat along Pebble Creek, Aaron's hand shot out and stopped him.

"I won't be going to the cabins this afternoon."

Gabe slowed the horse and waited.

Aaron pulled off his hat, and ran his sleeve over the sweat that again pooled across his brow. He peered down the road to his right.

Lydia was there. Was she waiting for him? What would she say when she saw him?

He wanted to know that more than he wanted any other thing. But there were times when you had to put off what the heart wanted. He'd learned that too over the last few weeks. There was still one thing for him to take care of first.

His father's words came back to him, as clear as the water running through Pebble Creek. They had spoken of it as he'd waited for the bus, moments before he'd left. "Remember, son, one thing you can give and still keep is your word."

And he had given his word, to his father and his mother, and even in some ways to Lydia. He'd given his word that he would do this correctly.

Gabe waited, not rushing him, while Chance began feeding on the grass by the side of the road.

"If it's not too much trouble," Aaron said, "I'd like you to take me to the Fisher home. I need to speak with Menno, and it would probably be best if I did so before I saw Lydia."

Pausing only to slap Aaron on the back, Gabe murmured to the gelding. Chance jerked his head up, and they were moving away from the cabins at a steady trot.

Lydia should have been happy.

She should have been satisfied with the ways things had gone at the cabins, not just that day but all week. Reservations were good. Renters were happy, and sales of their Amish-made merchandise were up. She and Clara were working well together for once. They hadn't fought since last week, when she'd sent her to clean cabin two and found her in the rocker, peering through the branches of a bush, watching two Amish boys who had come to cut the grass. Even that had lightened Lydia's heart, for it seemed more like the old Clara, the Clara from before the burglaries and arrests.

The cabins were full nearly every night. Business had been so brisk she'd needed to hire the boys to help Seth, who was now doing Aaron's work.

She should even be grateful about the quiet ride home—Clara hadn't worked today because she'd had a dental appointment. Their neighbor had given her a ride into town, and she'd taken the afternoon off.

But instead of enjoying the ride home, Lydia found herself stewing over her life.

The reins to Tin Star fell slack in her hands, and she slouched against the seat as her parents' home came into view.

Her parents' home.

Was she destined to always live there? To never have a home of her own?

The old restlessness stirred in her, and she fought once again to push it down. She would turn twenty-three soon. What sort of life had she envisioned when she was Clara's age?

Why was she never happy?

Part of her discontent had come with the phone call about hiring help for Seth. She'd thought to be able to speak with Aaron about that, but she'd only been able to leave a message at the phone shack near where he lived in Indiana. When he'd called back, she'd been fetching a cat out of a tree and had missed it, so Clara had brought her the message from their own phone in the office.

So much for phones providing fast and easy communication as the *Englischers* declared. She wouldn't mind a letter. At least that she could read over and again.

She missed him.

There was no denying the hollowness in her stomach and in her heart. It gnawed at her each day, especially when she arrived at work and he wasn't there.

He'd been gone for two weeks now. Maybe he'd changed his mind. Maybe he wasn't coming back.

Stephen walked out of the barn as she pulled into the small drive leading to their house. It was hard for her to believe he was done with his schooling. She'd spent so long fighting to keep him in the classroom, that now she wasn't sure how to feel with him out and about.

Where would he work?

They had no fields that needed tending, and the few extra hours she needed a man at the cabins—the hours she'd given to the boys she'd hired to help Seth—weren't enough to provide for her family. Not to mention Stephen wasn't interested. She hoped he wasn't running around late at night any longer.

"I'll brush Tin Star down," she said as he reached for the horse's reins.

"No, you should go on inside."

She sat looking at him for a moment before getting out of the buggy. Stephen knew she preferred spending a few moments with the horse. It helped to ease her mind and relax her a bit from the work day.

"Go inside, Lydia."

"Is it *dat*? *Was iss letz*? Is he all right? You could have called me at the cabins—"

"*Dat* is fine." He took the reins from her hands and began to unharness the horse. "They're waiting for you."

Lydia's pulse began to race, and she resisted the urge to run. Why were they waiting? What had happened? Stephen had gazed at her with such seriousness, but if *dat* was fine...

She practically ran up the porch steps and pulled the door open at the same time her younger sisters burst through it. Martha, Amanda, and Sally Ann all giggled at the sight of her, but only Sally Ann stopped to throw her arms around her legs, embracing her in a tight hug.

"I love you, Lydia." She was gone in a flash of blue dress and black prayer *kapp*, running off after the other two into the last of the afternoon light.

Stranger and stranger.

She placed her purse on a hook by the door. As she turned toward the kitchen, she noticed Clara uncharacteristically standing by the stove. Something was not right. She was actually smiling as she stirred what smelled like potato soup.

"You're cooking?" Lydia asked.

Clara started to answer. No doubt it would have been a retort worth hearing too. Lydia could see now that Clara had cut the biscuits and put them on the baking tray. She could also see the smile blossoming on Clara's face as if she were hiding the biggest of secrets. It did Lydia's heart good to see the smile after the weeks of sadness that had followed Jerry's arrest. But before Clara could speak, Lydia's mother walked into the room and interrupted them.

"Lydia, you're home. *Gut*. We have company, and we've been waiting for you. What kept you so late?"

"I'm late? Company? Stephen said you needed to see me. Is something wrong?" Her voice rose with each question as her mother put her hand to her back and turned to usher her into the sitting room.

She didn't need to see him though, because suddenly she knew.

It felt as if every nerve in her body had come alive.

The scent of him was in the air, stronger than the smell of the soup on the stove.

Lydia turned and her eyes immediately found his. It was as if he'd never been gone. As if it was two weeks ago and they were sitting at the cabins, and he was telling her that he had to go back to speak with his father. She closed her eyes, and he was brushing her lips with his own.

Her fingers went to her lips at the memory.

"Lydia." Aaron stood, his hat in his hands, his eyes still locked on hers.

"I...I didn't realize you were back."

"Aaron arrived an hour ago."

"Hour..."

Her feet were moving her toward him, but she felt as if she were back in her room, having another of her dreams that made no sense.

When she sat down, her father reached out and covered her fingers with his own. She looked at his weathered hand on hers. The tears she'd held back for two weeks threatened to spill, but she blinked them away. When she looked up, she realized Aaron had sat down again, and Menno had placed his other hand on top of Aaron's.

He sat between them, laboring to pull in deep breaths.

It was Ella who explained. "Aaron came here first, Lydia, because he wanted to speak with your *dat*. Although it isn't required, he wanted to ask about your marrying. Do you care for him as he cares for you?"

Lydia met Aaron's gaze. She couldn't have resisted it if she'd used her last ounce of strength, and she didn't want to.

"*Ya. Ya,* I do."

"*Wunderbaar.* In that case, your *dat* and I would like to offer our blessing."

Aaron's smile, which was more beautiful than anything Lydia had ever seen, should have been enough. It should have been, but it wasn't. She stared down at her father's hand, on top of her own.

"But, if we were to marry, how would you...that is to say, where would we..." She closed her eyes, focused her mind, and started over again. "I mean, I couldn't leave—"

"*Gotte* will provide for us." Ella reached out and touched her softly on the cheek. "He has provided, and He will continue to. It's not for you to worry."

But she was worried.

She couldn't simply marry, move away, and leave her father when he was so sick. She couldn't do it!

Menno patted her hand as he pulled in another deep, rattling breath. "What...what is faith, Lydia?"

She knew the answer he wanted. She remembered when she was a child, and he'd tuck her in each night, always with a proverb and a kiss on the forehead.

As she glanced up and into Aaron's dark brown eyes, she felt the tears tracking down her cheeks. "Faith is knowing there is an ocean..."

He finished the saying for her, finished it with a smile that was genuine and sure. "Knowing because you have seen a brook."

⁓ *Epilogue* ⁓

October

Lydia resisted as Aaron tugged on her hand.

"I want the house to be just right when we move in, and there are only three days left."

"You know Miriam and Mattie will help you set the dishes just so."

"*Ya*, but—"

"Not to mention that all of your *schweschders* have been pestering you to let them lend a hand. They want to help."

"I know, and I mean to, but—"

"Come with me, Lydia. There's something I want to show you."

It wasn't his words that convinced her, or even the teasing in his voice, but the look in his eyes. Would she ever grow immune to the invitation there? She hoped not. She prayed not.

Pulling her shawl from the back of the kitchen chair, *their* kitchen chair, she slid it around her shoulders. Aaron's fingers wrapped around hers and sealed the deal. They walked shoulder to shoulder across the kitchen, through the sitting room and out the front door. She paused on the front porch, turning her gaze to the swing.

"I know what you're thinking. I can see it in your beautiful eyes, but we'll come back to the swing." He tugged on her hand and pulled her down the steps and across the lawn.

"What do you want to show me, Aaron Troyer?"

She thought they would turn toward the creek. These days, with the cabins doing so well and Seth taking on an increasing amount of the responsibilities there, Aaron could be found more often down near the water. He'd even begun serving as a fishing and nature guide to the *Englischers*. The same creek that ran through the cabins ran through the back of their property. It ran through their community. It was part of what bound them together.

Instead of following the path across their yard to the banks of Pebble Creek, he led her past the small barn toward the pasture and the fence that separated their property from her parents' home.

"Come watch the sunset with me. It's beautiful, *ya*?"

A kaleidoscope of colors splayed across the western sky—everything from purple to rose to blue. The sunset reminded her of walking through the quilt shop in town, when she'd been a young girl, younger than Clara. Her mother had insisted that she choose fabric for wedding quilts, but in her mind those quilts might never be needed. God had known, though, and now those quilts lay on a bed in the cozy two-bedroom home behind her.

"It's *gut* to stop working for a few minutes." Aaron turned and studied her face. "What do you think?"

Suddenly she wasn't sure if he was asking her about the sunset or about all he'd done to ensure she could marry and yet remain close enough to care for her father. During the two weeks he'd been in Indiana, Aaron had sold his land to his brothers. He'd used that money to purchase the property next to her family's—the property she'd often passed and stared at with such longing. When they planted in the spring, Aaron would split his time between the cabins and the fields. He'd also teach her brother, Stephen, how to farm.

Presently what they owned was small, only a quarter of the available acreage and the home. If they worked hard, though, and if the floods didn't come again, maybe in a few years they could purchase the rest of the adjoining fields.

Lydia's mind went back over the home of her childhood.

The ache of what they had lost so many years ago was still there, but it was replaced now by a hope and a promise for their future.

"What do you think?" he asked again.

"I think I'm happy to be home." She kissed his hand, and he stepped closer to run his fingers down her cheek and across her lips.

A shriek and then the sound of laughter broke the moment as her younger sisters, Sally Ann and Amanda, ran across the backyard toward them.

"Looks as if we're about to have company," Lydia murmured.

"I might have said I'd take them night fishing."

"*Ya?*"

"Uh-huh." He slipped his hand around her waist and walked with her through the gate separating their two properties.

Lydia realized as the sun set and she was surrounded by the childish banter of her *schweschders* that her life wasn't perfect—far from it. Some days her father's illness was worse, some days it was better. Clara still had her times of depression, though her friendship with Mattie was helping both girls. Jerry's fate was undetermined, largely in the hands of the *Englisch* legal system. She hoped Stephen would decide on farming, but there was no guarantee he could make a living from it.

All of those things were secondary, though.

Gotte had given them each other, and that was all they needed. What she had learned since *Gotte* had brought Aaron into her life— Aaron's love into her life—was that it was the people, not the place, that mattered.

The people in her life had given her a home.

≈ *Discussion Questions* ≈

1. Lydia reveals some of the reason for her attitude in chapter 4. She doesn't believe Aaron will stick around. The *Englisch* customers don't stay. Her boyfriend didn't stay, and she's having trouble convincing her brother to stay. Lydia has some trust issues. What barriers do people put in place when they are afraid to trust?

2. In chapter 6, Aaron felt "the full weight and responsibility of being an adult." This happened for two reasons—he finally understood the grief and needs of his *aenti*, and he received the drawing from his niece. How does God prepare us for adulthood? What does He give us to help us transition to that responsible time in our life?

3. True friendship is a major theme of this book: Gabe's friendship with Aaron, Miriam's friendship with Lydia, and even Grace's friendship with Sadie and Lily. We all need friends in our lives. How has God provided for your friendship needs? In what ways does He want you to provide for others?

4. In chapter 13, we see Lydia's family gathered together, and we finally learn about her father's illness. Farmer's lung is a real disease which has been around for hundreds of years. The mortality rate is nearly twenty percent and usually within five years of diagnosis. At the end of this chapter, Lydia is calmed by the sight of her father's hands. (In chapter 18, we see a similar scene with Miriam looking at her mother's hands.) What do someone's hands tell us? What does the Bible tell us about God's hands? About Christ's hands?

5. In chapter 16, Grace turns in a report on Jakob Amman. She's very proud of her work, but her teacher's response isn't quite what she'd hoped for. Have you ever worked very hard on something only to have it rejected? What does the Bible teach us about hard work and finding approval in this world?

6. In chapter 22, Miriam reads the words from Matthew 6:5-8 when she is struggling mightily with her mother's illness. "Your Father knows what you need before you ask him." Has there ever been a time when this verse had a special meaning to you? Does it hold a special promise now?

7. In chapter 25, Grace and her grandfather discuss the promises found in Jeremiah 29:11-13. Joshua tells Grace she's old enough to study the Bible and not just merely memorize it. As they are walking back to the house, they talk about prayer. Grace confesses that she sometimes has trouble focusing while she prays. Could you relate to this conversation at all? What should our attitude toward prayer be?

8. We receive a small glimpse into Miss Bena's past when she is bird-watching with Grace in chapter 32. Until this point, I've had little sympathy for such a harsh teacher. In this scene, she says to Grace, "Some moms are shy...sometimes they learn to hide so they won't be hurt." That's it! That's all we learn of Sylvia Bena's past in this book. Sometimes we don't know all of someone's past, but God still calls us to be gracious to them. How has Miriam shown grace to this woman? How can you show grace to someone in your life?

9. In chapter 38, we learn that Seth had made the decision to join the church and be baptized. It seems that Jerry's predicament has had an influence on him and moved him toward a stronger faith. Has there been a time when seeing other's go through a time of trial has increased your faith rather than weakened it? How does God use us when others are suffering?

10. This story ends with Aaron purchasing land next to Lydia's family. Some of us can live near our family. Some of us can't. What are things we can do to support our family whether we're near them physically or not?

Glossary

ack	oh
aenti	aunt
boppli	baby
bopplin	babies
bruder	brother
daed	father
daddi	grandpa
dat	dad
danki	thank you
dochder	daughter
dochdern	daughters
Englischer	non-Amish person
fraa	wife
freind	friend
freinden	friends
gelassenheit	humility
gem gschehne	you're welcome
Gotte's wille	God's will
grandkinner	grandchildren
grossdaddi	grandfather
grossdochdern	granddaughters
grossmammi	grandmother
gudemariye	good morning
gut	good
in lieb	in love
kaffi	coffee

kapp	prayer covering
kind	child
kinner	children
Loblied	the second hymn of praise
mamm	mother
mammi	grandma
naerfich	nervous
narrisch	crazy
nein	no
onkel	uncle
Ordnung	Amish oral tradition and rules of life
rumspringa	running around years
schweschder	sister
was iss letz	what's wrong
wunderbaar	wonderful
ya	yes

If you loved *A Home for Lydia*, you won't want to miss
Book 3 of The Pebble Creek Amish Series,
A WEDDING FOR JULIA

⟳

Prologue

Pebble Creek, Wisconsin
March

Julia Beechy stood next to the open grave and prayed the wind would stop howling for one moment. Next to her, she could feel her mother trembling. Ada Beechy had turned seventy-eight the previous week, two days before Julia's father had passed. It would have been perfectly acceptable for her mother to sit, especially in light of the mist, the cold, and the wind.

Ada had no intention of sitting.

She did shuffle one step closer, so their sleeves were touching, as the bishop began to read the words to the hymn Ada had requested—"Where the Roses Never Fade." Ada had stared out of the window of their kitchen, attention completely focused on the rosebushes which had yet to bud, while members from their church sat beside Jonathan's body in the next room. She'd gazed at the bushes and made her request.

Bishop Atlee had nodded, ran his fingers through his beard, and said, "Of course, Ada."

Julia tried to focus on the bishop's words as the men—the pall-bearers—covered the plain coffin with dirt. How many shovelfuls would it take? Would Bishop Atlee have to read the hymn twice? Why was she worrying about such things?

David King stepped back, and Julia realized they were finished. Bishop Atlee bowed his head, signaling it was time for them to silently pray the words from the passage in Matthew, chapter six, verses nine through thirteen—their Lord's prayer. Julia's mind formed the words, but her heart remained numb.

"Amen," Bishop Atlee said, in a voice as gentle as her mother's hand on her arm.

The large crowd began to move. Words of comfort flowed over and around her. There had been a steady coming and going of people through the house to view her father's body for the entire three days. Julia had become used to her privacy, used to caring for her parents alone. The large amounts of food and the people had surprised her. Some of them she saw at church, but others came from neighboring districts. Those she barely knew.

She and Ada turned to go, for their buggy was marked with a number one on the side. The white chalk against the black buggy caused Julia's heart to twist. They had led the procession to the cemetery. They would lead the gathering of friends away from the graveside.

But Julia realized she wasn't ready to leave.

She pulled back, needing to look one more time. Needing to swipe at the tears so she could read the words clearly.

Jonathan Beechy
11-3-1928
3-6-2012
83 years, 4 months, 3 days

Now she and her mother were alone.

Chapter One

Six months later

Julia glanced around the kitchen as she waited for her mother's egg to boil. Everything was clean and orderly. Why wouldn't it be? It was only the two of them. Except for the days when she baked, there was little to do. Julia was hoping that would change soon, and she meant to talk to Ada about it. Today would be a good day. She's put it off long enough.

The water started to boil, and she began counting in her mind—three minutes made for the perfect egg, at least for Ada it did. There were few things Ada could stomach on the days she wasn't well, but a soft-boiled egg was one.

As she counted, Julia walked around the kitchen, and that was when she noticed the calendar. She'd failed to flip the page to September. Where had the last six months gone?

Six months since her father had died.

Six months of Ada's health continuing to fail.

Six months that Julia had continued to postpone her dream.

She flipped the page, smiled at the photograph of harvested hay, and vowed that today she would speak with her mother. Returning to the stove, she scooped the egg out with a spoon and placed it in a bowl of water to cool. Slicing a piece of bread from the fresh loaf she'd made yesterday, she laid it on a plate and added a dab of butter and apple preserves on the side. She set the plate on the tray which already held a tall glass of fresh milk. Picking up the entire thing, she turned to walk to her mother's room and nearly dropped the tray when she saw Ada standing in the doorway.

"I'm not an invalid, and I don't need to eat in my bedroom."

She weighed a mere eighty-nine pounds. Julia had brought in the scale from the barn last week and confirmed her fears—her mother's weight was now below ninety pounds. She was also shrinking. Ada now stood a mere five foot, four inches.

Why was it that the body shrank as it grew older? As if it needed to conserve its energy for more important things. Her mother had attempted to braid her hair and tuck it under her *kapp*, but the arthritis which crippled her hands made that difficult. The result was snow-white hair sprouting in various directions and a *kapp* that was tipped to the back slightly. She also hadn't been able to correctly pin her dark green dress.

In spite of her appearance, the blue eyes behind her small glasses twinkled with good humor and complete clarity. Her mother's health might be failing, but for today her mind was sharp. Julia was grateful for that. Some days sporadic bouts of dementia robbed her even of that.

"*Mamm*, I don't mind bringing it to you."

Ada waved her hand, dismissing the notion. "When I'm too feeble to get out of bed, I'll be praying the Lord sees fit to take me home."

Julia didn't think it was a good time to remind her she'd stayed in bed three days last week. Ada remembered well enough. She simply chose to ignore the bad days.

"Let me help you."

Setting the tray on the kitchen table, Julia was relieved to see that at least her mother was using the cane Dr. Hanson had provided. He'd suggested a walker, but Ada had insisted "the Lord was her strength." The cane was a compromise.

Julia inwardly winced as she looked at her mother's hands. Some mornings the crippling arthritis was better than others. This morning her hands—wrinkled, thin, and spotted with age—resembled claws more than hands. She wondered how her mother would be able to pick up the utensils to eat. She was tempted to offer to feed her. The last time she'd suggested that, it had earned her a twenty-minute lecture on self-sufficiency.

Ada must have noticed her staring. Patting her daughter's arm, she murmured, "I know the Lord is always with me. I will not be shaken, for He is right beside me."

"Indeed."

She bowed her head as her mother prayed over her breakfast. While her mother thanked God for her food, Julia prayed for strength and wisdom.

Was today the right day? And how best to broach the topic? Why were her palms sweating?

She waited until Ada had finished the egg and eaten half the bread. Some part of her wanted to believe that if her dream came true, Ada would improve. Another part knew that it was only a matter of time until she'd be left alone in the big two-story house beside Pebble Creek.

"My baked goods have been selling well at Lydia and Aaron's shop."

"*Ya*. That's *wunderbaar*."

Julia nodded but vowed in her heart to push forward with her plan. She'd thought perhaps she should wait until her mother's health improved, but after the visit with Doc Hanson last week, she knew that wasn't going to happen. It was imperative she not wait until winter. The tourist crowds came for summer and stayed through the fall foliage. If she was going to do this, she needed to do it now.

"*Mamm*, I'd like to expand my cooking business."

"You don't have a business." Ada fumbled with the glass of milk, and they both reached to settle it. "You have a hobby."

Rising and walking across the room, Julia fetched the herbal oint-ment the doctor had recommended. When she opened the jar, the smell of mint balm filled the kitchen. Pulling her mother's left hand across the table, she worked the cream into it, rubbing gently with her fingers to massage the muscles until they were straightened.

"I'd like to make it a business, though." She looked up, peering directly into her mother's eyes.

Why was this so hard? Why was she so afraid Ada would say no?

She was thirty-eight years old, and she was still worried whether her mother would approve of her plans. "I'd like to open a café here in the house."

Ada didn't speak as Julia reached for her right hand and began rubbing the ointment into it. When she'd finished, her mother reached out and touched her cheek, leaving the faint scent of mint and summer.

"Dear Julia, how can you open a café in these rooms if you won't be living here?" Behind the glasses were blue eyes filled with calm-ness, sadness, and determination.

"I don't understand—"

"Do you think your *dat* and I would leave you here, after we've gone on? Leave you alone?"

"But—"

"*Nein*, Julia. It wouldn't be proper. It wouldn't be right."

"What..." Julia's heart was racing so fast she felt as if she'd run from the creek. She didn't know what question to ask first. "How..."

"We'd always hoped you might marry. Your father spoke to you about this on several occasions."

"*Ya*, but—"

"I know your reasons, and I even understand them. The fact remains that you can't live here alone once I'm gone, which accord-ing to Doc Hanson will be relatively soon."

Julia jumped up from her chair, walked to the kitchen counter, and glanced outside. Her gaze fell on the rose bushes. They still held some of the summer's blooms—a deep, vibrant red.

"So you're deciding I have to leave? Just like that? I have no say in it at all?" Her voice rose with each question.

"You'll go back to Pennsylvania. Back to live with my family."

"I don't even know those people."

"They're family nonetheless. You've exchanged letters with them for years."

"This is my home, *mamm*. You would kick me out of my home?"

Ada bowed her head. She didn't speak for the space of one, two, nearly three minutes—long enough to boil another egg. When she raised her head, her words were gentle, but they still made Julia want to scream. "God is our refuge and strength, *dochder*."

"The psalms are not the answer to this!"

"Always you can find the answers in *Gotte's* Word."

Julia closed her eyes and forced her emotions to calm. When she looked again at her mother, she saw the same quiet, loving woman who had been beside her every day of her life. What she recognized, in her mother's eyes, was kindness—and it confused her as much as the decree her mother had issued.

"There's no changing your mind?"

"*Nein*. The papers were drawn up before your *dat* passed. It's why we agreed to sell the pasture land to Mr. and Mrs. Elliott. This home will be sold when I pass, and the money will be put in a trust for you, to help support you the rest of your life—"

"Support me."

"On the condition that you live in Pennsylvania with my family."

"Why are you telling me this now?" Julia's voice was a whisper. How could her life have taken such a catastrophic turn? When she'd slipped out of bed this morning, she never would have imagined that her days in this home, her days living beside Pebble Creek, were numbered.

It was true she hadn't been overly social. She couldn't remember the last singing she'd been to, but then she was thirty-eight. She wasn't a girl. She was a woman.

Instead she'd waited. She'd done what a good daughter should do, followed all the rules, and waited. For what? So she could be turned out of her home. So she could be told once more what to do.

It wasn't fair.

And she hadn't seen it coming. She had never expected such an answer. She had never dreamed her mother and her father—she mustn't forget he had agreed to this plan—would betray her this way.

No, she'd been busy designing a café in the bottom floor of their home. Where should she put the tables she would purchase from David King? What type of sign would best attract customers? What would be the best location for it? Should she advertise in the *Budget*? What design should she use for the menus?

None of those things mattered if she'd be living in Pennsylvania.

"Why now?" she repeated.

"Why? Because you asked." Her mother stood, gripped her cane, and shuffled out of the room.

Leaving Julia alone, staring out at the last of the crimson roses.

When she thought her future would never know love...
she saw him.

When he thought his future would forever be empty...
he saw her.

A Promise for
MIRIAM

VANNETTA
CHAPMAN

Amish schoolteacher Miriam King loves her students. At twenty-six, most women her age are married with children of their own, but she hasn't yet met anyone who can persuade her to give up the Plain school that sits along the banks of Pebble Creek. Then newcomer Gabriel Miller steps into her life, bringing his daughter, an air of mystery, and challenges Miriam has never faced before.

At first Gabe just wants to be left alone with a past that haunts him, but the loving and warm Wisconsin community he and his daughter have moved to has other plans for him. After a near tragedy, he hesitantly returns offers of help and friendship, and he discovers he can make a difference to the people of Pebble Creek—and maybe to the Amish schoolteacher.

To learn more about Harvest House books and
to read sample chapters, log on to our website:

www.harvesthousepublishers.com

HARVEST HOUSE PUBLISHERS
EUGENE, OREGON